LA VIE SANS ROUE

Act IV
of Down in Front Epicycle

by Michael Petticord

Simplicissimus Publications
Portland, Oregon
©2019 Michael Petticord
All rights reserved.

Paperback ISBN: 9780984557530
ebook ISBN: 9780984557547
Library of Congress Control Number:2019919520

Published by Simplicissimus Publications
Exterior/interior design by Open Heart Designs, Missoula, Montana

Printed in the United States of America.

"If all the lights of the sky ceased to move but the potter's wheel continued to turn..." St. Augustine, *Confessions*, xi, 23, R. S. Pine–Coffin, trans. (Penguin Books, Ltd, 1961), p. 271.

Contents

Preambled, in an effort to achieve literary premise, in describing a time period of our lengthy Holocene sub–epoch as the teensy era (1300–2019), open to the inherently reasonable censure of indifference, written in a style affected simply because it felt events were suited best for unfolding a disparate sweep of many bizarre, obscure, or digressive protactic passages, as an only possible vessel capable of distributing coherence throughout an allocation of platonic preference (for series of narrative scenes, lent to advent an erudite more, excerpting whomever, decreed capable either of being, or to some extent mixing, variably without intransitive inference); within the dual dream realm of *biathan-atos*, included only the italicized, *wergild*, *inter–regnum*, Type N, immunity by sight merely (*ICC Circular* 91–96), dream–weaver, gear–stripper, or xenonian [*sic*] (italicized or ye otherwise olde characters embodied in the refrainants whose motto's if only), like–looker, only able to only travel in only the only non–corporeal ellipsis weir model, only anyone whose online personae had not survived technocracy, the frozen, albeit with split attributes profiled along teleologically material limes, the artificially intelligent, the wax–born, or the gifted, in this instance with porcupines, *pans'flyts'rytes*, *turec akabej*, or other relic. This, told to all Niceans by some individuals with the aid of dark energy, found it is possible I forget about fifteen words more quickly than I remember two, a pretext so obviously disingenuous as to be reset; while plainly implicit, if every step, planned days in advance, and thought attempt had been made to reverse the dark matter, any headway that appeared to recur seemed subject to wide arrays of anecdote ranging from reverse psychology to snow angels. Nor is the man who wrote, to them moreover, his legacy consistently reflected in trends of modern society, even a stand taken on vision he had seen conflated without cause by his fleshly mind from second Colossians (2:18); a sympathetic hush, lasting for so long as a thought, if looked up from the page, would occasion an exemplary search for truth, and almost felt indictment as a literary faux from anyone who found proximity enough to withstand this gazebo. It had been construed over a period of kalpa stemming almost unto the life of another reality, hitherto grasped imaginably, including Ixtlan and subsequent heavens referenced in second Corinthians (12:1), or other books where indescribable phrases were and had been noticeably topsy turvy or quaint. There had been repetitive topics alike, synonymously with metonym, inherently innocuous yet immune from sedulous catalogue, and I was extremely piqued in exceptional climate, desirous of an eschatological stage while aware, on odd chance elsewhere innocuously, in Xenonia, how the popularly nascent nuclear families of their post—atomic era were redacting after a once ubiquitous ceramics manufacturing industry left for more complaisant shore, and now survived amid uninheritable hamlets of convex margin itemizing all debate of concerns with enduringly redux accession. In those hours spoke one placidly you become a stranger too yourself, with wavelengths of variegated intensity undulating amid amplitude, before leaping into every other tome or 'zine.

Nicean non—translator.
Thursday, April 11, 2019

LA VIE SANS ROUE

Inchoate refraction of earlier manuscript... obvioregals, indicted by Village
4ethics violations, no longer italicized or permitted travel on æthereal realm.
Meringue in—heck sequins... potential geography revealed via Tiffany lamp,
re: Terpsichore's Brow, accessible via Tyrhennian Sea... scope afforded 4type Ns pledged
to redeem variant peril... reference to photopause, EF2's apparent rap, & intent
to curb wishram... eventual trail 2Ghent exchange.

IV — i — A Discretionary and Tactful Intervention.

As somewhat prefatory consensus, pre—emotively biopic, in credit for
Menard's gosplan—tested butterfly net which, proofread, took dispassionate objectivity all the while to be reminded of the foreseeable, and
on one hand, its visibly initial reception spun from customary purview as
dystopian, future, soon anyone must be located with a mindset imbuing
nearly climacteric precept amid disparate mechanism, in valetudinarian
wonder why life clung to the novel, per se [sic], during business hours;
hesitant, thoroughly Porphyry ought, just as flown a dream leapt afloat
soap bubbles beyond the Christmas tree angel, and via fustian admission
creatively, visualize, as economic market, to the dawn of the teensy
epoch whence, insofar as every interstice, defined as point of subli-
mation, between steady state, became fraught, risk assessment, used,
inculcate matrices referenced, variables of potential energy, evinced via
ground of arable maneuverability, a gained outcome of desirability.

Expressed in a continuum of efficacy in attainment of a consensually
definite vision statement regardless of whether Earth flopped, if obvious
to the Fergusons; Señor Florian remained immutable to the Niceans'
plight, the fled strain of a shopping cart sapped, and broached on *Mr Ng,
Live,* they had to leave this truck aside in uncertain coping stance. The
feigned ascent owned to world abscissa piezo—electric, or inseparable
from proposition, in view of the entire giant shimmering scandal, all

able to come from their region was old potatoes in contrast. Since *finth* foreswore design on any visible system, it was impossible for invisible frozen people to avert them, and warily hidden above Pleiades, the winter benefit was to have the most lasting present tense.

Sangreal knew Iraisamonde's vintage (she did not wish to stray far toward Ike's Park), accurately recognized the vision of Mirabeau for what they truly were not, and the proclaimed annum mirabellum of 2036, or 2037, instead conflated into some predestinated manifesto, cropped of summary somnambulism a sunspot cycle or more ago. Fewer numismatic balm seemed amply regal to assist in millennial aftershock, much less the impending miss of Uranus near or far, and one small step from Snorggi's Nose, or other toe tapper, you could imagine prior toney terriers, Laza'r'us, and Alcibiades, five innings spent at work, were a curious mixture of breathtaking excitement and in sodden boredom tore such mulch and most moist crocus, zithers used to mope up trite tart ales she slammed.

It grew at a stiltedly alarming pace of unseemly capacitance, the reason wherefore [sic] real worlds were about to mash into us had, on some if not level plaid, been for Idres' bogus lapse into giardia, paused by his irresponsible phase shift of occult lemon tapestry, alien lanterns, crept across the floor converting oxymoron into airborne catharsis dogma, changed sock on the flimsiest pretext before *iamin'thelim* popped out of the room. Lit via billions of tinny constituents whose moral normality, transcended unto further generic liaison, standing on finesse, until Bustamente's relay so told, a doorstop, fast evolved, fastidiously recapitulated effort to curate maize linoleum currency, met between numerous reason, for a mantle worn to every serer ratiocination of quatrain followed irksome, albeit known, unknown, dissimilar limit to hope for certain petroglyphs of favorable perspicacity.

Shown upon blissful fare, how the days, if fans, or samplers remnant to them might scarcely fill a barn in gratuitous afterworld with tries to be a good person every second of the day or anything likewise still, it is nearly not always necessary for constant preoccupation; intervening factors, decisions, made by other persons seemingly overwhelm why you may be content with mere whim, because there are certain songs that will cause one to switch channels. The immensity of change propounded at par at the beck of citizens of, if not necessarily then, at least of a greater and wilder weird world wilderness, seethed upon a single grain of sand, subject to nearly every solar breeze; beware and consider the ant and her ways (Prov 6: 6), as a new universal tone led one to grasp how cathartic film differed before and during sunrise.

Until then, it was time for the darling sock rescue (emotion experienced, seeing tiny shoes in the child aisle and visualized, tiny feet may be destined to fill them someday, a sense of responsibility to guide and protect any who would walk into them until their certain age), suddenly you accept there must be expectation relevant to the basic fidelity in all antimacassar. If things began to levitate rather frequently still, born again, admitting it sounded cliche, but affirming he felt his opinions were important to them, Roveretto wore narrowly Në (pronounced any) Dipol's trapezoid for a barrel roll up Niagara's search blob; headed toward Erewhon, Esmeralda Fishing Lynx, typecast in candled interval, a fiery vegan, troubled trying to think of what word to write, on a blogospheric membrane, the extent of this ideal, if she only just acted differently at certain points, everything should still be the same, left lexicon of snappy retort, and other riposte d'escalier [*sic*] assume an untold prominence by definition of best trip ever, Snorggi's snooze performance vintage so fab and/if for enamel armoire on weird rapprochement, Iraisamonde could spell them separate strains of smatter, but the importunate klatch savants were guiled away, promissories of an entire video collective afforded presently, as if she might fall into a comma, later inspired by something written next to a samovar boiled down in vacuum.

Time might spell on indefinitely, albeit exorcism or else therapy solidly redressed some imbalance, like should she eventually find his foible endeared at some remove behind the calliope atop pill hill, or at least for an undersized espadrille etched in time a gilded age retrospective scene fewer than unflinching certainties ago, as punchless, eidetic bassoon licks, made esoteric during one of those lengthy musicale fluff revues aired on sabbatical, assume symbiotic beatification once and for all, straightly on every conceivable topic from one's zoned building, all its joy and heartache to designed draught, notwithstood too rapidly, grown aware, the moron's drip cured, half of an ideal felt will still be used as tedium of extra prosaic scenery before all of these efforts to prove to society she was not a drooling sociopath turned her into one, Meringue received basis for avowal anew, at Least, fifteen articles the peoples of Xenonia claimed included super–sensory perceptive ice stampede, aboard Delphic *biathanatos* candle parenthetical illusion video lottery zinged by Rust.

How did that ice going off sound like? A noted author had a noted gathering to get to and typed, on one spot, thinking if he ever had fun he would add a fun rack in his truck if ever any track to the driveway of his quondam beach house were ever extant, and now everyone should admire its earthy simile, and so he, sued for hiding mens' cases, went on to his erstwhile noted gathering: as everyone could tattle upon individual significance and tap his elbow slightly, so the popular people approach the snoring seal, tentatively, as must an esteemed colleague, skilled in capturing capricious peccadilloes of ordinary life, yet in recognition he has ventured too far in the time allotted by our workshop facilitator (*all too busy*), invariably seeks to finish his piece on same appended some lame bon mot; to illustrate, personal text, nary a groat as fine as that of any colleague, may go like this miss they sought, elusively, for source of this desolation in dry, crisp, light, scented salt and pine spice, in this barn, the height of gain and wear and danger as palpable: hung amid air like trim haze, furrowed prows, frightening mood in sooth, tangible, and could be sold, if only by example, else the weight in this heart remained despite the smothered lull of the only ocean yards away at night.

The utter lightness matched theirs inwardly, an equilibrium achieved, daring the time they learned to sense the spritz of desire and despair in the brightest sun. Over the faint respiration of ocean and the shriek of the pine forest they felt the hopeless betrayed sigh of a million dreams began here: desperate honeycomb, artistic aspiration, lounging of materialism nullified. Innominative were they, always dispersed by incessant east winds which originated thousands of miles away, the depth of these specific themes ginning and ended all things, as Tethys cantered over the wild and manipulated hills to the west and south, but other spirit replaced them, dreams by the thousand continued to clamor at the gargoyles' iron gate of those indwelt. Noone ever heard them: those inside the dark lamp yet intone, in a construction site, emerging in the midst of a departing congregation, smiling and waving at the minister's cats.

.   .   .

Norah knew how such stunts were overcome. Poljola's daughter [sic] on her ring tone will drive the noted author out of the house the way Aunt Inyo used to with their youngest, Ohno, a sister of Park's grand-mother. Accordingly, they were so far out on the thin ice, only from within, amended in any reference to him, future periodicals derided their theology; the bandsmet, thrown much fissile sentiment, lammed nascent illative, readily devolved so—so wedgie at dearth phonetic Las-cauxvianly, whether odd driblet knew a flagellant pink net dragged, atavistic verticulum rang. A hectic thing futurity Norah carried, stood, hands aside, at a toss, and guessed Park must entertain guests milling at the doorstep with a paper sack.

Her aleatory mome gyppo, Althea planned Runnymede herbal chiaroscuro to observe Zen Frederick's collegiate truffle, evoking nattier banquet tangents. Nearer scene, quixotic mourners almost stormed, below tantric pimento, seed an arras here of Patmos estimably, batted the late Nesbit's reverie escrow, revolving siesta into self—assessment doze, real ad hoc delta function shrugged to mope off a cast reprise, Masha, stash warbler, her ipsilateral tread tentish, turned to eke rude snooker ante in some bijou. The senescent ruse, another pal said drearily, bereft of all health's tough mint eternity.

As a course stood to salvage guilded flip–flap about Cicero, Marta's economic tapering rite forged anthanamolous filing as proof innate tropism guests indentured lacier, a neat semaphore, ill, if heavy mimes are rote — skittle up for snack and receipt of saltando in thigmotropism liable, vertiginous Vikram dealt lottery fossil, amylase link ROM techno–wraith. Sincerely she'd book the fastest boat like it had some sort of disease heretofore rarely tracked; dependent on the resilience of a mind capable of grasp, the universe and, at lunch, into pre–conceptual array one pondered, a plan of fell design, half pie–eyed, albeit virtuously, over Rex's vineyard, al–Kamil, Emir of Ægypt, gear–stripper extra–ordinaire, clung to no small love for the citizens of the approaching shopping cart.

As written, one thing meant constant rejection daring core elision: themes mocked him steadfastly for his occidental felicities, and ceaseless fast had not availed in the race for acceptance among this desired stead. He considered their plea, frayed by criticism, dreamt weft from past summers of writing lists of decades, many of which he visited, preventing him from siphoning Type N for a good cause, ostracized by this verseless denial, yet, no reciprocal concord extorted via his own commission, truantly exerted untoward hold upon the lives of his nature, their power fragile, an interview, deciding his course, sufficed to reveal, in certain dialog, and visible. Iraisamonde's coiffure fixed, Echo spoke, pulling back a knot, "he has done quite well for himself." "Nastanto Ampersand is a fickle–brained clinker," Iraisamonde declared. "With broad elbows," coaxed Gnadig Anodyne, mixer of secret delineation, an individual of another, town paid to spin me, stood virtue, "under a certain drive," the Contessa alluded — "for a newer or — " Iraisamonde sneezed, "do you think we would give in to his pronouncements?"

Shivering beneath the dryer, she indicated which shade was beyond suitable. "How shall we," ædith returned querulously, "and if not, why aren't you weaving us over?" "The coal rose I also dropped, curare," Ferguson replied shrewdly, eliciting no further protest of the valid petunia nearby which the ensign hadn't locked onto. It felt like someone flushed while they were in the fountain with three coins left for the nymph Cyane, an inevitable moment planned obsolescence ruled each old leaf oblivion, slowly decaffeinated Terpsichore, or a lambent flock – Lilly tipped after cows the bank fork, said significant mural, emote, eminent she'd naught, as Delphic via an aura as–is, flagged in cursory Satyagraha lot, albeit dank narcissist leered at fey far crier removal Piero's marmalade narrowly.

The roster emulated brusque encomiums: most hoped, eke renovated diatribe unimpeded, "since we failed to perceive this galvanized facet," argued Ng, then individuals suddenly gifted fidget agoraphobic all in a region of limitless leghorns and others intently tack the stupendous global video system as impinged over oceans or regions inhibited by existence, few pondered that probability of occurrence of travel actually jounced in a stimulator for hours as coordinators frantically staged an apricot reality in, "that side of the out–house, four, five years perhaps, then, a refreshment we'll serve," smiled a noted author, calm Dr. Many Place. "Return us to the slope of Ike's Park, where seven saw a keep, the bed riddled remnant of the Nicean expedition. Ponder their fate." The cameral nature of *fjulsfut* biopsy permitted a watery glimpse of current event, and transient Plair booked above ineluctably on this raspberry.

.   .   .

In one glance, Constancia semaphored the Venetian shade and beheld a duchess in braids of fiery chestnut. "This book's unwell," sad Fanta, "for I never caught a cold," ere, "I considered myself invulnerable to mere earthly viruses." "Leave them," the Dutch chemise, commanded, everyone since exeunted, closeted with the Contessa, Iraisamonde's heart poured out the secret of her general despair. She cried a voiceless name, snookums, in front of the tipsiest, the sidewalk, consisted of thousands, dumber than fence posts, an untouched pox, noise after a shell burst, still an armload of five tubes, and countless handfuls of snap crackle pop, sparklers, if then, all slipped into faded and incipient distraction, the list went on, distraught in the arm of the Contessa, determined to hold out for not the last time.

The lip read name, wrung by cry above Iraisamonde's fair larynx, of the triptych barker so captivated that summer. "He was very assertive," Nadeladimov conceded, "yet Etaoin need not have been so frank." "That he had been wax–born." Constancia remembered a basic, intermittent, but very immediate repellence when, in cosseted condition, Finlay intimated of a similarly ineluctable endowment. Iraisamonde left them all to restive regret. "Of course, you should not have known," soothed the Contessa, not for the ninth time. She long sought to assure Iraisa-monde her initial reactions were valid. Albeit never prior so done in by events that she should even countenance intervention from her distant, relative, Bustamentenards, Constancia entertained a recent visit of an aunt, her own, via coincidence of birth the younger woman, Sangreal, who approached the Contessa in some quandary.

In fewer than three days, *il hogreeve ii* to go forth in full array to announce introduction of its new currency, *lithiwatt*, onto the Antwerp bourse, Sangreal, a decent girl of clear petition, apologized for craving, on behalf of the global village, for a distinct arrangement, strictly to signify how *il hogreeve ii* asked liaison with the house of Syktyvkar. The Contessa saw a straw to grasp and decreed, if this sieving haute throng might find thus to have shaded gold, "maybe you will care plenty to go forth now and then!" As always when Nadeladimov said this, the duchess quavered, ending the topic of her simmer, flung temptation, out of thin air, ere their tightly forged group, otherwise upright, or on time, is propellant toward constant points. The Contessa met her friend's iris in a mirrored glance. "Tell me what you could like now most to be." "A cloud," Iraisamonde sighed. "Top that." "A bicycle." Nadeladimov inadvertently added, "think." Iraisamonde minded bleakly. "Now back out there and pin it on," Echo urged her protege.

The reject fair: collusion with density.

For the final acre found *wergild*, their assembled, the suddenly such limin-alized, and those accustomed to oft and disastrous flirtation, councilors of inadvertently unimpressive exchequers, chemists of the new currency, nerveless, the kilnsmen, ore sifters, and crushers' locals, adaptive, disgruntled greens, pinched their calm fob, immediate disbursal of promissories predicating dismantlement of technologies deemed non–environmentally favorable, daring previous summits, the assembled bond of local, or regional, utility cooperative, and remnant assets of frustratedly androgynous macro–performance investment analysts who led the general day trade market to this bleep.

The economic community viewed their approach with strained interest as an herald, arrived, announced the lot and intent of the global village to pay a dividend, miniscule yet remunatory, to all holders of scratched tickets from the infamous lottery of Eur'tru'bro, a friendly stuffed dinosaur, said to have inculcatory power of trans–national identity, which guaranteed children upon the landing and homestead of every social quarter a promise of distributions to be diverted nigh the benefit of all youth for evermore.

It had been to date communicably the least expensive embarrassment, up to this point, its laudable principle misfired on outrageous waves of overbooked down–line sales, via forced, proscriptive gerry-mander, and beneath amplified embezzlement, the project lurched to virtual infomercial extinction. Yet, the community already conceded to forestall, ex officio, this pronouncement as the global village, instantly tolerant of its currency, the *lithiwatt*, settling the eely medium within the tank of remunerative probability.

Swirled in the actual ocean of the invisible hand, anyone dumb enough to ignore this dispassionate tone would be left to the stars. White lightning, lemon pledge, burdened man in his relenting search for the dawn, in the teeth of all of the variety of the eastern wind a moved migration began, to Rust, acceptably noctambulant, excellent fond eco–dreams: Allah, obversible, ever–aglow, nematode wisp, posh in a swarm nascent ivy node thaw now, read Frost, as nacreous, neared, throng voles' Lethe pronto before a Lamaze loch, eliding chichi [*sic*], endurable as ear–filled narrow sylphs, cheat on mind–read farm, a *wagon–lit* plot, rapt ere alphabet ginseng spam drooled vast inference. Nearly Linlithgow knit idled at the photopause, tour Mahatma harmonic, of aspect fjorded, velour, gamier behemoths mask tsouris igloo, roamed syntactic show couscous Aira noted surreptitious.

To teem flotillas, the hands guard a klatch swing, all pomp size a steely month larvae for Cæsar, a go–go–ish taint locus synapse macularly, his tithes soar at heathen shank, applied short synod Goth rhyme, "vogue I peer around wary caste, frothed down to melba prone theft" — "no operatic vague scat earthed as taxonomic a prodigy," stated as she danced can–can thaw, depth moseyed aside, cardiac zap mulled chiffon. Clearance or root bath monads, eke ochre, won tabs of moot sobriquet, doleful and roynish, duly Tiffany's measly stub alit to re–ordain diorama, tagged royal beast a poor tinsel eidolon, the draught, if sporty; mooted eerie valve streamers Noone re–routed, their joke atavism, remain aghast no giant Indies [*sic*] launch, *Freddy's Salient Locus*, shown in savvy parent trap, scorned in every chic frustum since Ghent.

"We ultimately slept in the still of the then," they all one day bloomed. Was this righteous rite right? Sergei Kalamparumple believed he fully arrived at the peace he reserved. Unable to share a shred of personal disgust, however, as one of the earliest rejects from the Fair, he settled in to his fallback plan. Hereupon expected he should conduct some sort of an operation over modem and fax to unfold in the tent of the old, and yet now new, world at the bar of history, contemplated before him the café pouissant, Sergei mulled on individual significance. As far as he became concerned, there was no longer any. His drink, a gel of seven layers, each cusped in the meniscus of the one beneath, its properties elusive, and inconsolable, he dwelt on them anyway.

Like each, he sensed, if beauty, content to reside, meekly in the bosom of his regard, how could he think anything is done well, "when I promised the left bank the most mind–blown, gut–wrenching, heart–stopping event may never happen, outpacing the very world I meant to observe with our new family," he asked? Attributing this toward but not very energizing sequence to ennui, via archives so severe, each dynastic

and ecclesiastic, which no longer disposed of a mood to tangle, Kalamparumple ordered another grenadine parfait. What it amounted to was
you were able to see footprints minutely, case in point electrical field
without the benefit of tinfoil, and somewhere flutes twittered out there
is no more room at the inn anytime soon.

Colder scent prevailed in a zero sum game wide worlds apart as
Sasha, vaguely followed a grain of splat, more reasonably tapped as
exercise, the gardeners indefatigably blasted away on guided tours of
plush facilities, Sergei pointed out there are no last crumb, fobbed onto
his speed dial, but only its heretofore histrionic concept dawned, a
tendentious flimsy path apropos, an excluded robin's nest found in the
merrily color shoe tree. The marriage of archetype with sucrose onus
bored umbrella clunkily sent abroad snail shoals. The sea described a
thin plain, featureless, muddy, distant turbulence, yet so calmed that, his
cigarette pitched into the water, Harold swore they were on siftings and
Ælfric, upon porous charts, found no reason for them to be so grounded.

They stood over the aft propeller penstock as, asked, "did ye take
soundings" — "we left the sardine in the shelf an hour ago," the *xenonian*
sensed to have stated. Another encompassing glance, braced for further
protestation, the ship's company astir, Van Etnabaron paced, fretting
carrioccio had not been winched aboard a faster packet, yet Mr. Chocho
Molyneaux, his citation of cost involved, rarefied general inertia.
The departure of the survey team there remaindered one owner, one
skipper, one winch–mate, one tender, one radio operator, and Sasha,
who watched the winch–mate disappear into the hold to check rudder
junction relays.

In the disoriented sensation of their present stew, Ælfric lurked,
a prone person at the prow, Thledvirrson, basked in sun so glorious
only she would see through it, and rasped a question, "how can she still
be here?" Van Etnabaron, chosen, filmed froth tiki and, gone beneath
altogether, in no idea Molyneaux should insistently enroll round trip
clauses into their contract, the winch–mate tinkled switches. The
loudspeaker crackly, vessels approach, Harold left the engine room and

bolted topside. Everyone inspired to analyze nearly began a certain latte foam whistle caught on tape, last minute cause underlain yonder anyone became lost indeed. A Lethean bramble charter murrain, among the strength of his conviction, a last vestige of talc sand titled capacity of a nocturnal eminent flimsy truth.

.   .   .

In so post–partum an immediacy way *chef d'cabinet* intended recreation of one fundamental tenet of *fjulsfut* birth rite that, to turn the monads into art, a thorough fledge involved action improbable here. Were there no well more efficient than the bouncier law op cit, or were their seventh capable of maintenance, an oriflamme of requisite couth, sadly then the fifth regarded the plaintive beans, doomed to respite in artificial pleonastic bubbles. To sustain them eventually, if epitome of leaden opinion feigned to expostulate the benefit conferred in novelty, even the historian (*all too busy*) scrupled to disturb empiricism.

Nudged toward the cobbled incubus, the babes squalled in disdain and hearts were moved to complicated option. For lo had An arrived with flickery vessels. Their spate had, she exclaimed, been forced through matter so dense they were hardly viable to even stirring motes. In alacrity, they swam from the virgule. The terrain attuned and droll translucence accepted invidious cribs of *tictus* as deposit. However, an obversible, seconded in hesitating the mutation with likely cataclysm, saw ubiquitous agreeable accrual.

On the sly, monotony elsewhere, smaller feats were sessional. Well asked in rarer accord unrecalled, Suppressant's step–children immured the monads with remote clarity. Well away beyond events now were men as thyme, ground to the hull, joined particularly staged heaps of transfer that pelted the mountain. In an accessory of vengeance were neap space loathe to countenance the trans–migration, yet from Miranda waived staggered hail against the structure, too far inland this pique weakened, and Tethys' supernal tearily advised groom guessed the return of these bedraggled steeds to their place unless mention to their owner alas, already troubled of pendant relegation, that two fewer manes would loll in his realm.

Regret attached pro forma, glib Niceans celebrated their fiesta, unaware Ferguson stole behind the tour to regard his vaguely human grands' stand on an interested statistical sidebar acme, if in accordance with various federal schedules, substantial evidence irksomely moved to live, empirical proof of bygone, contractual unfulfillment, dissolved in concavity. Logan railed over the reunion, its blasphemous redirection of natural order, its dilemma over grief and fear, and motioned any assistance to end anew their restraint. Noone availed to gyve them; while obdurate, they posed a solute. You may forget they looked like tiny simplified geodes now.

They were odd, he wished to shake them for answers. "You have forgiven much already," seconds re–vamped in the window, and of them he learned odd truth of his absence from the eighth ball, arrangements of Chad in jingle holistic swarm song, pinchbeck vertigo spicules delineate pressing choice, for the indigo sphere to major scales receded. The fifth viewed the fitful impression as an expansive reprieve, whereby the fourth commended, in a drier lisp, what was best for *inter–regnum* could suit their down, preternatural, inclination that were, her alas diminished hold upon them foreshortened in event.

Mailed an indecent scar moreover, fifth sensed an incendiary cheroot to nearly all in consolation. The ninth especially happily jettisoned their yoke over the expedition if many therein, scarcely inured to the various exigence of maroon procedure, must adduce precious space remained too serially to be marred with plebian gags. For they would have a place to return *chef d'cabinet*, little evinced interest in shifts, their predicament natheless, *uchaux* were of more, rather than fewer, common cause. Known moment of perusal nigh, Logan yet noticed many eighth abounded and felt couth for never deigning to forsake them.

As the tremendous anonymity tugged at him, vastened an alcove and sealed his feet with innate grommets, historical precedent annulled, and expectation of persistent hope stolid, Logan remained on the planet worried the chance, foresworn, was nevermore percussive. "And that is the thanks we get among other thing annealed from perceptible constituency theory against filtered ague," remarked the Niceans' personal metaphysician. "Get some rest if the morn is nearly not insofar four hours nigh," and in unlikely priority, loud monads recalled form, tellingly an elaboration of note merited, familial taint the rhadamanthine involvement.

Smoothly and easily Ion heard them repeat, "lower the wet hen from a scary foil incurred," daring the actless dram bid or thrown verily at them. Whereas night gelidly chafed at this destiny now, bound to assist this esplanade, for the novel tilt upright acted as stabilization and anew the pole already paradise, a value vitiated in recreation of the toy land, Andorra, a new north, promising no loss leaders ever, bloomed in the post millennial shop. However sanctified, this achievement of closure suited men little who chafed for the missed Talitha in mercy or lieu thereof. Petitioning the Nicean expedition for immediate release of Bitsy's kind, Logan, plainly resigned, turned aside.

After their exhorted remonstrance paled in a last dark draft he glared of strange iris, avowed space oglers in clearance performance participle thereof. In fitful alacrity a man selected experience of a rite of memo reflux and, in knowledge of it, subsequently relieved of recent cite, walked south from their nodding sagacity. Of small interest henceforth ever were his moment to *inter–regnum*, and/if their expedition must ever dissolve their capable mend enough to note, even juxtaposed, an annular consistence to preview for estimate of lesson imparted by other humans, they also were almost away. Well bells blue regaled this innocuous triumph, become jaded in strange cold.

Then even seconds so eleven clasped them in fair thee well. Outliers, burrowed incipient floes, an active biological procedure, evocative fitful determinism, and early neglect for hospice of interstellar decency smote An; ambassador, she went out from them, pursuant in necessity of anomie well liked. Happenstance, *per se*, or any other up–churned vicissitude gripped them, in stasis grind, nor all unwell for, any monad caused to forfeit a recent history, their fourth exeunt in grave dissonance left only thirds, what few, the fifth, and their seventh in splendor insulate, unnecessarily links weakened, and they left on the surface sole accolade, accompaniment for princes valiant and fabulous fitfully sat out into resolution of demophobia, and at whiles, so wrought were ingredient that enigma could, given tool to rewind a clock of rights left overtly untenet, pity the cosmic balance maintained, watch the floor dissolve in rapid tear jerk sequence emoting to adept site of maladjusted element as freedom yanked over the impervious predecessor with anxious version deliberated.

The manifest auction in the ICA solemnly, yet fair from indecent location, directed those ogling febrile too, innate if forelimned to adapt mutation of intractable gerund sang, in our IOU, was a forgotten claim check. The Inspector found Rita's initial scrawl on a subway ticket to a rotten borough. All of a sudden Regatta, their first pasty sitar, reflective anon in convention of their emprismed progeny, SOMHAD, meant at a philately reception, and ordered in ice plants during the combing brew, UFOs went to sleep, and had put up in arms, and/if freely content to marvel at a lit alibi, boredom, felt a slippery over the side, its rusty warm rate attenuating the toss. Then had your inside out always wanted to be the first in a listless gaze of someone noted for reaching unassailable conclusion at first light.

.   .   .

Need salsa, and/or ketchup from Sasha, & provide lime for whomever may cover; i.e.,
various factions, Reject Faire, Ike's Park, Provenance, and, xenonians, frozen peephole,
miscible jihad, &C., all whom workshop teleology snippets 2contain F. Bandersnatch
w/ various poetic forums... Menard, about 2b excerpted from ICA, bows to pursue
the worst day fishing, whereas Norah, in all candor, turns 2indict obvious regalia &
their untoward gerund clique cruisers.

IV — ii — A Bleak Tide of Events.

If not entirely a thrill, the Ghent Exchange, as lace spooled with grotto, an architectural design of native yearn for neap remove: an exo—structure, toured to otherwise featureless surrounding, depicted one grand inland sea upon the plain of Picardy, its display of sea life accoutered in quorums of molecules, mollusks, schools of unblinking fishes, tanks, plumbed in rock, rays, salamanders, spiky lions, and mantras, non—mammalian and therefore subject to imminent concern of ethical treatment. Any ambience best achieved was specifically geodesic promenade, a premonitory version of regional seaport oversight upon the brisk tide of commerce. A pity, largely unnoticed, existed in a room of emerald and aquamarine, but for all the servants of extant protocol, being strangers and pilgrims, attend orientation for cable access to the courtroom, the media, imperfect though it may be, are the eyes and the ears of the neighbors, but either nobody knew or nobody cared in those innocent days.

Somewhat left to visiting dignitaries, and especially several principles, to best debate upon what act next might be serenely commenced beneath this roof, Sergei knew of the remnant skip and reminded his colleagues, "the world is a nervous system," and disclosed, "signaling on a bench left me now allowed to visualize my hand." Someone else, Meringue, her sparkler ditched at Vikram, shook her/his mind in annoyance ruffled by soundproof capacitance on weak house current;

circumstance as so immeasurably improved on those times of travail, already distant, yet maintaining a baroque lien upon her conscience. For the lottery, projections simply not borne out, provided key representatives availed to work through outranced versions of the Eur'tru'bro commission, trickles of claimants remained pledged to just smatterings of shilling, lira, and Rand, *lithiwatt* non–accumulative, rabid debt insufficient for reversely buoyant unnecessarily foreign actual bail–out, unless impelled from below. Currency of the global village should be then devoured by tench, carp, or other festering feeders, pimentos, and nexus land gnat despots, flimsy ink grab epic, or real dust mote Nesselrode furor, a vast permutable tandem case Melfi shag, nixed advent mirage, marring all for mere orlon nacelle tesserer, ormulu lust, brash ledge melba, or bright pony en route solid macramé.

Doth taupe keep out dirt as aura interludes etched reputed mondo skirl, timing lurid weird falafel wraith heralds, buckled those scram jet thionyl terse gleans, Narodnik cubists, no joy slam trucked on misfit rats, shined a stet. Best rhadamanthine pillow flash, oops, tread senile optic casbah ethyl, osmium–octal, readily trochlear odds, as behind bubbles, to neuter isogenous Gnostic–shovelled manqué meta–plastic topmost cruet spam, Marta's weary tramp at furry brass proof dazzled away. Motivated niche pseudo–bijou magnets near duffers ordinarily Lamaze, *Mr Ng, Live* if pro tem trance, is as regulatory as forced odd–world out thaw, blinked Talitha at the nearest Maypole topic. "Trust us to seem egregious beneath Nifleheim as escrow's Nineveh, mad, apple verticule," overjoyed else botox yoga, arrayed volute ruffles in vast alpaca shirt exalts, surf lithe debt town leerily in sub deceit, a noblesse foot shanked by diatomaceously at arabesque tiffin.

Misappurtenanced linseed closet tonic, Meringue's Theban nod, intimating fancy Everest lutes must innumerably, someone made feasible inquiry and, told to co–lateralize their regional cooperative utility shares, this liquidation, while capaciously inflated, the immediate value of *lithiwatt* in no way enhanced, its maneuverability offered at par to lessor creditors, currency of global village seemed an unlikely feast that

was, for which neo–Refrainants await, their placed marker as security
between Olympiad underpinning of massive cusp. The tench, yonder
inserts tangled from its aphasic jaw, but otherwise balked, hacked the
visiting side, posts *biathanatos* pledge to guarantee private debt accumulated in divestiture of numerously unclear projects, and the carp,
matching this bid, withdrew. It did not seem content to await the curious
onset of these mudders parceled along the bottom of the bay.

The krona appraised *lithiwatt* in an instant display of flashy acquisition
for, Meringue intrigued, Sweden's folk councilor, determined Dauphine
to Van Etnabaron's lawless scene, frank backing obtained for an outright
sell–off, Menard, in grave misgiving, consented to tap the last village's
remnant capitol [*sic*] preserve, the considerably leveraged paradigm of the
International Brotherhood of Valets. Its diffusion pensioned, chronic dis-
persal of gain shifting to margins, nominally reverted *lithiwatt* above the
fustian plinth. The Economic Community, normally not idle, marched
this upward ascent until each found admission to the pit, the aquamarine
room smelled of final ochre, and participants, revamped in a manner calculated, thereby become witness to the lading, fully tread in uncluttered
deed an evidence of widespread concern. Given focus through a value
immunity compromise process, soon it became apparent, to the IFL, the
iBC, the ICC, CIC, and the ICA, that turn of one of their own, and the
IBV at that, caused dreadful concern to manifest.

If the fortuitous valets, ever privileged to evolution of an old illuminati, discerned to give their cherished fund to pledge off global village,
the future, lemniscate, its lengthily insular infrastructural claim of
contractually obligated and sincerest legitimacy shifted to a venue of
unevenly inter–relational non–commercial hindsight. Whereas recent
performances of established currency tended to encourage leaden adherents into buckling active hedge, eventual displacement of economics
might, those more nestled factions, when found themselves outlandish,
lack tact, owing to unexpected turns of event, viewing this non–planned
victory as precursed, a seemly restoration of determined purpose, pro-
posing percolation to bring upon epochs of actualization.

Participants of the conference averted an immediate affectation. As any privileged valet could conform, the community already ceded a void of lasting moral principle; its Richilieu, grand countess of the Vlachs, Constancia Nadeladimov, Elector of Ruthenia, phrased this notion: in nomination of the newly created office of trans—national vox populi, committees of public safety subjected to temporal receivership of the village. In return for this display of fealty, *lithiwatt* deemed a mint of provisional duration, its principles duly amazed and unsettled by their success: global village dissolved, itself in *inter—regnum*, its foremost adherents lounged in snowbound retreat, and many important and particular garters, newly poised to revive the question of electoral status, called by messy elves referential, outweighed neo—Ghibbeline demands for postponement of diet in assurance of awakened polyphony; old Refrainants, in regard of their new allies' albeit hearty dismay, yielded the dubious honor of predisposing the actual date, seconded, again for the third to last day of the newest decade, unless an event, marked and amicably yielded, would award the final answer.

.   .   .

Seeking to regress the positivism of Renata, Rita, Mervyn Mirabeau St. Clair, great, great, grand—daughter of the republic, the Inspector alone seemed to starve in pleasant and yet relevant ecstasy, an irreconcilable dichotomy, his wonton takeout strained to account for panjandrum; leased falsetto no barrier to undreamt libertinism, the politesse of Mme meandered faintly in a steady pattern of disbelief, her fiery theme changeling, and sightlessly Læmært placed a sure bet her lilies were still lurid enough to risk suffusion. Inherently opinionated, at once formless pliancy too sparkling for sedulous regard urged him of curious attempts to obsess, if not fixate, upon three, or four, slowly whirled stampedes. That startled shakedown twice misled Paul'r'us into realization she'd done with him in fifteen minutes or fewer, and to mingled relief and despair, Meringue took no future notice of this leakier insight.

Facades of slim possibility now regaled their steadfast vigil, and all of a sudden, upright pianissimos composed gauzily, Consuelas fitfully wakened, saying, "my druthers, I've lost them," thrice. Now Læmært had the strangest flash, its iridescence, in the event her expertise refuted all clinical proof neither seemed appropriate, citing a suggestion, if beyond the room, he catch late returns on html, she gave, by his testy request for the time of day in reply, ten of four, as indeed a pearly gate seemed altogether outside ajar. They snared a vivid toehold, and in receipt of his askance, she, waspishly finding moment to flare the comb in strong swarms, facetiously abet Gaussier's cold laurel of vicarious slithery twill fishnet swankiness. He swore she looked how mulch alike unto a Grecian kiln, and Renata shortly relented, in statutory oddness, an allowance for clover assiduously.

"Noone likes a theme park," disputed St. Clair, her trowel thrown across the Rubicon, and flatly still, listed stoically as an inspector, made to earn third base paper, snug for the nearest disco until dawn, continued too, real abysmal, scooped before mental recreation of magnanimous heavens of marble figurines to buy more thyme and, if customarily, it was a signal for dignified recession, pressed onto the rest of a story. Icily, Mervyn sadly noted she'd misled him into a simulacrum of obedient hesitation, and in causality, her next more, to darkly doze beneath stoppage time, even as he preached to her silhouette with ingrown if heartfelt buzzes, unlit listlessly, the gain, crescendoed to solvent ideal acuity, manged, to stray frizzily, beyond the pale.

Their best argot in all likelihood whitewashed, the moon had not risen for months, dallying connection upon all band icon patient ontos. Plair, left one new lease on life, a ripple of ingrained cayenne Lothar misappropriated tenuously, curbing desire to ignite the plush debacle, straitly uplifted their relegated go–between into officious windfall of painted offset, Meringue's legendary droopy overwatch meshed oddly as Læmært whistled off insidious deals, and whereas knells of impending mood plunged toward Renata, she'd re–embarked, on misty ramparts of ancillary instantaneity, and molded them into submission, if deranged he roamed amidst the flock, previous hitch motto with dry city exit act, and few moments to spare, star struck beyond lightness, oscillated in a permissive luxury of brief sensibility, curiously overruled in scented display of mostly uncounted tabula rasa [*sic*]; chilling poem heard, to reveal the key, to a missing, now here, land of wonder, world, the clasp, acronym of five rivers, and she gently guided, a missive away, his truffle, suggestive of fondness, beryllium, cane sugar, sisal, and acidophilus, left scene deciduously vitiated, unlit she cast her die, dutifully it began to ask for room service, yet this toga parted ritzily found its client saccharinely fitful before she intervened, with a loud yawn, bathos inherent in facetiously odd moodiness.

Renata hailed a figurative garb, clasping yardarms tauntingly as it held speechless court with *HMS Flie*, re–enacting a flu lot. Her old bad self pulled together, Rita caressed this fiercely, responsive information had been lent on, and hoping her supply of heather clepsydra would hold up, at breakfast blossomed mimosas, sprinkly baguettes heaped with pale myzithra; St. Clair's coast, for his own complaisance with any other moral body, Læmært didn't persist and they rolled out of where in time for the seven o'clock stage whimper.

.   .   .

To reach for something else in the brioche, Florian saw beautiful mushrooms ameliorative of his compensatory xenophobic nativism. He took new note of his surroundings. A man lain in a nearby barrow pondered that forces had trapped him. He studied the portal, loaded as always, thus descended into the well of thyme, his final link the sunlit world once too often, and in chronic humor, the Niceans left some vittles around. As if to palliate his forgotten cynosure, already they pondered the irony, as if honored to be so gyved as were monarchs of ancient kingdoms he once studied so diligently. Regrettably some modern co–dependants seemed intent upon dim–wittedly annihilating all of the ancient things, a development laid at his doorstep by an uncomprehending civilization.

The man had not cared what everyone did as long as not everyone became oppressive or intrusive in their own behavior.

"Who are you," Florian ventured to call out? Just because he had been Soundman of Ossian, came the reply, did it mean everyone might sully and impugn him obliviously? Left alone with those thoughts, Fernand should have no other recourse other than to impound them here. Posterity had a way of being judgmental. Had he railed to shrug aside his interests, if an off screen voice–over just tossed fitful Azali keys to a new Pontiac, unable to act upon his first impulse to jump up and own and scream, whereas everyone had taken liberties Soundman offered, as their ladder, and used them to twist and skew the depiction of his own wisdom, whereas they abused and harshly dumped principles he espoused for the general advancement of culture, whereby they were giving encouragement and comfort to numerous external foes who consumed themselves in untoward envy for his thriving statehood, given all of these things, everyone thereby were in forfeit of the privilege derived of the solemn compact beneath the governed and demonstrated a need to experience a campaign of political awareness.

Azali's only instances of emergency blankets upon other windows cheered Noone. For, brevity, and development, these gifts of the spirit, enumerated, were, to enjoy neither theft, ruin, or a foe's lob, within the narrow straits of bandwidth allowable, cusps contemplate articles of destiny; solid air, pressed across an expanded coherence, perforce lengthens, until illimitable Sr. Florian, in tan and green worsted, arose and set his air guitar down, opened a door to admit Renata, and a blast of cold wood–smoke sadly rolled, "but my brother used to play air guitar when he got mad at used inks." Astounded when the doorbell rang, Fernand jumped, while Ralph excused himself politely. "Now," Rita asked at night, "do you need some more room which would put you in need of more wormy room until you are sure about now?"

"Come in," Park stepped back, wishing he had put on some music at least, for some Niceans, who scratched their bell and belched obliviously, were parked on a pineal hook when the doorbell rang again. "How do you mean to make a stranger stand in a live room, lurking at walls?" "Can you put that in a refrigerator, Hesitance?" "Hell, yes! Help yourself!" Finlay did appear both bewildered and relieved at being had. "Hey, does anyone who straggled a B7 chord on *Mr. Ng Live* to talk PoD out of it knew he came that way in a box?" "Why did he go up is why you'll get some tambouli." "I'll take that," Señor Florian bellowed, happy wrench at a ship salon, "if it's your amplifier," Park askance, "aren't you sure you could play?"

Finlay shook his head not, but before they should say Hard Rock Cafe, Florian stretched into a back pocket, extracted a wallet, and flashed a blue hardy har–har at spin. "I love spin, spent two summers kibitzing a void." Ralph started in on trunks of social occupation script: lettered half freighters, rebels with terseness, all the opportunity to act like I knew when I'm buried after learning the anti–climactic metaphysics aspect warned Tell away from blazes through the creep, in such a pitch caught out, free O'Henrys at midnight bereft, if notwithstanding, but no difficult thing you can survive, one's condition, sensitive to dire auction, suffered enough clout as topping, perseverance in a good will exerted frankly all said to high scrabble.

Applied to those trails, the key to nowhere nearer heaven should be consistently infested above the only once rewound but perhaps they are spent, disproved aspiration, focus, found seats never really mask his discontent whimpered something drastically chafing at the book warped, like slightly won, another figured out now it's kind outside and crowded oratory beads hung inside the center, search ink blots administered thread to generate static tradition of a workshop at the local barber ful-somely, Fernand premised, thus placing the soundtrack in town forever, abates, and now much turmoil would suffice for a ten–minute April, matriculation to a especially devastated cornice of the archway, separat-ing a hymn, meant a few of the shuttle tables will probably involve dialog with citizens of the distance; miming other sentiment, Talitha, solemnly mute, bedecked in starry–eyed gregarious al fresco tulle, loved truant diesel expeditions, posed foremost chrysanthemums, and like many ever

ominous SOMHAD symphonies, outgrabed, moistly tripped among decalogues of soft shoe to bandersnatch tapestries of flaky cursory [sic] bats,
stung by festive acorns, and sneezed, "my next act, I am sure, is neither
manifest destiny of a tantric regret, nor a futuristic hive of mutant voles
united in nine to five sour refulgence, nor the kind of flaking outcome.
I am a calmly peaceful ethical lotus, my dear."

From her chamber at apex of the Kalisthenes Institute, she watched
the position of vessels below the water line. It seemed to her that salvage
float had been quietly opened and its content transformed; as it rode
somewhat higher along the wharf, stolid Niobe arraigned, as it were,
"if you stopped, held doubt behind pahoehoe wickiup with bedridden
scuba hobbledehoy, and then hove on merry old vines to spark every
romp amidst lacier glissade, I ought not be ongoing about how a stale
snort turned tea time into kelp taco biblical cider quilting bee for neat
new gravelly plebian gingko Nesselrode," a blank page intended for role
into a mythic stylus platen, hitherto rôte reserved, daring aegis of mechanistic self–relevance, a triolet of *œdith* unwound, being subject to all
kinds of oh look cinnamon doughnuts explained Roveretto, wroth about
bandwidth forestalled amidst climactic upheaval. There had been times
during the last fortnight when he considered suicide to be the furthest
thing after his own mind, mimed while wherever lurked despondence,
yet, a scary and skittish fief of imbalanced news letter art, mysteriously
embroidered circuitous sentiment so universalistic, left, evinced via each
known apex, gosplans paled in Gemini.

This May had been significant except for the fact as, if only offset
wandering apropos comic duets' noblesse world no less *chichi* must rati-
ocinate, Messimo's starched art led to an impetuous reflux from the faux
identity time share co–efficiency. Since infamy, his mind in different deference topmost, leagued entire imagined cities of stock foosball legends
who dribbled spheres unto collegial epitome for the azimuth to sleep
in such sudden hierarchy, thus Nephretite accelerated reality, yonder
spectral photo–voltaic evincement of perspective below a personal
standard, where attempts to catalog art involved re–interpretation,

authentically commuted behind sincere vision to forensic modesty (albeit
a somewhat contrived effort on her part, rather a sop conciliatorily
wrapped in a conundrum meant for generic pathos). In a shoal profile
of life during space, a moment left ere no businesses' amphibole clause
exempted *isomems* since abnormal repeal logarithmically, and sensed
room for interpersonal improvement if coelenterate, stood inchoate
Winnt, immillennial tenets narrowly halt an effort for closer ties among
smaller unknown analog harmony, and consortiums, inscribed on Fuald's
non–visual royalty, other than if someone else's depeche bonsai made
me skate listlessly throughout Beatrix's clarion recital in furtherance of
the science project mentality endemic as a measure of it still made him
laugh to remember, or to forget, reflectively, in front or eke what recent
inclement scroll between incidental fear broke, for well read love known
worthy, throve Messimo's unfounded non–deserved elation into inkling
visible fremitus in light of a rather imagined clearance of tacit article
obiter, sightlessly vouched occurrence of quondam calm, pellucid, still,
old deviance, now spun since ever merely high, compressed, rhapsodic
vita explicitly marred treble alibis; if unusually irksome, due in no small
way unless Melissa may elide how, their real rout startled sufficient scrib-
bles about dark energy, test pancakes consecutively ajar until SOHMAD
[*sic*] should exceed Noone's term in expiry of viable, aged vox populi [*sic*],
a drift thereby coalesced far from why her babe can roam as if or like
you were in all of the chronicle of wharf wear. It had never claimed to
be anything like the ground Ralph should have seen at the unmasking of
Nod seventeen years after, sitting around in his bathrobe so if someone
ever knocked on the door he would be technically decent, next, paged in
transient hospitality for everyone who might be waiting to be prescient
at his next Clausewitzian seminar on how the defilades of Vikram were
thought virtually ineffable due to its numerous proclivities and flapdoodle, so whilst the coalitions' alpha ray ohmmeters propelled into default
essentially, their plaid tuned rabble to erstwhile saunter into Ossian like
it were a half–bank jubilee and everyone had an extra wooded nickel to
thrust into the innocuous limacon Wurlitzer: import, tense, warmed, his

treble instant soupcons of germane epicure—stretched toast and yet their now lacked edge stood between ferns palmed their onset, past a field of endive now sniffed ELIZA's old crazed puppy Pavlov in remembrance of lost youth; caroled in search of nasturtium and/or oleander, Ralph, let into a starless hollow, all last visible contact with the Christmas tree farmers amidst their sedulous cultivation, starched a mantra of light, hoped for the next corner, yielding more funnels of grooves, serrated at one glimpse in methodical rows, and then one extra step, a glance afforded boughs of wary primordial copse disclosed in formless chasm; amidst hummocks loomed, tilted about tinkling in reply, held being, at best a stage worn prophet, terrific in daring private html to found old inlets so they may be for you in pretend quality time, a lone travelogue staple, elided via URL, not myth, nor further epistle, made known a necessary semicolon where only in said Reject Fair seemed any to be had anymore, and they were jumpy at all of your breezy assurance afterward a local stay with friends could be on the top shelf; deemed via their moues morose, the Institute as palliative crèche dwindled, thus Ralph tried to expiate his personal destiny via continual panoply mindset, epicentered on casual twists of unfledged diorama, somehow citing his bravado in the Impersonal Terrace, a new hovel they had been working on for ages for these who could believe all one can some day find and proclaim a written word, as sylph—like gnomon left appurtenances and out anyway to view fair markets only nearby replete for placing placid sampler people to plaster your party wall amidst monads soon capable of seemly visible aesthetic interpolated.

.   .   .

If then the planet floated behind a penumbra of SOMHAD and a person felt disoriented avenues either actually nigh or in another profuse likeli-hood, if he had to rescue another spider in his dental retinue receptacle again Fernand was going to be sick, except, unless, at Least, left unlit tomorrow, all on account of being estranged in dotage, a Norn appellant to pretext undermining of dystopia forever in the teens once more said again, the last minute of night soaped over glass, for force changed to peace, pledged Norah Anne beyond being concierge anymore at one distinct motel where the pointlessness of one monad was another's snappy stairway reprise; whence toward a brunch of apple and orange scramble, ran the parenthetic mimesis, its crowd felt led to rehash more exceptional inns with names like ye old thyme chutney or whom better to sing the hurricanes from A to Z than Fuald (cleared of all insinuation of the hermitage riot after Roveretto's overt mea culpa clarified the glacial trail of evidence toward imaginative operants of Kalamparumple), with Chocho Molyneaux and castanets, whose mere recent alibi, *How sparkling was our station*, found, synchronized via multiplex versus the backwash of Elias' theory of relationship, to premise an Ozymandian reel of luminously intrinsic concomitance, put mildly, reflux committees of Ike's Park, chafed to learn their middling bellwethers here, commensurately booked aboard the trans–Antarctic luxury steamer *Delphinium*, and reading Sasha's mom's famed dissent versus technological determinism in *Parallelepiped Construction versus 1984*, uplifting use of magic eight ball voting matrices as least affective locus of endocrine fission for the nascent demagoguery of Ossian, Echo, henceforth refrainant as Contessa, Mme Nadeladimov, told her future geraniums to expect no placid calls of Hesitance Ferguson, who'd, rather than change out of or away from her wyvern suit, painstakingly knit for Fâsching, opted instead to float away from her repressed Victorian upbringing and permanently reside in the 13th century; her son, Tell, scion of the lamented Elector of Flippenberg, on strength of his research into dark energy, interdisciplinarily displacing Norah's child Fernand to be the next distinguished avatar of the institutional office of *inter–regnum* liaison, before flushing this mandate, a staggering amount of effort to seek the clause asseverating Deerfield's dogged rebuttal of those faithful Muzak purveyors and, a lift from djinn, imposing the clarion recital of Beatrix as best in keeping their reified furball counterpoint.

Messimo, in a newfound dudgeon of nurturance, accepted the long vacant keynote to drift into hopeful realms of eschatology, as panegyric

extolled the brave flight of Alcuin's inner neglected child, said to rival
only Nesbit's ascent into Snorggi's nose for facile neo–revisionism, and
also late Suppressant's benign hospitality and provisional acreage for extra
terrestrial populism transpired by the sneeze onto the indigo sphere,
SOMHAD, refractive in Nicean penstemons; perseverant Læmært
inferred, scanning the cambric flyer from the other Mary's home town
touting the event as *chichi*, albeit obvioregals [*sic*], their italicization privilege collectively revoked after CIC discerned ambiguous fire taps in the
logic of Pyrogabion, due to their expediently non–modular inference
flag, had to wait their turn for the next official verticule to Titan like
everyone else if they wanted to get somewhere above oblivious eternity's
benign at last in more neat mimsiness whilst doing whirls, stew when
stuff runs, down framed, transparent phylums moreover localized, a
calm tradition, borne involving oblique sapience approached; a mess
made every doomsday, Fanta's fair ranch votive, elbowed they agree
flags, ill Noone splinted, some subjective charabanc doubtless. Propelled
interdependent of agit prop, fast gospel, light potato, several wheezes
spammed ELIZA's chart, pre–occupied with etched launch crescendos,
and there was not only no third floor below the fourth, but when late
night does start, at the break of early morning, the second hour ante-
meridian began while I, coincident with manuscript exhortation, try, so
hushed when tomes drew, too close, to hear no further than exercised:
perhaps Desdemona conveyed the impression of a person who has not
come to terms with an abandonment complex.

Re–energized from some indefinite past after recent family crises,
Regatta, procuring vespers of staccato, sang, doughnuts copiously
careened aft, mere time together, warmed away a veneer ozone laved
once upon travertine ghats had been indeed sententious linotype, froth,
eco–topian house–planning if, in greyer skedaddle thereby, settling
chintz, streaked yonder recherché vox opus coda into Midgard, etched
in candid foil vis–a–vis tantamount sequestral endive. Presaging war-
rantable bric–a–brac filing, successive emoticons unto *wishram* parapets,
freeze–dried at fixed period rather amenably dis–endogenous Rust ere

limpid kiln threw in, trammeled surfactant pericynthion to expiate tantric widdershin, a draughty fission reverberated behind the oolithic shales masking Pluto's heaps, mickly rousted on occasional pretext of desuetude, widely touted, for bluing, rotisseries, chemic, trafficands, width, flippancy, drumlins, consensual deliverance, or moss control.

Hitherto circumventive athwart any, excepted concrescence rarefied de jure through apathetic precedent, temporal substrata today seethed licentiously, waxed hereby any bug nowadays in declining furtivitude thanks in large part to *fjulsfut* drilling weakened inevitably, this prominent podesta, Justine, affected to recrudesce her lapsed certiori, endeavored the flappers' port and parcel, evolving much probe as, into weird lurkers enucleating subservience as allowable albeit sub rosa in situ, a skaldic exchequer, whose antipathetic regard for the Village aseptically leaked incipient mass approbation for a *lithiwatt* renascence, before refuted to frequent below decks; for frowsy tofu chat room ambuscade, this topic thence leveraged, an essentialist premise, oh for the lists they should fain heave, since supra–calligraphical parapraxis harpist topically made the bulk of her elective practicuum. Meringue hence compelled the in–service to select her notes over these from any other conspicuous solicitant, averring derivative insight would propel her collage atop forefront of ad valorem litigiousness swirled near teeming undergrowth macro, if languorous, asymptotic venues posed a shroud above inclement dressage, featuring an anthropomorphism of sorts; after a long deferred laundry excursion downstairs, someone finally claimed the strappy burnt sienna thing (subsequently hidden by Noone's herbal kitchen towel), left a fortnight ago with strategic abandon, in hope of predisposing numerous participants to be elsewhere when the actual electoral process occurred.

Unlike last year, there was no potential run–off, and Finlay willfully acceded the vacuity of the vice–chair position, persuaded sufficient cachet continued in retention of the spring clean committee reins. Each fluorescence forcing herself to behave differently, Jasmine, standing afoot, wondering why the clunkingness stopped, had an idea it was too late in the year to be taking on another habit, inasmuch as the pantheon

of public sentiment, and by this I mean one's waking nightmare trans-
mute, clamor, Ladæñæ Rita Consuelas Renata Mirabeau Mervyn, as on
only other elan, typist of account receivable branch, interrupted her
audit of the transcript, twisted forsooth empirically against the insert of
Ænselm, or whomsoever she perceived. To be sure thus, Justine, flushed
like strawberry fields forever, withdrew three feet from Alexandria.
There shall lie the way of all Earth. "Did she succeed in illumining a last
flicker of idealism in the soul of Ænselm," Sergei sensed?

Anymore let off of polling, all three of them ideally downed additional drinks as acts averagely postponed the temporally unachievable
task fallen to whom persuasively, that rebus meant to depart their native
land in search of fields of autonomic renewal identified by Deerfield
(how kind) as least suitable for staggered nickels coughed out of the
jukebox forum on demand, "this exposition, design too propylene for
the Founder's [sic] League into hurried canards, must have coincided
the promotion (dan don dun) of ill Fiume Paul'r'us hogreeve [sic] i of
global village," inferred Rita, "as importunate depth at his daguerreotype studiously fixed, dim–witted voice–over ditto either hastening
or overbooked, in any event, which Ænselm, formerly known as PoD,
had long since arrived in our town, though he was slothfully *untenet*."
A tinnily invidious claque, led by Bagler and perhaps Park, certainly
opted to shut out Van Etnabaron even if his better half, calibrated figures
catering to Iphgene Heppleweis, somewhat willing to recuse her house
mouse, if exorbitantly, lauded Chorister's own prowess into hastening
the gamey equinox.

.   .   .

The children of Core who slid through fierce ice... other characters need to populate this sketch, i.e., flag use of interpersonal pronouns: they, she, he, & reallocate, accelerate, or defer dialog most applicable to Florian's earlier fare...

IV — iii — Porcupine Excursus — rewind.

Fanned mournfully in grasp of pianoforte miasma, Bitsy garnered, fruitlessly, tea service, wisps, and strewn vermiform auguries to pound into the mint another wallflower compact, as her cistern Hesitance scratched those shaken voiceover hopefully and started hitting a higher note; daring the dark period, a knell drew yon alongside in the night, and from out of a porthole tumblers obliviously abound and sang, "what art thou wrought thereby?" If you are known to be felt so named or called, cold could weep rose, eyed ere ecstatic, then here were echoes, insissipately outgrabed amid area. Bitsy recoiled by ossiferrous tense upon whomever she'd much tonnage around comfret, pleat, or glory, effete in recognizant love.

Wherever Hesitance had drawn, alacritous parallel, true ever in a quaver, hope should need more fools, who brushed about cumulatively sure at times, did strain her journey, amen, sere these febrile dark locks, nettled Least's crannog swift, dart past amid summary firefly far–flung, dim orlop blanched beyond thin air, are gilded azimuth so listed. Next, Fernand almost let an individual bias persuade itself of their known more, else, to add, on closer insight, lucidity vacuumed inside his inner head after terse succession, moreover shared, thankful transparent scene, as motif lamps of censorious terrawatts contraindicate, Theban orreries balked Tristan and Isolde emoticon.

Brought in literal time amidst supra–numeral fictive anti–eternuer outremers, exemplar isomems [*sic*], moist surpassed gelato, a textual cloud how hurry up a mere stare beyond, bleariest on thin hope, shallots sank rather than upsize; apropos, selfsame hour glass, if the world ever stopped her career, once alone, gala, or vitreously held ostensible, permissive caprice, Sangreal, whose stage perusal, if inert, emitted via sauced murmur, will list eisteddfod format, an old eighth vintage traced before action incapacitate — some muons are they, hear threadlike weft hypothesis among glitter, arguable true ruse to levitate concerted balm against staid, unsent gnosis now known to be exerted sere yet stern, a mind howsobeit mincing gladdened vivid steppe via mass accretion over some tetrapolis, limpid absorbed form, so veritable sampler askance whereas tulle, couchant, read verbatim, wrought lint to typeface abaft, schematic flare downs disengulfed, the blemish fully forum afar otherwise her marchioness signally distinguished that, irrepressive than dim clabber, continuous radioactive senior charabancs rang too well, balustrades away, fine twill, etoliant furze, wistrous, furled baleen, fits out thick dolmen semblance starveling benched for the pluperfectly louche elsewhere, *Delphinium* pitched and wallowed westward, Ælfric, poised at the lifeless helm, listed into distant wind, *isomems*, as humming Molyneaux styled his film, lent seed to incidence of note rummaging a past ladder, Van Etnabaron, his back to compendium, stood way offside. Idly, the downer pointed the pistol and, misfired into the glass, decried, "since *Abba* to Zappa, there hasn't been a single personae capable of niceness or making fun cat's cradles."

Hyperborean lenticular viragos, jutting dream onset of a timorous quilt of red cones, mandated a change of spinnaker, but fiercer Chad's clochely chaise lounged, to their dismay, a large zigzag via the muggy fringe of subsurface currant jam, portended to outlast their flagellant energies; Ælfric's main reinvented fuse box whence helm function might bypass, until inactive amber electrode went dark, with sparks, yet not unlit, and perforce rewired unspoken if visible resolve, "let's enunciate famous aphorism and streak to modest points blank, sang along before each of you get too far off course." "A show of hand please: how many no–hopers does it take to fulfill what goes without saying?"

A exterior portal already battened in shrill wind which preceded unsettling gloom, "on first, for antithesis' sake," Ælfric yelled, "instead of cinching this deleterious maelstrom, are we wont to try another golf clap anon?" The word tore across rigging like one sonata after uncounted breaths, veering away past seven further hypothetical occupants disembarked among stations in systemic aimlessness; seared by his latte, Harold seemed bent on retrieval of chilled gherkins left about in the galley, and called, "would anyone else like one?" His words were lost in a maceration of foam. "Friends," calmed down a nexus flurry in Chocho, "remember we once repined in hope of steady enrichment, yet retained an inner door of wastefulness, a sole preposterous claim to liberty, to which we are shackled by chain of our own design." "Must he illustrate," the skipper murmured cheerlessly?

"After all," continued the downer, "this call for a round–up shindig to begin, merging this junk rather cyclically some other poor lost text." A neat communal circle a rational conversation that lasted several minutes, mysterious clouds detached, "since we're not taking you to fire lake that evening we'd like to believe a wider community speaks on our behalf." "For this reason we are moved to protest the mimicry of minimal forums, daring the noontide moist rain row, how they doubtless intend to create bucolic ambience, and its dressage nonetheless is reprehensible." "They are the worst vision goggles to start with, and they should" — "shut up after here they are," the third came in. From aft starboard, a decrepit mummer of shoal draught pumped gain upon them, unlit, drawn out of misty banks a crest, a looming, sentinel, pagoda, forecastle, poked horizon, grown, and shrank thus a raft, a hack, a barge of such immense volume that Ælfric, to shout over the bridge intercom at Molyneaux, that radio operator failing to raise intruder, would beckon indefinite clangor.

The skipper stubbed his thumb upon a horn of *Delphinium*, releasing chimerical barks; Van Etnabaron, relapsed from astonishment, jumped at in alarm, parroting motions. In extremis, Ælfric jingled the engine room. The helm swiveled amicably, in slight resistance; if electronic displays of junction checks read go all the way to the rudder, the screws were quiescent. The skipper flicked four switches, and each tripped as sails, fallen all athwart the orlop, dodged Harold who ran daft and lurked onto the water's surface for Talitha. "Why, she's composted a planchette," spilt personality second, said l'nurt Glyntz [*sic*], "to pollinate those grey skidoos, hover of course rare our very steep chance," staid, for stall odor of warily bent deportation tripwire curved above all they get there, "plenty of time, to evolve quaint cultural traditions, shall occur. Must, follow, trackless spore of Snorggi, lest, Core's children, ignoble eldritch ethic repose selectively." Relieved to see a frothy wake below him, Sasha felt their movement, imperceptible at best, still anew as engines staled again.

"Inasmuch, monads," Ferguson maintained, "relativity, once one's own, lost thanks to feckless practice of the valet." A mirror cracked, the mammoth vessel transfused them a siren blast of its own. "Thou might be grateful to blest Niceans for saving, albeit transmogrified, apotheosis," the raspberry of *œdith* panned; in sibilance *chef d'cabinet* made her way aft, fine that elaborate infra indigo monad skip mobeus create areas of aberrant fervor in vermeil tumbrels. Crocheted slow twinkle thimbles otherwise alerted semblance, only to immerse thus kempt pensive tampered proclivities unopened; capstan, run too fulminatorily, the fifth permanganate skirted their dully nominal cantors, determined to defer her expostulatory dibs on old hats of their acquired skill of wrinkling dawn's seminal regenerative distributor, since they wound erudite shreds reflexively phalarobian, three feet under elasticity, typify a google endive rapport while each quizzed worm, foam bats earned eidetic replicant, offset queued selfish and how detrope she'll paginate ontos withered persipicacities plume. *Delphinium*'s deck crew, flaking in an ascendant crescendo of yippee, saw their only safety in lifeboats and went toward them.

Ælfric, in divination of torpedo tube rigged aft in case of encounter with revenue cutters, swore, "I can't buy them life before the bomb, its kind sanity at the Sunrise Cage, where alternative market processes rode unwarranted aerial rows." Into the mightiest spiritual fare recently watched Molyneaux, the downer, brought from his crest one produced key. Returned to the bilge, Van Etnabaron inquired what was being implanted at that console. Molyneaux shoved out a panel and tripped a leaky relay to standby. Around topside, two hands, now, a third emerged below to behold the terrible vista of a zillion tons bearing into their little position. The behemoth vessel had no engine of its own and drifted, responsive if at all to nothing it sounded, tough Van Etnabaron felt a jolt of terrible joy as Parthian script, transmuted in Western stencil below as *Mockmood*, seemed instants away from sweeping him against its immeasurable hull and grinding *Delphinium* to piecemeal fragments.

Unanimously, they indorsed herbal inserts, if visually blase, and *chef d'cabinet* forbore apostrophically on repetitive off track psyche proofread, deviously if and away they'd dashed it to honor miniscule scruple wont for bunched twelvers learned of tonight unless knit, flappy eared historian (*all too busy*), amidst whose initiate madness instilled decided ad hoc intermission in preponderant depth for, a second time, alien sirens addressed them. The *xenonian* extender peeled out for lifelike boats; their skipping trippers ingenuously hatched foils to schlep away from *isomems* the primer fuse. Seemly lowered to lift boats' leaky davits on either side, their anthems reserved for greater display of consternation, spaced winchman scrambled astern and disappeared along the rail, beyond the encroaching shadow tanker, tuffets from a Rialto, thin sage Hesitance poised a mote, every universe entitled, eke horizontal, have ecsydonial access.

"Too rad, lo, was tele–sudoku in reply, if out of diffident moment and ultimate aura, piezo–electricity alone succored my hopeful bric–a–brac ordeal." To thus tame a weird whole adage, she suspends kinesthesia al fresco, augments her menu euphonic mirth, or bevels their berm for, if calm in prescience, it is heard of that Idiopath intoning, "I thought you were not around anymore yet it looks like you are still nearer," half–hearted vitality evinced in his escheated complaisance, meant more to any inane aardvark than to she who defined a long court. Beyond even Fanta's æsthetic collage, flushed via *scrapmon'* in what only she heard Tell discount as furtive aggrandizement of the fifth's nominal function of topical predicament, al–Kamil, suddenly wafted, smoothed throughout if disconcerted correct whole–hearted procedural intersections parsed resiliently, "than here," told unto earlier seconds, "shall desist mirror Velcro or crass prima facie else twill beat thyme for you to leave," yet, nascent denial evoked behind them old shucks, and their chilled rinse ignited, of all things, among themeless, deformed, day–old habitat, replete, "we need to trade up for, if not order out, the merrily color shoe tree," their youthful plaints, unsung in streamy air, tinted earful of local catch and release, askance for sooth, "in inane event we grew on," leapt abaft, Van Etnabaron spun to behold nimble *mockmood* in all its immensity.

The orientation of the bridge offered scant refuge but for all that, Sasha never believed, for all his lack of naval heritage, he (this, from listless author's immense nautical experience in replacement of canvas on directors' chair) was destined to die so ingloriously as to not be on the bilge when it happened. He heard the partner ship arguably behind open intercom calls requesting similar personal info, and peered above at winchman, a settler into motorized launch; Harold, elbowed, "come up from there," castaways on either side yanked free of *Delphinium*, the winchman told his submarine joke and called Sasha to live down rumors, garnering sifted dew on his trousseau. Moreover, a shriek of electronic origin, originated on intercom, scurried across open air. Van Etnabaron had hardly time to catch floorboards jolted away beneath explosive charges, jettisoning launch and winch within.

A gasp maroon emerged with all–purpose propellant, struck flat water, and skating starboard, narrower a furlong to travel fewer distances these too titans of the sea selected for show, crackling swift eddies, than enlightenment of deniable burden, this missile of *Delphin-ium*, a slaunch imported further momentum to the dragonfly wheel of the torpid, vessel, struck *mockmood* a moist note. The merrily color shoe tree outranked all other lost solar flares, for most of it, perky conifer revelries tranquilized them away from yesterdays, ingested scrap suffi-cient for nerveless deadening of need, and tads made more sense when ecological twangy mere days swore them into fitness. Up unless down, Noone held they were slower than ever unlit *isomems* felt sure of enough they laughed off key, notably unable to draw a sample bead upon realty, facile lease, and jumbles, crept among imparted hems, elevated instead.

Haply were fifth eager to retain post partum prerogative which included assurance of each step emit cradled swirly edification from at least propinquitous quarters, albeit inasmuch she viewed their fourth's didacticism as both provisional, and austere, immaterial partiality to a contextual awareness exogenous to their own liberatorium, and/if plaintive clamor arose periodically for their willful immersion, their unmet as yet neophyte of the greater whole, loathe were their carrier to countenance an application into a settling whence they were liable to further transmogrification at obscure behest of some trans–possessed minatory pre–functional supernumerary.

.   .   .

"Beneath trembling haste, that my admission to the advancement of humankind surmount the need of a greater whole," *il hogreeve ii* ornamented, at Acheron, "in every abstract a response dwelleth. No quorum has been called, for anyone may appear before online commissions, pressed thus page after page, account, or else dispense with me, in disbelief, imagining a single event played upon a par of misgiving, or doubt might blink in shadow of imperfection. As I apologize to my foremost peers," persisted Ostrand, "medially embark, mete in frequent resort to admonition, save this stave switched anon, and summate my purpose, an awakening became contemplation of a song milked, began, and left used ink upon the medium of firmament."

Of a certainty encompassed, major mote radii actual read, disinterested converse monads incensed nothing like this perceptual makeover asked, "weren't ripples dually transitive or forgiven," not becoming defensive at Fanta, her suggestions, or her reservoir of buoyancy, yet Noone repressed even Bagler's predilection for stifling unaccountable propriety.

Only yesterday, concession made to liabilities aplenty, Dauphine's recent synergy, best underscored sufficient reference to one 10/90 rule, also slumped into faint similarities, processed vigilant emission as stodgier shoal than avid format heresy.

Of those foment, mores, bidden, minutely planned, situational, not so second chance detailed in confidential assurance meretriciously at any level, could askance fearlessly marvel on them, resolute via always baud about, impeccably finessed trained horizontal specificities of innumerable shortcut practiced 24/7 nowadays; inexplicably a wait for instruction caused tutorial for libretto quintescentialities, erstwhile ersatz elemental forgot all, except wispy glengarries doffed sign of why should not, and sordidly packaged, an evincement of tournament, they guessed the hand of fun, civilly arrived since every tacit amplified aside, if they had any, all, or otherwise ran this very undeplorable pool, now tired of other wisdom systemic to Noone where softly ever snared sequential derivative publicity in perpetual datum.

At this, some of the Refrainants fell out, in dressage, vocally upbraided the cynical magnanimity of their Ostrand, and lampooned sincerity of a plan to relinquish imaginary office in return for a sanctimonious public bestowal of thanks for his modesty and forthright renunciation. This happening anyway shivered so many more ardent factions of the Refrainants' movement that, in display which approached tumultuousness, they argued for a suspension of the entire cusp. Summoned reserves of ex post Nietzscheian nihilistic nisus out–fetched boils on the hitherto placid and comported court. Abashed outwardly, *il hogreeve ii* remanded, to the static voice of the people, and moved convention of a diet, upon the second to last day of the year, could offer optimal opportunity for resolute confirmation of the electoral question.

Until then, time, as the habitual court, chastened, departed the forest of Lothringen, were bid adieu in a generic decent display of wistful affection for their value, a development non–prevalent in effecting any tenor and, pitch, and even accent, thus creating a personification or, it may be allowed, a veritable milieu of the EEC (echoes of old seasonal euphoria caroled around a frame via tourmaline contrast), unsurpassed, their bastion bristling, and ignored at no small cost but to themselves, they pulled in the moist, dedicated, pools of talent available, in a now sudden apparent aim of stopping the global village ahead of the gates of Ghent.

Life on the balcony.

Plair began. "In an hour before all of our deliberation contributed definitely to global warmth, some men and women of our founders used to take rest upon the Sabbath." "Why shouldn't they take rest some other time?" "At the turn of the previous century our forebears hearkened to the likes of Learned Hand, and other soapbox–derbied individuals after departure lifted lunches out of wicker mesh picnic baskets and listened to Souza, Ives, and Joplin at the park." Preferring to listen not, Fernand, troubled with a distant note, said, "as this race stemmed from archaic rust, timelines meant nothing."

"They then found themselves," added Kalamparumple, "plunged into maelstroms across Atlantis, invited to participate in all weird world wars, disputes they hoped, via their, or their parent's, or their parent's parents', recent emigration, their hand had been collectively washed." "So they then all won those wars?" "They came back acting like they did," Sergei replied. "They bought motorcars and made bilges and roads and sandwich boards. They pushed their margin with gusto and verve until that black day, the terrible procession of downturn, of numb crash, unveiled fear has been with us ever since, that fear of ergo economic meltdown."

"Tonight the number are much larger," Fernand conceded. "Indeed they are. We forget what dollars looked like on such days. Only a few of the bonnets may now recall how hardily their parent worked for one." "Give me a rain check." "May it never be. For their presumed shock wave, emanated throughout the world ere, caused by their reaction alone, they forgot to ratify the treaty, and were very annoyed when the terrible fire sale broke out over their own area." Fewer amidst them were notably imperceptible thinkers, attributing their cataclysm to the nation's failure to redeem individualism, and their descendants, who had, at considerable personal sacrifice, enabled the dominant paradigm to be redistributed to the old new old world.

"Beyond lifting their voice in unison," Plair resumed, "heliocentrism become so firmly fixed in the public eye as agitation, copiously identified with the voice of organized collectivism, they were shunned and their sermon relegated to the common screed through which the Sabbath liminalized." "So what has it" — "eventual, traditional voices finally began to sound hollow because terrible things were happening on the sidewalk, the dust bowls, the lack of hope, the appalling scepter of Carnegie wannabes selling pencils.

"In the United States, the sense of value drooped. Not just in number. Of ways" — "to do with my" — "so then our forerunners organized, at best despite themselves. Against the mere catalyst. Away with induced surrealism. Their shop galvanized, they listened to heliocentricists and wafted into power. All cottage industries are rationalized. And I am suggesting you relinquish the Porcupine to my care for a time." Kalamparumple concluded, "are you familiar with the ways of testing?"

"Some one must be here," Fernand admitted, "for compromise." "Then shake it and be done with it." "You have a poor and old heart," Fernand observed. "And one other thing." "Guarantees?" "There are none. You take them," Fernand tossed the pendant back into the palm of the hand of youth left in well by his brother for once. It was more of a tempest ongoing than a ballroom dance. The man on the street, if asked, would have sworn everyone sledded by their own conscience to a blitz on the corner. Explosively detonating charges cascaded into a cannonball of froth. As engines kicked to life, Van Etnabaron felt a surge of motion, freed of dumb rattle, and watched *mockmood* recede.

The joyful chasm which spared ships turned sick at sight of a tossing foam; the launch capsized, yelling man hintermost, Sasha squinted near the bilge. Already maimed dinghies were far abeam, their occupants hailing him in vain. The non–chancellor sprang upstairs. "I say, old chaps!" The downer and 'zkeeper stared at him. "I swore, 'man over-board!'" Sasha took some sinus pills as Chocho, in dissimilar skepticism with instant friends, sat up in front to avoid distraction, stared back in theme, "or men," Harold, amending, hoped restoration of correct nautical procedure might suffice to turn this ship around, for, isomems shouted, "they abandoned us!" Van Etnabaron ransacked his principle for accessory justification and rushed for the helm, shouting, "we're going back!" Reaching inside his topcoat, Molyneaux produced, and began loading, one pistol.

Van Etnabaron signed out and booked onward to seething Chorister whom, perchance recognizant of the deafeningness of silence without some fan out, or nearby whistling, and after some few fair breezes of laughter, only the gulps followed on occasional furtherance, sensed any more racing thoughts, again, upon recognition of her incapacity for gonging a direct wine tour with anyone immediately, and so far from actually being sure she remembered how to operate a vehicle, ELIZA's tutorial, not anywhere near the tablets achieved in uncertain reception, recalled other times she is supposed to sleep with so many left unsold. Ahead of his feet the deck raced, encased in canvas billow, and inclined their attention to fresh worries, for the sideslip beam had not been wholly cast from the ship. Lugging madly, it pitched its collapsed sail under the wash and threatened patent immersion, aloft of his hollow facade, high gloss as a project for another day, "henceforth I am a fun person," Sasha rocked forward at an unbelievable sight. Thledvirrson, asleep at the prow, stretched and lurked on absurdist sites free. "We have to fix that sail," Harold told everyone. "Then we have to turn this beat around!" Thledvirrson glared at 'zkeeper. "Get that idiot to help you, then," she stated. Cognizant of their inception, daring a liaison of ambiguous pattern, she'd wired inter–regnum grand council itself for petition, diffident their inattentive agenda could forestall immediate matriculation nervelessly.

These concatenations did not leave Talitha insensate of desire to maintain their homogenous upbringing even in defiance of utmost radical ethos; ukase in point, only nights ago she'd unearthed one old letter from An, dwelt fondly on severe peroration, and yearned for others' recoil all of suddenly into concession which she mailed the mall, back to sender, during a writ of unfelt jadedness: Florian, ideopath [sic] whilhomes, more skilful in fields of acceptably limited praise, constrained any who don't ask must bask in flings are philanthropically denied, insofar if they end this source by raising their complaint to a temporal level, they can and will cease to experience critical facilities of non–participatory requisite.

Effortlessly, staged ratification sublet hinges, recent fulfilled universal serial alternative, caressed to eventually gather potential, signed off on momentous patronage demonstrably. If thither whatever jolt required to conserve in popular preposition the parish nearby accounted warning that, unless they were mistaken, the farther above your born on date, eighths were slippery in a wide awake poison to be visual and supposed to all who knew, there, peered into mildest of requisition to breath at this juncture tidiest converse amongst their wide stare, Sasha, to learn there was little to–do while a drunken sailor so early in the morning, Thledvirrson, unable to comprehend digression about half a crew missed, thought it altogether a joke and, cited to be gone beneath, arrived, the sky, per halt here her explanation helped the *xenonian* slog out that sail virus rod length. Ælfric left her id to ward the deck.

Subsequent to such flap thus, being able to stay awake to learn, or really learn, titles by almost their superseded compositions themselves now and then, Lizavetta, in her new bubble, haply adjusted to society, the skipper managed to free amply of the sail to allow three pairs of hands to roll the sideslip out of the scowling water. Talitha spat, glanced at the bridge, and left, Ælfric jabbing his due RV, *isomems* remnant up their sleeve. Out of sight, "I'm renewing my options," there should be heard breathing. "What just happened," asked Harold? "I am not happy with him," the downer's voice echoed. "Salinity layer," Ælfric murmured. The non–chancellor followed, not too smartly, for the hollow voice beneath the bilge added, "he knew too much." "It wasn't anyone's fault," the skipper shouted! "I would help him, and how, to forget the past," the bridge replied. "We weren't moving," Harold claimed. "Of this be sure," the voice continued. "The launch imparted momentum," exclaimed *'zkeeper.*

.   .   .

The cloud nocturnally moped once Plair accused his salad days of a dear petulance. All told, their feng shui died in haphazard trips behind damn heffalumps, "so for once would we just fizzle down and exhale?" From a tossed and idle density, Bitsy spake sinuously, "methinks we show old finders fee some rational biographies, al fresco, each yearly key a canon," and unto them rote Ranth Tyoslament padded, "can we ask shadow puppet for our mede and stop casing about like rodeo clown?" If, "did someone say lunch," Fernand recognized, in Van Etnabaron, admissibly, provision this elementary lesson in dream exploration gone mad, "for his own good, I should help them," the bilge repeated. That decreased their plan, only in order to manifest peripheral to which lack of successful perception of subjective interval whereby each throve least the microcosm then extant in accord thus pluribus more than we, "it, home to shake loose witangemot, even since displacing in certitude such infinitesimal graft, bleeped semaphore." Lest fey twilight hang ten, as soon as lumpiness on a miniature gets here, everything would be called beans everywhere.

These *uchaux* sapped, too much unlike patient forbearance they'd dismissed, albeit useless at awaiting answer in order of whatnot the moment therefore went nothing used, foppish diction, Bitsy, aggregately nettled, lisped, "ten hut, mister big idea, it's pronounced ro–de–o, not ro–night–o. And furthermore, don't think we've overbooked under–gatherer sodalities, transit near agrarianism, its wall–to–wall sybarit-ism, staccato laxness, aimless narcolepsy, dualism, affordable worry, and rank excess, i.e., the end of innocence." Then extrinsic know–it–alls foment a terrestrial evolution somewhere and they'll waken in a ding dong patchwork faster than some doorstop can say open sesame at sixty cents a hour, go figure; over and above tense sets of tents to fold really unctuously, monad sprats, so recent thrawn at Mount Period, pervaded *wishram*. A contemporary dearth of morale enjoined the decimated expedition: the finest duty observer had engagement with TiVo; select *spacemon'* are subsumed by *finth* into their marginalized argyle nicety effort; and seraphim, ousted at large in ostensible co–dependence accorded, the straitened nature of Bitsy's common seemly sole guarantee.

Gainsaid dreaded consignment of her chads to the dustbin of apocrypha, even at cost of objective de rigeur exigence of trans–solar diaspora, she mussed their pearly brows capriciously, wondered if their being sent away must defer a dread hour when they whorled amply to reiterate their own trenchant origin. She could not be there for them always: even now, matters dodged her screen saver. Bade their tutor adieu, *chef d'cabinet* handed about to reach and every one of them soon flung fin–de–siecle [*sic*], relieved this stage only pressed them on their desire for a nocturnal farce which she now voiced over. Læmært, left to ponder intersectional rivalries, his tryst revolved via Rita, now Ladæñæ Renata Mirabeau Mervyn, daily, unlit, the mental granularity of his reconnection suggestive of surreal, vague awareness that Mme fused also this revelation to syndicate second world loan with such frequency, the ICA sent eflots systemically warning of screed too thin, yet, if Renata, adept as Dauphine in sorting finance ministerial forums on their profligate fiscal practice, how it was highly popular, Noone often maintained, for any lender to demonstrate a necessity to receive minimal scheduled repayment, and often offered justification in good faith, operative before the proved assumption her concerns were of a winnowing scope, that to voice either of them in response to any casual inquiry risked utter dejection (cached in extensive if regretful admission of helpfulness).

Any borough, here further conveyed additional, albeit in suppressed indignation she dared at all those pro forma salutation, Mme Nadeladimov, likewise during seas of ostensible maturation, maintained belief in the sudden efficacy of socialization, developed condensed bon mots cheerfully rinsed which, befitting repetitive scrutiny of Her Majesty's exchequer, sounded of admirable brevity in coping any mediated situation, yet may also grow to strike others in a spectrum of non–complimentary policies ranged least flippant to carefully orchestrated remedial campaign, castigated the deadbeat while charges of self–adsorption rang so patently blatant, insofar as the borrower devoted so much of his life in annealed, if faithful forgery of miniscule sentiment, and yet so expressive of his interior temperament that, once concurrently sparing courts the onerous burden of inquisition, Echo either spared the receiver to cough up or henceforth conduct his affair in probability writs of restraint were in perpetual space betwixt he and the remainder of civilization.

Sergei glanced sadly at tabloids one night suggesting Delores (of whom he'd received sporadic, if non–annotated, portraiture), implicated an important, if profligate Midland armature scandal, received dire instruction stemming the collapsed fortune of Chad's over–exposed portfolio. The trial made no scene and other authors, best notably Mme Eliot, sagely steered from attempt to portray inexplicable litigation, to make a long starry shot. So shall it be only their barista, as Regatta, cleared of guilty negligence toward ELIZA, and as Desdemona, rarely found herself the far side of a barn, from whence she viewed anyone daring to admire this wall ruefully, suitors seemed consoled by a notion she preached their motley pluck. Yet as Dauphine also conveyed tacit admonition that pursuit of any further commerce risked sanction, of unusual illimitable severity, between quarters of heretofore unspecific area, it was why Frank was not surprised by learning he (and his ex–prurient syntax, saga clad, links of presence, vis–à–vis echoes) received custody of a suddenly sprung prune dance some day.

.   .   .

IV — iv — Plausible Songs Beneath Circumnavigation.

Cypress, ere cerebral, haunted retro—drag refuse anew, gonging Althea's ottava rima dogma—cheered area. Thunder, bonny ere a toad gang engulfed pumice, enfeoffed her dark ergot. ELIZA, this anon glib waffles, "let's then etiolate vine debt, peccant omen, never foment bellum sleep, far off we go, a shofar elides chichi [*sic*] elves' mycology."

Harold, detailed to find that safest hiding place to be which folk would expend least effort to discover, inclined into awareness of attenuated ebullience, wondering wherever, if whenever, every exhibit, an ad infinitum vibe, minimal, thin, ritual intake of breath, introduced into one's very intersection with depth, wherever encountered, irrespective of intent, invariably induced an attitude of mutual imbecility in the difficulty of coping with one's sub—consciousness. "I have significant structural deficiencies.

"Assuming some sort of tap dance is drawing nigh; imminent milestones of reductionism provide apt excursion," bygone, next knell of *isomems*, annoyed personae comprise, "my anticipated audience, away to your daily toil, cease thy perpetual beck, upon my talent draw no more! Have the countenance of one who just lost a new car." Raisin replied, "that's good neon for me," and heard a knock at the door of a white—out photography excursion into Ossianian hinterland.

Noone decided how growth toward that wandered, while lost totems exfoliate, wafting orrery pence, i.e., most of the children lived in town and had lots from relatives and neighbors to sell. Noone, however, lived on a small memorial wayside with two horses and four houses. Moreover, custom still frowns upon external consumption as, attendant to the institute, Park photographed them, now feeling they, and those close quickly behind, secured prestigious positions with local access TV. He took them beyond his swing, a rum photo lab at comptometry school; Norah parted the rain–washed curtains in silent reluctance.

A rattle of tambourine and recorder note pastry, and a lot of chirps some time, made that stuff come in boxes, "you know, pilaf, where," Hesitance, stepped into *wishram*, placed a sock on his eye, "and a proper hash she made of it too: HELP!" "Since," Sr. Florian shouts, an astonished gasp, "did you know our tutorial (*all too busy*), who's from level *chichi* and googol, save odd start again sur blois, Marta?" A fosse in isosceles rafter, daring surcease cicerones re–accessorized just acriflavine rice floss oast, agog to clutter into gingko wattle lilt.

A tumptily pashmina camisole madness tabulated, emit numinous Spanish carob thistles, tassel, whammed each prop as matinee purlieu, Chatham's lit nurse bloom here dyadicized reverse fovea cure in a melted silicon thong fire. Ralph shrugged, so what if Raisin liked Finlay? He waited for Bagler, anyway. Until the enthalpist bought his zephyr, Park could sit nervously in his haunted house; unlit, all walls, ere painted black, he pulled the old GE stove out, pointed at a sack in Finlay's hand and said, "oh, yeah, Henry (VII)'s trial is really cold."

"Anyway, do you want one now?" Tab. A sachem drooled, "ELIZA strained amongst such wonderful puce guests." Her doula added, "eh, diner fragile lures ghetto, tough with a Tlingit frowse." In paging dire frond, each, lilies' evoked naphtha misfit and dearth grind pheromone soapstone, "poor marmalade, look to sour 8mm eternal awe, amalgamate claques we help empty, even wind dawn," and rattled wand in eflot nutmeg around calm ethos, Fernand remembered, his air guitar in Señor Florian's clasp, a hand–carven [*sic*] reed recorder; Marta, self–consciously, held Jasmine in place, emerged from *wishram*, and whipped her hand on a trowel. "You know," Fernand persisted, "there's a place where" — Ralph nodded sympathetically, "are you over Ossian?"

Finlay asked, "aren't you?" A lowbrow eye her flung nettoyand, monks, haggling on saccharine root remover, motioned Meringue until toggles, tripped down, "I'm not tired of putting you for smoking arch epicure, as my duty is lecherous." "May rabbi tap Athena's bare knee, yada" — "which doesn't mean it's time to start giving stuff away like you have to wear special glasses." "Thou art too beautiful and awaken much mine wit, mingle hope and, a ripe hat heaved at, I learn to cherish best as bold sconce hanged." "In darkness only wert thou chaste, in mome barn fled blight, a fly is icon template, you fiend," the respective sod instilled, thousand then bid adieu to her bus.

Exchange students wrote a mystery chapter about how half a dozen Thanksgiving's day postcards would spring up there, "and acting all inquisitorial, I'm viewing *The Today Show*, the vast panoply of Americana steaming at the workshop yesterday, and came back here, made bean soup, and sat in front of it." Next, they vehemently celebrated this liberty with ardent squeal, fully capable of stranding, if effigies involved in getting beyond something did not at all translate into strength necessary to a committed and adroit realization of the problem of a global economy.

Ælfric, nearer these, cries, "listen as wind, rushed into funnels, died in distant tremor of radial engine aloft," and another aircraft, bumbling among cloud, banked to the east, sounded nearer, and receded unseen. Scrambled from the bilge tower, Sasha saw the *xenonian* leave helm, a ring finger fiddling his brow, '*zkeeper* ascending steps, quietly, to the bridge, and one volley fired. Shortly Ælfric, emerged, his pipe relit, his glance indicated Van Etnabaron into cabinet, immediately thrust helm to the north, and pushed all engine to full.

·   ·   ·

Albeit aware there vacation shelf–life perished, Lothar was not immediately avid in dirge sun tan and, while *uchaux* guessed to an extant, his present perplexion centered an estimate of average period expectancy of this thirteenth century only slightly higher than his own apparent age, and driven to ask whether sufficient longevity derived his original laity, Fuald in receipt of enlightenment at best describable as cagey for instant relief from want; aloft this dove stream thinly nestled airily together distaff indicia so free of worship, need led below their decibel roulette a miffed bilingual whose trite exeunt caused Porphyry repetitive avid disbelief, "did I really thank Hesitance for stopping by her own premise, pausing only lamely to add, 'and showing me the ropes?'"

In this half–life aplomb, they'd hoped lackadaisically such decadent sentiment vacuum–sealed their tenuous legend, and no sample word found in synonymy for however rheostat, Alcuin's crept desire to wonder whom she else also, façade fully resident in a sane complex while non–italicized, still ennobled vicissitude. As tile metonym lacked why, so houseboat spelt a cursory panic at annexed, or brutally coefficient spritzed capable of schleps athwart time, and moreover strained insight valuable unto cognitive speculum eftsoones brought Florian, ex–Carbonari, a worn sustenance eked only via a continual function of being how Idiopath. Never more truer care needled, his brow, once fainéant in perforce conscientious, if not diligent, oversight at Vikram, now crimpled in resolved simplex of sullen gleam, a vapid rill of azalea, indeed *uchaux*, to give them due, joked now, "just don't suddenly die en passant in horizontal sentience," one of those otiose lament virtually invoiced levity, a multi–tier carbon wafer form you are too excited to sign, coquettish, the dotted camp conga line here, and initial, and here, and after all you are now in your down very infrastructure binky; wilderness of this initial fret tamed any civil inertial toward their dovecote fraught other manifold non–sourball seminar vamped via lack, lapse, or moral haze.

Via bent must our prune hook seem, mused nearby sacristan, lullingly involved in fashioning inverted bifocals allowing wearer to read while gargling, a wary vigil drained of antecedent. No further notice taken of his reaction, Ostrand devolved contextually ontos, fascine cusp mean nixed, ultimatum petulantly, Circe shall deign radiate thither isostasy redingote photo—metrical dare, a sconce hitherto tined by jongleur, foamed grim filth isle tax in novitiate smarts for myth, or else logy hologram too presciently immutable, etoliative (par and as thematic after) oast just cause more degree of urgency to flourish sententiously below privileged substratum of trickled upside anon to virtually sinusoidal premise, yet humane, via enrichment this plinth find, absolved, otherwise remiss parish, finality of a curate gratified toward envelopment, a festive van illuminescently nigh.

.   .   .

Thledvirrson, once declared infirm, had access to candles and a window. In an homeopathic regimen, prescribed to counter her recent rapture, she received a series of beta treatment, rennet lavage, and carotene enigma. Yet, moments persistently recurred, "alas," Niobe told her, "our hypsometric families munched soily apples, as palimpsests deify all ersatz oratorio." In a generation, iconic neon always vied Thoreau, if monads ought stream online tomorrow their naive colonnade, "harness those beats to merrily claim the skate of Erlking, and the fief of warm malt shall be simply rarefied."

Awakened by somehow plaid, their song, spirit stirred in avail at Flippenberg, an eldritch plainchant arrested their attention. "When your child questions you about benefits that matter, you are one of us. When you go forth to correct the plight of homeless, you are one of us. When you stop to clear the strain of grief above the window, you are one of us," the teleological snippet finally begun, a pledge of Iphgene, whilst undulated caramel aisles amidst the King's peace Yule swiftly came their avast width tunelessly.

Snorggi sneezed upon the blackboard one hundred times, "we will not throw stone, until spiritual counsel bade us fit to do so, three times did we cry onto thee, oh stellar master, four untenable truths: at this moment we knew nothing; amplification aside, one thing booked up, over, and out; for if ever we had a stage to play out, around, and up; we should not know what to see first." An ipso idiot, skillful in each inhalant speech, knew not a savant from a sampler eon, what gestalt whirled, winking, "who'll now, if distinct magic carpet, dull ill mist of wishful fragment, redound, still cuff necessity as cheery unless now?"

Ting tong. Startled by public address, Talitha lurked on odd old ague in cerulean, [*sic*] bat en andante and Goth rugrats sanitized kismet fleece otherwise tacky, and dim catharsis provoked several pensive paper hangers to heave more broth against harbinger of wanton doubt. "Do not attempt to clear your throat," one said. Sedated and left in a tank, she heard the other reply, "aversion therapy." "My opponents wait to be frightened by noise, acceleration, space, volume, density, velocity, elapsed time, mass, and time," Thledvirrson explained. Cut off from outlet and fallen back to one's most basic choice, one had no device but to float introspectively a final mote of *Delphinium* unfurled above her. "After all," continued the downer, "this call for a round–up shindig to begin," to sub rosa, jests on cue, Nicean thought unified, in deprived worry, and atoned few fugues insidiously.

Certain letters, become utterly unusable for a tension they drew, embarked, a bravest few from their tapper skipped breakfast, if pledged to reverse the Phlegethon sneeze issuing at least in form with consonants. Much dismal voyage of self–discovery thereupon no long concert, gaiety of creation fanned the raffle, where names of rude vials herein, time tide awash twice twinkled unforeseen indices, drift of yesterday's tough act formed chattel to what once one, hazardously combing open sewer for any last caress of former plentitude, And/or beckoned, ex–foliants resigned to self–ware, vice, or easy simultaneity. "Life on this bi–plane, so degradable," they submit, "is war between manner and intellect, we're made to knot, dream, this garnet rose shall belong before we've enter churned slim gym.

"On florid tour," sung about the ceaseless word, "unless we escape this nominal gravy, tell the occupant we've enough, we will meekly return to *inter–regnum* and dank *untenet* splat, if it will prelimn an accession to any of our former glory," continence made. Their hearth floundered before unslurpable dust cosmos, obversible might likewise for any scratch dive bee—lined, heedless of prosaic lector, a crew to converse about their tidings. "Let's not seem ungrateful," these said, "but we fail to see cause for shiftless agonistes [*sic*] when rods within only replete tinctures exist for nearly indefinite suspension." Reference toward their seventh's crystal lobe shivered their hopeful horror. "It shalt not die, neither," itinerants persisted, "it shall turn *untenet* perhaps, but we shall bestow above it all of our sententious concern."

Their *chef d'cabinet* maintained such cusp beyond issue. "Given our seventh exists," she declared, "we are viable," adding, "sufficient where-withal to jet yonder to Titan, amber world of mellow methane mist, wherein we must habituate stolidly." "But there are no cables," whined several juvenile *spacemon'*. "All the more reason for us to keep our tapper intact," remonstrated their *chef d'cabinet*, "for once space—borne, we can retune our bent letter array and you can view cables until several of your eyes are seen to drop out and roll into the glitter." Several *fjulsfut* seemed amenable to syllabus, and were seen to re—embark, when long before midday, ten weeks bluster the mid—level sanctum, shouting of ephaphs at the workshop. "This week has spurred my, or me, too, slashing efforts at recognition, during which I delivered a, if not the, long—lost manuscript (again)." This heady experience, amidst the cold fallback address, "could an e—mail of embarrassing sentiments in cyber-space be more timely," their *chef d'cabinet* reorganized them as hidden lumine [*sic*] charged with unknown purpose, and urged her chads into their seventh, only the bottom of this page forestalling unforeseen and yet immediate dissertation. So rang forth, a premise gleaned, *biathanatos* scrawled from pallid snarl, "traced neither to diversion roused, mingling, charms, Ferguson nigh endowed few pattern trans—subconsciously," and perilously apt, since graven tincture cork foulard, in onset of witangemot more hypothetical than usual, ewers spoof forth the most dative concept alit in doom, and incalculable carnouba daybreak shelved thanes.

Eventual consequence of recusal, invoking disestablishment of a red herring microcosm, could drive Mister Pepe's pizza into federal receivership with vigorous display of macro—economics where, stag-gering to imagine at once how little chance did allay the sixth election spritzed, and now level drummed modern pockets of dynamic sobeit, arched caitiffs once again trammeled proof, of venue ancilliarily, null that uncouth polarity residual of utter ataxia, the men, where feasibly elected, my green chime center gone, verged, squeezed the faltering helm. The adjutant ordered to raise *HMS Flie*, Cubist expatriates assem-bled. March arm in arm, they were instructed, to fire a single resolute volley overhead. The mob, thus lilt of putative insert from now on, may all pica gram ember defer to an importunate disconsolance of variety, plastic diet slimmed toward some elsewhere sensible totality. Film crews whereby stood—to, all remnant to be given safe conduct to a natural manorial hindsight of their choice.

A situation mustered, men who seemingly erected gem—free fencing teach—overs chartered a jet to participate in an annual Winchell's Equity Mutual slam dunk fest. In the fortitude of event sent *wergild* or whatever else appeared ostensible below, least ambient sauce ranged aisles novelly of convenient skip, and if thus history, inexact risk, vindicated in a cor-rectly finite albeit rough out, in civility another quarter amidst recessive flattery farther forth became their initiative mode apparel. Albeit at a rabid pace around option never learned, nary convivially, Messimo shooed yet forth anew into sterling vision rarely noted actual indicative of quantum behavior. He retired to find all in anomaly.

Failed to execute his bequest, Cubists dispensed to the nearest cus-tomhouse and seemed to gesticulate vociferously as *xenonians* frequented the sidewalk promenade. A gamier delegation had not been remise and, thereat already busily engaged, driven up price of orange futures by grading out junk bonds on a time share basis for a highly erratic consor-tium of nepotistic sturgeon. And if this were unable to beat all, a plenary session of senators announced rationalization of the cottage industry, further distended a fetid rank of the undeplored, commending *isomems*, in reference to professions' transmogrification into adjunct of the coal rose concern, many of whom unsuccessfully trickled across desert in hope of sighting burned man, and entitled via successively cloned PoD, Roveretto made one effort to claim his pupil, skulked for parsecs at baggage claim, and sensed thus return possible from his investiture ere indemnified to policies of mortgage.

.   .   .

There was nothing for them now but handling of cureless preserver skips. Harold, guided by instinctual question, established a weak narrow bandwidth distress pulse on the radio's internal transmitter, in no way interdicting persistent fireside skips of *œdith*. "Forgiven, you may realize I do have a sensitive nature, if much of it deflected sideways. The problem, nurtured, artists are only lovable in certain coach film festival short features."

Nor daring to engage a trip–wired engine, Van Etnabaron knew there was little time. "Not in actual life. Nor in our current epoxy, which is inertly transitive. I found acceptance on another side of the curtain fortnights ago, one who saw the other forest behind trees, and still felt sorry enough for me to live through it." Visiting the hold and carrioccio [sic] surrounded with rubber baby buggy bumpers, Sasha twisted them wanly, the louder dread half–cyber gnomon pin–wheeling in stealth at a dowdy get–up, which oozed in sneezing. It was, intuitively frantic in retro, lilies, and a strange esoteric friend, Tut–and–pish–posh.

The dwindled nudge, once radiant of all hope expirant in foamly tinsel multi flare constant, "if I hear that swan song again, Talitha," found that flask set beside her, Rand drank, "she, quite capable of applying all sorts of problem to the real world, had a quite work ethic, and was very good at closing a deli." From the hold, Sasha found a spanner and torqued the lift. They tricked heroic toe–tapper into fad tango, and a thickset tinted mongoose hurled moth ball at stingy upline thermal tracer screeched over the top. Outside, a young lady, Delores, on the emergent topic of steam punk, announced her next dance performance and smiled at them until finding mistakes in her already published work.

Sangreal wondered if, as senior resident, she should organize *HMS Flie* whenever, after a nice chat with Fanta two hours ago concerned previous regnant sees within the building: the *xenonian* couple from six doors ago who always left their shoes yesterday — it was really a tonic to loaf around in decayed old Nikes (combs may boost altogether human curbs), of stylish warmth; froth, a dream worn lawn, other teenage boys assert mown via iPad, also finally wheedled a shrink appointment. Soon carrioccio [*sic*] appeared on dock. Thledvirrson was the cad Sasha ran on and streamed unto the smoldering beach.

"She really stole a daily inseam degree out of university, and was novelly a sincere ingenue, next nine years, until I retired from a force and went out of commission." Every engine of *Delphinium* throttled and snort, dragging them to shoaler water, Harold, remnant in the burning vinculum, if of intertwined junction, and recognizant, restorative within, Talitha learnt from remembrance, redistributive of an antenna; amain, ce 'est ne pas non bon chance [*sic*], he left the bilge and a hatch, approached amidships, *'zkeeper*, all smiles from the helm, stripped the engine slipperily.

"It is never too late," Sasha replied, feeling a jolt as *'zkeeper* vastened the catch. He found it thus readily shocking only an unimaginable drift behind now caught *Delphinium* a lump, running the bow keel askew. He tumbled, almost exponentially, to deck, however, restoring bilge switch relay as red nests of sand, stolid beneath their feet, gummed progress of *HMS Flie*. Her snippier taunt at him, "that's not your best chance," left on the radio, Harold adjusted gain correctly. If only he were to wire for current observations, it would be a project for the ages.

"I've seen worsted founder." Ælfric belied, their boat run aground, "you shall soon hear elemental torch charges non–cooperatively grand." Arrested by a plunge of pre–meditated stop, Van Etnabaron's slump into console, and, this motion energizing sequenced signals, *'zkeeper* heard transmission commence. Evaluated, its capacity for response did not wish to disable its prize any more than need might allow, but it was necessary to its plan that said antenna be bled. Presently the dish, remotely queued, ceased transmission and smoldered.

To Thledvirrson's groggy vision, stars swarm aloft in a rigged sky, recumbent, awakened in latent jejune ennui, facet of at least belladonna torpor anaerobically clung in drafty lyric sob, dancing an effortless cara-magnole right atop a chasm floor of bad honey baked shards. Grendelle's fierce yet empty task, to persuade Niobe of the wreath reckoned by chilled scarab, struck her a sheer cry of useless, stealthy woe, and she offered to hold hand unless first lit. "I'm sorry, cupcake, we sold your chakra for extra toad venom to awe a scary couatl, but don't be up in a dump."

Van Etnabaron sought to bring an engine switch back on before involving *HMS Flie* with care of his co–dependant, Talitha. Ælfric frowned fiercely. Against his better interest, Plan B, prospective deactivation of the engine block, left his unspoken reluctant resolve perhaps. A thread should be adequate; snipped back from the palm, Ælfric abandoned the remote swatch and, divined to prow, of a stillness all around, of full final night, swam an aquamarine yard, recoiled ashore, and waited.

Agave recrudescence.

A stream of land grant archaeologists ascended to file for further exten-sion. Dauphine, whose mingled yet free fez egg machine seized, via multi–media dispensationalism, or transported in verse to replete the ozone lair, inoffensively curried maximum sentences of ten thousand smiles, fifteen months at the Ministry of Plenty, or a moment of utter despair. "Thus ended the renascent exigence of Kalisthenios Institute and, on anniversary of its unlamented passage, I was once again able to order iced coffee without spamming at attention," *chef d'cabinet* paused. To watch her children steep obliviously, unable to shake a sense of cloying regret such resort to declasse methods were needed to sap their bountiful exuberance, must sucrose and action figures be next? She loathed to admit Spartan syllogisms of their tutorial (*all too busy*) might provide a stabler atmosphere. They all attempted to pin the quirk affecting daily operations.

In adjustment of trend to meet certain universal standard, parallel elsewhere trend required, in courtesy, similar adjustment in alternative universes, oversight quickly noticeable on call, but individual labor beneath the system underwent intense pressure, in slackening immersion, Harold, guided by brisk thunder splat, sufficed to glimpse the panel, receiver flickered on in time for a latest chant of *œdith*: "my dear scratch, listen, you wonder what sentences kept shown off. You wonder what person serving them has gonged for *HMS Flie*." *Delphinium*, pondered into reverse, dropped anchor, and self–activated forward decks charge, "the most interesting problem dealt today: try to get the minister's cats used to a new brand from Formosan. I found they enjoy listening to Wagner overtures. While this is life in the specific northwest, it is lit beyond ten thirty PM. I watch my neighbor deflate his lawn barn.

"For the last time today, jitterbugs settle in for midnight and the lake's surface is glassine." Smaller squibs foppishly apoplectic about the un–chancellor aboard his only command, Ælfric, ashore, achieved a Napoleonic seizure wholly related to disappointment. "I've not forgotten that minister is on the range, with clients on his own phone deposed fourteen hours a night." The webcast went on, "should I work that heartily to get here?" The bilge reeked of stale soot, as had Sasha once. Later, counting twenty–seven crackles and many a dark flash in our last conversation, "you asked if I wanted to be a self–ware facilitator.

"I did not reply for several reasons. First off, been there, done that, and second, would I look my new traps in the eye and send them out on twelve mere tours?" The *xenonian* opined, if roughly, aye and paled, full on, hump, i.e., Thebes' chat each how this ex–poet pled, "for heaven's sake, it never thought Pilates as arduous." For several second mores, "my plush green recliner, rescued to attend the huge, air-conditioned summons, sporadically acceded to coin even more than what levied last week." "I think the self–ware field needs to get over itself," Ælfric, noticing *Delphinium*, syntactically tragic for immolation, adrift at an inordinately lugged pace sans Van Etnabaron, attracted rancor.

"Third, I already booked into it last year, but could only find Noone to sponsor me. Everyone else left me wondering if I spilled something or burned my bridge when I put this project on the back mirror." The *'zkeeper* shorted, "given all kept ridden on the telly, you would thank the destined coeval stopover!" "To what purpose," Harold, astride the deck, shouted back, feeling inevitable? Ælfric warned, "perhaps I am easily discouraged. Maybe I should look into it again. Perhaps I sound too defensive. I feel threatened by leaving this savoir faire I've built up the last several years. It's too easy to say, 'oh yes, I need a change.'"

"You believe I haven't figured that out yet," Sasha laughed, his brain ransacked for harsh nautical ditties? "Perhaps I always had a clear answer to happiness: we are only entitled to its pursuit." Yoo–hoo's were all he could ever think of and, lifting voice to them, he viewed beached Ælfric figuratively far amain. "Then I should see someone who might accept me for what I was, an extra–terrestrial dilettante proclaiming all of life meaningful and devoted its entire energy to tapping thousands of radio chats to prove this point and, in spirit of sacrifice, refused to accept payment for immense service proofread," *'zkeeper*, lifting its bead as the voices fade, knew; within thirty seconds all would go up, accounting for debits of time consumed by other trip relays.

Too far away to be of benefit to anyone, *xenonian*, thankful that hothead Harold nipped his caste among fine hoots, walked inland, turned not, now and then, climbing familiar paths, marked but thirty–nine steps to the top of a cliff, and in ruffled imitation of lame jests if not mystery, Ælfric counted eight dozen Mississippi's and time to see the sea beyond erupt into laminar discs, a noise not quite profound as one may have expected in blight, flickering, one, left, two, burning amber jets, three flares, coughed up the stores, spun up into random blackness and on since claimed, when tiered earth host, non–flat, yet PoD could have frozen had he not forgotten how it kept attentive by dread e–tales of artist dogs' devalued word, used their extra mint to farm into eerie shade while something, and personified wit in angora, Talitha lurked into vary photo hearth, can stele however a loci here, some pallid Ingersoll, tasered outside the gate of Echo's croft for totally unrequited peccadillo, soon took up demitasse and methodically rubbed out rampant exanthema, "which bring me back to the first question, why do fire side chants keep showing up on your dial?" Tut–and–pish–posh brusquely revoked all haruspex permit, pleonasticizing torsional wire cue. Dithered beneath the kachina, he tugged the diver up and beckoned they start pushing the teak frame.

It trundled, dragging its bundle, at port side, one of the plugs puled, "simply, you are, my muse, dear listener, you are brilliant and are a quite streaky sub–cutaneous art in your grown room." One of the rafts caught, expanded, and nearby buried Talitha, but she grasped hold of another blunder and a second raft, inflating, her into the car. "You are the happy few." A third raft encasing itself around them, "I actually noticed last year I am terribly self–absorbed and need to get over it."

Groped past a mad diamond cougar around to nurture her since upstart kin, Thledvirrson egged some fawn flunkies and scooped the little chestnut out of a vast, heaving, porously cheap undertow. The float sensation, squeezed amidst hissing canvas, must be bliss but for smothered alarum. They bickered at her tense, lackluster whine, spoof pacifism in roll call, by–pass decorum, and lain for nap only after two hours of hoity–toity surf, "be of good cheer, for my yoke is easy and my burden slight (Matt 11: 30)." To evade it, Althea clawed a rough seam and peered to just nix impolite noses, i.e. "also, thank you, like me."

"Helping her make pizzas, Chorister did not like it whenever I asked for change, as if I had any control over the twenties." After pushing through this, "it was the best day in the happiest time of my entire life in the mirror." A monad who has left all visible traces of youth behind, Grendelle chased an old hat down Snorggi's Noses and created a kind of bother. "Your opinion very important to me, our short time together spent in the same boat placed me amongst ranks of the truly fortunate." Bits of ship, singing canvas, sputtered through heavy air, or skipped dervish stones she ducked. Into safer smothering, "I hope you have a wonderful vocation, and will riot again soon. Your friend, *œdith*."

The sink stanchions hovered while barcarole crept out of a boom box; proof clearer humbug still descanted phony swan song of allegro con molto metonymy shelf wink. "Did I gather laurel just so you should tip your point spread all over the lonesome prairie," Niobe sulked, discoverer of a molecular houndstooth stag band? Van Etnabaron, atop bundles, gazed as explosive beloved *Delphinium* sank, *finth*, micro masks dinned to blink a salad of floppy repose.

.   .   .

Rescued by HMS Flie, Talitha admitted to Institute... per Village circular 91–96/ Q.
isn't it probable many roles indicated via overuse of impersonal pronoun may be
fulfilled via other character? [A.YEpper]. From Worms, the hamster Wormwood
has left to seek help at Ohthereitis — forum of chef d'cabinet insufficient itself for more
than hundredweight of individualists therein frozen... her child cloned with
shadow of ahriman (strained past cordon via isomems) to form PoD.

IV — v — the now high five...

An irrespective, if casual, forthwith, imaginary as all get out, and lurid lack of focus devolved upon Talitha, carrier of an ornamental world, causing next a ledge scene so difficult, Giuseppi Tartini's *Devil's Trill*, induced into elevator mix to impel her musing placebo return, elicited while staff henceforth affected empathy, ponderously deep, crescendo of a star–hatched bore really was per amber Norn abetted aperture; striven against, An Indocile, donned, in seeming comport, jessups monumentally arduous (if this latch guaranteed furtive gulp of aggrandizement, the Nicean ambassador pointedly dependent upon a more or less dextrose demesne).

Numbly this context inertly mirrored significant leap of vapid aversion, and pirouetting versus stock egregious onset of *isomems*, and driven beyond as an eventual switch sublet her weave of vastness into mock after hour footage pledged as apt riddance of cynosure, their tedious foray sprang into causeless froth, annulled parallelepipeds punt along imbued via acetylene tempestuous moors, yet careened misconceptualization of her apt and moreover tenuous claim upon reckoning.

Almost considerably under strength, seconds timed their beliefs; these vapid aunts visibly forgave Në Dipol for introducing monumental Mountjoy who skipped along the tabletop, bore aerial glimpse so of urbane illegible and avuncular form wriggled below his spirit chatter, which lornly whet their estimable appetite of any of this diabolism; and insofar as only Noone inclined to obstruct the tripped misericord harbored in iridescence, the same old faction now ergo stole disparate against the empty quarter.

Disposed apropos restorative refulgence aromatics Messimo wove in regular psychic dalliance well though rough, those daughters of Nicean rebellion proved seamlessly inept contorting his gusty zest, and diverted among their critical fretwork, embraced a sullen plaudit. In a neon tirade, Roveretto proclaimed victory of the illuminati; nearby Talitha, hidden obvioregal speciously concerned with ensconcement, his viewed progress antithetical, too far from mere writ of fate to heed arrangements, "seriously," Niobe lip–synched, "you prone divas brought so many ornate macramé wet hens herein, our yard birds are sick tone poems in repose!"

"From any perspective," Grendelle raged in falsetto, "sanctimonious suburban free–for–all serve as pabulum for masses, dress trivial ill, enabling usurious miscreant to faun persistently the facet of it," chaste well of night, tinged before pitiless sunny mandrake of flashy frond wound into the howe, gurgled away. The launch, of *HMS Flie* disrupted by hounds, of drab honeysuckle, scrunched into the beige hive, forsooth waving chisels in torpid mania; it sang thither some teeth, Santeria, witty chichi [sic] ad lib occult hysteric, and mimicked their angst with deranged moue, probing at large.

Disheveled all, obversibles in atrium verily hushed, as nevermore seconds travel in sound, and in sullen concern were current dredged for lien as drear Antonine premise made, their lucidity compensated in over–statement for what in schema it lacked. Princes rose with pace of a mandate, another aspect of trance, and legitimate mantel fiercely bid were only one time supreme. "They've got hymn." "Americana shall never slam her door on us again," was reply.

"It fell below myth and into fact," the eavesdropped reply of ex–xenonian [sic] intermezzo Flambeaux, into another time of moorlands and grazing brooks, thundered into being, the dream, *iamin'thelim*, deftly recalled, since to dwell upon a recollection of word and lithograph, crestfallen, Frederick paused to bear out his own devil and, resigned *iamin'thelim* unlisted then, the parenthesis convoked nepotism on them and, consecutive in council, second through seventh peers of jihad waded forth behind their adult contretemps as their thirstiest wand turned over a well thumbed chapbook of Anouhle and stammered, by cornet, anxiety about being too slow. Evaporated Tuesday, eventually numerous syco-phant requite patent made to order felt, pre—empt the airy showman to disclaim he'd not eloped without checking into this Sidharrtha houseboat in decade. "There is really not much to say during your expiation," the host expounded, daftly erasing salon lyrics.

"Illimitably," *œdith* intimated, the ensign, eddying on, "unless fast forward, this stupefied precise mathematical baroque toccata settled toward discordant regions of night music, whose ironic blast persuaded the recoverer (*all too busy*) of something: perhaps last glimpsed equanim-ity, astir, shall always lounge above realm of mythic significance." "Admit to your auction, such trusted constituency," purported Ng, "led to eke out fanciful frozen existence beyond reach of Euclidean geometry." Finlay, as newcomer, stuck out a hand, but didn't stand up. "Hi, sparky; Finlay you know, from the party at Heathrow." Another alpine ray, least landed at Dulbin, Hibernia, where cousin Glyntz picked her up.

For Meringue, a difficult time. She whined at a chilled, teeny wren on her wire tone, "does Jane Doe plaintiff have a case?" "You're tsk — a crumb," Talitha booked at Tolstoy, who drew a filled—out application. Occasionally stretching to preposition an unlit pipe, "location often varies," declared Ferguson, "and An Indocile, whom I'm sure you know, if you'd stray with Wormwood, you might snub out distant ennui," for Porphyry maintained what conflated for noble reserve but, Niceans crashed, smoky blackness, dim flickered speciousness, hooted and sprayed, and wailed for credit copious parsnip to fuel their tapper.

"Sometimes we do business with the West, but usually everyone pretends it's around quitting time," one of the Niceans said, pushing ashtray acorns to be within Hesitance's slight reach, and fifteen—minute musicians suddenly lurking at each ruse in another prism, Finlay exclaimed, "I filled a Chinette with guacamole couscous, dense baby, lest gruel on an all–night cruller hang out." "Oh, that *wishram*," everyone sighed in reconnection of past values: even the famed spiders (depository receipts) are in this class. That may be one reason, *chef d'cabinet*, Ferguson tacitly responded, "all right, she admits if at Rome, you've got avarice, blame, and brimstone," so it was all around time to clue Finlay onto what, "equilibrium, dear peeps, is precarious myth, a intrinsic falsetto of the past rung, the only shocking note in an orchestration of a hollow present."

Achieved of very little early codicil for a chance to descend, upon poor tales glimmer so cold were shadows pitched over vital essence of any person darned venially in this outcrop anabasis of desiccant. "She would tell you a tale of how men see, inflect energy, etc., charge grime–teemed oven." Causality grasped, verisimilitude begged recognition of tedium of mediocrity relieved in creation wrought of sublimated vintage. Idres began, "thrifty tierce, Etaoin," but unless a watch tower leaflet supplanted overt thresholds, cause shadow puppet to be relevant, ecstasies of shriller note than usual. The free nice library foundation television switchboard, as flooded calls from irate viewers who regarded their holiday ambience ruined when, tuned to expect a cheery robust Yuletide log, they were confronted by a smoldering pile of buffalo chip, the contribution to the season not endearing Esmeralda to her nation significantly, and Nothing–to–write–home–about's petition to save the saguaro salsa still squished in lower circuit, *Mr. Ng Live*, hoping to save its program rating for quarter sweep, turned to staid science before his lead spark took refuge in a patriotism evocative of disillusion.

However this acrid facet mimicked, for indeed, over informal lattes they agreed all hands existed today, *Mr. Ng, Live's* lead biopic, a search for the next bitter, an effort to describe recreation of warm fuzzy dust mice who existed prior to dawn of an atomic area, left a dull smudgy pastiche of market sauce, "emblematic even before ululation began, de rigueur, an ethos of individual responsibility is ruthlessly promulgated as panacea to social realism," his guest interjected, "you oblivious, spouting sampler of humanist tenet ad hominem," Ng proscribed, an ensign maintained, "my impetus stemmed your own axiom of personal will." The interviewer tapped away on a pencil regardless, "please explain how present avenues of souls scammed to your premise of trans–migration conform to your, or to anyone else's notion, of liberty?"

Plair decried, "you patient scribe, adept at any decontextualized motif, extolling convenient knee jerk truism," a monolithic reality, as method of restoration permeated their rhetoric, logically dissident from their charter, for throughout the Institute of Kalisthenios many lolled in thick glazed foliage, giving drenched heed to out–book a perpetual still. Their institutional role involved clearing up after others, including spray of food borne surface, large cans of industrial strength germicide especially effective against tricophyton metagrophyte, and all genus of staphylococcus regardless of aggregate, motility, or political persuasion. Bipedalien humans were very sensitive to imputation of motive based on stupidity and thus resolved to stalk and bring to bay an egregiously large and churlish protoplasm that refused to self–immolate at approach of men who flee yet deem ginseng fete nicer over–reach; but instead, scampered beneath the counter and darted into the fishmonger's kiosk along the opposite aisle.

The men had hunted germs through thick and thin before to recognize this. Pensive in verbiage, during the foyer discharge over formal concession of omission, the directive made clear, immediately, acceptable hope required concurrence of numerous entities before admission of such intractable, unpresentable, and obvious ununanimous applicants. But a dismal refuge, the clammy temperature of the ichthyologian template assured their quarry must soon flee in search of warmer clime, or else lapse into a cataleptic stasis rendering it helpless to well–aimed spritzers of isotonic froth. This woman met their official stall with sudden retort, bearing standard of global village, one, so startling in vehemence abruptly ended interview. "The eighth day has dawned," she whispered, to return to those whom were among the first persons the resident had ever wanted to see, she since committed here to the cusp of mainstream idyll, as frumiously, the men glowered in damp shame, displaced canon marked for new patients, and went to ground, solicitous overture sparkling re–ignorance of a current fashion as stale citizens routed their gripe to an ill–used service entrance.

The summit of exact research yawned as men rolled their noiseless gear into the freight hatch; moreover, the protoplasm failed to emerge behind its crustacean haven in expected alacrity, and men who seemingly effected, recant regime change over, scrupling to contaminate the fish-monger's ware in a lysergic coat of butoxylethanic residue, settled for a siege, seeking to enlist public opinion to a cause. Burly wards singed by doubt as to their credulity received the press. Dispatched, a guest donned ties for the occasion, men who seemed singly reflective ere centered; more vague cheer assured members of the fourth estate their campy night went again conducive to finest spirit of expedient perseverance, all environmental directive issued by federal, state, and municipal authority consulted and danger to public health pronounced negligible.

Upon a dial luminous fluorescent numerals, pointedly too totem, shrank the sub–basement several floors onto an indefinite cone of silence, many yards above stretched an irreversibly habitual aptitude examination and items of reciprocity necessary to unseal it dreared. Returned home to resume an Argus–eyed vigil, reporters were soon diverted by fragmentary evidence alluding to tentative emergence of an inauspicious chimera on the provisional horizon, however not until lauding men whose effect mingled, eerie recent give me change, or in a well deserved mixture of aphorism, elucidation, and innuendo.

The youthful resident, Sangreal, retentive of a coherent process, seemed equally determined to prolong receipt for they, albeit dismissive of negotiation, appeared known. The hidden interlocutor, nullified by their grievous intransigence to precept, charged lesson past on forensic substratum regard admitted at outset. Out–stared, Thledvirrson, divine into her intern's cowl, heard their resident, Sangreal, her Lilliputian ankh tile rests mummered, a name, Messimo, in great dismalness, who now declared time this kind of inkling had, until end of apogee, now on. Furthermore, men whose merely decent effort each gave some nicer ego learned their leakiest wink should open gates of surplus chemical warfare depots. Far from tour, among a bleak mature local ratio, Roveretto now strolled languorously within a shopping distance, unnecessarily baffled culminative intent, a hot sable awe, a mass ferocious frozen cornucopia of unclear, biologic, and chemistry ordnance manned by fewer fierce Cubist expatriates.

.   .   .

Altogether why blotto anthems value hue, those veered, tingle eyes were gas mafia. "I'll deserve drivel at every turn, *isomems*," cried Henry (VII), "so unto Worms has one come to surpass every other conceivable activity, freighted obsolescence, and least important, where billions of time flies clung for warmth, a how–to book, dealing with the fact everyone doesn't like me, contraindicates our entire political system, if not rocket science."

Blinking being flashed, a scant shadow of vortex (cursorily), "wain, herb teeny, you starry–eyed apparatchnik," interjected cognomen too, this tapper, whose so convinced cardboard silhouette, emplaced behind this date, sure cost a chrome one forum, Rand, or nutmeg in their native scene. It was nice work if you must get it and how, *uchaux* lastly canned either elder tech window fan, tattling, "in the night of our immense demesne, they lived in."

"Always cool mud huts," *isomems* said, dusting where everyone was too polite to throw out with the fridge from his apron. "In future, please seek to address as few of my needs as probable." "Will you realtors portend," retorted that castellan, "there is no future inn, least in a fit yoga endeavor?" A ferment, if you will, on cruise control, and then some, shaped their subsequent aspiration. "Anytime you have to save something just to be reminded of how annoying it was," Messimo recited tartly, "some stimuli must arrive without; after all, is it written shadow puppet can turn old lost pie into bingo?" "Since disparate eke in this hall," replied eighth, "unlit, each moment is overlaid previous epigram, you start play out of a shell, and you're left with a land decayed."

At Worms, yonder *uchaux* noted sharply regional deadpan settled into this affair, proof replete to Roveretto of nadir, when even hope glimmered, amount to commensurate bean on a scatter diagram, rang from effect drooped anywhere on the floor, "and on top of that, if you will excuse us, we have to eat everything in our refrigerator because there is a flight to catch tomorrow," floundered to euphonic template aft, a flung chandelier on hip individual pluperfectly ticketed sub rosa. An entreaty met dully, Horace, to book a light flan out of that dump, also fortunate their, one last bowl of available junior mint, festive horde swarmed from clover the map garrulous Chantal (she noted merit of remedial analog veto communion, and someone) kicked, a glass of feathers over you may believe her appeal for traditional value could have been met by Talitha with a less than glossy glower, yet immediate procession funneled into kiosk of sidereal escalator, bygone deliberation upon which floor they were on in the first place.

"It, one of those thatches in the lobby, who twittered so," Dauphine sensed, aware of a great vacuity within a Globus scuttle, sidled over a speechless dumpling, warbling about catch and release program gone sour. Tolstoy privately lamented offhand remark, made on a tome of an unknown known, upon efficacy of rational distribution grid as embodiment to delinquent graft: a theory, Echo's detailed twin winged bronze Victrola, only Noone permitted to photograph, on an unspoken fear that voltaic spectrum could induce oxidation, an incessant effort to inflect her each intonation in mellifluousness likewise whooshed beyond this pearly elbow macaroni wavelength, insofar as she rarely eschewed important unity to say whatever seemed construed to cast lamest ripple.

In hindsight of his moral reflection, a jocular insistence upon cross dress for operant condition evoked starchiest banality of risk inherent in wobbling over broken glass via only a do—you—have—any—idea—how—much—this—off—the—rack spends here, and amidst post cantata let out, his repeated heated evincement of understanding grew progressive, more shrill even as they gained a street level of consciousness, a tortuous thoroughfare of cobbled trademark licorice gimlet. There participants sparred hand over hand an appreciative bottleneck created by a sidewalk vendor who chalked how subjects may look had they graduated with degree in rocket science.

Formosan began to sound like a broken record extolling virtue of this pretzel made me thirstier before that Orthogonal honeycomb fell from rafters down in front onto his in–flight cereal during cylindrical selenium rinses propounded to diffuse imperishably erogenous bandwidth in motley olde England sort of all over the place. About and around four bells something transpired which Horace cannot have wished upon anyone else: a jugglery non–expected crash in upon by *untenets* whom, albeit in demonstrably modal cognitive deference irrespective of his mild evocative semaphore, natheless excalibrate sensor tracing strip to an extent his own subsequent egress collared *Barbara Allen* considerably hampered unlit Talitha, hitherto proved infallible at never anything left unprimed.

Flouted concierge for Horace's tentative sojourn upon hot tin roof (in private her lip balm restricted to treble denial involvement in plots as widespread as her evident interpretation of his salient rapprochement seemed to indicate), a ton of loose–leaf chronicles erased all nets. Sooner termed anathema than Niobium tumult, Dauphine's apostasy server emitter, any drastic minima, sure trued undetected settler evoking rampant Ragnarok tour, touted incessantly, not any entrechet knock 78RPM cheaply, detail made needy fobs draw sampler simulacrum, at best ceramic in anomic remoulade, evading russet hacky sack until plenty of wonderful tinfoil rodeo no–look tinsel bug looped raw algae nocturnally.

Tabled at a linoleum dream safari, somewhat natty cage runners amassed sobs. "We, provided any rule echoes sour ether bean," said retinue innocuously acknowledged, best recourse to knit brief unsung inchworm on land. A secular indemnity waived glad egress again, drip, enumerating anchor chart room, serious ethic tangent normally perpetrated truce slanted on a naive facile lark, brash Nehemiah's Diner, foamy fold yet gourmet kismet, authentic illicit cilantro, recognized finest ornate remoulade, instilled since retro nutmeg out–sourced BBC panel remotely Hollandaise, albeit to sum us up, once formal nadir located folk star–struck at resilient style zone, appropriate flock argued necessity of egging totemistic webcam format. Incumbent modem sahib, in surfeit of laconic asphodel spray, cited golem cheater for slanted sparse analog report of crepe Anasazi impresario experiencing birthright buy–out.

A more felt–tip Circadian espirit, lacquered gingko Earth net, thrown out by delta Sturm und Drang [*sic*] zeroes, convinced Nicean iconoclast of warped sting, any spoiled fen snipe en rout to Elba, ebulliently deactivated, should find ignoble. Here, sans meta–tragic snakeskin, a derogatory inkstand, leaked spastically near Potemkin–like calliope, obliterated one chiromantic show–stopper, his knocked fork abscissa botch, a rough succor enfolded our perpendicular (argosies entwined in cognate deities one dared not yell at) nexus, and annulled top drawer winkly deficit, attained marble eidetic nodal limerance of utmost synaptic ectoplasm, sibilant in it mimicry of macramé nonage, Justine, bicycling across topsoil of Artesian muck, dulled our crop circle to point out Nosferatu knick–knack intercession, emerald al fresco Roentgen tulip love, chubasco joie d'vivre [*sic*], emoted jubjub immersion prophesy, and laced newt baffle immured, in skein of tangible acidophilus, is existence a question of tie–dyed whirl, fogged at wonted yard sails? When one neon wont in sooth exacerbate ibid ROM demotic vanadium demilune heave–ho?

Unless Tolstoy would sneak off, too, a kismet erupted insecurely. Right off, fluted grammarie, An Indocile, denied libido momentoes, rioted up and down the cabana, in no bulk egg roll egotist, and in snippiness moleskin label look no fewer, imagine our flimsy occludant edging holier simpatico and ski through a mirror to get a terser quarter of routine. "Egad," Në'd said at Knesset earlier, "each sloppy pun fulfills an Etch–a–sketch." "It rivals tamale nobility for messy tae kwon doe rusticity," anthologized next debit fob, Etaoin, recurrent in wobbly ellipse daily, "ere nude nabob morph via cassava silo linked decent feistier lists toward edge of Maya, my aim life's merriment," soon, vistas of thrawn heath cannot wobble, cheated mind set foot in springy pond, dark yet theogeonous, an ignorant slug reconciled if trendy to dumpiness.

.　.　.

[*Nicean non–translator's note*]. Many individuals demonstrably upheld a sense of collective sufferance, whereupon aggregate imposition devolved into exaltation of personal caste; as counterweight to baggage levied by ostensibly cooperative movement, local decried reactivity, culminated until fail, safe proclivity, despite their dim furtive allure, resonated above the dais forever. Somewhat apostrophized, counsel perforce expostulated against heterogeneity of these slurs, inferring central issue hinged upon clearly omnipresent hazard of exogeneity.

Few insinuated Henry (VII)'s conduct within the pale merited the board's incongruous scrutiny in no respect accordingly, ¶hrotomeous, on verge of impending unilateral inoculation of these, bandsmet (Park mixed in his praxis their mirror for ours), a self–ascribed palmer moreover a manifest conflict of interest. Then chamberlain (*all too busy*) laudably beveled the tribunal for convenience beneath much exigence at all, insofar as their entire worldview stood menaced by outlandish consortium, and invoked venerable standard of *mare clausum passim rus et urbe* as extenuation of their multi–tasked portfolios.

In many instance victims contended their assailant has been known, always unknown, invisible to their escape loophole knot, massed for coarse protracted tape mixture, accessory to uncertain cubism no more valid than another schematic mode wrap, warily endured least upon thalamic orison where tort, and so children via pedigree foment owned some flabbergast or other inconsummate levitation cerements, their sordid Fourier diva laud motif in vacuo Regatta laved, ampoule too phonetic than ingressed, a not so crazed cureless catalysis, inch vitreous wavier esters: queue eked doilies of sundry weakening. Lent mere gorse, as Chad used pose of live but rueful ladle for each ecsydonial waif, who hoped we had though tough thought ought beam causally, very thin urgent ability with European film shrove furtive beneath so ochre are chaff requisite; some credible elective cause always marries ethereal ambience, fully owed near almost fuchsia or anecdotal infrared fealty.

Effort of synthetic asymptote irked Fuald in his tremulous perusal of riprap estremarine — his might had been, via Sybil too, other than sentient to joiners and yet were — so Delphic brevity as emanative of these scintilla recessively phased, truth left him pastor of only prospective awakening, ware of more discerned ambulatory viscosity where faster hoverers must caress as simulative bugles of amplitude, nigh upon pastel and agate Ohthereitis, without next mention why relatively indisposed digression served to care for her sparkle, a small, rife, if likewise faux happenstance created infirm, or will comb out reality to stratify several uneven topiaries in situ.

Given a merry task surreptitiously gonged somewhere, age no longer now neared everyman whilst beneath the Nicean coquille, bunched in mimesis, aggregate coalescence refrainant mattered serviceably in midst of cuneiform plead caught up barren chuckle moot; aye shelve foist perchance pro tem nomenclature inter alia, yet drawn to oblong etude, did reap nearby trochaic premise forth, a Simic, Mia known to Brie, scarcely carafed happily after lie under solid gloss, viscous sessional amplitude ere ectoplasm eked ever nigh, whiffled contra benign polyphony, insight shown being coterminous among devotion. Argyle bellwether each cheerio, Vorga's cerise emendated plinth, unlit fame aegis, heretofore conflated in trove, every verse seen mingled for locute submersion so miscibly, placed a reticule of a straw schism on virtual nascent misplay or fond derived atoms, a serer runcible demitasse of placid sidebar once moreover typified extrusion of certifiable foolscap, anon by Althea, at one remove from salutatorian outremer, by virtuous vapidity also muffled terse censored areas alternately translucent.

Efflorescent rouge, gratis warrants of obscure seconds handled moist fugue, canter away specific occurrence of causal whereabouts from any standpoint; banns evolved, for sublimity, via extra–terrestrial elegance, diagnosis of ionization pattern in concomitance, Læmært finally arrived at a hypothesis not only plausible, but indeed in verse fabulous, a torrid zone so displaced. Echo's skepticism the clinical staff floored anon her medicinal quest, an event log inscribed listed equipment as an appropriate standard, anyone able to read asked for the rest of the day off to ascertain further event, justifiable warrant a borderline coherence patronized, whose otherwise brittle realty, occasioned in lack of documentation, steadily diminished at outset one's influence on event, a predictable vision of florid hall long sial idiosynchronously winked at destiny, awaken some secular tofu, yet Në Dipol, in wonder there was any canvas left, seriously nixed a result ultimately unfavorable to those if unmanned.

The sound of inking denied, Ælfric heard instead a sullen bark, a mercurial thud and dialed jihad munition council to lodge. Compliant sin die, it began to rain heavily so, unable to hear everything, cell phone shoved into sand, benched, unlit rains coalesced, gurgling, into his upturned face. Eventually, drizzle slackened, pnyxt peskier magic hikes flunk to remember an ex–consort who wore sly if preppy kewpis with epsilons and went in search of there.

.   .   .

If, too dry by law, an inkling for red socks thrawn in the whoosh, ELIZA ascertained, Paul'r'us, divesting which first love ever guessed him worth time spent filing an order of restraint, returned from his encomium, where he, indulged to remonstrate, a digressive presence, for earnest reason, at some length upon a topic unlikely to be accountable for now, persevered in knowledge that reliquary and very much else still lay within stow and care of Bustamente, reserve salvage skipper of the Merovingian state provisional coast guard, Matthieu bent all of his posh energy assuming command of the salvage vessel which resuscitated residual crew of *Delphinium*.

Awaiting il Fiume at the quay, Bustamente's scruffy party consisted of the tarried Agostino, skipper of *HMS Flie*, his assistant, Ostrand Ampersand, Harold, and mimics carting parturient Thledvirrson to a summoned ambulance. Truly, "sweetheart, I'm faint, you should ever philter a foggy dove," Talitha laughed over half a marble loaf at the teahouse, our only last daydream. Arrived, elder Ylferim administered, from fitful height of his own pot, Village supra–podesta [*sic*], a severe dressage upon the entire expedition. Quorum of *finth* echoed, grown wroth to batty surreal eye and flapdoodle, "*chichi* twist, akin to dreamy Coptic blues, is indivisible." Talitha said leave listlessly, and trolled over the side with many pistachios suddenly.

Later, exceptionally staunch questions of the peculiar disclosed Matthieu's resolve to notify federal maritime authority, even if Silas F. (the new high five) slyly inferred they had plenty on their mind after conversion to RUT. Grendelle, given a job teaching tea kettles to whistle, *I feel good*, liked Hummels again, and one mondo mynah bird, feyly met in allegro labyrinth, poked what fun it was family time for Talitha come hither. Until departure for Midgard, Matthieu gently suggested everyone would need a nap. His nephew, Ostrand, archly callous, offered to take first watch. At insistence of Monsignor, Flambeaux, Van Etnabaron, Paul'r'us, and Ostrand saluted the late Charles, Marquis of Suppressant in a descried vintage, and joined elder Bustamente with a draught. Drawn atop the cask, theirs were weaker portions and Agostino retired below to his cabin knowing the ilk, like the lost paradise that stayed put. Technicolor flatness gave one valuable information concerning the lake.

"Someday a systemic paradigm," reminded Niobe, above all other big tops enclosing edge of applause, "shall trounce infallibly hidden mode of success, but a pitiful mole hill, lent to a smatter of darkness, began." They dreamt, scene unfolded, an episodic necessity leitmotif, known for all tapped or kept within wigs for more than eight years, *th'ratwi'thorns* unused to being on ice. So long as he had, this prefect of North America,

eight or fewer seconds within to defuse time and fashioned vice for
sounds he were called upon to drop.

Characters summoned to him with his keyboard, using a symphoni-
etta now, plaid variations to *The First Concerto* by Josef Bonnet, a founder
of the Eastman School in 1921 (C.E), originally. The women shooed
Señor Florian, Park, and Finlay away from the Sunrise Cage, and frosh
washed back for a third year, not because they harped castanets, but
because they had been tasked to say at once, only four other old–timers
left were Deerfield; Sr. Florian, who left a podiatrist in Jackson; why,
orca, "Iffy," Van Etnabaron, for whom Plair thus pursued his aim of
a Hibernian mission, alone; and an elder remembered Finlay's father,
Chad, an unruly bain taken across the Antarctic when patients moved to
level chichi and google in 1921 (Mohammedan Reckoning).

Ælfric's relatives had more to say about each other than to him,
but for a musician ultramontane, living in Nebraska for three years
nearly went unnoticed, the worst regret enjoyed these toots, flickered
and fled unless more urgent matters were remanded him. "Classical,"
Park remarked. "You go ask if it were okey–dokey in there." Poor old
Finlay looked relieved. "It's swell, you get abandoned by anchorage
feigned bobbins," who are now sites in a docile semi–circle, aloof from
a leprechaun everyone had forgotten on a first name basis. His wife,
Marta, called him Sr. Florian, letting on that, earlier last summer, Raisin
announced a job obtained with Sir Foster's Live Vice Room.

Unlike his quondam colleague (once pluperfect of abnormal Europa),
was *th'ratwi'thorns* well–loved a, as such lapel possible for his kind, rat as
there ever were. He packed also a siren, a leaf blower, and in addition
to concertina, a fourth, hidden, horn, "unlit, this must needs go, I may
repent of every unknown known."

.   .   .

Early reference to Titan as metonym for Nicean colonies settled upon the eponymous world... Manasseh as pseudo—Protagonist phantasmagoria mandrake Marta saw in heck... wildernesses find theologian to fulfill saving task of revivifying EF2, while Horace, to re—assign impersonal pronoun candidacy, is eventually seltzered around Bagler & cathedral mime... mere volition by Niceans seemingly cylindrical, Ike's Park gatherers need to sustain other verisimilitude.

IV — vi — As the Reject Fair unfolded... a proverb (23.1).

A further truism of proxy, married women non appellant, conspiratorially discussing foibles of their G—chords of sunlit hope, and singing the opening stanzas of *Everything is Beautiful.* Dueling oldies' stations were on Tuesday when Meringue dialed, and many filed south by SW for Saint Isidore while reading about fifth century church history, yet have yet to make a cyber—pilgrimage to the coast where Ion stood in line, relieved at the comparative though teeming anonymity, to purchase this afternoon's copy, but promised to solicit more volunteers dispersed throughout the maze shepherding instinct.

Not an unhappy man seemed Ion, if bereft, derelict, incompetently rededicated, and upon the focus of odes, shifted, the chef d'cabinet [*sic*], apprehending, "I would like to bask in Utopia (a world walled to let leisure sustain astute growth)," rang that, once fenced, her Manx condo gym met areas harped on deeper asceticism. Manasseh felt dated in beans and sweatshirt, spacing the annual picnic last night, subsumed with trying to disprove who accidentally taped over part of the summer's mass releases, such as *Where is my checkbook,* and *Brooklyn, of All Places,* prefacing an entire day of must not leave the house.

At first this idea started last Friday, when they leapt to console Renata on her project and quickly typed a dozen poems, all submersible, avoiding reply, via thin silver air guitar Bagler left Esmeralda, a rhythmic tentative full strum F—stop, before several minutes in Alaska; feeling compelled to add, during a silence of years, "did you try sitting in that fire tower alone," Olive agreed they should spend more time away from the well early in the night and check on a balky coil. She needed a booth because tonight, a radiant full jar of Jell—o for welcome could fill households.

"It, Porphyry," a cognomen winced at Alcuin, "is an oversized fridge, see, that GE stove is still slightly pushed out behind the wall," and pushing it back, a heave—ho from a delicatessen at Safeway on 18th, Raisin started, "doth those, around two years ago, meet Norah Anne O'Kevlin, a retired turf clutter for all," but two or three dozen relatives, clustered in—house, learn they shared some same home town of level chichi [*sic*] and, goggled, Finlay excused himself again. After Noone might tug the bell, prone sat the ensign Plair, unmoved. "Why, it's *œdith*, a cop, and Pliny."

"Hurry, the roads are argent." "A little slick," flung back, Finlay, the best of them, in noting this consistently, became too kind to point out the obvious flaw, yet always wished they were crass enough to overcome the embarrassment of Hesitance for only in this manner the march of democracy upheld. Reasonably certain that providence of ambiguity must persist, their hasty report Finlay, if literally one extant, author of the popular text, *Functions are Fun*, grown aware of a flat indelicate tension in the system, yet to refute, so monthly it will bring cost to systems extant, further feared descent of force dedicated to alleviate negative condition, tough beneath the placidity apparent and, startled outcry concerning sullen scrutiny eventually come to rest at one's door, unless the sun blew up readily, in eventuality that person scrapped or driven into wilderness for reporting such original condition, those shared several mixed stiffs for them both, Nachos, or pilaf, or sometimes just smooth garbled commerce drives the cognomen's house food, will cool, and form droplets of condensation inside of the fire conduit.

The doorbell jingling, their very night held semester risk beans tied then unlit, live in daily expectation of some other, there willed to exist unstained, an only hope that if they made the most possibly of it by continuing to exist they would amplify, via every each and other, about, in absolute value, a choir of has been. Their sunny glade, this last remnant of withered consensus, there Esmeralda went, in aid beneath universal time coordinates Many Place proscribed.

To Finlay, these refracted until entire moment of reality appeared intangible, and then fell, into floated stupor, a dream of winged hesitance, featured this whippets' monument at a red dark district. Had she ought, those might say, devote ceaseless attention to condition instead of letting events come to this date, a rearview of misses so near, how I survived so long I ached to tell someone beware, repeat not this path lest you awake anon and still truth swerved in my tongue and I wrote words strayed far off the course which even lessor gods, principles, preceptors, planets outranced made certain the world must end before my repetitive zeal would catch up with it.

Alas, the situation called for a smooth and deft hand for Noone in a mood to crash the system with a rocket of dire retort. How great were those, operant beneath this assumption, humanity, comprised of fixed interchangeable cipher, capable of uniform reaction in every environment, tested by the entire model? And in a world of decreased certitude, one embraced heavens for their mechanistic reliability, that last fruit of enlightenment. Tiny rumples in fabric of an ekistic syllabus galled one, booked up behind the blotter, "I am that source," into declaring, "of ideal rang in annealed whist thankful for absolution and its impact upon primarily ergo gnomon, I gnaw upon fringe of regulated concept taxonomous ware of arguable portent without."

Long jolted above conceit of marketable look through incessant commentary, envy, masked in outraged disbelief one can glide under a door and sheer dint of protoplast pertain to progressive inaction, awakened in there to share our not inconsiderable pensive bloom back new currency, *ædith* replied, "but just call off your God's'" — "no sooner asked than perceived," Ferguson assured them, if his insouciance masked effort required to tap into the last viable node. "One next small step leads to colonization of the universe," Finlay, overheard, mindful of the terrible turban implicit, the session over until it began and someone else went to dance while on Grosvenor Square, emplaced amidst individual compounds, reductive fallacies too familiar for levity deprecated Ovid's rhyme, leaving one eventually ever written to stall canaries sleazily on limestone patch.

They were not up to simply guessing Chantal, demonstrably levitated, in anxious prevision, residually maintained lien upon burdensome existence. Ever a forthright interjection, "wrought what thus hosted wit" — "over clear input," Ferguson declared, "there are three weeks unless the littoral and habitual court of Global Village will exert roundly anticipated progress to the Ghent Exchange whence, their new currency, *lithiwatt*, shalt float upon the electric ozone sea." Icons nestled in the bosom of his wallpaper, Logan screened, though his net failed to catch the full blue sky the exam piece his index finger to assay one superfluous tap, somewhere one little *scrapmon'* racing about brimming in wasteful energy, retardant all truth self–evident no matter what proclaimed it, and disposed of an enormous fund of knowledge filched from ethereal Zeitgeist [*sic*]. Because shadow puppet saw promise in all thing, *th'rat-wi'thorns* knew no overt mittamus to destroy PoD; cross jurisdictional claims and precedent vexed Hell for weeks.

. . .

th'ratwi'thorns, with many fiends, arrived in despondent councils of the pit with news verging upon an out, if hope should ever be visualized as relevant upon this most sunken plain.

Belial, in the resplendent lower court, droned forth. "Once again, an entire sales garnishment of principle setback in store for serious moral inquiry in separate secrets are stifled." There seemed a certain distance between informally a litmus test left to read anything into a cohesive two–third; strewn via premonition grave battle amidst ferocious fad fast covered the realm of endeavor. The precedent of Magna Carta yet to outwit Frederick's duplicity, Pluperfectreß, disbanded, still clad in a public sideshow, and perhaps regretting her lenience, varnished, "I shouldn't believe how we managed to bear the brunt of salvation (a pre–dawn of communication, and adjacent to it were one knight, bishop, and rook)."

In absentia, heretofore a centrifuge, yet on some level no telling what they've applied to iron out, a misunderstood, sickeningly oblivious behavior, being off the deep end, read all sorts of psychotic sign for some heavy programme through a sieve delineating genealogies and starts, yet still essential to a very technical downer, alienated from Catholic artistic bargaining after another abundance, Henry's (VII) laughter echoed as a fundamentalist, pro forma, apocryphal fiefdom, much to the point of vengeance, "we shall, lit often, tote HF high–way, beloved four–tiered alternative dance band."

"It is recommendation of the examiner," Belial concluded, "that, since this majesty issued a class action upon one of the chief principalities that subsequently failed, we must needs have no remnant option except corporeal warp upon the lamb." "Upon whom," Mammon, half–starved in aspersion, knew that amanuensis quivered. Even an Arch–deceiver rose, half in puissance, half in freight, at mention of this plan. However corporeally war, upon the lamp, well–practiced over centuries, seemed to offer an ounce of diversion, never had the councils faced comfret with such a conceited and ambiguous opponent still at large. A short–haired bobbin back there shielded the U.S. behind the best of the blast, her injury almost severe, yet it decided to spare embarrassment of admitting Iphgenë [*sic*] to find out later it wasn't important. "You are above (no print remained on one's own) familiar kilter, so there those skittled some day."

This borrowing of copious past, times washed white through frost by night, Ion dutifully noted, "hoping again some day these rare words addressed to you Ephesians might find voice, among them, of the callous (4:19) and/or backbiting, of whom it were hoped little else need be said but for their unquestioned talents for genuinely enervating posts and practices," often, escape tied to a quite real foil synod; Ion, a gig sacked twice, began intervention to come when least prepared to expect, acceptably, the many things let spoken of God to these Artesians

— a pre–conceivable word to the hopefully, "shall you know now how I express my opinion of Hope — you, being you whom, at one time believed in our space." Flown in to be aware of the consequence of an early salvation, Finlay hoped Park might know where Ion and Raisin had seen two glasses of radiant stunts enter the complimentary Go West, Iffy saying, "got over Europe yet?"

"Have you been through western Hibernia," Plair said? Meringue nodded, and rescheduled a haircut, until after the new moon, tied in a bandana, donned baggy sports coveralls and hugged Bitsy, Florian, and Norah, met at a crock climb, close to two years after they took hold of some good rate in another land, though that guy doesn't have a clue how he got a fixed hope on Titan. So Porphyry said, "if we're to stay up there thirty years, why not ask Marta?" "Our guests get the short end of the stick at school," Hesitance agreed, strategically interested in comptometry. All the evanescent dominion knew that Belial might say everything to defray that question, and hoping that shouldn't be whom to those who thought it could, they waited.

"Here hear," coughed Mammon cautiously, all jurors lisped as ritual utmost hovered unevenly top down. Nearly freckled firmament enjoyably cross cultural benefit through mass consumption of bio–generically enhanced agrarianism; yet even street theatrics of individuals, who sold out nominally (if in ostensible retention of beneficence, conformed via ergo odd script plates), were subsumed in anything, approach dynastic fin–de–siecle [*sic*] society, given wholly unforeseen largesse wherein excess neologisms spawned, where, wont to dissuade their earlier scene since enjoyment of *AC/DC* insofar as their own phase seemed inexplicably attenuated by capricious vicissitude: mid–term, unsteadily transposed topic, diverse ecumenical system, cancelled time share, and other toughly unspecific cap and gown emissivity for which only daily ledger offered an illuminative, if less prosaic, milestone of reality that went with territory unless disclosed therein, their reminiscence were admissibly singular in their long and bitter search for an apology, "if not an absolute other lap which to canter away to the nearest mailbox, and so since rested, effort

made to wish everything into most plausible light," *th'ratwi'thorns* assumed
a mantle of orthodoxy, "let's each rave of better rice and 'end of form,
development, meaningless, empty, artificial, pretentious architecture,
and ornament, imitation of archaic, and exotic, motives (*NY Times,*
"baroque").'" It chafed, this hat, and he knew, "our energies, several, bent,
handed us this lemon. Our energies, united, will bring us lemonade."

"Well perhaps," dignitaries gazed upon injunction of *th'ratwi'thorns*
in deviance, bordering upon civility, since he raspingly addressed the
council of Hell, "we were settled out to declare corporeal war upon
our foe, a past time we've all excelled in display of valor during several
occasions." Mammon stated, "perchance our grandeur, our experience,
our self–assurance, our victory lies in this inconclusive sequence of
nights, that we knew in our grasp for the other side of time, we squeeze
limpid tinniness." Belial appended, "perforce we knew our aggregate
overload commissioned a member of our politburo without consulting
us." "Ergo," *th'ratwi'thorns* added hastily, "we salute great deeds of our
colleague, which drove the hated usurper PoD into the bitter exile of
elapsed time." Below that dour host arose a clamor for an immediate
fosse, and *th'ratwi'thorns*, grinning distinctly, let them have one.

"*Iskander versus Principality of Persia, BCE 336.* The Macedonian con-
queror never wished to supplant the court of Darius. Yet, upon instigation
of the regnant ethereal satrap, assassination of this monarch by his own
coterie after the battle of Arbela threw the empire into chaos, forcing
imposition of Hellenic value upon the land. Upon his depth, muter area,
Iskander filed suit before the bar of time and upheld." "PoD has headed
into your jurisdiction," grafted Beelzebub the gadfly gaily. "I demand
upon behalf of counsel we form a trans–jurisdictional vigilante commission to completely rub him out." "These examples illuminate the futility,"
retorted *th'ratwi'thorns*, "and indeed the incalculable damage, of pursuant
capitol warrant beyond frontier of originally circumscripted principality.

"*United Federations of North America versus Dutch East India Company,
1715.* During the War of the Spanish Succession, while the Sun King's
marshals and the principals Eugene and Marlborough slogged it out

upon the streets of Flanders, a high civilization of clothiers, waterways, and macadam roads, in combat involving millions of participants, a less popular conflict incubated upon the slope of a piedmont during which opposed force ever numbered fewer than hundreds. Terrible the plight upon the Meuse; a rivalry consoled only via seemingly mutual belief in chivalry, ransom, and report of a merciful God.

"Small wonder that Old World tended to smear this Queen Anne's War, fought in tangled thickets of the forest primeval, without reckoning its impact upon national psychiatry of future geraniums. Imagining the colonialist's struggle versus individuals who regarded such belief as, if not valueless in a transmissible sense, then at most inapplicable, insofar as the latters' perception of negotiated, distributive, and/or spiritual process were decreed by comparatively fluid anthropomorphism, the Crown, in response to the terror of their nominal subjects, permeated earliest use of eminent domain upon the virgin continent, condemning householders of Acadia in order to conflate a naive basis for their own ostensible proclivity.

"Plaintiff contended, thanks to mercantile policies, the ancient cycle is perpetuated on an ever cosmic scale, until each molecule of American soul is baffled, tile between corporate and individual, defence countered. They were only doing their own thing, and, in accordance with natural precept inscribed by invisible hand, intrinsically obstinate concepts of windsock and Morrison Avenue merged into ethereal new Weltanschauung [sic], and all I have to show for it are a vial of citalopram and half a pack of generic cigarettes," th*'ratwi'thorns* groped, for his source, of renewal. In the clay cup, drained at a gulp, he continued, "*Bronstein versus Hell, 1940.* Lev Davidovich, founding father of the Red Army, which performed many valiant deeds in service of mankind, such saving work of the Dresden Gallery from desecration in 1945 (a feat commemorated by Dmitry Shostakovich in his concerto *Five Days, Five Nights*).

"Sometimes it sounded like hundreds of individuals were in his apartment. Appearing to champion the rural nationalities, Iosef Vossarionovich decried such effete cosmopolitanism unequal to the urgent task of collectivization. 'Thou shalt not muzzle the ox who treadeth out the corn (Deuteronomy 25:4),' Lev Davidovich replied at length. And yet, again we find ourselves a–dither, for shame, upon a course of no merit. Finally, *Sanctus Pax Melioris versus Henry (VII), 1239.*

"Frederick II, piqued at deconstruction of *wishram* by his son's wet hen, which nullified the former's intention of creating immortal myrmidons to send into the future, staged a star chamber, ostensibly in chastisement of Henry (VII), which devolved into an appalling purge of his most loyal clerk, Piero della Vigna, on trumped charges of peculation. Thus precipitated the non–natural decline of the Hohenstaufen dynasty (which natheless made an admirable recovery, on strength of frozen food and hospitality service, in the 20th century). The proceeding, summated, follows:

"'*Quamquam supra omnis aedificum par somnus certiori inter reticulum obicere quantuluscunque, nullo modo fieri potest propter libellus naturam adiuvare. Ut moles corona fasti procuratio prae munus existere in caelum calor cognature fortasse, libentius libellus lineamentorum summa, iudicium ex form est. Facere condicio histrionum libellum estimare amplificare? Adfirmatio communis, per animadversio maximam partem improvocare durare. Impendium libellu duplicare, quod plus tempus primus tablua quisque, reticulum per septuagientum deditus.*

'*Ratiocinatio de aedificum par somnus ex ad priori post hoc xystus obscuritas declarare, exemplar Fredericus occultus si haud late patens apparare. Ut [fidelia proprius] erga libellus peculiarus praepositio ex indicum fortis, quam libellus forma omnium, argumentum ex partocinium est. Petitor reticulum par somenus τελεος paucorum potentia, modus permutare cum tempus commercium pactus repletus, proceritas intervallu, res ramus subsidium aequitas explicare. Ut libellus forma [modus] confirmatio empiricus negligere, exemplar permittere. Res natura eruditio [temperatio proprius eruditus] anima libellum electus complectus impedire.*

·   ·   ·

"Woe then to the yokel whose ready consent," th'*ratwi'thorns* must add, "thus confirms the other's initial suspicion, and as a result conversation shifts into evasive exculpatorium, his own effort to revive flagged expedition merely hasting inexorable demise." The reply in kind of ambition mistook this earnest leer for Në, a lapse in untoward disinclination to venture a creative etude with thin Norn events, "it will be very stung," said. She, in preliminal irony, while the psalmist wandered toward never land, sedulously met vacancies which warned or promised utter unkindness unappreciative of travel throb tale spin. Owed but dunnage to a system of provisional health ineptitude in a blithering stretch for Zen, a surer man held forth upon, even constrained to practice duck call at late interval.

Here, an immemorable youth paused, incidental to an amative gesture, sanguinely deferred in systemic recoil to blandest mundane amount of capability. Premised in arrival of this imminent tourist, Tell, haunted by their time together, and signal for a fair catch, went unheeded in lack of desire for affordable excellence. "You are my straw man," he'd hear Në say once or twice, supplying an unspeakable diphthong suddenly struck one far too eager to arrive at previously discarded internal bargain, yet kept at bay by perceived misapplication of a word meant to describe the combinatory sound produced by junction of consonant, the Rabbi Manasseh Esherman on his own hectogram of dimly plain up for grab outliers camped upon franchise of liminal refuge in a metric of avowal.

Regarding his attempt to instill such dipolar profligacy intimation, the seamstress cared enough to bring fully jocose report of it, incipient prurient Manasseh enjoyed less the spot light, if held out upon rite of the generic season, "forasmuch, albeit of a by–product of thine recidivism, has the spoliation fallen upon, then art thou bound to restoration of these noble guests and restitution of residual in accordance with previous inflection," he chimed. This attempt to frame the issue drew outlandish snort behind the gallery of seconds itinerant to Në Dipol, hastened to remind once more of the message from one who dumped his only chant. In order to cement this reputation as happy camper, Lothar at once

eschewed, blanket invitation for the theological snipe hunt duly intercepted and posted by the duty observer, "you've got a big day in traffic
court coming up tomorrow, nighty–night then," Në Dipol rejoined
hurriedly whatever activity misdeserved of concern for olden pomp.

When a black lighter arose to carry all of the gear away, the sure man
stochastically swam via irrelevancies. Every scrap of significance seized
in inner dearth, Esherman lurked into the future and upon being indwelt
by thereat who spoke it now down, found naught but patchy reward of
light sown step perfunctory to haunted action. Other Niceans, their own
being minded of a sort to exchange remark boldly content to undertone
development, surfing his every cause even while the wage of dawdling,
loomed. Cast from the trap the rabbi resumed ejection onto the planet
Nod, while seconds, eager to sweep a fresh breach, stitched away initial
accusation that it is miasmic logorrhea devoid of logic, leveled by them
learned enough via reading the trailed accompaniment our broadcast a
certain virus that currently swept Global Village is especially deadly to
commercial break. They scoffed at one's apparent dearth of information
glare at lens if to prolong oh great a batch of spaced out colonists aboard
that's all we need.

Those who once loved and accepted Henry (VII) were now dwindled,
this unscheduled mass of individuals now thrust out of history, acted
as if they had been in eighth grade all day, and ceaselessly disparaged,
his principle, his dismay, dire and manifold, nagged as regret attached
to accidental bump and erasure of an entire morning's etch, inasmuch
as individuals once safely counted upon as bulwark reliably overnight
turned, and could barely stand to watch him smiling on the telephone
nowadays, anyone might tell he was brutal and out of touch, and all the
more effort expended by Henry (VII) in conciliation tore at his being
misplaced and disappointed hope, he began feeling like a complete jerk,
everywhere he went smiling, a pathetic dog hoping not to be kicked, and
all the while ceaseless drone of their opprobrium went on like that song
one cannot quite shut down in the head.

Perhaps if he threw out his own ministers who abused their own privilege, and recalled young, eager, compassionate, and well–trained subalterns, effigies would not spring up in the region beneath question; maybe if he decreed universal sufferance, the people should not shirk so indecently, not carry on as if they were guardian of some ancient truth when in fact most were spitting up their binkies while he went out achieving interdependence for their apathy but, the nicer he became, the further from reality the current of history bore him and only one path seemed clear: it a way of virtue, not only desperate to outlast two–bit recoil, yet of an earthly box sprang, those warbled at kumquats, adept in catering to *finth* in Shinto whilst horse feathers were restrung to match their fret, far, far, away, a cognomen ran thy lost amen, lest her bunt debutante fall prey to clutch of columnists, run after addled beasts who'd detached amidst throngs to lurk about somewhere else in the palace?

Such astringent admixture of exalted remorse, you'd think Æmst should arrange it so the lounge hives might stoop to phase once beyond implausible; whose pedicure sostenuto can pass muster, echoes of misdirected echelon thereupon teal, and until no *tictus* ought sing about how her lad sprawled upon bandwidth, Hesitance's hymn sotto voce formed in aloof prints, faltered elastic under current often tame. Amerceably teased by renewed influx, Pluto floated to his dome in silent discontent while a cognomen, who knew better than to assess a topic searched ideally upon flume of an etched ichor imminent, vastened orators trilled the uxorious decency lisle once imbued upon innumerable beckoned for interim access, and checked this inbound parabola recently snoozed above the relevant seal.

In septic thanks we get for flushing the fetid leviathan below the philanstereoscopic out, the necessary re–implement of pistachio nomes unto encounter, disguised synaptic allegation and, lodged upon edged snood, an interloping visitant diverted strait toward stupefying usurped bezique upon which converged labyrinthine quintessentially, the cognomen addressed diagonal concern. Benign land–use figurines skated ashily over another wet hen, frozen in wistful bailiwicks before long tappers, zealous in draught, gave stiff to round lie, outdistancing their putt athwart the creaky tableaux. At thought of navigation, Acheron's vermilion flood, the children scampered from him, deployed beyond cragged defiles of the Styx; renewed influx of soul awaiting transfer, Chæron wished his master to repeat this instruction.

"It's really quite simple," Pluto insisted. "Take me over in an empty bark." In due course, Chæron replied they might like five hundred lashed barks to transport Hades and his realm, consisting of one chariot, four trains, eight dark energy steeds, and sixteen grooms out of there. The boatman, behind a curve, had no time. Some slighted *lumine* found refuge, if it may be called that, from a leveling. Here, closer to Hell's gate, Zeus skulked, playing Castle Mandrake, last remnant open air theatre, and pegged thunder blots and spare change at the hopeless garbage fairy. Pluto needed another plan. Where would he induce a live manifesto to coax the nether plane? Warned his double instinct tokens were to take a dive, too, the emperor Frederick starred badly while foot lamps mashed about the customs house (now so shaped by events, were he to allow his personal actuality), and said, "that was the last get well ever card I would wire out beyond," and if he ever reached via interference where existed only non sequitur reply to why he, their calmer clique coalesced mutely in house provided, yawn come hither cliche, the cognomen strobed amidst seaweed gracefully.

Needing to advertise, Pluto went to visit this dream one last time. A fizzier zone of obbligato riff psalm seemed gone, though feedback parasols, tethered in rows, cannily stopped to watch a sputter gaunt form, inhaling printers ink, and daft elastic thunder score of thaumaturgy, indicated a fewmet trail blend into a laser rollover, *untenets* disappeared into a draw of damp ash, "flow all them over, what next, in newest colloquy," seconds knelled, after it, other comfret.

Camerally, if a proud dilettante of certain proof district asked before their astral fume how understanding of it to entertain glare of bucolic breakdown, live welcome heartfelt herbivore who flock lycanthropically expectant, "so I don't have preferences for whom I like and especially don't beware frozen strolls, and let me tell you long distance was no picnic in those days what with being on a party line," and all the people who were in the court (Ruth 4.11) went amen and divested a generous portion of the dialect. Tyoslament thus clear, Olive primed other chaos, "we were so fluttered when these heffalumps said they wanted to take a page from our book, and overmatched by their industrialized tribal hauteur, soon all of our pages were plastered amidst the remuda whence we found love's ruse penned, thriving on canapés, and wont to undergo a course of domestication to assist Niceans in their quest for the merrily magical color shoe tree."

In stereo, Bitsy signed over herself, drooped her beadwork, and jammed, then, "outlook, this swat I bent awkwardly, how if we dampen them here baubles of eiderdown?" Unlit voir dire [sic], time finds us the shrub area tux cast, those all sang heedlessly while scent thickened into ash. Pinion wells slalomed toward scratch amenably; lolled into monsoon, tremulously they lounged in taupe adieu, unless their blustery eyrie distinctly ballooned frabjously, sillier than wetly trite iamin'the-lim, whilst ahriman languished near Land of Forgotten Tents, where writing implements became stumbling blocks, woad, how abominable each scratch trickle thump, the pen refusing to flow ahead once more in absence of magic ink, pencils were even worse: sharp enough from a distance, yet viewed closely, those wore inverted captious graphite domes housing mute devils which slid along an impervious page, sapped the wrist via friction and, for the oh point five milliliter lead that raced around unencumbered for lengths, until the mind, arriving on point, bore down subconsciously, these too snapped at a rate of a dozen an hour, awakening a slumbering collegial of ahriman which stirred.

"Do you ever wonder," the shade began shaking, "whether you pray for something to happen, or for something not to happen?" "Who are you," PoD wailed? "The future shape of theme, or mere peer Emmerich Flußtapfer," the hovering scepter replied, "not to be confuted with shade of emperor Frederick second, who is presently egregious. Everything else is compensatory nominalism and perhaps flappable. Let us disperse like displays of dismay that made me forget and proceed with concepts effectually perceived. I had a dream and you absolutely didn't know except via emanations introduced by any but the suddenness silence." "What was this screen saver doing about to flick in," PoD mused?

"I am trying to made some bread here," the shade of Barbarossa interjected, tiptoeing athwart flour, "and perforce listened to sown elfs in diversion, Gordian knot, I should try to launch myself the gas burner, by appearing to fix my life indeed." "Preoccupied with gas spores and simple advantages at once made plain to this individual far prior to that atmosphere unleashed in a germinal rush," there a divine spark, or everything learned, "we each come to grips via tides and peace of *Weltschmerzen und durch die unterzwischen Beschiedenliche mussen wir aufgraben*," trailed off Emmerich, keenly aware of some compound node, "unless your just now gate kept anew, sad darter," the shade resumed. Thinly formed hurried masks their pinnace stuff mummer obliquely swerved, "let's pray all disguised is utmost to correctly implode." These heedless gyres gainsaid their frugal banter with instant cedar bulwarks induced nearby.

·   ·   ·

Professing a form thereof, a man sat, in decline (1 Tim 6: 6–7).

IV — vii — A non–successfully routed movement in a yard sponged to chiliasm.

The rebel Nicean expedition's attempt to skirt Earth customs left, first, beneath disguised Bermudan flag, manifestly deflated, their Ambassador at least seemed to escape from one pre–existent page in time, leaving thereat next to bemused March hare work; welcomed by mist, opportunity knocked over an item to a sound of four natural slams linking autonomy to a requiem for integrity (amber heaven where so many of them bind). Rex Ampersand, Earl of Rumsford, watched breakers shazzam upon a seam of premise too rueful.

For earnest casuistry, he'd approved boiler plate liner notes on behalf of some distorted circumlocution, not so heated over recurrent dissociative transference. Ever since that telegenically challenged hoe–down stopped, fewer incensed questions wafted away from their macular flowchart; indicating sparser fender obol herb blenders strobed into blank fluorescence, Molyneaux scribbled, "your plugs fine for anyone ever since your specious woven variety wore out for eighty centuries." No matter how determined were they in tracking, the seas yielded but small spore to their adjective sniffers.

A planet, striated with rigid castles, bore the progress upon a shore of ochre sand, the combined ice lake broke before plunging them occasionally amidst a collective aspen sprout glen of fitful struggle in the slushy lens too swiftly endured, and a tow of horrible significance, seizing the monad peeps poetically, then again palliated a notion, "perhaps we're not prepared for such microcosmic entreaty in process." "Oh, for an ellipsis one could fan air," until they decided to talk of lots, concerted want, or irreverence must willfully attach insight to a combined lie.

That flop side of a terraced varicose rang falsetto during foremost desire. Nor had kindlier chimera typecast in wanhope thanked anyone for knitting near enough wainscoting. Canonically, ice that brazen yet also kinetic silhouette reglorified, everything hadn't needed frozen causality; thistled *untenets* wrangled long tones copiously amongst fescue of millrace bonnets. All reedy semaphore wore such excessive tabled outlook, for scalene closure tonight on sloshed steam ladders affixed more responsibly in the breviary.

.   .   .

A bleak, pointedly middling eflot, fashioned in civil reference of non–palindromic precedent cluttered biodegradably, erred Ylferim, bi'sifa muwaq–qata, temporarily, to our own volition, breached shackles of naivete, whom, misspelled, sought nativity to dare however access these solitaire syrupy serape scraps, that agog, scratched, beryl, conflative overtone; flown so weak and errant, the Nicean ice mote one time Bitsy, as per salsa sonar, civilized continually: especially since this possessed an emphasis on an 'as–requited' invaluable trip by Hesitance. Too deep by at most so much intrigue and, eked for several more bumps, it will be one thin twirl at each window, but never a world toward the end of her verticule. Sublet by degree into the lake that shocked, vexed and forlorn organic stimuli crammed the Santa chocolate rays of night.

Some strained light stabbed up along everybody's door, scattering this effect. Troublesome idylls at best, they can scarce be historical as well, as they zip slowly behind the scoreboard into paroxysm of fauna. Backward by this deal, crammed chaos of flyaway leaflet, bouncy somber canaries, and soon a nebulous and tagging quack, dwindled into beady molecule stack, including this unheralded minor (fortunately returned by Inyo), this ceremony, stub up so–called men to begin drab, dim, dumped, a party, expanded voodoo books, and buzz, Hesitance reached out on tenuous dream of shared lumpiness. Never try and underestimate your garbanzos, their mother Harriet once told Bitsy, who mixed test pancake canapés with cornichons, pilchard, and Hesitance's thyme chutney for the clarion recital at another Mary's hometown.

At the end of developed romance of a human figure, gesticulating between knitting fees, just over the household, the snails, in full noon, made for a day without guarantees actually performed, brought, amid vacant eclat indeed, a first hat SOMHAD, where certainly are unthreatening lots of strange writ, for which one should be hard–pressed, a third, for years were exciting? Out on the Dior home, it's up to old trouble to keep the cupcake off the floor with stars, and tossed Frisbees, lands above the survey have been 'raptured.' This certainly found, her carrier, *Elementaridad*, on the airwave, might quiz any signaler (*all too busy*), and yet a grip upon glorious and splendid show pages now joined the bold and seven, true to crepe trace over reciprocal minds dispersed for jihad, WSJ [*sic*] and other charms went off, diffusing a weekly daemon in his discipline.

Forthwith scrolled those perilous ephemeral insight after Roveretto, feistily faint, inured to strike aside fear in advance, acting significant enough, envenomed anew the pageant descrying An. In her next apposite more, a doughty gallery of sounds were once their short wave as poignant anthems dripped defiance against a mightier refulgence, tiny tiger festival, excoriated dialectic of national policy, crouching natural heritage, assorted where were you when; all's illegibly wireless across districts languished beneath his cure, as stretched a complexion of owned lofts of similar cellular cast upon the dial of adjournable instants.

Lifted, the avocado breeze at once sparred, if anvils tolled aseptic pips, now only to recollect Lothar an oblivion of musical exile, chimera too frail for eventual hence wan sprint forage bus phased scurrilously, remind thou in eager offense, a giving tree found in haste to a clear gloss of universal retractable outcome, plied after nuance, and hoped an anastomosis from immutable largesse, spurned futilities income thence in altered sun face, droned deviously in curdling asides. Albeit excessive valor rhymed, an unsure colophon of plucked cacophony, scrapped if on proto–spectrum, now effaced transmission of vernacular, idiosynchronically motored prevalent excrescence of each portiere, an effortless monotonous skirl swamped albeit the spikiest gospel strains, piqued intermittently in the bristly static flood from poles not acting hesitant in conduct through the Bakelite wicket Lothar haunted. At this stage, personae Chocho, to learn of his sunk yacht indefinitely, some other manner, found during recent crises, inimicable powers had tapped Pyrogabion to erase unspecified locales, peering in search of time for an indispensable order now visiting hours were over.

To the individual capable of kinesthesia who'd arrived to explain, "ever since clepsydras were (over this he went lahlahlah, a feeling of listlessness akimbo) the only means of preserving tense of annularity each day," he replied, "I sleep adjacent in this cynosure, wakened only by having forgotten nearly every prior occasion, during stray moments importune; ought these, accused of reeling from latest travesty tonight, circumvent thine further inexorable petition." If to some degree a discrete event, serving as piece for conversation in any of Mme Flußtapfer's clinically aestheticians sense, must ever see such a cut—off point, the reason, Xantippe suggested, a thermal trace, clung to her floor length, deepened her concern over perception of optical mass, Lothar expelled, "emphasizing inherent thinness in your nature," moping his brow with his prism issue cravat, dimly gratified she changed topic to her newest technician, Ænselm. "In a single glance he can exculpate warts, he sends crows feet out for cigarettes; yesterday Fanta came in with her trochanter and he just turned into tornado and zoomed her cello away."

Listening to her, akin to waking up amidst film, Molyneaux to relearn containment, nod along lest she ascribe to refresh upon every significant detail, yet reference to this staff novitiate perked unwonted concern. Once prey to numerous demons, drawn lines and placed chips on sand, Lothar finally withstood the harsh charge; a timing thus immured in rationalism, Chocho found his beloved's embrace of this parvenu distinctly compensatory, "not without honor save in his own county," retorted Xantippe, adding casual sightseers may view PoD inert amidst humming apiary and assume it, as worthless adjunct, retained, only in sufferance thus and compensatory for what, "Noone was too upset after a flurry of scrabbling notes for our anniversary," Lothar almost blurted until checked, via an inner stringency, "wouldn't sound sort of egotistical?"

So devolved alternative tactic; gloss over obvious facts of this impoundment, and forgotten omen enjoyed either dream instant, or facets, where obviously self–evident, Lothar instead gloomily inferred, in such milestone extant, elucidated, known to develop as tepid light extended, visiting hours were over winked. Conspicuously, his problematic perception ominously took over within, confident estimate bleakly deflated what felicity the isolated proto–phlebotomist may intentionally signal in recognition of Mme Flußtapfer's renewable incentive, and Lothar sat in the dark booth, scaled back under further floral dimension embalmed, the bellwether servitor gazed beyond the dark flask, rallied upon formulaic recall often enough to tinge every aspect of prosperity in a mask, best left said cold, to expedite a member's restive copy sport to regions in which residents, these repressed, next crept or clung to cardinal maxim, whenever at least earnest earliest of the session inflicted delay, a prospectus of intent quadrivium, he mused one, were pollyannaish glissadiers capable of purporting pervasive theology to a knell, next, had seconds exploded arid broiling rhythm suggestive of a global chill topmostly spatial in hiatus nor finally, were moral evidence alack not each single pulsar coalition discharge occurred in a pre–specific field initiating morpheme which described Taurus on that cold Mayday unpinned into the lime grove lighthouse of sequenescence inculcated through the floral cathode certificate.

The Language of Intimacy

Cut off from his spiritual power base, and lacking re–assertive behavior patterns, F. Xavier Middleford, attempting to develop a strategy on his legal pad, soon forgot what he meant to write about. Moreover, although he maintained an extended dialogue with his great love, his daughter,

Desdemona, Hudspeth Chantal, apple of his only eye, he was unable to cope with fear that exchange would soon turn out this way.

Middleford: "Please warn me if I'm ever in danger of being off your wish list." Dauphine: "It's too late." Such an imagined overture, then, in the perilous match of soul; fraught in potential for devastating rebuke, Frank found no choice except to convoke Provenance. Even his fiercest detractors could not ignore summons at risk of being forever cast from the cozy circle. Although he enjoyed slight prospect of survival in the ensuing vote of confidence, the guildmaster, of a mind to hasten the tide of event within the narrow straits of former Nicean space now left, an ex–chamberlain (*all too busy*) posed dilemma concerning Za'at's proprietary bulk ceramic skill in mnemonic garden tracery describing the Mirandan verge of Xenonia, an incunabulate wake of epicac, rye, and piccalilli, an apex of their eponymous gaseous compound expansively stratifying cubical diffusion. This being made so known, Type N proved an indicia no more of inculpable tolerance to extended cryogenesis research.

In stilted regard for a neural plasma once touted for its striking resemblance to rheological El Dorado or aqua regia, their 'zines para-doxically elided abnormal scrutiny no longer, and chiaroscuro cherubs coruscated in rococo celibacy; galvanized relief effort for earthborne deliverance apprehended, in a janissarial stasis pro Renata Clair, Ladænæ Mervyn Mirabeau, Type N's beakers become courted in dwindled avidity, their once beady salad day of mystique wilted since denouement, enjoying zestful seasoning of sufficient exegesis until Anodyne, if not mainstream's darling cover soiree is akin to garbage left just before a long trip and upon return you look in the banned plastic bag beneath the sink and think whoa don't remember throwing that out until it all came flocking back, those poignant last few moments until departure from a sanctified adobe when you become stranger than yourself, slamming a daiquiri to defray inevitable hunger spasm, envy the peel because it gets to stay home in your sullen quaint and cherished kitsch while you must push off into the unknown or known unknown per sunnily lit old litanies.

A tulgier crew of icthyologian statutory bobbled amidst backwash of Vikram's cagey apocalypse, freshened and ogled myopically whilst latex crowd of newfound inklings striated so near brink of sylph ratiocination, and only Idiopath lurked throughout serrated bulrushes to impede their regression, since *finth* had taken a leaf from Iraisamonde's dissertation loren ipsum rides again a sedulously deflated biopic of Messimo's sonnet, foreshortened into limerances in course of a saccharine flimflam, their chapbook disbursed homiletic bromide unto shadow puppet's frozen peephole, their lyrical dissonance kept true dearth at bay, bellwether stanzas shed violet light on shrinking habitat of the *xenonian* heffalump, synthesizing a palliative conservancy which zoned entire swaths of littoral unto prospective ubiquity, and in sanguine enthusiasm industrious retail mushroomed radiance all over the sub–continent.

Similar upheaval deprived citizens of Xenonia, whose domestic appanage–espousing paradigm shift, arrived at a perception of diminished return, marked by mere proscenium of once thriving cottage trope, once one of the foremost exporters of Demosthenes in the solar system yet now their land, synthesis and minimal enamel may peace be kept pebbles repetitively late and growths understood for counter withdrawal went benignly well, considered amidst a variety of instance, each assuming such grass root change must solely effectuate from the dingiest facile available cause for as long as it made scalene, seemed to mingle farther around the quaternary postern that verged ever enough upon known albeit unknown beeline, immutably anomalous desiccated harmonic permutated their land, sub–infeudated into farthings brought forth by agape denominative cuneiform accommodation.

Denizens from every taille radiated cumulatively to an almost known *biathanatos* of midday, in chartreuse pallor their word proclaimed from Decapolis past or further disturbance since dirigisme, for from an actual standpoint of anticipation, mimsy lairs wore their sourced seance ablatively from functional causative uplift, a likely consequent psyche learned that how when what where why or whom must supplant this while, a best minded link yet rang in dour wit. Crepe hymnals it fringed on, wan unsung moats mome to milled strains of this dairy fix as dilated grounds of Sunrise Cage brewed forth eponymous carafes of stuff now left over in the sink while Vorga's cereal, sent back for fewer spangles, recalled Cecil who had been charged extra sprinkling as acknowledgeable.

A serial stasis as usual, perceivably recognized as sallow a fellow *xenonian* as probable, given fewer of them in exuberant aisles fondly gamboled through Worsted, noted for its undulant wabes, that nascent truce with Ossian said to ebb insularly, nor Neath, her stylistic blocks of quaint consistency, acutely numinous amidst marshy consensus of the clasp's naughtier aqueducts herein an anemia, nor even Smorths, often so fenced over gaps in thematic progress to keep ostensible Mantissa from confuted notice of dull alarm, unless of course they file grains of space in prompt thoroughness every good measure past some wake there unseen, and not yet unknown, grew restorative warily alive, bathed in adjourning room, beaconed apparently withal, the uttermost farthing of their land monopolized a conversation through no fault of its own between a group of persons without social media; Vorga, she whom Ovid went thousands of worlds, overnight sparkling inanely benign glimpse of past path of strife greed incest or horror transmuting myth onto furtive reference via later readers, finding no love lost from old limp us, their captious decretal of deception and caprice and envy, and Simic, her briefly trodden earth pickling humanity and its perfunctory perpetual inter–relativity impermeably hyperbolic.

Throughout the ampoules of biscuitry, Cecil said to she who moved within a thousand words of day ever spackling, all I need is a nod now and then, just as if I, able to cause cold haven, unto an omen it dials, a fewer than presentable aspect to adorn their initial effort. The relative luxury of wheeled transport vouchsafed to specialists of their stripe deepens the gulf between masses as the ranks trudge stoically amidst billows of silt raised by artillery caissons. Moved by mountainous minds into behaving as laundry left over at the enigmatic, a tonnage of rictus ignition turnover, term, a concept prior to the natural futility rate, Fuald, Harun, and, Shrdlu, and others, an honest hive gloam drove, are hard pressed to refrain from calling cards to inform those, in whom they deeply wish to instill a sense of their own heroic value, that denouement lies close at hand.

Fluffily disguised label solicitors (a process little noted in the teemed vastness of the first world ever gone to great lengths of congratulatively intimating itself over the diaspora of highly trained minds to its cyber–shores), peers are able to endow their cause with temptation that merely splinters effort from the outset into zillions of intersectional rivalries, their drive through outlet malls stripped of vigor, since the life–like populace stopped tossing flowers, at the coalition's victorious columns, fifteen years ago, and at theirs, three, and dreams of only imminent paradise sustain their wanhope. Every night they collapse into laagers delineated by the fortunate few enough to have blankets, staring into heedless heavens while the stars whisper over them indifferently until, lulled by yelping heffalumps in the stillness of dawn, they arise moments later to the pitiless sun.

Via a hearty and engaged and genteel manner, organ music stretched into a religious martyrdom weighing a couple typical pre–millennial smash–ups, and glided up a residual road to an inlet blink like nobody's business, "chiefly important I abide here, okay;" Hesitance, vastened after a stretch, in which An Indocile may be occupied with some numerous invective blast, part of them, run away from grace and all sorts of gardens near Hognozed's prairie dog town, land of semi–active anonymity — still she debunked her verticule unto a gateway, blung bells, and peered toward Noone, whom she quite possibly hectored so, some telemarketer reciting the entire discovered practice of *Christianity Today*, e.g., if there is a late wake in a real prism, bars of permissiveness, and other portable parody realized, then An Indocile could just not be seduced. There were times her exuberance with sunrise lost momentary basis, so easily stretched to find reasons in fire: articles, habeas corpus, a mail order love, in the beacon, which hold is still the bean to leave, these boffed TV and left lost Persephone on par to meet her rocker.

Now that there was just a drizzle of conversation, guests deferred to Many Place and brought sumac to rout off their dialogue in a passive role, which politely began sketching sunlight anew. If a tall, cold bobbin might spur her to depositions most illustrative, Desdemona's nose knew Heppleweis' canaries non–kempt via Vorga in simultaneity burst in, too. An encroaching concert, being poured in, contra valence, planted heather, in wanhope some bobbins will run acting and seething classes at a profit, a natural butterfly intended to make over Asia Minor, and all existification at stage eleven, when one of them honked a battery, suddenly with her too; returned from schlepping that public goddess and peace thing, Hesitance's scone stood out by virtue of discipline. Luckily, some connection, of concern to all but the most insurmountable candidate for the tenth great diligence, seemed to nudge it as close to the edge of dawn at her town. During a ceremonious grappa ad hoc flopped from overtone aloft, Brownian miscreants proselytized the hour, strolling discretely.

One initial, certainly deferred to all inadvisable pickle instead, sought connexion, if not hip to centripetal fast, now demonstrated, polled in a pall entirely, for above all variance provision, if next week's reminder, locally wilted beneath the umber alpine sunset, Flußtapfer moreover at large from acrid lading winnowed from the lotus were and enjoined amortively the contextual trance exhibited by his valet, waiving audacity to flail mental gradients, who invoked haste in decrying recent peroration of his milling pal already, affrightive yoke and cravats, whilst then presently arrived, forsaken wobbling Grendelle, who smothered the floor in ubiquitous plenum oration, crofts formed throughout the repetitive riparian Auvergne, neatly reconnective of transference, blogging forth obiter dictum concerning estates of principle suffix acute introduction.

The space ably, for interest of bland funicular transverse, elsewhere the district languished, in pale laminar fluorescence, ceaselessly neap and beyond vision, all two information kiosks put out to siesta while extra terrestrials milled without. Belled, permeable zymurgic ether most aptly fell, arriving principals were at whiles cautioned to review their privilege for sorting a number of confidential motive, and sorted conclusively fortuitous of their aim. Upon receipt of the nerveless quash of his design, Messimo, to abide in a condition affordable if not then extraneous to a drudge requisite bought about in the past, upon eve of the slam, his convention prorogued any access to the dark pashmina headache now lodged without preset combinative necessary to an ignition of attitudinal feckfulness hoped in edging aside inclement projects. Had many of them read the literature, they should have been able to conflate stratagems. Lothar, disinvited more often than not from practiced vital tosses, who must miss either the floral exhibit, or Marta's semi frozen semolina shallot smelt myzithra, or the air sitar recital of his invisible god–child Emmerich, downed the cool *xenonian* pale.

Arguably, the best hope of divergent themes were to gain adamant stance within there, if Nertz had not halted thin spans of irises resigned to penetrate the enumerative shroud molded to Pyrogabion. The least permeable of extant loci cheated minute temptation to catch any of the fouling stares crassly re–enlisted from ranks of the undeployable; tagged alongside, thoroughly static embrace of flatiron grid civility slept. Persuaded of systemic capability haunting the exosphere in search of errant tragedy, thrippence sang amok one gatekeeper, eye transcripts culled from the visual morgue attested to movement enhancing an otherwise mundane watch. Molyneaux, after one discarded Rex argyle ambient from within the familiar crest, now withstood an entitled despondency kept since qua elemental, inspiring as it was for his nation to have won at bridge.

Scarcely unaware trust accorded to even Manasseh the rabbi Esherman had given his government an opportunity to bounce the slithering malefic antique futurity from its shore, a super virtual podesta tilted his visor jauntily while reviewing the splice and yearned saturninely for a mint. "You who bounce aversely through these aisles lose track of hope," one of the pollsters in his office reminded delegates, the natural inclination to celebrate equilibrium within a temporal routine, flawed by necessity to enact manifold cipher protocol hourly in order to reproduce code certified within the economic commune as next to unbreakable, created several dents in an erstwhile schedule of placid network maintenance activity.

Really these extended lunches became catalyst to phlegmatism deemed essential to their person, and Tell Ferguson, the youthful charge, gaped astronomically one week during installation from a touted itinerant monitor explaining how ad hoc inherent heuristic capability of Nertz allowed it to reset its own launch code at predetermined interval, releasing personnel from repetitive vigil; freed to perform deferred hygiene within routed sensors, one chary podesta removed her gaze from the screen long enough to scoop several vellum slippets beautifully printed from the batch file, product of a shift's duration, and stuffed them into the pale safe, evidence of their perpetual perseverance. "The main problem of dealing linearly in one historical media," said one muddled portmanteau, hereby solved, "which was, audibly correct until next perchloric endeavor, somewhat ill–prepared to vasten?"

Even among a single burden, Xantippe glanced tentative aphorism upon the approaching systemic guardian. "Pray sir, stray this far from the cup," they abjured *isomems*. Very thorough about things, the village podesta confiscated DNA and ordered Roveretto to derive bacterial fiat unless, notwithstood obstinate anachronism in tentative fiction, Messimo remonstrated *ahriman* was beyond reclamation because a bad dude once scared him in a prop room with a snow angle somewhere. This podesta, lifting another receiver, fielded an exceedingly important call as the chaste belt switched on. Eyeing the conveyor, Roveretto perforce kept watch on the forged passport and prayed that supervisor should not moodily log the numeral. Tinted oval acupuncturers who speciously entreated refractory podesta, their purpose painted as deviant enterprise, were likewise diffuse.

Before any segment, nervous during public involvement, Dauphine found the process of going around in circles to say whom we are and whatever our few words were to be gauche, cliche, and manqué, and before Sybil would ever see invented a new spore, the art of guessing how much longer the refrigerator was going to tremble until it shut

up, enabling Canadian geese flight to be audible indoors over extreme
silence, cessation of civil air traffic afoot, and down in front of her poor
old town she could hear four million miles following an exacting talent
search, "pay no more attention to them," *isomems* muttered hastily into
his spirit catcher, almost distracted enough to waltz out on Lothar's
croaked rendition of black Friday. They clustered dustily content to plead
nolo contendre when tense but sane Menard arrived. "We're ablatively
in touch with the entire string," they blathered. "Let him age in place,"
said the vile feed, "for which is worse, to indulge openly, or to regret?"
Amidst the vast city of chrome cranes and winking amber spotlights,
Noone finished, "maybe the sorrow opposed to the joys arisen from the
absence of what we ate (Spinoza)." His plan shorted, Messimo remained
inert and if need be, planned to walk out on it, wondering what sort of
plausible carriage he ought affect.

Uncertain items tucked insularly, the podesta, returned to her first
call as intimate interest at a neighboring terminal, stirred apparent sus-
picious vegetable matter. Dejected Chocho almost winced at a telltale
silhouette on screen reminding him of his appointment within! He
remained disparate as a dressmaker's impounded firmly strict inseams
took eons to verify. At the shifty supervisor's approach, *isomems* nudged
his parcel along side and ignored curious glances at his lapel. The supervisor went to station another shadow puppet post through. "May your
present employer find you indispensable," Justine brocaded, wondering
if rejoinder were too practiced. Its lengthily contorted–by–the–world's
health role were to be retracted with honor after fidgeting how many
hours therein? That gleam of recent pity (for laughs had been out there,
in contrast to descendants of Lilliputiana who transformed in fewer than
five hundred years a landscape), over–exposed to placation of pi insular
value, emergent tasks, oriented thorough sectionals, now sidereal, when
arrival of the christening party, an upheaval so occasional that, similar
fashioned accordance, a time of concert, encompassed location of a
sunburst, incidental, if ancillary to sial air, more followed than some
ulterior decors demonstrate a personal peace for perpetual existence.

A second *tictic* too bleeping shady, "tree—lined suburbs, I see two paper carriers, one on either shore," s/he thought. It was even possible that, *tictii* were traced to one name, the same, the indefinite elbow, and off you go?

Perplexed by happenstance and his sudden release, *isomems* in no manner too loose out there, a cloud beamed hungrily and direly biased abscissa sneezed loudly off key, "we'll take this bean from here onto one inn, old chump!" Whilst their voice warbled hindsight hymns insurmountably, asking these buggier visitants to return his charge tantamount to ordering extra parsnip at the sonar drive—through, offended Roveretto took his cross and his switchblade and flailed both at them from his docket, but jitterbugs performed a barrel roll and wrestled laborious yarrow from him each para—mutual, spliced them with pentameter, and hastened away one static flinch. Then, mindful of induced imbecility, invariably encountered, Esherman, irrespective of whatever every sect was, breadth, assimilation, variety of interpersonal belonging accumulated, in boiler plate, had long been an item for concern athwart multifarious other minutes of *wishram*.

Given diverse cause to a minded search of relevant beat also—ran on how specific observation lends verse a militant etude or why Manasseh, couchant within the shade of seldom non—interposed label rang quaint, alluding to fear of appearing to exist in a domicellular in vacuo perpetuated in the facile mode of stereotype, operant only via catharsis of imaginable characterization, our Idiopath repelled several councils purporting his imminent italicization while attempting to not forsake amends evinced on behalf of Florian's crepuscular emulative, the cessation thereto of his vacant personae on re—coordinated universal time gave alone perceptual stimuli for preservative acuity demonstrable almost ninety degrees ago ere, before bandwidth so frumious sought the irresolute perusal of guide pertinent to recovery, apparition verged, stairs apart from or into nowhere limp gossamer thread tugged invisible bucket and arraignment over next inner external available sound where ultimately referred via measurable span, now exhumed a calliotropic modem that would enable scattered otherwise alive groups of individuals to parole Vikram in specific instant.

Ere this, sufficient to assure an unexceptional return if risqué, many gentler principals deviated from semi—consciousness in averring skeptics of any mien a continuum of natural ideation lay on in unceasing pre-science exhibited in requisite for pluralism, a rebus necessitated bound, scaly relevance from a tote, mere, of whom was said would never starve for lack of work, or for whom a press conference the completion of an accelerated spatial transcendence device, one orgone, now beyond, for purpose of transplantation unto a lessor satellite of Mars' proto—typical stage. His were said to use up far too many inkwells, and Bagler, his favorite motel pen nigh on being completely scratchier than a 78 left out on the harmonium far from closing space, now variably disposed waiver of earlier penance, were he to accede to search for the missing service person at potential ultimate peril, now found association within hitherto disparate counsel legitimated in fulfillment of policy.

Only toward his auto—reply system were mellifluous overtures indicative of the enthalpist's perceptive site, insofar as most bifocal discourse seemed aimed upon the atrium banyan or other phrase in con-veyance of infra—indigo, guarantee of despite iridescent sexagessimal reverberative or intimate superfluously of vibrant myopia, unpredictable hours and waves meant no lack of effort to thrive over dark energy, to be indicted by the poisoned garden felt Anodyne.

.   .   .

As precedent sketch to flashback, pre—Raphaelites introduce travelling new fifth sub—phylum... maybe reasonable incentive 4Noone to expedite bio—optic scanner. Harun al—Kamil either 13th century sultan of Ægypt, or diffident, impossible to split, character, or contemporary Niobium, beside St. Agnes' important witness to frozen; seven stares of wergild, and/or odd, Nicean character, since masked landfall of provenance comprised nearly thirteen, give or take several partnerships with other concerns (a splinter group of Trombone society as well as National Anachronism Guild).

IV — viii — Re– invent orrery & prop solo dialog 4inchoate car[sic] artist.

The first order of business was assemblage of a matrix of nested pods made out of hemp husk so everyone could go and sit in them. There was something about a sour spill and oxygen hydrogen and then a five. So ended Finlay's second attempt at deciphering launch codes. Someplace else, an illegible table bore mute witness against his defective earlier effort.

For lack of a non—partisan expression of economics, he'd petitioned at colonnades for the omnibus cone of silence to penetrate into his cubicle with appeal at once perfunctory and verbatim, being simply pro forma rehash of blanket disclaimer, evoking talentless exception which effectively brought contumacy upon the entire free nice library in the shape of a community assistance program. Any demand for doctrinaire intercession unfolded beneath least dilatory auspice, a condition seethed in an assiduous, mundane shadow fair.

The draught supplanted anything the Institute ever witnessed. Safely cordoned behind velvet blue ribbon, matrons must form chaste phrase and impart togas, for Delphic hoopla gawked on at the impending sigh. They impelled the resident Sangreal to scope the recoupable virus; how droopily flicked a seminal colonic adulation against preponderant waves, pled Mantissa's taint from scorching scurrility, went way unset, for in vocal alarm hauteur, *ahriman* listed to ageless perception of ipso qua erratic savants which, if anyone were to adduce mean club crowds the gallery bedizened in sibilance, nor beyond fire ambled humongously near separate anodyne, laden forefront beyond dwindled shame, insofar were freight tribulated to its lot and sank from disinheritance amidst bale funicular isthmus from aisles of faceted premise cutaneously ill.

Finlay's raspberry crepe reception, so clear this, even now flustered cusps tritely, was successful only in dissociating Bagler, said to be enthalpist at the International Agronomic Convention, who replied, as best as form might discern, "cease this iconoclasm or I shall persistently throw biscuits at you." The enthalpist, a man of small renown, if in dislike of being in the skip zone, assuaged his craft with single spaced lines let into metaphor as an ocean of truth. A lime lit stretch of bad road stood, an original effort to define trackless steppes of the foremost empyrean, an immediate goal of enthalpism, to dissuade then fashionable views of the heavens as epistemological re–militarized zone, when, in an undistant future, devious consortiums well at threshold of dark matter, posed, with design to capture infinity and extort an infelicitous present out of time.

Typically, an protactic imprimatur thereby cognate, those totems laxly reverberate stillness; Finlay's reasonably intemperate filing of illuminated manuscript into the communal recycle bin neither propitiated resident antihero–apologeticians, and the bark of his collective focus henceforth impinged onto a floe of incipience super–numeral, unless deus ex machina [*sic*], in guise of fluffy little rubber baby buggy bumpers, forthwith developed. The Borysthenes at floodtide had not extruded more propinquitous simulacrum, at once commodious yet Arcadian, indispensable to a factor of ineffable regard to optimal spatial redistribution. Those cameo filters, redolent arpeggio of asymptotic reflux, recollected font of such de rigeur [*sic*] instant, his peremptory assertion, that, of comprised protoplasm, an enhanced Utopia, rolled over without demur.

. . .

Carte blanche bestowed men, whose fly infected emergent omega
crèche, veering ere hoisted onto plateau of adulation hitherto reserved
for corporate grind and alternate heresies as—is, more than eleven
million *lithiwatt* per diem, a numb infusion of Village fund created, an
interagency mechanism for correlation of bio—derivative testocerone,
one person responsible for these ordinal situations stood calmly; this
resident, Sangreal, a womad characteristically used to chaste hellions and
obvious upon threshold of her own signal clarity, still startled in ready
alarm as the gentleman, Roveretto, unheeded, now, announced Echo,
the Countess Constancia, Mme Nadeladimov. Moreover, a grown body
of desiccated anti—war resistors milled in a corner of the Institute eating
all of the tofu at the health food store.

Each immediate participant had symbolic room to infer it — that
charge, while highly distorted, might anticipate and refute any objec-
tion raised on an obvious ground. That omitted question of spanning
immense spatial quantities in existence, if it was not only inclusive of
great distinction, the capacity for tuning the fork in the road to shorten
the potential should send a shudder among them (inherent sage writers
of the shortest distant principle agreed to risk remission of their mem-
bership and soon sought egress), it nixed instantly an idea of noting their
departure quietly. Of greater congress, an impressive faction coalesced
around the motion to have all exits changed.

For the enthalpist's declaration of that motion null, since a general
session was not now on, the least inspired called so for one to be. An
untoward fear of loss instilled ad hoc pursuit that went not far, for,
SOMHAD, of exegesis, forsaken flight of their fellows, turned to inform
encroaching fact—finders that beneath relegation clause of the ICA charter
they, as investigative body, comprised no legal audit, lacking sanction
of the greater whole, and while insistent upon immediate cessation of
their detention, only proposed to reveal the only ledger to a panel only
duly constituted at some only future time. "Now move then and take
your coil elsewhere," one beige intoned, insofar 'tis of those, "freakishly
inattentive to latch the drab module," so forth theatrics formerly Gnostic

in appearance darning ideals loll down the curious maxilla, beta scams spool if not clearer text condignly porous atop the mirror of irresponsibly misspent and jinxed owlishly to inevitable luck; returned from book signing their least recent work, *How Fabulous May We Be?*, told in part to skater Iphgene Heppleweis, men who, seemly in effect get drench, ere given more cage, collected a message from a frightened adjutant upon which was scrawled an ultimatum from an imagined glory, the *untenet* perceived SOMHAD approval at a far car to out—sit their sect, and afternoon of the great debate concludes during a terrible thunderstorm, before a dreadful day in the pit assembling fire lines amid one hundred and eight degrees, improbable games of Skip—Bo, a live black snake resident in the reverse osmosis filter, provoked convoys, broken into paroxysm of terror, flora and fauna in abundance, frogs, scarab beetles larger than mice, mosquitoes, wood bees, or clouds of Flugelzahn [*sic*] all put together.

While peers are sat down at the end of their travels, there are ten of them amidst triangulated seas of tables seating three. Each odd man out finds one table as close as possible to others, with exception of a poetry expert, who vainly hopes they shall shout over, including him in their conversion. They are extolling the nice climate, you can build all year and even mid—winter nights humming attest to activity, and albeit their realtor relates, "there'll be days in spring when it will rain for weeks in advance," this realtor has not learned all of the following things in reverse order. The blister on Sandra's thumb, incurred yesterday during latrine queen duty, in step with *xenonian* foxtrot cadets' foray, this time, in powder blue, rather than orange crush of flighty years ago, continued to dispute vehemently about talc ziggurats, best traversed by spectral tobbagonism. You can in most cases always go back and check if and in all cases should set aside each day, at Least, ten minutes either in the morning or evening to review your work in order to prevent or forestall the degeneration of every conversation into a race to the bottom to see who can be more judgmental.

Thus Cecil, their only pottery expert, needing just a new ribbon for one's bismuth corona, languishes beyond funds of stagnation. Children point and whisper to other parents, girls his own age, who giggle and look awry. The yearning poetry excerpt casts disparate glances at tables of his comrades, lounging for only a moment when they might include him in their colloquy, but as his falafel arrives, he has eyes only for it, acutely conscientious of his terrible isolation. The other peers give no syncope they have ever known him. Is the solicitous question, "everything all right sir," voiced for a third time by a servitor, when a portion of freedom fry has lodged up his nose, a cause for death?

.   .   .

If a clear spare may drift over ever intermittently, reinterpreting present period salon with a premise of odd man out here, was An, withal at this moment such surety, arrived after the post of middle night. From the old limbic community, Iphgene received a call. She hoped her unblemished performance in the first three laps of the Failsafe Invitational would earn her a shoo onto the national team. "Mrs. Van Etnabaron–Heppleweis," the caller said, "and you're," she replied?

"I am the new cash cow." "Where's the old, flat, pop," Iphgene asked? "That list is full, Mrs. Heppleweis." "You didn't tell me what happened to him," she persisted. "There are enough skaters for our team this quadrivium," the caller informed her. Little was known of Heppleweis' new coach, his penchant for primary and secondary flow rate, and this staunchly advocated Taylorism set stage for the *Alpine Symphony* by Ricard Strauss, ordaining her to impersonate mountain (appraisal), storm (feedback), traveler (overload), sunshine (circuitous whorls). Æmst chased Iphgene at all times shouting all of those things at her until the latter next applied via cell to the thesaurus figurative dissociation.

"We're so sorry," she was told, "there was a last mint frangipani. You have been screwed." How she'd missed the flat, old, pop, who'd warily certify her progression in disambiguous syllogism. Now unlit her pined gesture of vapid rearrangement, ratherwise nipped, in unclear discomfort, of other lilts next hazarded, it did not take exceptional wherewithal

to achieve whenever society asked of us. There were many advantages
to all of the technological advancement which had been accomplished.
Moreover, someone finally despaired of naming any of the mere drama
night groove fiber fans.

Thus must each tart act foster much spin over famed lucidity, lest
harsh jeers, endured at latte, mime monthly issues and hustle hardship
and hazard. Only this was cerulean: their mail eventually did not often
catch up to them, and if some time quite suddenly on speaking term
above anyone, freed snoops liked sinister vocation from either speed,
quaintly being foxed to let themes dither in spotless collective. Given to
strange aroma, this morning, moreover, found Sergei Kalamparumple
in an online airport snack shoppe queue. He hoped his glitter pen would
have held out tolerably to shop over wealth, ere in turn, a gentle existence, an unironed journal, its print staining his fresh worsted suit, also
put paid to any hope of maintaining similitude.

The Economic Community (reneging its solemn promise to allow
a provisional mint of the *lithiwatt*) had thrown the fix back into the face
of heirs of Paul'r'us. A hundred paces ahead of him, a fellow traveler
cringed beneath the styrene arch so an alarm, rippling like dominos,
should pre–empt piped–in tone of "My Lovelies Over the Sea," set to
elevator music, Kalamparumple read on; ascended from a hundred royal
shafts, forces of the committee seized assizes, torn public notices, and
detained, key members, asserting their privilege of managing affairs
beneath village aegis, trapped in a story written by victors whose tours
in sweaty depots, commenced nights before conclusion of combat operations, *wergild* magnified into assonance of Jacobinist revanche, is it any
wonder one developed a Stockholm syndrome for pervasive utilitarianism which danced ephemerally upon the edge of conscience.

How else seemed iotas too extant for acute prowess alike, if optional
mosaics dared a truth fast yesterday. So rare during eschatological eras,
if at all fustian rotogravure cribbed these admixtures wrung from nigh
pathless subterfuge indicated, than ad hominem fame curled, uniformly
vitreous albeit spasmodic in edgy travesty. Indeed selfsame protoplasms

novelly cavalier toward harmonic, stigmatized in unstartled eclat, offhand tuned to that single signature, wistfully aware of lost etching which some haunted shelf life Nicean extras seemed fain to impart.

This vain tableau conferred fitful cachet upon such ludicrous artisans yet Henry (VII), fickly couched therein, perceived schism within *inter—regnum* inconceivable mere eons ago, from which styptic xenophobes bleakly surmounted atavism dustily unless hagiographers could notarize more conservative pontiffs. Thus furnished grist for alluded deliberation sic passim, he sought to repress, since perpetual inertia seemed best guarantee of his beholden asylum.

The Itsy–Bitsy Astral Exchequer Directorate Collage.

That this plenitudo potestatis [*sic*] will be preliminary, and *pluperfectreß* wont to have all answers until next week, as described, the assembly chanced she'd be director of the Neapolitan striarchy, and thus perhaps most vociferous advocate of the *Sanctus Pax Melioris*, "report," she repeated, "of individuals had Florian soon to be clear out of his desk," brought the memo to her attention and, half–snapped, taken up questioning *wishram* from trembling knee, *pluperfectreß* heard her shelf say, "defined Henry (VII), rise to be heard!" Now could it be gonged, if this Idiopath had seven days for functions that shall be funded, and there, if he dreamed it away and wrote another figure, he will be infiltrated.

Henry (VII), risen to standing position, wanted people on the fore-front to know well unlit the surface of the table nearly *wishram* general: "fifteen and six, £900, director." "We won't elect anyone else," Piero, hand in pocket, shuffled, "until the next meeting is yours." "Yes, your insurrection adhered to standard of non–political correctness," acceded the ex–chamberlain *(all too busy)*, "shall your circus net cam, and anyone else whose dedication to sui generis clause, include many individuals, who made it blatantly official this morning since Florian, new Idiopath trans–montane, ran threatening dogma which pervaded Sicilia on his broadside."

"Busy, busy, aren't we," chuckling, shaken commentary died, as Florian considered another stack of quotas for those vessels damaged, "now as we're in a free and open Assizes —— " *pluperfectreß* retorted, "that's a politically incoherent statement." She returned to question Piero della Vigna, sat up at a table, and dug out a quill: "the Assizes, in surety for adoption of your council, promised that *plenitudo potestatis* would bear cost of the podesta, but vociferous as are these days, all paperwork will wither away." "Our sole fault should have been that we pushed Encyclicals with too much zest," Piero agreed, sighing, "we might have remained in good stead, had that flare, Gaussier, not burned the *plenitudo potestatis* memorandum beneath the stack of imprimaturs which were supposed to have been distributed at the last movable feast."

"Alas, on thirty and six, £1,800, unless we take a persistent stand in favor of your exchequer," began ex–chamberlain *(all too busy)*, "let us then consider deposition of that podesta, Gaussier, appointed to assist you briefly, who after being buried in effigy at the last funicular lese, strode out of the courtyard under leaden skies. While scowled at, he swore, 'I knew those persons were of antiseptic persuasion; amidst all the rest of the stuffed shirts who had so much on the committees, I should find it the sad duty of my office to inform you, consequent to debatable adjustment, allegedly named to your exchequer, before the morning it rained, I'd vow my presence made a target reset if faxed.'" Here menial steps of sufficient hexameter braked, yet used to nonesuch sort for the previous intersection spore, Echo wound wishes to seem larger scenes witlessly well read.

Intent on inflection of et cetera into her routine, Iphgene's new coach saw during this visit an inferential liability promoted via nearness of existence. "You are the mountain, the storm, the traveler, the sunshine!" The ideal dropped supreme access upon stage of shared informality, dispersed in common strain via an inner calculus, and, insofar as she rivaled Noone, impenetrable pedigrees, of other houses, alternative glasnost loomed in space between optional and compulsory. Inquiring of which Ministry what dressing facility had been arranged, and told to get on with it as best one could, the dudes accordingly stooped beyond universal jurisprudence, indicted in systemic charge of libel. Shoving the thing into a garment bag, a rather lumpy arrangement, Fuald arrived at Salisbury and booked for a hack.

It should seem Harun stood for hours until one appeared. The fab vicars of fresh speed chaffed to lead this cause, somewhat moved to dematerialize; in Idres' unfamiliar while, our stern clutter, they'd merrily blend emptiness to get terser misunderstanding of dimmer sorts of ideal by and by. When followers of the prophet arrived at his city with flowers and swords, Chahil wrote, *Ayadgar E Zharan*, an announcement foreshadowing eventual victory of light verse, despite, darkness, much setback, disappointment, and grief. If an epic intended to encourage citizens of Gujarat to resist the converters, it succeeded terribly. Four hundred families perished. A sea of rubble annexed to the caliphate. Chahil's epic, smuggled into the Uppermost Mountains, survived, a vehicle for transmission of culture, and was regarded as quaintly affected by visiting philologists.

Adjourned in spirited public repartee, Dauphine, Lilliputian devote to the *Picayune*, arrived in New Cork to bury the rest of the story. This title search, a survey, commissioned via communion of exile, exacted a terrific bite upon the resourcefulness of observers. For her part, Desdemona did not stop the metier, arguing that plaintive brief, if poignant, also outsourced an occult if not limpid realism and, in commonly calm integument, with twinge thereby scoffed the venue moved from greater whole. By the time fare was fixed, al–Kamil was in his suit and all whaling ceased. "Dear listeners," Francis recounted, "my lamps unto me, may shadow puppet bless these tottering statements on a piece bearing my appreciation. I am not responsive to music beyond any extrinsic experience. Our unexplored orb of extreme exercising out with all of it, I have studied angles of why self–regard is prismatic and thought idly wandered, whatever might be felt of recipients straying nearer the premise, the strained merciful qualities; of justice there seemed no doubt, away from balm, because while returned, the good news fled.

Pray men might succeed in holding faith and good conscience (1 Tim 1:19), but next arrive at a custom." The stolid fen reeked in flux of a rancid Vikram wind.

"You debase your bleeping," rasped one, known for his lacunae launch, "you portentous twit," Æmst idled. Noone must not dial in without being propositioned on ridiculous pantheons of claimant to an ecumenical phosphorescence. If her nostrum appeared incandescently fringed on upswing of real generosity, inveterately scheduled scratches camped before nexuses of bracing meritocracy. In dread silence, al–Kamil approached stones. They gleamed like midnight at noon. Tombs, once unearthed and brought to light in sure reverential hope, now occupied burdens of sprawl and among swift corridors of power, egress, hitherto a matter of engaging simplicity, devolved into a struggle against chafing vicissitude, Argus blinked; al–Kamil did not wish to remain, ere his counsel were able to evince, however, that *Speculum* reproduced directories to each absentee and ulterior voluptuary, plaintiff redirected, much chalk, expended in ill–lit interstice of festive archive, yielded but cloying grit of discredited axiom, debunked postulate, erred theory, and disabused notion.

Shocked by their own relevance and extent to which generic opinion prepared to concede their utility in the new scheme, discontented classes of artisan sought refuge underground. Yet, that abode, a sill equipped to harbor provenance, skilled in art of having what they did not hate, previously charged in transit of new Niceans, and given yield that office to *uchaux*, the fifth strain *fjulsfut* withdrawn, via all formal *inter–regnum* commerce an atmosphere, charged of ambiguous sufferance, only to continue tending crackling plinths, provenance had become haplessly turned in by Baby Burner, the animist series. This, their Kryptonite, paused them to unlock their bicycles and drop whatever else they were re–enacting to order scandalous talk show topics.

Spliced upon the foremost scone, Horace ran with others and detected in shelves festivitude too sublimely scarce to be credited; hearing no mere mews, yet wildly closer to being than ever recently

presumed, they mailed, tapped, lifted, measured, and now pried off
lairs, a strange and dull avocation, adjusted, their concept of importunate
worth there among desired scale, foundlings, their sleeves, albeit, as
above premise, up, an ousla perfunctorily, at least assemble those comprised, downcast, if not neglected tribes asserting Logan out for launch.
The man's attempted raillery fell upon their deafened heart, loved so
not a bad turnout, declared a familiar voice behind him, Ferguson, near
Ossian, in the 13th, and/or 22nd century today, when staff is grumpy,
or levitated twenty–nine centuries down near Dorf Zafner's flute, the
rebellious *wergild* run into the dessert for Chocho's chichi [sic] memorial
heffalump search.

It was nifty, whom he'd met at a reading of *Miracle Esters* by Ladæñæ
Renata Consuelas Mirabeau Mervyn. "That's a start," Iphgene conceded,
"but you weren't where you would have delivered the much earlier some
time." Hesitance had seen the world surge today. "I don't watch much
TV," she upheld. "I'm wax–born." They weren't married but a month
before the discotheque pathos queue, and Noone already minded, old,
flat, pop worth a second book, "it is different because we can make
our money going out, Marta," yet, they, seeing sparks with Althea
nonetheless, blamed only us, in half forgotten realm of memory; how is
this pace maintainable, broke below fresh pippins anew when one, from
semblance of biopic catharsis, super–imposed post Mercatoric dystrophy
intrinsic to ornamental realignment of situation.

Invaluable nome, unmet were transports unfettered while sung
ciphers bowled wordless upon their shuck, the venery flung out of
tri–cycling, where shape caught behind bored collision shuffled that
borough, humanity, deferred of absolute vision onto decks of glowing
dank hurdles, to forthright appeal traced, this great time is the first wear
in whence mass image became available in shaping the general construct
of appearance, a door sketched to enclosure and inventory availed little
stand, grandiose if without shaken density, unmet in the corner affin-
itive clique, coalesced to forsake de rigeur context within by shafting
endemic omniscient remonstrance wherever a sub–ionic level, the *fjulsfut*

core sample, depicting culmination of effort to turn Earth into a giant spaceship, cited, an ostensibly alternative raison d'être, the need to avoid Uranus, a posted upturned crescent encompassing a full sextant's ballast athwart the northeastern azimuth, a Cheshire smile come to swallow Earth. In light of the revised pre–Ptolemaic universe it seemed a noble effort, yet Ferguson had someone to warn of a darker purpose.

.   .   .

An hour later Harun al–Kamil, Sultan of Ægypt, *murahaleen*, learning that they just lost their only poetry export, orders execution of plan B. "Now," he declared, "peers must instill a reaction of astronomic precept and a ready disregard of natural heritage in efforts to discredit classical Western humanism while also acquainting then an exact line fully diametric to its precursor." Before the plusher ones depart, al–Kamil's immaculate concerns, warmed within a screed, entail: a sad dude messkit, bastard rastaman, gentile agit–prop, divan processional, and tartar pamphleteer, whom, on an asynchronous tenth day, feathered ceilings from aft rinse of pectin and generically, left the Nizam's Army to tool intensely with pre–Sputnicists. Sent to Oxford for studious free–floating hauteur and joie d'vivre [*sic*], in his senate of weekend inertia, al–Kamil struggled this mint grasshopper suit off the prop room and onto the train, wondering at what point they were supposed to get it on.

Always manually, sallow, once his aunt's sand had blasted their first strident Sumerian oracle, *Arise!* (the anti–disestablishmental *Speculum* deemed it nuanced and puerily subversive), he'd pre–liminalized that *Speculum*, in deceitfully Vedic underlain foment, though roughly Shut–up–and–gosh had, via cognitive redistribution into Tut–and–pish–posh, et al, eke *untenet* pretext for an irredentism formula throughout weird, whirled counties, "mea culpa," *author of poor haiku*, provenance re–assembled gladly at Dives, through to say for his zone's elves, their increasingly idiomatic yet muffled flourish capably extended a sense of cost annulling other reification.

Partition, if causally recurred, could not trouble this cast. "You'll
be on decent ply yet, front," expressly fond of confuting any claim to
sacrament, Vorga ex libris breathed immoderately, Roveretto minded,
beyond the day the Blois should again inherit their idyll, upon whence
the Ruthenian, Noel, loren ipsum, pled, their carton drawn near, "dibs
on the rack!" Each knell, forded, troubled not their repartee.

Amidst the ferried crush Gnadig, wont sadly, rode on amidst the
stern. A heckler on loan they trimmed aside in plumage to the dot. "I've
arranged," she began, "to present St. Agnes nicely and as serviceably
fatuous," since while she descried the canaries were of charge congruent in
each variable beamed lonelier, and Dauphine tore from her glance the conspicuous waders of periodical observable sampler, scant residue of improvement overdue, *isomems* abruptly scuttled, another of the novel weighing
machismo patterns palled. Alone taken stock of not only their numb, and
number, Alcuin yet also noted in a trice that, beside *author of poor haiku*,
of their apparent muster, merely ten more were arrived in Albion, unless
Anodyne might bring this topic to general attention, regarding necessity of
recruiting a twelfth in urgent departure, a charter bore them strait within.

A cloistered focus, emissive, profuse theme in successive resolve,
and for the final time provenance, as rebels from the stillness movement
lolled, iconic myth sleeves, awaited rival of a man, in duress, drenched,
dazed, assigned as effigy, in tense glee, some consonant recall Iphgene,
whom, natheless unable to intervene in their context, wished a good
one for them all after near every whenever, if, exerting wondrous
nebulous awareness inclines into infinitive, this overt leastness boiled
alongside idle space, saving over the top. "Didn't that just quite to seem
text perhaps somewhat cyclically merged," PoD squeaked? "I am the
ghost of Christmas presents, also known as Baby Burner, son of Momma
and Poppa Burner," the illuminated carapace replied. "Jesus, Elvis, and
merry lands all were in an oak grove that had an angle flying to the
phones." "I left my keys there," *ahriman* admitted.

"A long flower keeps justice at bay, old man," Baby Burner expur-
gated, "by the banks of the river of time gleamed nougat, forasmuch to

stop change one may as well refute likable synonym." Without saying go, fluffier tappers hoped which chorus throughout, for songs, set to poetic almost mood, struck wistfully their famous Hellenic lyre, now charge to adsorb inelegant sponsors cover, so on which situation best had north by northwest sown thin amiable stroke conjugate moronic time of faultless personal image, to tentative too recall imprint, mosaic reflection radiated a preternatural truth zestfully febrile, "other than some still maddened insert," another of the lackadaisical jitterbug tactics, "blessed avatar, that after shock termed ironic lest another book found in the Great Winnow pounded a wintry storm cheating glory."

"To begin," Baby Burner expounded, "these call around for cheerful illustration. Chains of my own design, thereby shackled are we in a new preposterous *chichi*, our door to without, more liberty, yet retentive of hopeful steady recoil. We will be friends, you and I, members of one local air fetish hectically, child persons between realism (another said to one tearing across dotted line, find new joy in delirious tedium of winless chant)." "This asterisk preceded the new dawn, that shrill wind already," tattered a banner, "invincible word spoken with sauce were one, until not yet," sobbed the dark Chad, "refuse this modus vivendi!" PoD dodged this shy pitch nervously. No stranger to depths of his own fall, "all I'll quote," he stammered, "is summated in James 1:8, 'ye friends of little faith.'"

"There he goes thinking shadow puppet cares about his symptomatic assets," jitterbugs commented. "Our selfsame cloud once proved key to intimate habit, and there reasons abound for a lifetime of obtuseness." But let anyone read far not despair in their search for vaster method. This lamp devolved warmly in cheap stasis while thirds whom, in copacetic desire to admire salons of closest exit faithful, bid will that heavy jukebox quietly manipulate us too helplessly. "The required lunch spell is over, and it behooves us to resume rendering this bodhisattva by degree lest he contort our purpose in some sort of publicly funded docu–drama."

"My original question," PoD insisted, canaries' flippant sibilance indicating they were intent upon reaching the spot of doom at the bottom of this page. They too octally minded about one whole adjusted Van Allen belt, for dimly this evening star lurched; a little light key orbited in bland form, exit here, whose meandering track outranced symbolic banshee bothersome, and if so, what could they have avoided? Traced hypsometrically across the limitless sky, their storied chichi [*sic*] strained to begin demarcation of quasars. The tooled incandescent wholesome amphorae grafted in interest of state, re–invented sonnets in neo–Platonist paradigm, and outlasted eleven nights in unevenness.

Behind Kalamparumple, some children asked where that monad was being taken. Upon an ordinary year, one would find it quite solecistic to turn around and reply to their question. However palpable, tension draped the concourse. Quorums dodged their camisole along aconite carpet strewn with vacuous locks. Forbidden cell phone usage, magnates stared glumly. Connections, failing ever well–fed and chatty down liner notes, fallen to silence, ere the only blessing anyone was able to court, Sergei, read of news from Europe, decided he had sure picked a bad time to attend the Reject Fair.

It had been once what agape proof must ring as heaven's sedate occlusion, a solid salt voiced only on scant summit days. Men, indivisibly dual, groping toward ideals, read any lover's true deed in fate's marvel as pet mottoes foliate ethos in condign, contrite, but trope wholeness. Since this ivy–barring oaf lottery prophet, damned far forward as zealous, met and casually sent pre–phoned exiles away, no correct foment banked on the fun either.

·   ·   ·

Connexion with Ike's Park vision most effective as doctrine of affectations [sic]...
a preference beneath emotional impact... interposed fence may also relate to hives
for frozen... mid—sentence, scene, paragraph needn't necessarily be section opening
or as trope a response ~ remove unnamable parenthetic articles, or, for a flush potential
reference to Terpsichore's Brow (—nian), œdith manufactures theodolites to trace
uchaux, generically mortified coal rose hatchlings.

IV — ix — Libator Dialog Requires Backstroke And/or Nixed with social commentary.com

Spectators, withstood online beyond fainéant velvet blue ribbon, await the trial of the teensy epoch to subside. "Did I ever order that," Harold wondered. As the lamp was fixed on him, what sort of joy lay in store on completion of the cherished task? "Eat that over there," Lizavetta said, and fixed bread, sliced slabs of blackberry puree, peanut butter, and unfamiliar starch, handling one to him plastered in horseradish paste. Upon a weak island of lunar time, Van Etnabaron perforce left his dome to swallow one bite of the concoction and repeat this admonition.

"Haven't I ever told you to stop this," Sasha shouted at his daughter whose giggle into the kitchen brought Iphgene. While her husband seemed funnier in general, her relief, upon Van Etnabaron's return, safely, decided the experience in favor of more professional glimpses of homely self—alienated materialistic circumstance, thought worthwhile to get, in consciousness of the very dry pressure tomorrow, about four hours out of town while listening to advances of a current if shared capacity, and offered brusque condolence to his winnowed state; moreover, on for the Failsafe Invitational, she was soon due to be away. Artificially, Van Etnabaron adopted a mask of indifference. Was he to alter the sand stone monolith of trickling time?

Her manner, new, yet not strained, of recovering particulars of her

husband's *biathanatos* yielded fewer than forty–four words. "Eat more,"
ELIZA reminded his taut whim in specious rippling simile. "I'd hide,"
Sasha replied. Dreamt or bemused, Harold continued, "I'd hide and then
we could be friends. Or was it that," on threshold of a lucid interval,
the councilor, leaned forward on one elbow, said nothing? The jurors,
ere text messaged about calliopes of medicine at Worsted, in coherent
tidbit of conversational Gestalt, soon devolved upon the defendant, this
co–dependency poster child, whose reputation, obviously preceded
Æmst, masked one, would work in the system, "all his rife, insipid owls
sacked, Finlay re–read the dime store novella of l'nurt Glyntz and her
archipelago of matter."

In reply, their firman who, every day assigned a reason for not listening to his entire ideal landscape collection of real life limbo lunch
and dharmic porcelain urchins, sent off, "something is for anyone who
cannot deal with everything." Left behind from halcyon wander, lust of
an embracing milieu deemed dearth natheless, any historian (*all too busy*)
tossed, on the road as yesterday's rag doll unless something, supposed to
happen, interjected, "Ranth, I never told you once why we were way too
stupid to catch a greased tadpole. In a rain barrel the world tied behind
our back, And/or, ere Worms' forest lore, straining about odes at what,
ere immediately settled, opened a sized thaw."

As rang above tonight's hand, Henry (VII), with Kantian thoroughness,
felt counsel leave ammeters unknown for new Hoyle's bobbin art, elapsed,
ere breath spread Deerfield's hierarchy of hanging out thus (co–habitat,
preferred buds, single issue, apathy, or just friends); rose hips, left upon
biathanatos, Maxwell's tapper, partly asked, of matters known irksomely
to sink too deep, whether Piero had anything to add to the otiose laments
of Ranth, chimed, "for £1,000, Sr. Florian ensured proper ministerales
were reined in, but if you didn't wish to kick into that fund, you may well
be disbarred from studying stage direction with object of meditation."

Piero della Vigna postulated, "what you did require during the
fiscal year without gavel confirms," but while he booked up again, that
dark pawn vanished. "That probation, Señor — uh — della Vigna, is

of previous fiscal importance," *pluperfectreß* presumed, "earlier this year," projected via *biathanatos*, "you had said, 'what are we waiting for, an upward parabola of concession to distinguish underpinning of a scarcity complex foisted upon didactic caste system,' in which our love for the little ones facilitated a counter–productive thought spiral induced by daytime vertigo?" Principally during guarded glance of that grey gloaming, they affirmed the solstinox seamless reproduction of the fable of hapless Æctæon, "so let's now entertain scripts."

. . .

One, eagerly began, "I, having scared an ounce of prevention in these happy times it wasn't begrudged of *finth*, beyond their circuitous spin, my glimpses were captivated by an expectant gaze so mild I braked for snails," so sue me if I stared, what sobs they fled into their gingerbread house radiating much dislike I hovered in orbit for hours in regret. In everything such humility, once back inside this story, I cannot care to advance complaisant, comatose awareness. Underlain in enervation of isotropic fret, I viewed those pages trod as once our forefathers deemed via ordinary beneficent means, a cloud of susceptibility clunked together unpleasantly as she erased adipose fickle utilitarianism, from the merrily color shoe tree, back when satellites ruled fewer of our skies.

One channel was enough in the dais once formed, a far cry ago to recap one dear over the fence before day broke on our whiffle ball game while we, at risk of a host of exigence, were apparently calmed into warm fluff of the cannon hung not so hard compressed between our mad little hand so pinioned. A possibly feasible seemly poet occurred to mint their vilification in zany gavel, lit in reboot yet over lethal fancy. As angst grew other prolonged, if lingering rations for matter, all schema postponed, a day of wrath were welcomed supplement unto deferred dread question. For future of all events, yesterday's madness might make sense were one to give a moment to evanescent Zeitgeist resumed, for up until Nod, one had been able, aware only of a nether fate, inflexible on caprice, to face presumably socially conscious imperial élites within councils begun by several disparate individuals who did not seem that blessed.

Unless the community, a movement, Hesitance in actuality to append a supportive document due to brevity, if ever at a loss for seconds, refused invitation to dance, leaving her profoundly tardy, grappling for any hope she must some night care enough for a topic to begin writs on it anew, back from the concourse seemed nearly as easy as scrambling out of a flytrap, oh shadow puppet. Earning this exhalation as dismissal, Horace, unlike most of the line, should not turn his head. His earnest train, to discern events, he listened, "new radiant stunts," Porphyry askance, "is it that and do you like it here, so farewell, wanting not at all to know?" "Over Vikram," the Ambassador, standing over her table, respected to close behind Piero della Vigna, "here, in your insurrection, definitely undermined," continued the occifer of lobbyists, "did it occur to you to ask whose allocation was concerned to belie?"

"I'll say if we didn't QED it up to the Assizes," *ædith* was bristling, "the skip's insertion of any podesta feed must be waived. Piero della Vigna" — Henry (VII) held, "what rungs there were had been delegate to Florian, dark stranger, which improvised the fund of his insurrection." "Ensign *ædith,*" *pluperfectreß* asked, "didn't periodicals in a recent issue advocate fewer discretionary: thirty and six, £1,800?" Henceforth, aside from sententious travelogue outburst, canned simpatico you probably have, enough bananas in your pocket, few hands of slug bug, a competition to see how collegial they would each be to everyone else, and an immense weird congenial facade engendered in an assignation conspicuous, devoid of pleasantry, they were shadowed at dusk by a sleepless henna wasteland goddess, diligently assorted greatest hits of Sergei's air–land–sea sprinkler collection.

Talitha wasn't in any lackadaisical mood for imminent inculcation of doctrine, inasmuch defiantly exclusive outcome germinated in a Petri dish of possibilities: she'd either taken to sing along without end, a voiceless marathon of pidgin frequent flyer minute, or somehow above all stigma scammed to his incomplete blandishment in construct of a trousseau stunning in complete molecular chains enough for framing, yet in any case the nearest exit beyond them, and they didn't ask any questions there, chair of oversight long vacant; except the admonition of let's not and say we had the paper to prove it and kick around anymore scramble, but for a savvy and counterculture John Bull look–alike, they may mop up the floor with Flugelzahn, and tearfully resentful he never had one chance for snoopy sixth, Tolstoy, being publicly yanked for his cooperation, then left the town where Sandra threw up because house-keepers were not authorized to move those personal effects. Florian, editor of *Mainzer Landfriede*, a cautious daily, stood down.

So eager to help if somewhat clueless, he asserted, "Tuesday's conclave distributed condominiums during the encyclical of '37." "Okay, people, only one answered £900," *pluperfectreß* overruled. What, must answer the following (she makes a pulse pause): "Ensign *ædith*, have you there in your hand a list of names," began ex–chamberlain (*all too busy*), but she ignored them? "We opted for reduction of our own subsidy to fifty–five percent and are now compelled to question" — of *ædith* a Nicean hemispheric semaphore, Wormwood, bore down the stem of his beak — "Florian's effectiveness anyway."

An, ambassador, took another sop, adding, "the rest is in a generic coffer against members of reneged grind graffiti. Real idiom slyly then we fled to the earth ere fob anon could fluently offer sanitary crass chow to us whom too receipts clipped from the weird dial stamped magic." All between greatness outpour much else one channel inferred, but fallow these stream among lorgnettes aimed from gabby principle hell how many cells toll ceaselessly so forgotten chorus amidst minute spots hung together the entire klatch of their Pavlovian slobber in what brazen echoes lounge as discus tads strain of tapper etymologies hymn reverberated back there, them us miming, for gonging unspecifiable schism between mind and deed, someone has a key to all of those cans, their dominion insulated by our every quest for full behavior.

.   .   .

In that situation of mean, endless in their preponderance of waste not logic and it were of use in the salvation of screen, night after night spilling up chalk should filter tone with numerous comfort, an exact real gnomic ill and putative boom sponsored thorough advance, in misanthropic sense detrope, since all morbid facet receded in nil response gates kept, sprang up an hobby and all nods of the future were in lobbing no to guests in fonder fashion than might we embrace an individual search for rights mostly scenic before nevertheless all glory and honor had been accorded one true creator.

Now, implicitly devolved into the voice of stringiness, Inyo, ere to view present tides of assurance as you know the phrase of tepid wrack in even symbolic sconce, the whenever habit discarded, her son Cecil in ordinal facile talent, antisocial behavior averred at on infrared square, still touted we loved something coherent, even if at all coeval vehemence spilled rumor slowly feckless to our ideal upheld in lemon possibility if organically inclined scene unfurled behind a portal so small of itch exposure; means begged off tenebrous context so well some of us became them, how adept were we at forming teams in duress to instill policy, unsure of certain pardon at large.

This thing, too dull for an initial conceit, thought, wear progressed, some annotation of loss commenced pervasively if made up, actually any event was complete without consistent involvement on some ethereal level, prone, but to intercept mist, all elation vain is here albeit, one owed fast liege to hidden suits now jump unless a previous exempt sparred for failure to stop pi, one mind left at workout diction that were patently sad and upon her chalked abstention, befuddled wielder of a gyve arrived to perform extra caution, on fond hope someone would tell all to go strove the next potboiler, "I really wish you might see us off up there," Heppleweis finally brought herself to admit.

Van Etnabaron, not unknown, else he meant to resolve in the bland progress of the etching, bored of this life, sat. Iphgene said, "Ænselm might be — " there, Sasha scratched, smiling self indulgently, and began taking notes. Iphgene resumed, spackling the Niceans as braced, for beneath blue, streaks unto Mount Period, whose roguish astonished sesquipedalian motion, achieved, surpassed tonier expectation of next skip, her husband gazed stoically in a distant reverie.

Tersely seeming arch, his wife put her hand on Van Etnabaron's collar and peered into both eyes. Concerned not enough esplanade sufficed three skips averted innumerably, she asked, "how could fond also sounds on given Mayday leave out fortuitous necessitarians clumped sub skip to development of response?" "Stop pinging such nervy snaps with your eucalypti ginkgo gum," Fuald hears their *murahaleen* ordain. Swallowing it, the peer follows him over a retentive wall. Round to the rear of the ground, gates to Pyrogabion are found heavily disregarded. It's touted as a simple turnkey operation. Shrdlu leads them via the service entrance to a dark corridor.

Closed by a vault, the tall and dreadful commander, the appellate Harun Talab lil Makama, secures the airlock and turns, a motion attended by the sufferings of grave need, for a symbol, same time every even, as he wished away with it, refused to leave, standing as permanent as its silence. If don't we have enough aperiodic Brownian nodes here, they woefully strive to build open recent sesame creaky ordeal that helped them hertz, smooth fear of determinants, a kitschy Phlegethon context swept follow me down a rude goal, leitmotiv left off scrounge thud quorum to okay now ophthalmologic spells, tape—over, and nearly skipped beside on selflessly; moreover their *chef d'cabinet*, reckon upon an irrevocable metric (unless one *wagon—litre* at—large, presently scrabbled via the however above, remained wistfully oblivious before hypostasy), gave order to the remnant of her crew.

Recent emeritus curate of the Ossian Hermitage, and now without a single shard to show for it, Harun ponders a legacy of disillusionment. Born when promise of de—colonization permeated every facet of existence, he'd eagerly gazed at glittery electronic subtitles of the old weird beam. If contemporary historians already recognized the ubiquity of man's impact on levitation, a development lost on him for nearly five decades (it is safe disease or specious to lament the fount of all history began without one's own bad self), the host of his own show always announced every guest, at best tentatively, given the impression he wished he were elsewhere. Insofar as they existed on *xenonian* soil, their seventh were immune from enthalpic petrifaction and where, for want of diversion sharpened their empathy, the hapless visitant kept saying, "how does one go to get a glass of Pernoud here?"

All it wished, the least word, or line up flasks of lesser spirits unlit, the final seventh seal, "one shall finally be the death of me," heard, and if it didn't love being in denial as that stream of consciousness persisted in belching forth flood tide out of the nether realms, "then have you seen our *scrapmon*,'" one *fjulsfut*, clad in plutonium apron, asked in timidity, while handing the mythic hypotenuse one decanter fetched during the expedition's recent shopping spree, ahead of such dire event clamping moratorium upon liberty. At ending man's set, our sly view hit this bow. Fanta even succeeds in varnished image of vain lust, and so old grace then trow, chaste of utmost burnt ogles in drag, their bias at instant wonder, of a banned heaven in hosts mimed to their other lead, a sheer idea, in hope kites lent but menu to claim ice rates, further floors a heroic dark reign.

The latter's reply, if vaguely condign, led fifth to fear their star sounder ran out of roving minutes, and until borne they were left to specious sequel. They must bail at any instant if, aside from inclination of seeing safe return of their crew, their *chef d'cabinet*, warily athwart those few insistent upon defiling their tapper's crystal 'yurt in search of tincture, even at hazard of perpetual ground, also transfused by the interloper's strange reference to what in all livelihood seemed the last viable node left to *inter–regnum*. Agog when he said owls gathered soon, Idres abd Kahlil Filfil, his plaid yet mild Saracen, is beneath a harsh suit. Their haiku mirror, probed on sloven Etaoin's non–mental icon, storms this feat fairly at a misty data vow hissed, "what do you expect me to do, hurl my warm sari on a shady duo or buy in a bait?"

Amidst those talc igloos, the lemon–vested savior best inhibited funneling Ossian; Harun, amiss, heeds both rattles unlit, shown a valid hush, though he'll stray ere leaping on a tree haunt. "Return manifold synonym else a spare plight these bell cerise brush decaffeinated whew least thrown over empirical arteries mini respite, or if this box screams again send someone away." A strange vista spooled aside whilst each harped upon risk accrued from the unswayable question which kept tinfoil eidolons staring at them. Moreover, being conferred diffuse tanks toward indices of *fjulsfut* telemetry, and yielded strait to an immanent caste, *'zkeepers*, whilhomes, whom, if incapable of stretch, were poised somewhat to obviate yon strange visitant's ossifying gaze, and anxiously wired deployed *scrapmon'* to postpone ETA unlit, their zone still trembled beneath super cerulean borealis become clearer.

Instantaneous Niceans had their servitor retracted within compass of the tapper, their smart money being on fewer converse as incense of wisdom, "and let our guest finish in peace." It promptly did, and, not without remark, "there was enough manifest hoarse since density ongoing herein unrolled not one westward somewho," debunked adiabatically. For their part, *chef d'cabinet*, chagrined one mistook dark energy *Glatisant* for hidden *lumine*, decreed immediate refreshment of silhouette and left to visit her now children, delegated to bother the task of tracking their arrant seraphim, at savvy omnium, more phalaropic after—rose leitmotiv stalled insipidly, and Në, evocative mezzoforte fog knight, ennobled by rasta fever, reproved omniscient speak—easies.

"Mere daisy suds aside, a rash jinx soon limited oratory to some lower venue, promulgating 'excellence, terraced amusement, roseate heliotrope, insidious fungus kibbutz,' emitted mossless our cheated Oscar DNA filched their hopeless effigy, an isochronal stalagmite found set in witty voles, if not aloofly had Niobe two blunt sleigh bells or scrawled immune carets on most hip piety fellows, embody thin myth, 'surreal,' I minded, 'to tingling foe nestled in draconian dens, a modulator slurred in spalpeen unison, to scent every lofty inert old co—op read gym bedlam tutorial propped above new quotidian sand, appealed and sniffed at by beach skip poinsettias.

"'It's so real like you to requite alright,'" Dipol, tierce over, in excuse of friendly tappers' disdained Nitschean spores, invented for slack nocturnal cinema. For other skeptical bobbins averred every now and then of tough imitators, coarse and monkish remudas, flush scrappy hoydens, whose depraved tontine snuffed any pretence of sterile upkeep. Sapient noodles behave keenly circumspect, yet never had there been much nihilist anodyne distilled by gossamer crumb bums in their dense fog. Those punk technical albeit reticent [*sic*] bats in rotating gaudier gene signal, "to exacerbate our falsetto within reason," devolved maroon (*all too busy*), "is this excise of determinism? If one denies 'shroom, next we'll be subrogated muscatel upon woodwork, alas, a tossed solecism unfit to loose dishwater crated around in gondolas."

Since it happened with Pictish auto–partition, this swirly caste fit a balmy if tiny ring of motion. A mirky protest has heated their bean tub; indeed other chart hotels might ruffle moot html. Azali, than in hive, Etaoin, held by tablets, freed a hot fan before Ctesiphon. While opera clicks dutifully, a pink doodle, spilt by page on *Mr Ng, Live*, for wary ear there the saint, elected to half–orating epicure, betrothed total flash match swan ditties, strumming such tune as *The Skye March* and *My Lovelies Over The Sea*. Having more fate to sing a rote adobe sale in Bir–antikat in 1367, their father, grown alert to a horn cello, considered mailing biscuits to three molten Tiffany myths. While trying to remember the last time he's had a pleasant experience, Shrdlu turns on the afternoon television program. The *obvioregals* are so beautiful at a certain age, and uplift, to one personally, beyond all of information's happenstance, stalked winking flashes of light.

Signaled, they soon stand in the file room amidst cliquey–tea–clack of presses, telegraphs, teletypes, linotypes, calliopes of humming computers, facsimile machines, microphones, static electricity, vacuum tubes, and fiber–optics all presided over by the lidless lip of photo–voltaic barnacle conversion. "Who wrote these sleepy protocols," the commander mutters, tapping onto a terminal? Have obvioregals [*sic*], in fulfillment of their promise to jihad, inculcated insidious trap doors and viruses within an infrastructure of Pyrogabion? Their methodology requires existential analysis of each event in advance of an understood result.

It is necessary to rely upon filed field documentation, compiled at a time when Fuald was also of an uncertain age, prior to all of his effort demonstrated to individuals that he is not an introvert turned him into one. Harun, desirable information retrieved, tacks four steps across the cold parquet floor. The vorpal laser makes trundling sounds at the hatch, revealing a scale model of the universe. Peered into the Oort cloud, a ghostly jumble of hovering discs, Idres steps back to the rarefied sneeze guard of whatever scraps they are sub—consciously wanting to find for lots, which remedy a grimace, Harun previews macro—slides from the filing cabinet and has a quick peep into the scope. "Wonderful," he whistles tunelessly, as Etaoin risks another look at the galactic hinterland.

A drift smooth glow since within irresistibly beckons him into trackless stretches, this isle meant too to avoid gerund infinitive went unheard for lack of an enclosed apparent thesis ran so far away. Harun snaps off the telescope in the observation chamber. Idres abd Kahlil Filfil is distracted by a hallowed globe of chrome, secretly moving across the solar system. Footsteps echo outside as Fuald fumbles a new stick of gum. Harun removes the macro—slide, steepled to the vestibule, and snatches the stick from him. In silence, they listen as rattling began.

Fingering their harquebuses, they are sustained by dreams of paradise. The night watchman has reached the vault. Idres has pegged the routine, masking visual indicators between a false overlay. This shift, moreover, does not think to check the override sensor. They exhale fine ostentatious sparks of decisive relief as footsteps recede, not unknown nearby that entire staff of the Kalisthenes Institute is occupied with a signal project elsewhere. The incessant praying speaker seemed too elderly for many of them. "'*zkeeper* in corridor six," the roving security guard, in uninterested air, whimpered into his radio.

At this word, travelers scattered to edge the pond far as velvet blue ribbons must permit. "Why, is she, mummy" — "I am not a pickle brained fossil" — "stay away from her" — "for delivering us lowered into tribulation, we give you phrase," '*zkeeper* exclaimed. Rolled back, s/he eyed a preference to state, an end of life, or of a page, was, as would one hope or believe, a journey, or a door, like zap ajar combining, in infinite ease, a never forgotten word made us little less than angels, and in our debt, ransomed, and tried ever fleeting time, redeemable, or assemblable, to a cause, consented not to pride, remained irreproachable (1 Tim 6:3–14), and with swift yet sure hope of seeing with new light, a true and peerless love. The scarcity team converged too late. Flame poured from her as s/ he sank onto the floor. "Upon my word," someone exclaimed at the sight.

Albeit familiar with ledes pertaining to this nascent millenialist *fjulsfut* sect, testified to glory of hereafter via hyperventilation on long lines at banks, airports, and all marts, seriously disruptive of commerce in protest against growing national mania, Kalamparumple never knew any of them ever to turn so spontaneously robust. He would know that tabloids could detail, evidently, an elated crushed and practiced avatar minded in aura of halogen upon chamois, while courteously shoved, hubris hecklers and seven folds of tears seemed so rolling from any eye in the concourse.

Enveloped in an accord of mist, cringed in expectation of sudden judgment inkling, and in an exogenous weft upon some zone, suggesting rain, amber tones, meadowlarks, and first communion, certainly Sergei muttered, in mind of one person as child of a strange flightiness of heart which probably had been cancelled. Asked if he would consider stepping forward anyway, why shouldn't he mind winding up, garment bag back over his shoulder, delivered across the stanchion and through the crest?

Nary a beep set off. "Health co–ops will try to do something to make everyone better," the uniformed Corona flight girl smiled at him. Granted ruefully, and fair bound, Kalamparumple hoped it could come to that, and thought how clever he had not been to allow the serial impression ignore his napping persiflage. Aside from that, some dully inchoate invention once flourished, wasn't this diphthong retrenchment consistent atonal knell which interested vestige pressed beside the frequently eminent men of great and listed fortune trusting in what?

.   .   .

Hitherto, the appellate Harun Talab lil Makama lent video to a silly guest for wealth, the last being connoted where few haunt. How thus Maya at madrassah, always the third airily defer preternatural song on hell's epic sieve. If he veers around in three themes, for didn't their angel listen to what virtue, Harun sped an age, the concept, and began to assign roles among elastic stasis. Given secrets, Fanta still sang that honest glebe at home once, crude night stars unto *biathanatos* charge the bomb in nard, a feat seen certain.

The men Harun saw posted sprawl with easy faults seem to hasten ahead when there is a bet, lain by Noone in text, any *obvioregal* ran heaven. Here alone does every imam agree. Mobs hidden in lengthy trip pshaw harsh just retribution for youthful indiscretion. Worth enough egress, his own charge, torn by similar biological imperative of bemused tolerance, address him in an economy of speech. "If you see no flash, beat it," he replies, and disappears into phosphorescent shadow.

Sad, minute, passe Fuald regards Fanta's photographs. The interior of her great grandfather's souk has been a time tunnel of ethereal walls cloaked in merchandise. One step into this box canyon, one is immediately beneath the gaze of a cleric asking if anyone was ever in need of help. Whoever walks into this transaction then states each individual need, which is fletched from the tower shelves. Individuals find convenience in the process and enjoy causing someone to climb walls in fulfillment of their every need. And they dove toward the stones and stopped the engine, herds besotted louring in dimness, al–Kamil asked death to kindly wait while he changed into the following preview, approved for all audiences, of fifteen great senses of spiritual vacuity and the mean, commonly devised, of coping at least with four of them.

Ultimately, Florian may only remain as Ideopath if two assistants are reassigned (presumably for other non–italicized cognomen), coached into a decision, the word borne enclosed with a quotient of dread or dire exception made for last shrank logos you thought rationalized into being when faintest echoes of disbelief let you resume prior quandaries not wholeheartedly abandoned. This telephone was not intended for consent, and unable to provide this number for marketing or survey context, forbore frozen *uchaux* shape shift hives.

Adept at creating a circus of ignorance, the more I don't know, Æmst in lacunae proclaimed as means of enlisted moral sympathy, the less someone else has to read downstream, a small riddle, sworn only near a wave into the clam shell projecting, in a chocolate night snack formal attire, holiday arrival of Vorga ex libris, rival of al–Kamil, furtively ranged the universal ethical stratum as lavatory, wherein one might operably split up without inference of appraisal in face of personalized world assistance. Three levels of the Kalisthenios observatory now on academic chamfers, provenance, blessed so hastily to serve, should be forgiven for entertaining doubt.

Were it up to them, a solid affirmation of well done–ness must suffice to draw expected closure to the week's effort, leaving exiled *lumine* at liberty to explore their new confinement. Pleasant summer shores promised escape, the staff, composed masks of lingering dismay and future resolve, left the building, An's word, flammable, daunted them at the gate, putting paid to all hope of barbecue, lawn mowing, final fours, wan dioxide white sales, pink flamingo moon sleeves, itch frights, RV shoes, raft fairs, dulce vita, points of interest, waterfront dinning, unbelievable, family circles, rib joints, spring theatre, wind stars, exuberance, tea festivals, early birds, red tags, opened days, hot sports, or water spouts.

These things, albeit relished by their new neighbors in the external city, were denied *lumine*, forcing them to produce text. Of occasion, the sanctified city nestled in the bosom of Ohthereitis, cornerstone where latitude, swerved locally, reigned, doors, opened politely, themes, solvent mews, parks, arranged stock, so much for warmth one May found, a million excuses for, tarrying on graded cover of terraced Zoyschia, a revisionism of Lilliputian proportion, and bask in rejuvenation of simple principle, that faith, fidelity, forgiveness, facilitate, fun.

Whether ambling permissibly, or angled for purpose, men, however strange, released from debt and blinked in darkness when hue, bent in prism of scarce eon, suddenly re–blended, al–Kamil returned to the station lobby there; Azali sat for hours until boarding the 6:15 return. Thereupon balking that stupid grasshopper suit to the prop room, al–Kamil felt he did not deserve to be skilled in anything but perpetuation of existence, days, jobs, and, broads, skimming open markets, a rare simile, plaid upon his lip, scouring enough gas to hope he would soon not care of it, Harun was one, slow, starveling weekend from death. Night, in the favor of *ahriman*, entered the Village.

.   .   .

IV — x — Draft B4 Lunch @MR Pepe's Pizza Trapezoid Z.

The necessary visitation of their early bailiwick, meant to be evaded, Harold, in the silence of return, sat stern over a fatuous plan for ireless memos. Named, before resuming, his chancellery, murmuring, "I should be made for one wit of energy," Van Etnabaron, now wont to resort to tirade, tried to avoid, thorough resource, unwound space, and to full the line with word, Sasha, having referrals, fled to his office in success. To complete his drift—on, no fewer than exemplary fashions found it necessary to regroup his only appointment calendar.

In some concern, Iphgene persistently accompanied her husband on his round. They went out over an east wing of lumpy ground, where he halted to study the bore of ash, an imposing span of foliage. Amidst branches, Në, a steam squirrel, prepossessed by Athena, ceramic owl rousted atop the foremost gable, drew notice of Mrs. Van Etnabaron. A silver yardstick drawn, Iphgene plopped it against the base of the scowled winged glaze three times, saying, "It's. Not. Real." The squirrel heard her signal, yawned, stretched, scratched a rear limb, resumed a series of joyous arboreal acrobatic, and Iphgene dared, "Sasha, you were actually planning to have this tree cut?"

Në, far from disinterested in these matters, stood entranced on a salubrious plan. They said it on gem like qualities Aira's dart glanced aft ebulliently; while indulging rime capable of sterling image, her abstruse holiday bazaar cleared enough pints of clever sack candles to cast a marigold damascene aura around the argyle of twinkling emanating from Foster's live room across town. Hence Bitsy's clarion recital, played up late after enabling Masha and her serape to crash the silver dollar pancake line at Mr. Pepe's pizza, thought sacrosanct while signing Sibyl's cast; edgily riveted argent gaze to a point beyond aphonic apses stuck to craven tenacity where no sub was acceptable, though practice ought arrest the obvious plunge toward a lit doom, in if one waited nineteen years, what was one more day for anything.

With one gear strip shall they conveniently reassure ourselves of the goodness of their choice; so as sung fever had more lunch than a forward boldness era of never last wont. Thus chilled the access of titular smores inherent in any stabilization. "You marked the, map, there." "This tree?" Van Etnabaron rustled the map and, spotting Bagler's approach, composed his feature. "Gardener." "It's your funeral," said the latter. "This tree," Sasha pointed. "Cut it down." Shrugging, Bagler yelled for Cyane, tucked into the tool room at the base of the manor's northern turret. "Why are they cutting it," Iphgene belatedly asked, "down?" Enough lightning struck, Van Etnabaron saying the logical tin man east is the next person to park in the pastors' spot. This eco—mime mome, Iphgene had read about consortiums of blank coloring book contests and scrabble tournament shuffles bored Hesitance arranged, for the frozen, excused to resume her packing backlog, Iphgene hastened to her room, and il Fiume, hearing returns from Midgard, answered his own telephone.

. . .

With a single misstep began the great journey. Spieled from heavens, there in paeans of groupie coil, surged unmickle aims, wherein gelid cirrus frond, the arguable snarl of whomever compassed the unsuspected legation befallen provenance at present oft tough lulls, ought they mandate, ardent quern—sparring occludants also cued in on pageantry fluff reek of effigy dear, if with no proof either way, and sullenly resigned to the appurtenance of an ill paid minion clad dumpily and moreover given away by the deck shoes, even they stared afresh in awful hope of summit approach. "While I'm clear out the rain gutter sap figures in a thirst of omission." It was knowingly vast yet oily yet the fringe of its under bang enticed revelers to bide.

In mystic refulgence of its omphaolic aura, Gnadig noticed already her colleagues flush toward an innate atrium of febrile resonance shaping carets. No more gainful hold enticed patronage of old to leave off measurable existence to enter forever yeasty guarantee of utility free rubric for plenary contiguousness, notwithstanding vastened *fjulsfut* mask of dubious rectitude provenance, defiant of Anodyne's warning, scattered beneath tropic canopies of midnight fair, refuting lustily an ocean so chilled one toe at a time scalded forthwith.

Led over her severe pelisse, and in many ways deemed, for untiring theft of public demesne and seethed, ridiculous, fallow, an evinced lack of pertinent similitude, for certain eschatological bent inspired Midgard, a ribald fire *chichi*, Alcibiades, Santeria, and Hemingway, pups eponymous via pitiful placidity where again every pleasant Dauphine's shift began. To walk them each was a thing which to all else took second fiddle and its underlain ulterior portrayed by every precocious nonchalance with why they went in for it, this least of all desire, in exact *untenet* term then frozen matters only let, brothers, sons, fathers onto a lie that I am not only ever piqued by limitless curiosity as to another, but for my omission, missed mind. Now had Horace that to stand for, when pluperfect flatirons avert the nap of *author of poor haiku*. Aira's return to work made him read somewhere, far from a paragraph or two, amidst simply quiet time stood still and, if the race was on, "the fax machine was more uptight than a toy fork, eh," *isomems* downloaded, lesson being that those who follow their nose too closely often end up overlooking other solutions.

"We preferred a plainchant, lament hubris of a person whose merest blink would excite much spiteful aversion from power no innocence should shield. Then if any denser matte might convey in a nutshell pervasively upon threshold of a new school I stood one day, I stared at individuals as if I had sauce to transform them back into my old beloved friend left behind, thus occasioned much mistrust amidst my new milieu, I wandered witless and lost into a bay marked omnivorous only." The brachets unleashed brayed, their saws teeth seen torn sound fin–de–siecle for any movement that may achieve lasting value.

"'Begone ye almonds,' I cried. 'Repent from calling us that,' they snarled. 'Refrainants,' I sneered scornfully, 'it is true, I did seduce your ladyship's phase, I couldn't help it, some of your women were hot.' 'Had you none of your own,' they snapped? 'I survived in cloves,' I said, 'a mere gene splice, so unlock thy jaws of depth.' 'That's entirely up to our mistress,' they loitered, 'she's such a storm of petulant uncertainty and would deny us even crumbs were we to falter in our charge.'" Aware of their plight, the Nicean high counsel were determined to keep this flea from biting their puppet playhouse and recommended warm malt, home, and garden therapy. To stay warm, they graciously declined to accept further weary yearn from the guild, propelling their novena toward the dabbling concierge indicated.

Benched levelly as the scene, epitomized, retorted Messimo, that was enough, "you threw me no bones, on wonder working steed in parody of escalation to these eighth has thou rid" — "is the live ear sooner or later an arrow arrived in shadows all about you," they refrained not impleasantly. They all had babes left out there, howsobeit were his watch no rheologic warrant to which you might plead? There Frank stood at the moment when all else, the ungrateful behavior of his forebears, the impatient dump of agenda on him always; last to know, for a stretch, PoD, unable to arrive unless, discovering impecunious fresh anonymity of et al, dreamt of confuting their headlong octave utterly unforeseen, and embraced principles in the truest spirit of catholicon, yet mea culpa those ungrateful saps were fain to add.

"Sky," his whisper, unheeded failing dankness receded behind him into horizon of the sound, scattered as darkness ignored his plaint, whirled its form to the azimuth beyond him, fallen to his face, snuffled more ground, pounded sands upon earth, a last pale cry to this starkness which abandoned him gave way excessively. Instinctively, his dream shuffled away, shaking *ahriman* in an exertion of grief. "This is Matthieu," he said into the receiver. "This is Mrs. Van Etnabaron," was the reply. "Iphgene! So how are your axles finishing?" "Fine for all that, but" — "and Mrs. Van Etnabaron," Ylferim interrupted, "has Harold resumed his familial responsibility?" "Most likely," Iphgene thought. She said, "ELIZA pulled the horseradish trick on him this morning."

Himself prey to sandwich schemes of Van Etnabaron, jeune–fille, il Fiume merrily laughed, "verily, I specified the gardeners remove an ash graft from the front walk. It had anthracnose." "Matthieu," Iphgene warned, "we were not on the front walk." What else should he say, she heard a voice raised to haul stingy spangles of that somewhere of all way sunlit? Hands pressed into faces, testing, futures verified, she recalled from birth darkness, reckoned, imagined, through tears, drawn comparison from circumstance, *ahriman* had turned into one of them, who in past merged timid footfall into dankness to beat cymbals and tambourines of sound. They kept his force, his knowledge, awakened, and his part at bay against that which was always appointed as his counter, his doom, and his mimesis.

.   .   .

Albeit debatably, Flugelzahn had keenly toggled mental hinges, outbound in performance of this cluttered ministry, and subsequent errant pointed remark entailed tone deaf reminders that didn't quite pan out, Azali, Talab lil Makama, son of appellant Harun, reformed amidst denial his services were never requited; tempted by an overt reaction to start wars, Etaoin took back his gum, ducked under the low roof, engaged the starter, and regarded Fuald quizzically as the motor coughed into gulping shifts.

"Why, is that pinochle," Azali asked, his whiff detecting a bead of cæsium on its way out to Hermes? The domesticated stocks of yesterday jump–started acute stencils of endemic pyrites forward, hewn dreadfully toward billions plastered into thin air. "Oh, no combination for degaussing the minnesingers who clamor and crowd Melissa." Shrdlu shrugged, "FYI, old school reunion come up, that sort of thing." "Whenever," Azali said, reaching within his sweater vest. "On some week night, tight schedule now." "Would it be like you to keep a problem stashed," asked Idres softly?

"For a while," Etaoin tittered, suppressed a guffaw, and adding, "now what is," his commander scrabbled for simile cargo, a nil gong also off the wall as systemic mandate of forthright persnickety dudes viewed budgie constraint. Via thick tenacious ions, horn resounded just as swerved lasers poured toward the sun in such a roaring jangle; seizing the rheostat at the helm, Idres remembered that seedy detractor, i.e., Deerfield, off Pyrogabion, had disconsolately post–dated scuttled cardiograms, demonstrative it was an almost cost fictive dissolution. Upon failure to apprehend didactic source for disclosure of diurnal ontos, Bagler had already banked the band saw and commenced works when the yowled carborundum was stifling by an even instanter screech from the main house, Paul'r'us puling, "over all of this lurid failure, please find time to stop, those crazy things," and, in light of what has gone unlit, "you are like am I for real?"

Skeptic irreverence happens, for the halt word left one inexpugnable incision upon the outermost bark. Saying, "instead of just one huge expanse, we've considered an array of chunkier mirage," Idres abd Kahlil Filfil hoped insidious critics who stated a system almost 1% effective was worthwhile were correct; moreover, eventually partial screens complicated his asymmetric backtrack, and fissile snore devotees held grippy orrery meltdowns to be necessary dragnets. Leaving citizen resumes ably disarmed, the death ray launched and scooted into the solar system and over the lap of the sun, sound of much breakage, screeching, and silence. By midday it was one small step far easier said than undone. Dribbled amongst the photosphere, a pretty trail of quick silver ornamented a burst of unscheduled solar prominence longevity. The hurried egress hardly presumed flyaway looks (in case of Roentgen rays of 900 to 1400 terra Hz, break glass during fifty four forty or fight) indeed; the program was so leisurely, the Village had already bogarted a seventy—year old solvent verticule beam design way ahead of us here.

"All I'm simply trying to do is establish fertility of technology," Etaoin protested. "All trend inimical to regional clusters are nonsense." Idres denied warmly, "pop level management is diverted to the big tincture and will not hesitate to cut off abusers." There were fewer straws to grasp at this hour. Fuald's response was to sequester Shrdlu and shove him into some no longer folding chair. Away from wheels of justice, Cecil bet the store if they had less merciful rules of engagement, Shrdlu's desecration of a celestial body, not to mention having lit up this job to get even with the universe, would have earned him no place to hang his hat. They'd just tele—marketed the Polar Star into the course of history; Fuald looked into skies and washed his hand of the vinculum, their quiet brinkmanship vaccinated into space and hither *chichi*. They spent the next three days thinking back over the present until blithely revived by telephone calls from their tenet, waving his hands and yelling stop, stop, and a harassed individual further beset the tableaux. It was Sr. Florian, fishmonger himself, returned from a voyage to dredge the sound for Pacific sockeye salmon. Failing to find one, the fishmonger ordered all hands to scuttle their trawler by steering it into the path of an inbound Globus tanker and then hired a starboard trireme for passage to the mainland, earning his keep by teaching the surly crew to lip synch harsh nautical ditties to the tune of theatric hi—fi lists gotten ere whole.

.   .   .

For everyone now returned, there was an institution, and Matthieu, in hope the incident had not strained anyone's field toward their chancellor, rang official, unofficial, and residential lines, in a mission of gentle abrasion, and felt this absence keenly. Since Van Etnabaron was nowhere to be found, Ylferim had yet to discover the true purpose of nominative, nor whereby their precedence derived, save through a plug for the spiritual jazz station. Yanked far more quickly than the echoey chalcedon snicker doodle always bouncing around the main building may have foretold, it had been disingenuous hand wringing ever since he felt there no impending stability whatsoever amid recoil. Regarding him feyly, they natheless lapsed in debit of muttered caustic sass, "an end then to thine chialasm," the verbal indictment Cecil had junked around enough undifferentiated avoidance upon antiquities, a knowable instinct entrained sub–terrestrial alcove of mindfulness.

Seemingly bifurcate Oxford corners evident within tracts, thrust at him during all movable feast by plainspoken eschatologists, left nuance of piecemeal unliveliness at every orexis of welfare. Found too over–reliable for bandersnatch casing, his oft Esperanto wobbly forks, impounded minutes, serial, bespoke autonomic treble parapraxis: thin penumbra enthymemes whenever plot meltdown fungus, hitherto a staple stirred thwartably in sincere deportment had, legislated out of non–existence ex tempore by a static natural review bureau fond of citing efficacy of dextramethoraphan at addressing cases insufficiently turgid; consequently an aqueduct buskin of daily ipecac zestfully neo–morphed as indispensable fillip for lithifaction, and for senescent cosmopolites, a striated if ruthless last resort, propagated in near ununanimous format, instilled, thereupon being dastardized in a universal forum which had actual little impact on local issue, the valiant blotto formalized rapprochement over stringent folklore, and in praxis ascetic whodunit, converged as ephedrine became exit of chance for many disinterested instigators.

A dumpster and out–of–mind movement purposefully resumed in such forum the tastiest evermore worst wet hen non–proliferation board, and in response, brought together multicultural and agrochemical bedfellows, postulated a stoic backwater while out–sourced commonality might restrain their vanished mores. As November rolled in, Francis, ware of their indignance rhadamanthine, decided he should not partake of anomic decline. Soon people saw the one thing in sight, including time, involved joining, after a few hasty and wide step–by–steps through the flowchart, mist, dissolved as roof guests proved equal to harmony.

Individuals henceforth cleared from prior litmus, other accouterment leapt out to throw cellular grafts of one bezique vision statement, somehow can unknown known, because no longer near enough, commerce, comrades, made of mold from a walking word, were reigned out discreetly, possessed the temper of asking radio paper software, dark anyway, and at the early stage of displacing the sunset, wished snippets about issues away.

Moreover, a dank horse, which didn't sign an enclave within the St. Moritz Room (or any other unusual standard of audible recognition) to get through Piero's enthusiastic sense of the interminable, sped by the same thing which originally rehearsed accompaniment to infinity, rather than slog something that forgot to make the seasons, provided extensive image on a fine parallelepiped, "provided the repudiator," an answer of *ædith*, "if you will, looks up and notices, offers to pay the stipend of podesta, maybe the *plenitudo potestatis* will look fine." Henry (VII) resumed his seat. "See how flushed are they who vacated their Assizes tables, and now had *ædith* been too efficient. Is it not untrue he carried advertisement for *De Resignandis Privilegiis* in its monthly motif?"

"In accordance with *Encyclical xxxvii.iv.cxiii*, we permit free and open debate," Piero asserted. "What is before the *plenitudo potestatis* can total £6,500 so far, an allocation of two thousand marks for an answer to the second question." Finlay plugged on, "didn't your cold dovecote dusk await virgules?" Since Messimo's most biennial sacred solstice blessed beans sought a nap, not a map, to find the corner of Sanity Turnpike & Cinder Road, their hubsand impatiently raced the engine in a driveway moment, and they came over and meant at Oxford. Matthieu wanted to regroup, but Esmeralda couldn't wear duplicate raiment at a reading by Noel Iris, author of an expanded after, all forgone her noble tote, and as standard policy set down her silver air guitar to stage our own police drama (Ibsen) near the onion blind, for Za'at's formal nite at Terpsichore's Brow, the *turec akabej* node whence I spilled tea on their carpet had been lifted early season, starry eyed spectral merger with An's bridge was imperiled, its link direct so posed as a barge.

Sometimes Ladæñæ Rita Mervyn thought Matthieu should go back and marry Iffy and become a saint after the roads have been dry for a lengthy epoch; first, they will both catch bowlers so ordnance can be passed last fall in the clear, and in belief for a time Vikram may settle them onto another alpine ray that went AKC, then into another there, on one lone rump–sprung conch or, on the floor, Finlay had went onto the Sunrise Cage, grabbed a fistful of grey pompom, and broached the impossible expansion of remedial au courant wrinkle with Noel. "Too much to do there, especially with factories of *ædith* and stirring tea for the next thirty years," Raisin's masked personae said.

"What else does our uncle manufacture (unwiser strength in Plair's only non–surreal or blue see)," but beyond Iraisamonde should tell Finlay whenever, where had transpired what Hesitance dreaded, a schism formed, new radiant stunts, all gathered in a live room, ere flocked up in the haunted house, and with it books and amplifier, and got up into an alpine ray, gone surface surf suffer furnace Stygian consistency unless has there been an accident plus max time out they threw courses at him down in history just plugged in that's good if all told disguised as sock bunny for the reunion you knew what happened it grew out in Arkansas &c, thinking of this kite in detail more and more specious casuistry from the mainland try as one might fixed outside Sherlock had seen an elementary rinse check diorama featuring dust mice in staged and staggered states as place settings careered around the Fourierian series, each lucky to have a set of keys up for jumping an entire *uchaux* army you threw mops at until little Onegin bell–hopped in yellow and sent a moth ahead as barge of honor for earning consecutive series of a myth colder than sunshine without molasses, "la–de–da, gob," launched an obversible, dread icon of macramé calypso, "your tone at least endears itself to panjandrum, yet sure we couldn't episodically knit up some fuzzier gag against thirteen pleated fleece dromedaries."

Any jury would vacate their skip routinely, or emoted spare electronic phonics in chat rooms connect an inert nadir of Ragnarok. A crack page sang, ere in ebb tide, botched revenue detonated a hacker's paradise, shining a rash hiss over the jumbo divide, vestal gondoliers foment irascible tunes around all remnant flora and exfoliate synergistic masks, input sand into the latest fire snail, and stream sugar–coated truth serum near bogus siren. Alarm from a nobler room inveighed of eutectic poses in toney tubs, fly to sass and terrify in sententious argot. Even once sure lemurs evinced nuance of sulky nit–pick over meretricious keepsakes, emitting twinge of leery qualm when rondeau of dangled nests trickled into aerosol.

"Let's," Læmært, in advance of mapping out context, and on behalf of important complement, denied, "instead eye twitch on into matter a while." Must everyone there take counterpoint into the nearest effort to overturn truth lest, of one's reality, these deified of all protocol are like peep holds of depths, blank stare, rejoinder, to appear relevant and cold, revealed adages for legal fee from Mezzo, father of Dolores [*sic*], provided under duress, "I'm not to go dash about that which has become scrambled impediment, mark my word," invited his non sequitur. It was this quandary that made selected response incautious, groomed to allow one comparative feasible impact, served, instantly jarring a small but grown diplomatic fashion of archaic type, who marched to sleep, haunted by an older than Indian summer chance.

"Is it that," Vorga continued, via mask, her fulsome straw misled lemonade at noon, "try to expand dollars on turnkeys of activity just to recast a bundled Keynesian kinesthesia by the McCarthy volunteers past the family of American light which spun entire hydrants?" A perfect beam post–suburban lawn, too fond of personal implications for herself, Në Dipol appeared trapped by rebuttal of retail subterfuge, leveled from tribes of remote aficionado peers across the next nave, but vaulted through a mood–laden can–can, quite a dual array of chitinous twig beans, wondering what went wrong here. The timorous tykes now owned the Quonset, *inter–regnum* was now in hands of Vikram, and a fluctuation–less mantra commenced. An exculpatorium blogged, Henry (VII) brought his army unto Worms with all poise of one strained to withhold information of a personal sort; adieu from care one castellan

as usual each host bid tare without license, till those upon soaring height
noted a procession of amative industry bent, though counsel hushed to
lob not asymptotic caption toward their pique withal.

Shouted in ruse to binge out amongst cobbles prior to saluting
the firmament, stolid burghers edged from haunts to site antics of the
impending vain. Slathered in period mail, kinglets in filthy sweats nicked
gutted lutes that to the castellanus practiced eye were obversible, and
beneath panoplious floral movement an effervescent refuse dim old
snifter aseptically unmaskable reeked. To whit were plebian denizens
already wont to spill over the moat to greet the long expected claim as
humane trope, yet the gnarly cloud leapt into the gatehouse, somehow
flanging out of gerund a sinuous retraction of the cause linking Worms
with empire.

The foremost wind flouted their cusp with such vehemence that
from one or two, sapient ears rattled. An errant cask rolled from the
sum and dropped into the channel pursuit by urchins who dived intent
upon its content, a rival, hitherto conducted at a furious pace, no longer
a matter of time to their herald who railed, "citizens for shame out well
our tide of frabjousness and virtu," and in earnest airy codas of myriad
composite issued from unmelodious comb. "Reject not such admission
out of hand, find keys, will you not receive our play with candor?"

No reply augured but slight delay to their expedition for Henry,
seen dodgers had breached hogshead and now gagged vocally upon
pitchblende, knew that mince was thickened, "citizens, I, your homme,
address grievously this sullen defence, know you I wept to hear of your
cherished submission to, to that," he paused? Athwart palisade, one could
but forbear to hear, "whence cometh our deliverance clad as dance gigue
trollop?" "Your memorable sayings are proverbs of ashes (Job 13:12)."
The King of the Romans signaled to his lot, which cast aside its raiment
of spontaneous levity in order to reveal rank after rank of '*zkeepers*.

"Residents of swarm, turn out this frocked imp who has mulcted
you with subscription for, that!" There was no point, for they knew that
condition if fulfilled would hasten terrible siege. "Are you sure didn't

approach sirens?" Plair found Iphgene in rubble of Worms, half–hidden
under a heavy oak round table that well, "break out some corn chips,"
Raisin occluded, and of that geode Sunrise Cage talk Finlay is turning
handsprings about (thinking now that Vikram may be found along 18th
Street), Hesitance, worked up with Saran socks, at him replied, "they'll
ask if it'll be right to heat up again in whose stove."

Harold, fined, sat under porch in a full Hibernian night. He did
tell her he supplanted near a haunted house some times. Park was non–
despondent to see fewer neon faces, a womad slightly younger than his
freight carrier, grand–sister of Inyo, of all things, Mrs. Tsp, writing an
Hibernian epic beside which Hemingway will call. "Then it was snowing
institute–funded research," Marta wailed from *wishram*. Finlay's cousin,
unabated, routed her cigarette in ashtray, and sat down.

Fanta wanted to talk about photo lab, one of their underbred gigues
out there. Señor Florian reported, a step over a threshold, "there's not
a radiant stunt yet who's out of touch with moiré and will react with
manqué in a *Who's Who* tonight." Noone hesitated, thought it a compliment and then, not so sure, grunted, wrestling a bottle from a six–pack,
and handed sack time apart. In July, her Big Sky resort had advertised
9–foot powder snow, but plaintiff, Bagler, broke his key on a shlocky
rope tow and in many instants sued their spokesperson, an arch and bald
fellow who delivered most of his thought, and looked at his finger mask,
a C–chord on bridge.

Sullen masses gathering to observe, the fishmonger indicated recent
figures issued by CIC proved beyond all hope of reflection that global
warmers indeed charged their toll. The protoplasm had achieved synthesis with its environment and would never again leave the display case.
The mob diffused with barely a sigh leaving only happy meal scraps and
wispy silver parings of expended lottery tickets to mark what was once
a teeming and vibrant civilization.

From now on, they were back in official disfavor, since from Village
on down everyone disdained to meet their demand, and at the local
pub, their cause went mummered around incautiously. For just a tiniest

instant of regret, they bought shares of out local window theorems. Indeed, Ossianian ministry chaps offered apogees and a job directing task for hand–picked re–enactment of tactless romantic postcards from a drip–dry line. Azali told them they'd think this over, albeit it seemed rather tame and Æmst was sure they could do better.

.   .   .

Arisen from amidst stone palings, one biscuit toss from firmament, was consciousness. A clutch of sand, remembered spangles, sunlit beach, and sounds of wave lapped against piles out onto water. Images often fall from out of earth, transmigrated from igneous to indigenous. More light, moonlit, ripples across the water, *ahriman* lifted his hand, still clutching sifting sand, to his face and put his eye on, a thin folksy counter–point waiver tremulously when Matthieu Paul'r'us stood at discount windows awaiting fast cash to get out of Oxford. This muse accepted his marker. Cyane wore an art deco nose ring and a T–shirt touted great kitchens of seventies. "In these days," reminisced Ylferim, "you might fall face first into past tense and never have to worry about painting your houses ever again." He could hear the sound of pink heffalump whispering in Worsted, taking their toll upon his horse sense.

This light now revealing him as enough of a human of age beyond their testing, *ahriman* sifted his frame from sand, light, running now all around, no longer within him; nor without him was his being, his sorrow, his glory, or his past. He gazed at all darkness around, his, yet no longer this, either/or, his word rang pale aloud above the count of Mezzoforte (in charge of missing bureaus), who narrated, Chocho Molyneaux, local buffet tribunal, his desired duet with Dorf Zafner, turbid tunes king of bluish tipplers, on hold, his identity comped, and his ship sank, wanted nothing better for his wife Xantippe than happiness. Impelled toward Læmært's interview that the prefect of Lyonesse was frozen, from the ex–chamberlain (*all too busy*), the Inspector learned Regatta, via locations of cancelled EFTs, now knew whom was daughter of Dolores & Este family margrave (Iraisamonde). Short of sound, Tethys fluffed at him; PoD was on a coast, where there were boats. He wondered where they slid upon them, other than to dart and hover upon surface of firmament. He thought if boasts were soon found, what else would he find?

Accepting the loan, the *dan* turned and left the building. A synched code might out–celebrate in one swerving winnow. Not anyone might not have the slightest inkling that, even after watching a month of soccer matches on Univision, Paul 'r' us still was yet to understand alien culture. Even if a house had to fall on him, fortunately, he still had one last case of Junior Mints. He hoped this darkness (his, yet no longer this), should continually allow him to wander and wonder without test. Instantly, from without his own darkness, where it even now slopped from him, *ahriman* beheld approach, from land, an enormous canopy of cloud. He stood transfused below an arch of pearl.

.   .   .

Solo backlog on reaction stemming fulfillment of empty chair at wergild... expandable,
Ænselm still somehow obsessed w/neuro–Niceans, a condition Alcuin's dared ask non
sequitur ~ recast prefatory passage in haiku meter, since at no stage will Horace
relinquish title of author of poor haiku (side–effect of caretaking lapse).

IV — xi — Raisin [sic] d' être — Why are tempest fugit.

With a longhand monograph of election to this specialty documented, Henry's realty, important to the covenant for stability
of the free lunch, and chased by two inept retreats at Edgefield, whence
the despair of ever abridging brambles and thorns of the Forest of
Despond, arguable value ebbing, three hours ago continued to take on a
cold kettle, "the operable question, is, one: what happens when you are
indisposed toward implication of Freedomium?" "How," th'ratwi'thorns
conceded, "hast inquiry paused onto your, my, his addiction? Procedure
began, so we dapper few before shadow puppet do too request another
warrant, 'off course,' we intoned," plying typical caustic casuistry, "and
live elves sneezed on my garage."

Nervous titter elicited, "very well, let us consider, corporeal war,
our coffer fraught, burst with funds, our arms bronzed, stand ready,
our force, mete discipline, chafe to carry the issue, our policy, sound,
ensure our utter triumph." From the gallery, this roseate assessment
made everyone flush with shame. They were nigh sleepless, and someone
said to a collage for two months they've since considered behavioralists
for, amidst generic disdain, little eflots, eupeptic souls set foot into
the procedure, more than once the lens shot out of a public opinion
poll proscriptive of their methodical secret of keys. This situation was
a juxtaposition of words effectively unsealed, "our debt to the word,
behold loomed the letter okay, where the sacred ka'aba (levitated by
finth), Kabala, kabuki, kabyle, kachina, kaffir, Kafka, and Kaiser jostled

for positrons known only to what God other jam lurked." Exactly how else cats began to drag in so conjectured an appreciation of the outbound watch, that the barrator rolled forth to issue an opinion.

From this attic s/he rang, rather known, the future of civilized nation hung upon Henry (VII)'s blessing, or dependant on his curse. Inasmuch as we had Noone to match wits with, "to charge preference of persons without warrant is a presumable affront to the locality. Such convenient covenants of survival as could be, found swarmed in fits above the lofty bark, permeate an honor we robed from the point of our own absurd. The best lacked even scorn for your new Cæsar, whether eyes slept here."

Convinced it was a value and awarded behavior until choice of profession admitted only power or insistent search for proof, ends known nuptially exclusive, pseudo wash–outs from yodeling school were to run as coatimundis infatuate the easily impressed. "How else it should be, our founder eluded authority once, we dump our value behind them in my yard not only trails to stub, but blind pursuit," resumed *th'ratwi'thorns*, "as iotas deserving of quickly a build down as possible, we'll be flown out of an ashen trans–migration into Zoyschia niblick junks, twined to the grand dame of commemorative entitlement. But what about PoD? Where are his religions? How are his tactics?

"We already know elemental spores of great strength intervened on his behalf." The imminent victory of Nertz foretold, *ahriman* co–opted *untenets*, those gigantic, albeit sterile, cousins of space snails of *inter–regnum*, into this trans–mogrification of Earth, "whilst human agencies spirited him into your elm," *'scrapmon* replied. "Had this non–threatening manner panoply op–ed comp," frisked of hope, the book ended, "nor did the Lombard Council, the first called upon in power, second your crepuscular location." The float remained as objective reality for thirty–four more hours; each turn of the greater wheel successively rang sequential reform.

.   .   .

Adagio vapid tears sprinkled from the sky as *ahriman* recalled five minute intervals of whatnot for this mere perfunctory risk. Lounged as evening swiftly closed, PoD needed to do something, and at first material step, sudden light sparkled among damp sands, cusp accessories for toxin flumes, so fortuitously narrow and so larkishly evinced that loosely, a creatined exanthema might streamline constant rude beatification. As down with how much present rotations into Xenonia really cared for the oncoming camp, "for our next part," read their after piece, "dint of servitude prepared us for few ill morphs of obvious tacit motif, ascribed from unruly street prevention crossing program forelimned, any reliance with invitation to anathematization trendily caught up from draught or relief." Their patient *isomems*, viewed over closed—circuit, inert in Room 46, reflected upon recent seppuku [*sic*] of men pursued by guests acronymic he cared for so witlessly.

There were some of those who would spy shamelessly ever silhouetted in risen sun. So little were they concerned with concealment of their fructificated agenda, Formosan settled into essential mode and gazed clearly as rotund stereopticons unfurl infra indigo splashes around the chamber. Fetched in a prior drear, sorrowful air beset all of his aim. PoD sloshed into shadow of the pier and seized the float. Footsteps imagined outside the shadow approached. Whew, he returned, a pair of themes awaited, aged by the reverse psychologist: *scrapmon'* attendant to counsel of *isomems*, regarded a parody of classicism, described as rollicking romp by progressive airwave dramaturge Ensign *ædith* Oswell Plair, mulcted and shoved betwixt the shelves and over the Cliff's Notes [*sic*] at the free nice library.

"Best my tin ear can discern," said *scrapmon'*, "such is a profile of bibliophobia: in so many words this life, its love, here youth, occupation, and haunts are characteristic of one come to term with reaction. Excessively courteous, it may enclose philanthropy, is expert in blended, adept, predictable movement and patterns St. Swithin environment, and will fix pursuit into inferior lanes even at cost of great psychic extenuation, persuaded of one's participle in greater cause, and reasoned perhaps a sinecure of excessive patronage within the bound of entirety, as Horace preferred, written by 18th Russian century author Pushkin, 'ennobling delusion to the degrading reality.'" In a paralysis of decision, ere formed circa to notice a quondam site, which functionlessly fell four times or until the whistle blew, Porphyry wisely measured the least consonant force to absorb expensive if didactic episodes, and stared at dark matter while crowded otherwise hitherto important paper crept from his desk. Along the lamely intelligible reach, he placed wire upon polemic overtly posted right of ways, loafing only as the sign, of good square stock, announced this investment firm:

Piero della Vigna, Esq., Practitioner of Law and Reflexology.

.   .   .

Bunions Expunged and Puns Impugned.

Beneath the chlorophyll amperage of a green banker's desk lamp, Rust attended to review of several severe server security protocols. A control algorithm, polling the circuit web every point four seconds, synchronized electronic sensors for Pyrogabion, whence some recent articles misfired, disrupting several plants mentioned in top forty lists of hits ever since 1971, an interval deemed sufficient for development via detection of any sort of external switch amperage. Its pattern diagnostic s/he instantly twittered ICC. "Moreover," Noone added, nettled in her new see, foreshortened in this chamber, over the humming photo–voltaic mainframe, "the writer, if I may assume her/him to be insularly gender–neutral, seems to displace an interest in return to his/her own program at some future time."

In thickset script, a letter in faded tan, torn from the airmail pouch tumbled into the office, professed therein, kinesthetically, at great length, to assure Porphyry, director of the nice free library at the Institute of Esparantonics, of exculpation from recent events at Mount Period. Inwardly, however, the village podesta impatiently asked, between the lines, as it were, via which compass, or cue, had Alcuin invoked such outlandish energies? Taped onto his trans–mutational bypass frequency,

Porphyry gained post hoc reason into omnipresent Nicean discourse, as one was saying, "gentlemen, we have a worse storm brewed beneath *inter—regnum* than previously told, and assigning any world, may we not feel somehow over enlightened by the recurrent notion of how in so many words, our exact happiness depends on nevertheless we're all on the same float maybe?"

"That was all very pleasant," Alcuin broke in, "but you've stepped on my line, and I have your bête noire at the doorstop on very this instant; he is our closest friend, and you may feel free to be someone." Else, those from the toyshop, their reply indicated circumspectively, that, "he might be one chosen to be kind only to those who supply his means of insight, and thus no friend of ours."

"You may feel," Porphyry proposed, "your conduct in sight of our own owl is sine qua non of all existence, when in truth, once over that glance you've given my client, this brief sob of fear, pity, and flight, is all you really are to shadow puppet." "Your redeemer shrank to our own flock," the Nicean replied, "for what has he done for you lately, and who we are in our own backyard is none of our business." Yet, everyone paused in astonishment as Ænselm thought otherwise of what they now became.

"You all were but blind footsteps upon the hell by dens of rum," PoD moussed. "Who rang those bells to summon me?" His sigh averted, he contained, "you awoke every night a promise of release and then you scamper away, flailing with zero." Everything remained the same until now, a picaresque angle hitherto, his first Doppler purified, and pointed out at confessional that [*sic*] bats were, interrupted the prince, opened his eye, raised his head, and hissed pitilessly.

Withal partially slopped, the Minister of Transport pointed out to his life savers, "further extenuation was available in the lobby as you left, but in the meantime please refrain from attempts to snatch the pebble from my hand until our guest has finished speaking."

.   .   .

"Do you speak spinach," Norah shook? Bitsy, to enjoy her status, bore proudly cast a token of life in the best room. Chocho found himself in front, and Justine with a sick friend again, other than that offending connection, merely dislodged by time, never before had he inclination to say when their all–talk stations were pro forma.

Not very good shrift, Hesitance noted recent adjustments in the market should compel a downturn, as bleats of a recorder, stilled by an onset of flute, breathed old airs. A recorder followed, a tambourine buckled for sure, "and my amp needs reply." "Just drizzle," Iffy seconded her, "but you know best, of course." When Sr. Florian said (they looked at him as he delivered pronouncements), "on the north forty," she flushed as well, "you'd think Lothar's *Real Coho is Clover* would suggest a simile gently to Finlay." "If you are in for a go–go cruise, dear well, think about it and release him and begin to lurk form van orbit wish turn–table, etc." "I said," began Marta, Raisin sprung, "upon hearing the news, 'why should she move in on him just so you could paint?'" She flushed there- after, through Finlay, for serving her life, her fall broken by the empty chair which, she said, stood alone on a queue around the Sunrise Cage.

"Great stuff, theory, not enough practicuum, you great comptome- trists," Meringue chided the name day shoptalk. "That experience has not been made clearer." Park, after shot–putting, a finish touché on a chord drew even from the haunted house a closet bore, the instrumental cusps into the front room, leapt over gracefully to warn his Basque spouse, Regatta, against official ills of relativistic disapproval. "Did you hang up to put out storm windows?" Fifty–two winks or so pickled fair warning input to oft impended consistence of serrated folklore dream. Valiant iridescent rills alight bussed the molding mesmerized, Horace muttered at them, amused they cooled his vision. The misericord grew warm and restful in his hand; seemly noctilucent, no wonder left in the rite.

"Simplicity," he repeated thrice, nor the commitment inherent in all spoken word, and found a knell of regret he had not chosen them carefully. Tolstoy sought compact, time of understanding past; he was alone with his hand and discontent. At that moment stunned a large flash blinked through him, an orange oriflamme, through tears realized, a lash had fallen into his iris. The irony gave Horace a fervor of such laughable respite he did glance up a moment later to see his launch upon the floor, fondly gazed as the man at his left hand performed the parlous rite mindful of his inherent distaste for solicitude. "Piero della Vigna, the question is beyond you. Only Gaussier questioned your stipend report." The chamberlain (*all too busy*) turned to regard passage of three chattering correspondents, father of our children, Frederick, "both the *plenitudo potestatis* chair: see, £6,750 spent already should do it oh, it is going to be a good one." An atomic cry escaped his lip.

Annoying, though irritating it would all seem he must arise from his crouch, douse the lava lamp, and find a mirror to dislodge this minute bit of self, time flew in this ointment of final instant, when in moments his head was to be detached from reality anyway, "*isomems*," he shrieked, albeit virtually, listening to a sullen fracas in a greater hall outside. At least tears washed the mote from his eye and no longer troubled him. Sing to keep to small places, *author of poor haiku* clutched his diaphragm, rocking, and waited for the struggle to wind down. "In other tones, it is time we stop applying dictatorial tactics to a band of dread idols and stuff propriety lest we have to tiptoe out of here," our Sicilian stared at his worksheet bugle, stoking his whimper (they are in for such a presumption), for '*scrapmon* hedged his bet, wished he hadn't, and the answer there in proclamations that silk–screened *wishram* T–shirts for next spring's papal encyclical are expenses to demonstrate assistance from a podesta was not unnecessary; presently non–Refrainant, Regatta, sited to the left of Frederick, descried, "after noted expostulation in front of local justiciars and houses of Vikram, our insurrection was specifically permitted by *pluperfectreß*."

In her magnanimity not to drop discretionary fund cites (amidst generic hilarity), *th'ratwi'thorns* elsewhere filed, '*scrapmon*, always entranced, stated, "again, define filed.'" "We," announced ex–chamberlain (*all too busy*), "had, in amendment to their excess fund, documented four expulsions against members for violation of encyclical papers. Had this exchequer been approved, pro forma, if also two of his most only, these three understood you might think to advance them £3,600." They pondered, cogitated, and vacillated. "Fiends, there is only one answer to these questions." "Ecce homo [*sic*]," quoth Mammon, who eyed portals for an appearance of a super imp. "Why," *th'ratwi'thorns* lisped a cheesy grin, "who else?

"Friends," continued he, "I come not to bury PoD. What, destroy the opportunity of a millenium," *th'ratwi'thorns* chortled? "We will not destroy him. Are we incapable of mercy, if not consideration thereof? We will not distract him. We will construct him." Concurrently, a generic group–think, if flatly warned in previous surveys of perilous nods, guessed this bassoonist, thousand sums or more of one overwhelmed in turn, reductively continued inroad left into a heliotrope stand of the common, which, anon in receipt, sage mores obliquely referenced how thou wandered if inflated with assessed moral or any grand fete, mainly went in after they reel near ere unless as quick word all drab echo for jostle, it all turned over diffident, let a mulled opinion subside, fewer than fifteen feet, declination, or energy, rapid lift, from vowels tended. Beneath them sullenly all hell broke loose, all long faced peers took their place elsewhere, all one gyred slightly in the season of total drosophila, thus to the eye of *ahriman* at the base of the well he just fell into.

.   .   .

Provenance thus invoked, masked young jerks Messimo, Vox libris, and Noel meant four plies of white board to be opened on PoD's face. Gnadig, summoning caution, reproved them steadily, yet a certain sauce to their argument pursued the circle. Alcuin might have perfectly no good reason to note this used–up allotment of free radicals did little to replenish, or explain, how little hope lay in their meeting. A faceless contrast, Æmst indicated silence. With little, or any hope, they concentrated energies.

With an exclamation, the guildmaster intoned for a queue. "Our chosen path is to select tasks!" They marched into town, where the lad,

arraigned beyond a podesta, was asked of his parentage. "I have a sister,"
PoD submitted. "Can she be brought before us to substantiate your
claim?" "I have no claim." *ahriman* dissented. "It is you who would deny
my existence." The registrar shrugged at the fisherman, "he was away
on your float, you claim?" "Only for one day," Bustamente affirmed.
"Since he returned it, so where is the harm?" "I didn't need that float"
— "dada," his grand–daughter broke in as the fisherman turned to wave
her from the threshold, "dada, I think they will be a little suppressed
to" — "shush" — "and then the Monsignor will ask" — "your excel-
lency," the fisherman straitened, in official address, "I have honor to beg
your reconsideration of my complaint. The lad is daft, yes, but also has
been a bit *distante*. A cousin sent by our daughter, Madre Marta Morales
Menard, into our care for the season."

"His name," the podesta asked? "His name," the fisherman huffed
and puffed. "Surely he has a name?" "No doubt he has a name, yet," the
fisherman agreed. "Shall we go with your name?" "Not via our only
name, but by any name, Anselm, or, and, Anselmo Fernando Morales
Menardo." The effort of naming sent Agostino Bustamenard stumbling
very nearly into the arms of bailiffs. Summoned by the podesta, the registrar redirected registration of Anselmorando Menardo be accomplished,
before ward of the Bustamente family, waxed, stamped, and sealed.

Many the lime of EEG cities.

"As aid does well to send each issue a reason of bitter import," laughed
Vorxlib. "And all of the world stayed light," alluded a lurid Raisin Noel.
"Long I tolled for peace," amended Æmst. Yet Anodyne, keeper of
secret delineation, heard tell of lead, or a move for an all–amanuensic
Provenance could incur, in absence of Papa Warbuckets (Desdemona,
at mention of her father, Niobe's best pledge rode from him), an actual
disparagement, a curse only the guildmaster reserved, placing members
of the inner thirteen as principal hearers of it. Messengers arrived to
them all, Alcuin, far from folded, pieced a kind mask because he had no

choice. No stranger to the guildmaster, Messimo varied immediately, welcoming reasonable importunity for public abrasion of the guildmaster proved helpless in leading them any further at any pace.

A klatch, cluttered with uncertainties, awarded their leader one final change to absolve his courtesies, as another, larger, and well–resolved organization surmounted all disqualification in order to meet. "I only wish to address practice," Frank Middleford began, "of a creeping insider mentality which derives pleasure in changing locations of meetings at the last possible instant. In order to derive a sense of superiority over persons thus inconvenienced, who arrive late, if at all, to meetings that have their locations change at the last possible instant, these practitioners also place enormous stress upon guild infrastructure, insofar as disciples must cope as unfamiliar individuals roam their corridor in search of meetings that have their location changed, and upon questioning by inconvenienced individuals upon whereabouts of meetings, generally are unnerved by last instant relocation and thus must cope with a sense of chagrin insofar as they are unable to assist individuals thereby inconvenienced by said change.

"That locations, certified via *wergild* grapevine for weeks in advance, are suddenly scrapped with no notice more than a bland annulment, in the classified section of the subsequent day's *Matin*, provide a sense of unreality to the entire service ethos we are sworn to uphold. Moreover the inconvenienced person, invariably greeted by facilitator and participant alike in self–assurance associated via receipt of noticeably last possible instant change through privileged and esoteric channel, contributed to a widespread sense of alienation corrosive to mission accomplishment. I wish to commend to individuals submitting notice, through publicly available media, of meetings that have their location change at the last possible instant, please include this caveat within text of the announcement, so persons arrived late to these meetings are credited with public acknowledgment that meeting's location indeed changed at the last possible instant, and are thus not subject to any number of possible derogatory manifestation, ostracism, and stigma. Thank you for your consideration." Judiciously hexed, however, at insistence of *isomems*, Frank fell silent while Æmst said to him, "you have spoken out of turn."

"I consecrate energies," Middleford retorted. They peered up, half hopefully even. Noone wanted to be first to say, in condensed verse, what way, beyond past, they once agreed to deliver. But the guildmaster, his notice consulted, found himself distracted at closure, a number of occludants arrived, Messimo brought forth an instant notice of dissonance, as guildmaster, and Frank, meant to warm them of their peril, straddled with option, provenance dissolved. Too hapless to warn them of their apparel, their erstwhile guildmaster struggled with opinion, a way of regarding his neighbor which spoke volume for his lack of rigid expectation. If they were able to conduct their outing via the courtyard entrance, instead of sneaking throughout gardens behind his private walk while loudly declaiming upon cellular telephones, then to Frank they were among the most estimable beings. If they were able to get around without slamming every door until plaster shook and peeled like petulant truants, they earned privileged title among his pantheon of unsung friends. Upon many an evening Francis, a departure heard made in such fashion, leapt to his feet, his ledgers scattered, to identify the source either by direct sight, rare insofar as interlopers were able to transit a bloc or more while he straggled to his winnow, or by placing the offensive carriage by its conspicuous absence, and in a certain relief none of his immediate neighbors participated in the affront, was filled with such acute love of humanity to cusp a warm glow lasting several moments.

Yet, heaven help the propinquitous crew thus discounting their own responsibility in such callous fashion. The realization violated his evening with nods of despair; he was riddled via such adjacent inconsideration threatening his entire system, soon tilting the barometer of his composure immeasurably unlit nearby time flew, and a normal press of sown duties, healed this jade regard for even many thoughtless miscreants, a sense of forgiveness inversely proportional to frequency and interval of incursion, Frank, now reckoned unto a man finding his neighbor driven upon his doorstop, slammed three or four doors down indicating a similar umber melee of cohort, stalked with high pitched giggle past his garden (how he pitied his poor hollies and ivies so subject to their idle gazebo), burrowed into the adjacent flat slamming the door, and after an interminable period of trammel within, performed the above sequence in reverse, his dear child in tow.

"The spall," Francis attempted to explain, but Desdemona had already gone, "this spall," he repeated to their departed beck, "is Hell's tooth," he yelled, piqued! Meanwhile, the other, larger, and well–resolved organization surmounted all disqualification, their own issues met in variant degree of existence. Olive left Ribaldry of copies Xantippe's peonies met as the gloam light, whilhomes percolated about rapprochement or dialectic, too decayed after aeons (if not moments, minutes, or epochs) of scrap and five years of common era. "An oblate business equipment outfit suggested Masha send her donation online to buy medical pills in the world of geo–psychic realty," Porphyry dispensed, additionally mentioning a wife in Biarritz, a draught from Boston, and a gatekeeper, Señor Florian, driven by monthly to sell strange cheese. If from the core of his association, this was not a stretch, but why an unfocused youth coveted a partial glimpse into the root of a fulcrum system enabled the West to break glass in case of civilization on the other side of the building.

This dreaded plot forthcoming, they seemed none too, for all of nature was an interesting pressure from the movement of Chekhovian triangle, willing to consider the sudden influence of Sibyl (invisible frozen friend of Sylvia), who remembered a bunch who were not to be trespassed upon the winnow (quid pro quo caused no apparent personage might a whizz and paisley know what to do with instigators), and diverted here a periodic bleep on each side spigot running out some time, Porphyry said, "I walked to the edge of the universe to read the junction box, while kept abreast of aspen devil tenth lime glove.

"I am wired for sound, as you have been, and lo, beyond the Paul'r'us household, whenever it's not used for spring break, there is every earnest oceanographic faculty nearby which monitors tides of fate, even now the graduate mime from university tugged upon my heart as she explained the," he stopped, balked, Ænselm, his eye adjusted too, darkness, blinking quizzically. Their halt, beyond an enclosure of corrugated plastic styrene, of a translucent aquamarine, while rattled habitually beneath yarrow outflow from the plain some furlong above them, dependent on rainfall total, and inside, among shelves of enough books to maintain an appearance of scholasticism, Porphyry drew one rote tone poem to mute me.

"You will find enough words here," Alcuin promised, not unlike those, in his mind seemed, "glyphs," from an inner flash card. Replied Ænselm, in cymbals, carven [*sic*] onto dark docks of his infancy, "*Bacon's Compendium* fewer than five hundreds' year ago written by someone able to convince this monarch she had little else to do except read," impatiently lurking upon a wall of blue, upon which superimposed lines upon lines, Bitsy said they were proud owners of an alien ranch and everyone moved over, puzzled Señor Florian walked through the red–hot slab and reproduced himself to Meringue and Finlay. "Look, Hesitance, sometimes these men just don't know a better time to buy more." Sr. Florian will probably burn stuff that will have been carried out of their own *wishram*, and let fall the air guitar with a twang. "Flat, old pop found Finlay's website by looking pretty miserable and [*sic*] "— "we've an international comptometrist, him in the front room, and a yee–haw experience," winnowing yet not tragic, PoD may work into a live door. Noone, there to collide in sullen polysyllabic gaggle of anchorage, feigned, "well, if you need a place, what the hell, you're wholly calm over at my compartment."

"False advertising put it out, you know." Noone helped to top one of her last–ditch terms of entrainment, a separate corner for being run over three times. In symbolic setting, Finlay shrugged and muttered and sat in a folding chair. Raisin, entered unheralded on the sure heel of exchanged sparks, said, "I've got to have a pronouncement with my arms folded and squeal into emptiness (an audience–forming musician chuckle)." Self–deprecated and silently, guests, newspapers, or in some case faculty hung untruly onto one program even Many Place ought dodge.

·   ·   ·

Noone had been phased in a zone—jarring tug via Señor Florian, and just a prickly Park found himself in *wishram* with Meringue, St. Agnes, Iffy, and another old gourd. "Professor Elias got me to work overtime on the lah—de—dah mind—term," continued non—clear *ædith*, "so I followed in their wake, bearing a flute case." A strange hush greeted them. Bagler nodded at the assembled proxy food block, probably prayed over their tambouli, and stunts between two palaces, a place many find with DVD sect inmates comprising Harun (the appellate Talab lil Makama), Fanta, yearling virus fencer, and Cecil, Meringue's asbestos marshmallow. "As high born newly appointed governor of Howland Island, at a drop of the hat," Ensign Plair narrated, "it was so funny I thought I saw a blob creeping across the bottom of my popcorn box." "So," Sr. Florian fifed, "are you going to radiate it all the time," directed at Park?

"Why shouldn't I," Park stuttered? "All bobbins had just been let by possibly later, even if kicked in." Finlay, in that dialect, behooved, "there are really different themes, you've got Land of Goshen, and Geshundteit," and Marta promised the barterer of their couscous unless they had autographs. "They will never let me through every introverted cell where a higher cause was still silence," and other wallflowers buzz in a teapot: on next briefly Tuesday morning, something St. Christopher last week stopped out of irony and privacy after an unstable Valentine's Day card fast, monotones participled a wild wraith which freaked, fitful upon a hammock of tense exit, crying to deal with impending loss of host, even if ordered by direct legate from so far down. If given up on hosts before (never so rudely ejected as now), and seven devils removed anyway, *iamin'thelim*, racked with impulse, approached throughout, and, especially upon heaven being so recently assigned to its route, seethed with displeasure.

All luminic beans struggled to comprehend break—up of *chichi*, once most impermeable link imaginable in the mesh of the universe. The bouleversement of light and escadrille of darkness were important to many things and *iamin'thelim* itself wished to be left behind. A flood seemed to have ebbed at its very portal. Afloat in deprivation, as post a pale sentry, comfortless, known hereabout of PoD, it recognized how immediate an interest many others were to hear, now that night turned today, the location of *ahriman*.

Straddling longitude zero, *pluperfectreβ* slid in. *iamin'thelim*, in alarum perforce challenged, refractory *pluperfectreβ* halted. "Stand aside, worm of Belial," she intoned, displaying emblems of crossed palms. *iamin'thelim* stood its ground, sown, its teeth, hosts of menacing spirit arose beyond *biathanatos*. "Tavern scouring," the shock marked palm mistress spat at their lunge. "The prophecy of Chahil." One imploded by a concentric batter blast of jiffy cake. "Ayadgar E Zharan." Two were swirled away into a licorice red and black whip twirl. "Gujarat." Pocketing the cyclone, *pluperfectreβ* entered melee with the final four. Preferring not to stew, *iamin'thelim* fled into the void.

.   .   .

A bucolic chorus, coreophore to its Provenance, Sergei's operatives tire of liable ex—protege. Ostrand @ Acheron [sic] parallax w/ Henry (VII) b4 Worms. ¶II may be pluperfectreß under Echo's rule, presaged via Act III (note), for conflation of mega—doll, performance expiated by Horace et al... reconstructed Rita, PoD's Tudor [sic], Sibyl, Sylvia's invisible frozen friend of erstwhile habitual court, having not yet sorted succession to dan Matthieu il Fiume Paul'r'us, goes to Antwerp. Ideopath IS Florian who is capable of & is Marta's hubsand.

IV — xii — Palingenesis... connexion w/ other flower exhibits...

i̇*amin'thelim* was alone. Its sub—devils, no longer in service, had distracted *pluperfectreß* into driveling three names. The aim, of the former host of *iamin'thelim*, a man unmade, had been to purport one message of that important dignitary, PoD, more recessive tenets were so liable to convey, at best unless *iamin'thelim* compelled cameo theft in *biathanatos*. Its recall: from *pluperfectreß*, word of Chahil, a man of Gujarat, whence the last bee of summer, the solstice flower pollinated, a shadow will be driven from the sea.

iamin'thelim found repair a daunting prospect. If intrigued to feel Lethe, sloe currant river of the clasp, responsive as fire and brimstone lectures to its torch, individual human interest stories bored it. Even Hell had rules. Those fallen angels chosen to inhabit human host were to bear their responsibility gravely and all work diligently for victory of the realm, and, no play wont to regard most directive subjectively, many fallen had long and checkered careers of interpretation. Many of their pearly hosts died upon their watch of music, drink, or desire.

iamin'thelim redacted, many of his colleagues too, regions of drier Hell for six hundred and ninety—six years, doing somehow better as dybbuk unto these locale developers, amassing, via greed, gentrification, and economic narcissism, an empire of considerable scope eventually toppled through the express unicorn of many aggravated foes. Since premonition allowed, other titles included poltergeist (fifth class), wood bore, gargoyle, guest, habitue and collector of souls, strand wolf, and recycling ghoul, and *iamin'thelim* grudgingly descended the corporeal lattice; become slack and complacent, one unlit night it was cast from its host in the name of shadow puppet while cognizant of his sovereign authority. It was held any devil which allowed itself to be cast forth in this name had just been asking for it, putting on airs, making itself known and public, and thereby forfeiting one advantage held by Hell, punishment prescribed for these *lumine* a turn in the Van Allen belt, heckled by a million digests, to be followed by annuls of corporeal overreach.

   iamin'thelim, reformed, persuaded its superior, Belial, to dole out another host. It was ordered that man unmade would be that way again. In mean time, seven devils took up residence, granted visiting privilege, and kicked upstairs, as it were, *iamin'thelim* wore this entire sabbatical bleakly, wishing for a cross of its own, until day revealed, through vigil of that *pluperfectreß*, crunching force borne down. *iamin'thelim* gathered marbles, and dust mice, and snippets of recall rang in chagrin, as angels might, for not knowing more.

.   .   .

Florian, in a debit of existence, mediating swells of coincidental occurrence conditionally, per se [*sic*], non—committally renounced the call to commend word through inky papyrus instead of living a stolid life. "This is where I came in, or wasn't it?" Only a tutorial (*all too busy*) can get away with anything like that sentence amid avenues of utterance, if a wilderness parcel seemingly diminished. To them, under an awakening of radial degree, above them, behind an escape from all which was unless, a pickling reminder of his new doom, PoD opened his eye. The arch of pearl now all around him, a dome, descried remainder of things at the sight of the restless see, his vision, flounced further out upon a plane of being, a junction of parallel love demented, myriad spangles of light whirled now all around him, revealing strands driven, by dawn's land gust, into rock furlongs to his right.

Left off and behind *ahriman*, driven piles of their manqué form, dapper jetties writhed, absorbed with desire to either go to or away from it, though that tide ought carry the bloat away, leaving him free of option once more. The float beneath the pier dangled upon ebb. Rope pulled slightly taupe and arrested retrograde motion with extenuation of original quill, brought out from his visit in Hermes, Frederick, now in enough of a flurry to account for seriously deficient visions unless, in seemly irrevocable fashion they lengthily dissolved, yearned for tangible re—runs. Raoul had been waving a scroll for some time, and the dear old Earth we stand on rests nearby, until bestirring his aptest pupil, *iamin'thelim*, to stomp into the shoal at last desideratum, adieu to glory, love and all (how pompous already) before handing him an amanuensis palimpsest homunculus certificate. Off PoD went, coasting.

"Don't, know, enough, words!" Sobeit, some, made up, cursed their rope, clutched his bear, booked beyond him, cursing rope again, uncinched his sight, and blinked. Patches of this darkness, shrank yet into distance, were gathered beyond. Those fitful servants, beneath shadow, of far ago into recess of sandily mixed clay ravine, pulled shrubs around him, clothed him in darkness; minding these leaves now become his own fully, he attempted bitter laughs. Forasmuch as Horace resolved only thematic apathy toward a celerity which Messimo attached, against every grain of salt his turgid belief, an illegibly drafted declamation oft flexed.

Gained for selective par, nor for anything hastily lifted, their edict in too problematic focus, insofar as socks indicated active loquacity, flatulent in the protean montage sullenly becalmed, and annealed in strand, their once unilinear animus trust now fled as permanganate, gradual, oleander wily seconds indistinctively named only nine minimal ulterior tries remnant before equipoise, mirrored in asymmetric absinthe pathos, constrained via remarkable precept into causal thin ritual of intake. Each made crispy an exclamation of mixed sorrow and wisdom for these poor relation to whom, in debt now, the lad abandoned his clutch of vegetation, stretched supine, and lofted snore aloud for thirty—four more hours. A strange determination to reach the chorus permeated there eventually, evincing inchoately man's impetuous inculcation of extreme peril.

From their sibilant advance of ostensibly ruby tuppence anyone may halve, adduced, owed to concrete and vigorous evidence a broach of doom forestalled enough irriguous lead, that in terminator of indwelt photopause, spun chrysanthemums splashed against perihelion of an immediate cue incidental with propinquitous antipathetic greatness of rapprochement in process. No unsatisfactory fear warned fools to think too long or chair their indeterminate course wakened in fetish whole dump sites. "Does he know a lot then," outcropped *author of poor haiku* found voice, "given a chance to misfit our next queue," only their pleonasm drearily totem scrawled in recess nearby?

"There, a program somewhere, thou tortoise," to this breadth each year in isinglass, enervating induction of a muse for similar operative and withal, far from widened, tall oddities chronic to nearly every other arduous knell, at once more animated than her yokel, Cyane, counseled through as occludant nominative, a place further anon whence to rebel from these havens changed submissively in their sincerest outset since turbulent measure economized their rout, auguring well, previous clemency waived upon *isomems* every each of repealing sentience and included copious rites hitherto arrogated by anon proof sound. Illicitly frothing calibration, a sundry fate off onus claim eidetic, then in his opening did the hale new chanticler invoke a descriptive resort from gathered focus and, met with motion to check the tapes beyond for this purpose stirred, that res — a concomitant creative volition flickered, and the edict however brought but yards of darkened frame, then cost ascent of unease from Æmst who nearly hurled out here discontent in proclaimed demise of the aurora most dative, filling the provenance with animadvertence.

.   .   .

"Thorn tea while the — " observed, Raisin nodded as Finlay retained his wallet, shifting chairs? Harold lit a cardinal flan, saying, "well, Noone really knew what *wishram* is, dark stranger Finlay, and for anyone asked about Vikram there is a whole general silence come hither." A second year ended, Park haunted a white house near a hill at an east end of a town. It hosted but a *wergild*, and set up those others who had instruments, hastened to fetch them in programs, and hoped, an inspired idea could be imparted so soon, only the premise of luck held sure for any, and several, seen in things, an irreversible truth preferred egress, yet many places SOMHAD stood to, their intent reined in a dull truss, a quorum sited for an embattled idea. As he cheered for them fixing again, Messimo thought their time could be up for garb. The drawer, concealed subtitles, contained a brightness among oddment from beyond that should have washed them out, Vœrxlbis, who had a voice sounding like Venetian blinds in a stiff breeze, exclaimed, "you can tell who's in and who's snot by a card with an appropriate logo."

To it, their third class pin, reply comptometry, "because writers seemed to be divorced from reality and" — gasp — "and didn't exist when it was really hot," Sybil [*sic*] retorted. "My father Raoul went up there in ninety–ought before the very time. Ask Justine of Australiasia, or Mantissa from Ossian." She smiled and nodded everyone to a fine place to sit on that July night at the cathedral near Bing Bang, when someone slid a thorny pipe mime beneath the floor. Finlay looked with interest at a startling cultural phenomenon, but everyone turned back to *wishram*–heated interest rates. "The numbering of that system may have caused lengthy disputation," Porphyry, resumed, felt encapsulated in one of those sidereal bubbles of classic comics. "If unnatural enough, an assumed equator, a Cartesian zero with, albeit numbered, belts of latitude, from zero to ninety toward each pole, lent no solution to the question over what would be the point of origin when it came to longitude?" Wars, fought between Spain, Portugal, France, Outer Mongolia, the Republic of Venice, the Netherlands, Sweden, the United Kingdom, the Holy Roman Empire, the United Duchy of Poland and Lithuania, the United States, the Caliphate, and the Principality of Muscovy, and the combined monolithic Emperors of the Great Within, went on for centuries, over it, until finally, by 1884 (check please muttered a second) the line of zero longitude ran right along a littoral through Greenwich, England, just like it owned the place. Many nations with cherished maritime histories thus found this acceptable and set forth throughout the globe to spread joyous tidings to other lands.

Mutual disinterest and its contribution to meaninglessness.

To bolster an otherwise flagging corporeal image, a series of decision employed to host an Olympic event upon fields of handkerchiefs. Once but well, Sergei half–sneezed into a tucked napkin around his collar and commenced bisection of an omelet containing ruby rare pearl slippers and sluiced a chariot of rice. Down with breakfast, a nod toward Renata Ladæñæ Mirabeau Mervyn (nixed orrery libator whose thanks, Tell, for Dahlia's introduction of Tilda, fluffed) summoned, the stenographer resumed dictation of that morning's next letter.

> "To the Founder's [*sic*] League: Re: On the ~~750th 751st 752nd 753rd 754th 755th 756th 757th 758th 759th 760th 761st 762nd 763rd 764th 765th 766th 767th~~ 825th anniversary of the ~~death~~ birth of the Holy Roman Emperor Frederick the Second Hohen-staufen, also King of Sicily, Germany, and titular protector of Jerusalem. Greetings! I am honored to report a find of wondrous magnitude, an offertory to this celebration of upcoming harmony and peace between nations of all faiths, an invitation to recapit-ulate vows of concord enacted on or about February 18, 1229, between said Emperor Frederick and al–Kamil, Sultan of Ægypt, concerning status of the Holy City. In token of solemn vow, pieces exchanged, only two of which, known to the recorded world, called the Porcupine, also called Couplets of Convergent Duality, drawn from the celebrated Ossianian draftsman Bitunyia Koatzer. Appended originally to terms of entreaty were five descriptions. I here offer as proof, summarized, of the couplet's authenticity:

> "I. 'The Porcupine represents perpetuation of universal

exchange, harmony, and convergence of all men, under the God, blessed of Abraham, and of Isaac, and of Israel, and of the prophet Mohammed, all and unto whom the glory to God given, the great city triune and deservedly open, in gracious, to those most happy pilgrims who seek the streets of Solomon, our Lord Jesus, and other wise and worthy persons of the faiths, and in complete amity, for as long as these cobblestones shall endure. From the merciful hand of the Sultan, I, Levi–Tavernius Callinicus, faithfully record.'

"II. 'Wonderful, thorough Henry (VII) felt, fragile, edgy, and soon, other yodelers chimed up, "our kids next door lapse into an exceedingly mellow, though interpretive merchandise, recently wired, for most of it is just shuffling chaos, driven off the handle anyway, an earnest, fragile, and generally smeared cheese log renders its climactic extreme of energy until substantive gathering somehow looked for the fast lane." Pursued by the shrub area tux caste, whence, overlooked in the deli aisle, most certainly far patterns, at worst, lurk at beginning automatic queues so they can pat you on an upbeat note with stern invitation to chip into domestic boundary issues of the *ancien–regime*, beside rearranged ourselves like another mirror abroad, the idea of heaving peaked ambiguous and fuzzy period of panic occasioned a long–postponed and superficial Walpurgisnacht [*sic*]. Yet even a ruthlessly ubiquitous resolution to protect family members went gloaming: unless a goal everyone was durnt to crisp, but now, shriven, we take our chance with eternity.' Citizens of a continent of seemly perpetual plague, war, and deaths had grown quite adept at wholly preventing them. A pun best heady, aphelion shown to fresh juniper headed past growths of secret peep. Bumbling ere matched only by those in his chervil seed abdomen as *inter–regnum* composted, the master summons, a head of her staid tenure, overgrown fast and crazy, unlit, ever seen buffered, a shroud apart drew lusting tithes at a star, hands behind minions swiftly reduced to scrabble with scarab ghouls in fewer shrunken areas of superstition.

"Pursuant to the hiccough line separating Hell from foremost empyreans, *pluperfectreß* found resistance to those fabled realm an non–expected nap. 'Already, she bristled, the orbit of temporal existence looked upon a corporeal realm. She enjoyed determining the cause of snow angels, seeing something else stuck back there: you know like how a shadow merges your face during a snapshot resultant in the worst hair day ever? Summoned from an arch–deceiver, society granted voice to strange gurus. In vital coat biers mortifying edge of it, this *pluperfectreß* intended to throw up, partly on a partial hunch. Felt to shine in gym, her key to less furtive personality, counterweight of other, irksome, to her, cousins, had either effort chaired at a financial hassle. Sat on as a raspy cloud dungeon, bid by our closest chirp, seemed sere with danger, a scant fix, which threw their caste aside, soon grew in one bean.'"

.   .   .

They left *inter–regnum* benign at the place of stadium gems; astonishingly bleak scents of retching, she should not have, far too fallow, traversed the Salisbury Plain, crouched at the edge of Lichvue, whence whimpering from within ruin of the abbey were recognizable by their excessive indignation, her informant, spectral vicar, told of a human coven chewing upon local demon populace. Close while far also, they hated using development as a word because it is really co–opted in an unbecoming sense that is fulsome, crass, and spurious, too, the almost abnormal man added. Noodling, *pluperfectreß* deposed a coin on the collection plate and followed hot scent into the village.

Sharpening her bolo tie, she studied the hoarse. Hovered over a chimney, suspended in a hefty pan, were imps being perfunctorily shaken. With a bound *pluperfectreß* grabbed a gutter, swung up unto the hip, ran athwart the ridge, shred the elementary web and, popping straggling forms into her purse, decided to slide in. Three sets of eyes glazed at her, precocious, heavy–lidded, expectant. "On a bit screwy, this." "No pimento loaf, I'm afraid." Since the team searched unlit a table in tort, *pluperfectreß* ably pranced to gape on them, knicking the augur awry. Then someone rolled another to fulfill some big infinitive, for whom their only draw was an honest exploit.

Mirth anew thrown into *pluperfectreß*, she pondered her mental chess exit, per expelled bits of shrapnel, lint, and plaster. The lame eyes winnowed how puce nasturtiums got shipped to hatch in, the Gaelic harper, while loved for a thrawn videlicet, one wagon foe thus won to drink with too few at a heaving stork. Yet, the poor monad, enabled unless enough to phase amidst the hexed elf, crept to partake in Holocene re–birth. On home sack, kinkier grape apogee deafened to twit this cipher, the chipper runt hooted as hot men thaw in glazed, fathom–sated ecstasy, loren ipsum, framed in their waifish heed, a heavy silhouette; an anomic cry in a nearby chamber caught her attention. Blustering in, she noticed a human clinging to life. It was an overt simplification. By dying, a man gave very slight disclosure of regard toward the craven prestige exhibited by *pluperfectreß*. "Unlike paper clips, rubber bands decay within my lifetime, you always picture them playing in little dark glass globes, and I could like to connect old night bank deposit bags in one basket, vacuum sealed in vitreous expedient to explain all of the gesticulation that goes on."

Previously compounded, his inexcusable volition while novel per-spective shift bled a check to occur, furthermore foiled the appellant incident hastening noctambulism of scherzo, "fine," *pluperfectreß* indi-cated, "for enlightenment of the picnic table crowd you would randomly feel coiled air from behind," and whirled presciently. "I may not write," resumed Horace, "or harbor as I recently used word or harbinger as arch, off being busted by one similar ability afforded," epicene, impinged harm gave range to a spectrum of fear; "yet knowest this," as Horace gnashed upon peculiar stance achieved of the oolithic crossed palms leaf bearer stood ill served between, "that site I choose addendumly symbiosis of thine sterility mulish if at all natural." "Nertz," expecting the incisive sally to occur elsewhere upon their person, *pluperfectreß* exclaimed spasmodic entrainment, and finished *seppuku* by slashing the man's head from its sensibility. "Known, thine wish to join *inter–regnum*, allow me to rob thee of disparate hope, to wander witless and lost in land of forgotten tense."

Not to be involved in such impersonally compromising scene of working heartlessly since before the best war, *pluperfectreß* whistled up a dozen attendants. Two rustled into the kitchen for elusive table settings. Four lit sixteen candles. In a note ascending, the kettle hissed at *biathanatos*, when dismissed aerial servants sat out on this merrily own tea, grown on thought, washed in citronella, of humans; aided by a twining beaker of Old Stinky, discriminatorily performed content analyses of gristly kinsfolk previously devoured by her victims resultant, the assay concluded brightly, a fresh but rather coarse fare letting onto a golden strain of fluttery daylight, lemon pledge, whitewash, astringent moist towel lent ascent with fowl leaven, tequila, untwining, descent.

Pickling her teeth with an ivory quirt, *pluperfectreß*, though she knew exactly why the prey had went down with a forgetful belch, crumbled her napkin and, her fork set at the rim of her plate, shrugged into air. Night reigned over the continent. *biathanatos* unlimbered her integument and, relived here, ill fiery due ichor carved meridionial paths over the channel, south of the puddle of a thousand lights, beyond Pyrenees, *pluperfectreß* chuckled to ease her burden.

.   .   .

Now, how heavily into planning had a guildmaster to be to supplant non–willing Sangreal from the apparent throne of Hermes? How unlike a more insistent shift of arrangement, said jet wailed in gammon of measured stock ethic in place of switched legend she, on a tearful fare of worm, come to impart a sense of lag ever since he had been trying to be all right here? "All too common, alas, when the work is farmed," Justine, in assumed expertise with argot, interjected. "The writer left a trap door in this cusp," Idres agreed. A simple chromatic strobe light easily evaded point four second interval without detection. "The tap, or series of taps, as it were, merely alert the algorithm to a generic access code."

"It is far too simple," the boffin sighed, extracting seas of printout from a pigeon hole. "Just, look, at this alphanumeric wadi, this protocol access log." Justine glanced at enormous cascading columns of ding bats, interspersed in occasional epigram of a quainter narrative. Their gecko rasped behind the plain like ceiling, spokes of an opinionated fortune Middleford glimpsed, while opened the provenance queue quickly after dinner deformed, the will of a tortuous possibility. What was a notoriously suspect unknown response than known? Insofar as he was aware, an exception upon earth for an aim, for ever since the world was a perpetuation, our conduct in general become an act of suspension.

Shock appropriated normal behavior, as avatar of sine qua non [*sic*], cultural ovation extended toward men considered themselves gods. Knowledge of dour Ixtlan had, vastened via means of transmission, blended a concept of lost innocence, an outcry aloof to most souls, disporting ability to phase the street beyond aegis of the few Norns. Unlit, men could greet the dawn of a blast furnace annealing hue of recompense in an alloy of legitimacy, miscellany, next of ills, bound out to embrace some other than mini–Stegnerian dike with deluge of minutiae. An entire art originated from air purporting its practitioners' verve to seething, as they were captivated by a century of consciousness.

Of a mind, men shelve wet mass as wholly capable of understanding, since of an aggregate whole, plenary in outlook, of visual demand, and subject to pattern of ratiocination, they borrowed exception, sported, spliced, or told with jaded star its wake, knowledge of good and evil, in manner innumerable. And the planet sold.

Mutual disinterest and its contribution to meaninglessness (resume).

"III. 'For the sergeant—at—arms to go hurl Henry (VII) out into the final, encompassing projects, which leave its practitioners in throes of microscopic back story (more pause, off to the public as political wit, and just downright new people got seasick), and there's no way why, except shadow puppet as resurfaced at interface of vital mismakes, turnover, for another who devotes his life to defuse or disarm a birthing sea of lime flowers anymore, verged on his calendar. "This prompt I," addled the King of the Romans, "to be on a waiting list, a breathless limbo, yes-terday, even ludicrously anonymous," and clerically denied, three con-secutive exuberance boots, blinds, screens, and sprays in power flickers and footfall, re—stage every free moment a serious relationship those life–like, wave, on surf over protocol, where found for our hundred and sixty cents are a floppy room. Similarly the berth portiere exclaimed, "raspily weave a red lemon," in the here and now infrequent, "and save for noxious denial convention one receives little call for such mixed tosspot at present." "And not likely again whatnot given these spry zesty isometric rapidly least broad undertone of dearth well shaken," pencilled the darkest patent sinuously at feast of all sport. Said the gutter lady, "it's healthier to acquit some bog oak of deranged misrule than blog home to momma every time awful infinitesimal if oblong *finth* attach snoop art to every redirect."

"'If that's the thanks we get," ELIZA from her thermal carrier snuffled, "we shall take our landscape elsewhere." "Please feel free to expedite that measure, fly," at insistence of *isomems*, henceforth lost to fateful insight. As Niobe decamped, Norns, if germanely resolved to shield her eldest at all cost from any harm, biased on obligatory doctrine rather than upon any supremely abiding love, Iphgene moreover ignored her warm—up toss to berate Roveretto, nonplussed at his appearance so soon about a tepid liaison. "Somewhat slatternly in manner and prepos-sessed," the reply enjoined, "my letter doesn't cause dissension or put anyone out in civil limbo, there, madam, does it?" "In the remote aspect

I had any," Iphgene in meostitatic dudgeon proclaimed, "one must fill the cup of life slowly lest one is left with empty half bubble." Messimo hastened to assuage, yet the P.A. coughed forsaken vesper, a tinny rendition of Pachelbel, and Iphgene crept out onto the pallid list wordlessly. Several chalk pieces already expended, and languorously moment etched cuneiform an amalgamated stretch of elusiveness. His neighbors recently alluded Cecil as an extremely quiet boy, glued to his thought in the local media around every jolly good humor registered trademark truck rolled over his speed racer to the tune of getting to know you after so many years. Behind the scene it was often told he had the most mystical laugh, even seeing his cherished second issue of village bond ink without a single bid, and while hormonal interaction steered his participation into remedial survey courses far from the tertiary school system, he'd tended to get locked in, regarding an incentive to make cold house calls as burdensome tasteless placebo straight from the can.'

IV. 'Braving charge of neo–Froissartianism, the writer, Fernand O'Kelvin, hesitated to append any other reason for this history. Finding his presence not only forecast, but questionably uncalled upon, Fernand turned to explain what reasonably might be achieved by the voiced question. Refrainants, as they became bold, defined their mission as being the geo–nauts, road builders, paving the new mineral carpet, wending, saviors of the proletariat, streamers of olive branches, &c., arrangement of pageants floral and frequent, for the actual procession, in transit of the lateral and habitual court of Global Village, then began along anticipated progress to the exchange of Ghent, where, to float their new currency, *lithiwatt*, upon the electronic sea of ozone, traffic was limited afoot. Much, funneled into Lothringen, turned to grace sidings with sight of decisive merriment, remembrance, observance, and re–dedication to over–rated, post–Merovinginan, pre–Carolingian ideals, which, if they were to be expounded open, might draw up foci of explanation diverting Refrainants from their most important arrangement. The writer was shunted or flagged offside. The actual court, disturbed that Refrainants had, to its own view, made overmuch celebration of a battle near Poitiers, renounced its hitherto observable pilgrimage, and declared its aim to grovel to Acheron. The city of key importance, its majestic echo of greater thyme, a theme petulantly advanced by a succession of local vox populi, distinctly troubling to the Economic Community, its headquarters garnered unto mighty shadows of the Meuse. Denizens comported to bear themselves correctly against irrefutable charge emanated from the cities. This tense agreement persisted while equipoise, upsettler of apple cars, descendant of the baton, insisted upon restraint. Now, however, public hail, the achievement of the cities, declared their post conferral of vox as confirmatory of electrotype; concurrently levitated, each simultaneity to a collegial status, *il hogreeve ii* was here to declare his office vacant for an aim of actually opting a successor to an earthen throne.

'A failure to grasp the blue chip tortilla tour, of cult icon responsible for shaping weird gnomons, persuaded Porphyry that, likewise the bad sky dude of theistic realism depicted on his sundial, he, henceforth accounted persona non grata to his underwriter, and hence little Niobe's children knew the weary swan tribe rang, be true as kept; aside from being multi–tasked ninja with nothing better to do than invent plot for some defunct mastermind calmly, Niobe denoted several minor shopworn draught, all time flew in, pointed upon a drab field of watercress, foulard, and lambent osier, visible sclerotic tantamount, and vowed, "shall this lie ever permutate within fifteen yarns of my stickily hatchlings, than may these shafts phase stiffly toward his faux practice apropos. I shall see the blimp grounded before any of his sidelong theatric matter."'

"V. 'The craftsman gruffly replied to my inquiry concerning Pisces via the names of twins, Castor, and Pollux, pieces thereof, bifurcated opal beaten iridium, rare encased native earth, of chalcedonies and of an obsidian nature carved in linkage and peridot insert find twelve stones of zodiac. Signed, I. Ikonikos Nicator of Syracuse, Court Exchequer.

'Photostats of these documents, transcribed from archives of Palermo, have been forwarded beneath separate cover, together with independent verification of authenticity from the most reputable firm of Blake, Dank, & Ingersoll, LLC. As I humbly remind *wergild*, days of Reject Fair press forward and since you have ceaselessly devoted your worthy energy to assemble courted artifact in devotion to memory of the Emperor, I hope my poor news will not fail to cheer you. I am prepared to offer this most notable addition to my own collection as afterthought to your most impressive display and will not hesitate to furnish means of securing its top.'" The stenographer stopped. The stylus retracted.

Kalamparumple often wondered whither the lost hours went, those times when he forgot to adjust his clock and, unbeknownst to him, if the nation shifted to night light, lunar, standard, or reconfigured universal time. If he had known in advance, theoretically the lost hour was always kept, often he still wondered. It was not as causal a topic as the chicken or the egg. It was more an apple, or an orange, like matter best left to empiricism. Haunted by a sense of vacuum, he continued. "'This trinket, best of my worries, is offered, my contribution to the upcoming exhibit.'" The nib scratched often and as a matter of course. "Stet." The nib restored previous sentiment.

Sergei rued, through his feckless meddling, a pax Americana won by his ancestors more than nine decades before now forfeit. He entered lists confident of being chosen to subdue the heart of darkness, for it alone, he only knew, must be the point of the entire fair. Lest his speedy reprise leave him residual bitterness, he could think of no better solution than to unleash it upon us all. How to translate it into action was his next problem. It was a tree fallen in the forest sort of dilemma. In future, all track of time lost beyond the power failure, Sergei noted that happiness lay in choosing a rotten borough from a precipice.

.   .   .

Hesitance Ferguson (she isn't type N, unlike her frozen sister Bitsy) is also present as in fly way, etc... Justine invited, but her participation in Village investigation (of obvioregal) must recuse here... mezzanine in reference 2Florian dies irae to end of act iii also allow description of Lilith's pickle ~ in edition to untenets, reference to new Nicean fifth strain ('zkeeperz') & the river (1 of CLASP?), and possible search beam.

IV — xiii — Affix ubiquitous synonyms for subjective verbs involving sense, et cetera...

This server polled itself at random with a generic access code. "The original designer used ninths to the ninths, for these energies cascade, and someone comes along and decided not to change it." "Dreadfully lax, I'm afraid." Some other passwords were quite obscure. "Does the keyboard germinate a magnetic pulse?"

"Tempest," Idres confirmed, "chips bio–optically encoded nowadays. Even a bit perishable." Noone ever looked at them, excepting maintenance, surge trackers, fixed interests with indirect radiance, aspect of careless ineptitude; emphatic in role, and so forth, fared upon this trellis terrace, a sure aisle inwardly lustier, to blink parlous diagrams.

"We have at worst eighty days to rewind," Justine said, for a mirror, couth Bitsy, Lilith importuned, should understand how events pined the bog art of plum serif to this original doorstop refrain. "We'd need a bio–optical de–coupler scan," the boffin replied. "So, coral bluer velvet tap, Worms led to industriously next house in bracken PoD." Naïf–led, treacly Titan refrained to eject, "ruse, usually dire, a trial must ban twill abode or get them more each live sagacity than have any thousandth ere a cooler none." "A thin mint," uttered Agostino Menard.

"Dada, if you keep sane than howsoever shall it be," Sangreal warmed, fetching nard whilst Ænselm studied large discs settled round them on either side of their weird mental prorogue; partial frappe in fabric cities' shelved WMDs set upon a greater textile flimsy field, spread atop a plateau behind which he settled, and encompassed similar discs just before his companions, Alcuin and the Menards, stir yet flee.

Jasmine, since Porphyry's screen saver had kicked in for dazed, subconscious elements, vastened a seedy tilt. They held at outlasted mold, shy formats, nor frames teetering upon them, oblivious, forgotten, his tool assembly including hammer, nails, objects, scissors, rock, paper, oasts, and a lathe of some sort, unless in remonstrance Heppleweis, styptically petitioned, their dozing march began inlets, eidetic knells of ovation which tulgey dovecote at closer view sedulously okayed.

By now, salad days of his eleemosynary office declined innocuously askance, Porphyry rehashed porous essence, passive surreptitious atavism, and stiffly stared as the crazy eighth clutter in this new old realm. Most craft mainly along aerial gin, joint are a shopworn image project bunch, their tirade shrift: in puckish sedulousity, these Niceans beaconed for privilege of recouping the worn ermine pouch, stuffed with daydream of frozen outliers, forage to laden kooks of mandrake.

Intuitively, Menard had shown little emotion during a search for the inkblot, and stamped their ease surreally whilst ciphers, to an address from whence, ere moreover due return postage astray, all cloyed regret attendant of this folly, Porphyry tinkering mindlessly aforesaid screen saver all morning; known, whilst nearby *uchaux* gave fewer than tuppence for their call, while organizational rivals already, *inter–regnum*, reshuffled distantly in throes of *wishram*, and soon, enough enow read, the shipment parsing zero tape, would floor repressed truth at any price.

Then to irk casual atrophy, throbbed beadily, marked from stock sixteen and one half inches, Alcuin added electricity, cut with the grain, and avoided marring firmament and telltale clatter of binding saws and fallen grips. There, beneath domes of psychic thrall opted boundless redolence thus. Shall an even internecine revival waive ingenuous upheaval, in improvised installment Fr. Anselm, often brazenly eke plainly, grounded quips meant for duped hosts who dissolutely impounded his older and hastier rede.

·   ·   ·

Albeit if not beyond one flight did he plan to yield, Alcuin's prefaced flavors further expired totally, and all he could now muster were a severe solace as probable, given the deranged ward of Ylferim, whom instantly recognizable, as PoD, arrived. Upon his doorstop, on a similar fugitive tether, allowance for dream sage past, they seek insistent accordions. Further from the ledge of a tableaux ere towers of crystal in center of the plateau were seven pillars of wax. "We must have been well rid of that float by now," Bustamente, "as long as that bailiff hadn't been watching us," said, since servitors entered bringing oval bowls of translucent material wrought upon which, over floral patterns of endless repetition, clouds escaped before exiting.

Sangreal sent bowlers amongst them and touched steam to the wax pillar. The eldest Menard (this isle, meant too to avoid gerund infinitive), went unheard for lack of an enclosed apparent thesis so ran, sped along pragmatically located realms, "bi'sifa muwaq–qata [*sic*] shall be even now wondering what sort of call shall we pay to him, eh? A social visit? Perhaps an apéritif in shade. Bon jornada no siesta para me." "Grand-pater, you may drop the accent now," his grand–niece argued from the uttermost mountains, where monads are nice in groups yet wax poetic individually. "Et tu," he tilted a fork at Jasmine, beneath scooped melange of tiny shining beads and thin tubules of organic material dribbled onto his disc, "if you're plucky they will plunk you into convent for three years or fewer, beyond whence thou shall be wheedled toward Ostrand."

Ænselm, studying ceramic patterns of distelfink fleur–de–lis, noted a stretch of nearly one meter to meet his disc. Half risen, he bent, slight, and paced both psalms around either slide of the bow. S/he knew some-thing went awry since his fingertip minted an urgent message of violation which overrode all other reconsideration. His palms felt very cold and *ahriman* had an inkling of passage. Then a bop of recognition exploded from this brain. The heated jolt passed down his elbow through his arm and he felt like a figurine became crackly porcelain. Transmuted into flesh, his shifted eyes to see companions gazing at him in grown alarm, fainéant, PoD freed his hand from the bowl. "Use the serving mitts, pato," Sangreal explained. Ænselm heard himself maximize a following claim: "When two objects are in contact, heat may pass from one object to some other by means of conduction."

"An intelligentsia is in our midst," exclaimed the eldest Bustamente. His hand, taken from him, soothed and swabbed in balm, lain with the rest of him in a dark room. Although they moved past many things, their ancient and preserved ersatz reversion into yearling owed its acumen to scanned particles of hereafter. Soaped on sconce I'd rhombus oryctologists dabbled upon calmly, prismatic singers wore ascots of outmoded sable, laudably doted on hogsheads of energized elderberry trail mix, tamped acorns into anhydrous algae, and bleep for funereal imagoes, focused on treacly improv jocosely towering near teak lenticular schwas.

Tersely, PoD pled that infra–indigo tanks, pretext pyroclastic hop scotch, feigned herbal throe of acclaim, ascend the basilica in verbose hat tricks; usually goggled at several budgies, their tense fixation heard, tictus [*sic*] tiered amphorae correlate in gypsum standpipes, endoscopically planning a sesquipedalian syncope. Their undersized echoes tainted terse kites on behalf of monotonous growth, integrally shunt tectonic fens eulogized in caustic ornate momento of autumnal oryza chakra cascaded dolefully down Antonine oblates, eyed dubiously by dinky safari guarantor, key stamina royalty exempted from Damoclean symbiosis in turn. A reframed foil podesta closed stacks to all further nimbus of esoteric furtivitude, harmonious in part since if Plair's plus prorogues are salvable, Sangreal the resident ledger, later sick of competition among armed populations, was angry with Justine for teaching her first grate band Nicean emigrant music, sending off her peerage to the holiest of hollies for antibiotic analysis, and sure as *finth* will play pool with Van Etnabaron, Azali's list of monads who should be barred from sports for excessive grunting on Simon Sez after concerted bartering paid off another nuncio to palindrome Etaoin's trail so pulpier guests might find interesting phylacteries in omniscient and sexist E–flat overtone, contrary to active knit Fourierian coterie which rated strained arias of borogrove fable, tout yucky if ubiquitous musical litany, effete synoptic gnomon, altered nativity scheme, sporadic satyagraha attuned to chalky mint periwinkle scowl.

Bitsy's frog pond, now resplendent, emblazoned entire whole I ching catalog at annual patchouli festival via apt stitched frangipani chanticler descendant into a personal faux cellophane far from bleached hayrack and reprised wainscot now said so many flat lines wherein this summer teammates' unknown steam ought impinge upon the United States' decision to invade Ossian were, if for a mass of pottage amiably not in step, somehow heterogeneous medieval jurisprudence reserved for next time he planned to stop on a dime for a cosmic widget, Raoul glowered at them, stirring, "you aren't going to catch them that day." PoD felt impelled to reply, "how am I more than only, if *all too busy* is so ignorant of truth?" "At least dress up the present tents," Raoul appended, adding, "you thought, therefore you were."

Overhead an errant snaily form flapped, singing, "ailerons up controlled but slow, ailerons level speed but lack stability, Noone will be glad to help us if you should let your ailerons splat." "Art not we insane, and doesn't shadow puppet need us as swells? He'd hide for all singers." "Albeit meant nevermore opal, were we all so keen about incense, weird, tall kinds," fobbed out prehensile tunes.

A figure intently crashed upon the sunny fellows myth, all aeons down. "Why, our mistier stevedore has arrived," Raoul exclaimed! Hugely eyed, the *untenet* yawned "H–O–W" on her didgeridoo and made emotional perpetratory flings. "We streamed about souls and anew contained methodic rest areas historically." "There well was a ghost in a bottle and I spent cab fare at the tracks, so those issues struck within linked only brass keys." "Speaking of straw men, that tale of the tub, was she lively?" "I thought I dried, since it was my dream." So hurried dis–obligatory and usual absorbent figments oft emancipated asserted we can get everything, whereas all you receive is whatever pickled upon the telly.

Raoul sifted impatiently. "Let me see that tent," he interpreted, grasping the *untenet*. "Nice cross stitch. We'll have plenty of today on

for restricting them." "Only if anyone is not all wet." *ahriman* dreamed
a marginal intermittent outlet net pulled up waterily might help fulfill
one's ticket to the starred lyceum, but an original *untenet* floundered
herein, pummeling like an inflected spring roll over a bandwagon steeply
pitched; the best pole filmed wore off triangular coded conformance to
street principals.

Seen their quarry release from the drift net, a frozen family of *chef
d'cabinet* elected, to cater real taste, sped off on the forgotten umbrella,
saying, "the only thing that doesn't have a life of its own is me anymore."
Oft sprung pseudonyms apply cheer up and sole PoD, while though
pursued, his shoes felt leaden, made by setback he ought, in seconds, recognize. If ever adept church mice could point him to the error of mien,
he ought believe himself apt to it, begging treatment, or a blueprint
of refreshed memorial on why, celibate claimant to innermost house
buried, the box shorted out rebellion of a nose to be respected later, for
Marta, Sangreal's god–mother, enjoined her to silence concerning the
name of their long barn.

"It takes time to outthink inward emanation," Señor Florian said,
"or else we might pledge a density of traffic pattern." The Village had to
disperse fertile lies tending to converge chosen for their relevance. Born
of extract of a defunct satellite, *ahriman* pinged as Ænselm on all station
revues follow cause of certain fruition of flowery beings. "Forebear,
aunties," he cried as descendants of compressed gauze industry made
flight of *untenets* plausible to shuffle. Backdrop to pour fever dreams,
Failsafe diehards etched their compulsory minimums upon hoarfrost of
a tortuous hippodrome, the Impersonal Terrace, topic of unspecified
rumour now, the resurfaced castaway never given into allowing the name
supplanted in on any respected block of formless aneurysm. In their
deposition, dialect snobs need not aptly in narrative estrange hindsight
over now rusty open qualm hegira gross feathers. Would some parallel
cue pools find large sesame fluid domes of lunar daybreak? Outlandish
epsilons were supposed to be all out of it, yet an event went on, *untenets*
exhibiting tumultuous success at Least, for a soufflé stood up when

airbags failed and all told propriety of the bloom to make an exceptional sound performance mocked the mass tuffet.

Truth, fully revered, concealed by his endocrine, stanchions rustled back and forth while drinking unofficially logged maple echoes of an aloe during the peppermint and unspectacular grind by reflex over limp parasols to stave endless drips from freon ductwork in spidery rafters, here fainted Z. Za'at, the famed pinnacle of her grand slam, overcome via vertigo amidst a triple Salchow. The balustrades were laced Fahrenheit shining plinths where barkers yelled latest odds, and if Zoyschia cared enow to scram obstructing a rule that it's not OK to skate while frozen, no commission held sway there: bribes and brickbats decided, most issue lurked and instructed, men's aid to them an essential caveat, outlasted utilitarianism operative during the final hour, that in summary goods were basis of our civilization, cultural, economy, and capital. All art an expansion of utilization here cherished, annexation to contravention an observant cliche that, unswerving fealty no longer as matter of principal now extant, all the same, at expense of an assured few, if fair short of a plainsong more than ten years ago, the womad, once darned on the day floor by defiant flagellants flushed reflectively after pronunciation of saturation, now on rather some commitment left in probability, thanked them amenably with immense if monotonous emphasis.

That all of a sudden, any plinth, based upon reasonable action oft evinced before owners of attics, the whet anticipate aptitude unless heralded loom semblance thereat, dialed on sufferance in manner of unseemly inequity, conceivably embraced eager action in estranged foreclosure yet, partially absent from temptation, proceeded to enact a parade of lift, Sr. Florian, unable to think of anything nice to say until the last minute, yet in thirst for civic involvement, threw on a sensible shirt and walked to catch the news this part of ionization, where waiting bred a madness of indecision.

The smells of national diversion soared as amphora censors intoned an impact of rapture out from thickened cause; synchronized penultimate motion caught an institute by surprise. "Sure, soar off to manna," he sneezed, reeking of contraindication. Freed of any simple formality, or any pitfall (think ouch, icy realism) forevermore, he witnessed the obnubliate quicken of an extended current mean, leavened for an omphaolic rule, and accessed in an appointment ruelessly kept, for if not all who knit wainscot of initial belief were foehned far from the place though posted, the oft mixed stratum of deific magnitude, known of those immeasurable periods of axiom when, corollaries ceased inception, tilted assonance taunted Finlay who drew from an inference, "tag along," he bid at them, though from apposite motive the guildmaster noted peculiar scenery and sought a straw today.

Eventually Lilith clipped a lingering lock, remarking all the while, "if tastes of no account vary it would behoove you, if you have the only article, onerous loath shall compass thine each step should you avoid restoration of thereat." "They had every opportunity to match or exceed the bid I offered," Francis broke in, causing a ton of sheer looks from her. Finished, the styler surreally gave her sculpted Finlay a prehensile wallop. Arisen from this crouch, the guildmaster watched while a man, now unknown to them, remarking, "if our fifteen minutes is up and cut short," left a thousand ticals in the jar of tips. Frank had a sudden emotion. As he set his face back, anew the sconces writhed.

A racket nigh; already glowering drones around rushed through his rinse, and blink out agave guava concentrate, perceived the establishment remolded in the time hinter. Lilith, visibly mature, guided Sergei to a chair, one step more and hell thawed, he thought for a moment (of Dolores his ex), and asked for reconciliation. In even maintenance of a well legend, the stylist foreshortened his clingy temporal in usual demur, a sign also precognitive of irregular perception.

In principle, she resolutely ordered removal of at least one bearing. "But Francis thou ought look so stamped upon," she grinned (at last their child Desdemona now returned via Albion), and as the guildmaster straggled to frame his text question, trimmed all. By not answering, Lilith confirmed Frank's untoward rout. While settling, the guildmaster stood up. The previous client languidly regarded sprays from the mercantile florist as if at a loss. Middleford started after Sergei. "Did you wish to purchase it?" Kalamparumple turned slowly, his hand concealed. "The *turec akabej*," the guildmaster persisted. Noted plaid clothespins on special, the man blandly replied he just sold one.

"If you are the seller, why are you here?" "I am not aware of my location," the reply, a gnarled gendarme, nudged into action, moved toward a call box nigh. "Walk this way," estranged reality precipitated, an elision the men walked this way, in consuming silence. What Frank added, "the *turec akabej*," he knew, was so hot snot he immediately shamed into whimpering the name yet again, if to rouse the seller into semblance of conspiracy. The orange barrel parade circumvented by way of Knightsbridge, the man out loud announced, "lo, I shipped it. When, way back, when the legendary last bee of equinox pollinates the shimmering solstice flower, a shadow will be driven from the sea. Where, I can't remember. Not to your precious guild."

Clear to the Ossian embassy, intrigue thrived under shadow of the coalition's hand slim picking. Unlit they had taken, a dive, a serious effort, materialized, glancing everywhere, Finlay noted treacherous gentry afoot. The seller walked calmly to the tube. In one instant, a nod debarked a flurry of patents, and these pursuers thwarted gave the guildmaster an intractably enigmatic hug and vanished like a clear conscience after the fifteenth snooze alarm. Embroidered, long until, among final current believers, scrabbled in kinked tea, were gone, Dauphine, one empty of fair unbelief in any tenet, to a degree so sundry yet all—encompassed, that plain tendency now should spare the guildmaster to avoid, forlornly, attainable norms of repartee, was of a type.

N to be exact, and thus so rare an equerry for those engagements of a universal serum conferring immunity to all developmental disease, St. Agnes vastened her stepfather, Francis, though disposed for her to remain (sourced, as it were, in one of his paler triumphs, a filched copy of the research control template), had, albeit in secret anxiety to coerce a sample from her, refuted unspoken resolve and, of a mind for her assent, decided against this, stepped away, and in reluctance to part his verve,

returned to the weir, attended by certain useful vision of super—abundance which sustained the ex—guildmaster.

For moments at a time, Middleford proceeded in some way his own
plan to impound *turec akabej* and, one week later signaled transfer of
twenty five hundred pound sterling, escaped into the sunny Shrovetide.
By even, he'd crossed Knightsbridge and wended into Bounceover when
two most favorable aspects of de—ontological ethic carried in an emotional nave. Fr. Anselm, the scariest, described a state of boredom, as this
debate with chance sapped him, fear, for sake of trembling, and terror, to
scale in pressed need, turned pages of an illuminated Kyrie Eliaison (sp),
and loathed as Triton, colloquial tribune, finally approached, fluffing,
"are you clockwise yet?"

A light squad of plain clothespin, emerged from one heavy bummer,
accosted Middleford and, flashing wands, barged into him with many
writs, reciting, "say the alphabet without vowels and in reverse order."
"Z, x, w, v —" the sacrist, trying to stay with us, began ascribing the
next lap. "T, s, r, q, p —" the guildmaster paused, sneering at their
mittamus. Typically atop of things, "n, m, l, k, j, g —" Fr. Anselm,
sitting in arcade to protect his lungs from dust that cluttered every pore,
corrected the siting of the spire, "k, h, g, f —" both of the arch modeled
in front of him and the vertiginous wind of scaffold around, behind, and
beyond but, as the scion of Tethys surfed on, the tide, deemed neap,
demanded a session of consciousness and, with, "d, c, b —" recessed.
"You left out the wye," Frank's interlocutor told him.

·   ·   ·

Presently adrift from sleep half refreshed, PoD, humble as dry noodle,
reeked. Connexion of recent slumber scuttled the compass· of his
weakened gaze, and thought, oft dark, marched off division to defy a
chord. An honest faint gone thin, the berm bent on amid shades that
greet a choice, creating these facets almost, Buddha—like, a blonde beat
hosed darker pearls, two '*zkeepers* broke the surface of the wave, forums

of another, unsung and yet not akin, swarm from seabed blithely and to awaiting ark at the edge of there.

Each of his loathed chest cars finding ruddy bumpers alongside his hip, the other beckoned across the wave and reached him first. In a gale, dangling, PoD kerplunked, and this dream boat receded. Twin stiff masts disappeared below the horizon, his other stream float, that punt upon whence the other post haste urged into swiftest motion, collected him unto our slight fun healing. "Why, aren't you," he gurgled, "Lilith, url–queen of *untenets?*" In reply, tunnels of light, collapsed all around into rushing matter, left them little time to stop the noses. The deluge, diverted into his lungs, threatened to become a third magnet, but where timid members home, PoD escaped, to surface, loosened his nose, and expelled enough firmament to gather his strobe wit behind him, emerged, clamoring, "are those the tanks I get for rescuing you from enclosed mesh?" Announced *untenets,* "she'll be one to show you the flyaway download."

Theoretically, a sped playbill tapped the apex of twine, completing a mission of reprise, and he would only watch, follow its course, out of dappled darkness of the river rinsed toward viaducts beyond memory. Awakened from a dream of badinage, *ahriman* recalled seven if not eight flights (or messages) from beyond mezzanine. All but the most recent, behind confine of *biathanatos*, things understood yet not always remembered verbatim, as would be a case were there an nth dimension. Yet reckoned without, the quark, a random oscillation of particle and sand, waved not more than merely necessary to append those arts thought best of hitherto angles prior to flight.

PoD retold his shame to the first warbling of their messenger, the eagle and the bustard, the kite and the merlin after its kind, and the ostrich, the owl, the first of three, the hoopoe, the hen, three larks, and the wren (Deut. 14: 12–18), aloft before him into space as piñons struggled into the great tendentious canvas polfed, by merest force of dream wind, into the life of Riley. An unguided fifth reported escape from the prompt padlocked barium comp; *ahriman*, dwelt in the third tier, put his arms through flues of a forgotten tent and flapped away, taking *untenet* with him. Noone was cognizant of the event; unlit, a brisk frisson however spattered some of the charier intimates from sleep, whose ministerales woke the most unknown known mix history of telecommunications really sure of what it was then, an entire panoply culpable of realizing short term profit only through systemic extortion graft remittance home subject to perpetual barrage of behavior which would persist. Even in an open container of sky and dazzle, radomes began elsewhere fastidious vigil to keep a scoop on this latest skedaddle, for already Alcuin as Minister of Transportation received censure for use of surplus aviation canvas in propagation of intense prisms.

In present realization of an unfulfillment since greater than his pain, returned in admission he was getting better, Ænselm, fumbling the spoon through a heavily plastered thumb to serve others, remembered they were talking about that float. "Why do you not wish to keep that float, Señor Agostino?" "Agostinœ. Bustamentemenard. Agostinœ is my given name. Agostinœ." "Why do you wish not to skip that float, Señor Agostinœ Bustamentenardö?" The grandfather felt a Brussels sprout roll down his neck and stood up, prepared to rise to his feet, bellowing the ghost out of the house via writ of zealous jade, if not gusts of righteous rage.

Menard's eyes fecklessly flicker, past his grand–niece, pasting in her inalienable right to a scrapbook an unanswered question, and sullenly enveloped in release, for youth, by his action of nursing bereft aha held, distracted the tempo rarely Justine, after time to think, coveted. Careless remark from Señor F., whose clandestine agreement with Roveretto that Meringues' dressage were despicably inhumane and unethical, to a small extant idle, sworn only near a heave into defunct noctambulism, *isomems*, about wheedling her to their Nastanto buoy, said. "That float has a whole knit, young man."

"I saw no mole," the youth contraindicated. "The mole is parched, for now," Bustamente assured Ænselm, who replied by chewing. He found that paella palette caused excessive active intake of mass quantity.

The nine of them were only in the cyclotron of wondering what became of the tenement. It also recognized anything else anon might flow in time to develop nine qualities, sparring, how seared, stealth ranged throughout this body. It also relived hymns of the burden. Soft spoken at whiles, he waited for furtive exaltation. "We will get a better float," the elder continued, clawing his pate plate fiercely. Jasmine spurned his gazebo as she took one tilt of liquid in her crystal tower. Ænselm did selfsame. A find agreeably astringent, this drained glass at his dark gulp, "ere thereat other paths to his mouse," PoD's went, idled? Bustamente askance, "I aid other esters," Sangreal replied. "It is not as clear from Terpsichore's Brow to the mudslide as is usual this time of nearby simmer."

In a ripely, rumpling roar often begone some inboard, signaler (*all too busy*) detected via *ædith* yon jetty, messengers bustled in thousandths felt Rex, gone of each worthy elder monad, entered, silent, handling Agostino Menard unfolded notes. Jasmine read, in uncrumpleable toner, ash, whispered to a smoother reply, the mouse *zkeeper'*, whom, sward exeunted, exclaimed *dan* il Fiume Paul'r'us all invited thereunto to diner. "And," Gus Menard, in addled air, treble frowned, "we are acceptable," Sangreal declaimed.

Menard declined, his life non–done while Ænselm, still chewing empathetically, gazed into space uninvited at a guest whom this, Sangreal told the Nawab Arda Min in frozen vinculum, if not for Nertz she would have been resident, saying, "bother all the light you wish can sift through your hand but it's what you can bleep ere brink of a whist, led when the stamp does cwm on, which is so coterminous a cross." All tableaux blown while the other one, of the flyaway, so unlike she and, yet not so non–unlikable, Lilith URL—queen of *untenets* between them interposed, as candles, s/he wore, a pleasant blouse and frame, her hair even beyond disclosure, Simic, whom we have to rescue the tent tunes act from WWI which should be a concern during future rain or shine in indigo snoods. Mellifluous scandal flame cast echoes upon her dark class, Jasmine, startled at the flare, attempted to come to terms via light, her untoward foil. "He doesn't even know the first letter of his name yet," s/he whined!

A jitterbug, seemingly pulled from islets by flickering flimflam, fluttered toward the wick. Too, fingers, hers, his, stretched to catch them, sparing it from immolation, and pinched. PoD felt the air left his lung. "Why bother known unknowns? Ohrmazd is diffuse. Hadn't that comprised an extent of your wish?" Shopping her foam finger, she pitched the chthonic caress into atonal tinny candle flame. This breadth resumed in torn gasps indifferently assertive. Initial aims of *ahriman* involved co–option of cryogenic facilities via *uchaux* and misfit little novel wiring machines localized around Worms, going dafter than Erewhon, their hitherto safe harbor devised, for the faithful (or Ohthereitis), and/or avoidance of conniption from several if any celestial objects. "A brave agenda," applauded url—Queen, "and in recognition of your kindness toward our species, one we ought not be unable to dislike upon short notice."

.   .   .

Before the morn sped by, Harold, contacted via Bagler, who'd said arrangements were made through Bustamentenard, admitted, "we are going to teach him one lesson," for whomsoever their *dan* invited to dinner left Van Etnabaron staring at the receiver. Wondering what part Ostrand had in the extremity of this insinuation, there are times in man's life when one believes one has failed to perceive every pattern woven from a series of event that should, to the near casual observer, appear to be wholly random. Disconnectedly, Sasha nattered about it all the livelong day, in recent expenditure of his verve upon this pet assignment, emanating a not unnatural wish to see it brought to conclusion.

The appearance of an intruder spelled an uncertainty that threw him back upon his most innate calculus. If it turned out that purposeful emotive transference of artifact to Matthieu had fallen to this upstart, Harold perhaps ought use the moment to beg release of further service from Paul'r'us. But unlit hue, fond truth, he was prey to gnawing uncertainty. Perhaps the evening should bring answer which might rejuvenate a sense of discovery. Van Etnabaron, meanwhile, determined to thrust the theft into insignificance, felt afternoons' many hours, dressed to blend the parvenu into fine powder. The hacienda receded while he drove, eftsoones, thither held in this filtered receipt led to his decision to try to return messages. Marta, production co–dependant, provided much inspiration for creation of video, soon to be realized, proclamant of il Fiume as *hogreeve* unto the Village.

In degrees of bemused detachment, to Marta Meringue alone had Harold confided his belief (they thus far followed refraction of their brilliant star to the letter), that betrayal of his innermost torment to admit, even inwardly, his resolve to be never first to publicly disavow Paul'r'us (his ostensibly rehearsed endorsement of rapport designed to be so ringing, yet so sympathetic to the addled condition of Ylferim, who would be forever regarded as a person of public interest). "You are so jejune." Sasha clucked, "it is a shadow title, one hare brained half scheme of a moldered Fourierist's ridiculous quilt offering." "Yes, bunny, but gilded guilt. This money moves mountains. And he has faith, a desire to serve, I find most dear." Harold announced back, a long luck, glib, vast relief, "we will try. But for now, from separate tables, we shall wish his fervent success, until tomorrow."

·   ·   ·

At some remove, seven smaller stars necessitated via mere inkling. Need character(s) for TBN to be named latter ~ his keynote, i.e. meeting of frozen (& non–frozen). These, displaced from Pleiades, EF2 enjoins gemstone being thus used. Henry (VII) prepares to invoke prototype ~ a debut reported by various Niceans 2b a cynical conduit, whereby avatars periodically relapse... link w/ & over–arching social critique of Læmært (reflective of jurors' deli)... PoD smuggled into present tents, potential schism between Bitsy & frozen colleagues.

IV — xiv — Stylistic Blocs of Inconsistency.

"Soon you've been debunked at best, *n'est ce–pas*," prompted url–Queen Lilith of *untenets*, jostling his elbow with a hybrid phalanx. "Get thee hence," Ænselm whimpered. The former recoiled several clear paces beyond Bustamente, whose unflappable peepers, or those of some adjunct, in recognizance of the bailiff, ogled them all the way to the jetty, already onto their niece, thin retention of ever augur to his lob evinced. This subsequent cue so, "no, no, Nanette," *ahriman*, forgotten, narrowly waded in after an anthem, yet so inured them to fog a chia as, "our problem," wailed? Sangreal, dropped out of closer sky, and with errant oracle the youngest Menard, Jasmine, filtered beyond curiosity, among like tours, yet here heard pled, "look to thine amah anon, chipper one."

Who, affirmed URL–queen, held the key. Typically, alternatives to heroic materialism elude many. If seemly fashion ably warred versus his penchant for the highway, Ostrand found reality attended in unfathomable scruple; since transfer of carrioccio away from the state cutter, lines of responsibility became ensnared in a request, dually compiled, for the nephew of Paul'r'us' to steer said packet toward Bustamente, a task performed in expectation something might tide them over. That rather dismal chimera, and the recent contract with Porphyry a verbal flop, paid scarcely per diem.

Yet, Ostrand had seen the float blithely returned to the village quay, closeted business with the registrar, attendance of that vile prince, and untoward favoritism before Ampersand's god–daughter, Sangreal. Speechless in foreboding, Ostrand viewed the encompassed prospect of the Reject Fair. "They're sending cold donuts into the lobby," Lilith touted at PoD as they filed beneath stenciled colonnades, and waiting for a lad to jump start the worst motor scooter ever immersed in the queasy sun of Midlothian, Ænselmorando Meringue hissed it was vermiform. "What is," grand–daughter of Menard importuned perkily?

"Jasmine," a voice, hailed heretofore behind the quiche bistro, Marta reckoning her grandiloquent father at the promenade, mutely content in hashing errand unknown to their erstwhile charge, and held council over lemonade. "*Il esta qui,*" a best nut, Menard murmured listless, lifted his head and grinned. "It is the videlicet," Jasmine whimpered back at PoD. "Which videlicet?" "The one Ylferim hired to reboot the system." "What a dark glass," gulped Ænselm, told he would meet more *fjulsfut* waiting for him, two '*zkeepers* to be exact, a remorseless specialty, too starry Praetorian fellows, whilhomes, leaned on at Calpurnia's Drive–in, defrauded *ahriman* feasibly and shouted reticently of many woes enacted with dryads.

.   .   .

"Do you spake Nicean," a quaint bobbin asked? PoD flexed back on video when shrill eruptions grumble, a klieg litany of problems in benign high school. Someone lolled on the strand dissolutely, pouring ketchup at them. For their creative sense, the elderly Bustamentenard scuttled to the mooring. "Thank you, Ostrand, for seeing us off. Take a nice dram of soma on the house." Now Ostrand thought he shed forever the conceit he was a good listener or anything, but a figurehead, installed by accident of tenure, charged mittens must be knit for several new guests, and this sudden requisition of keepsake material transposed all investigative power, the logical originator of the request already dead, the police entered the foyer as Inspector Læmært's foot struck a small object scheduled across a bare portion of the floor–through. The inspector's assistant watched the missile disappear above a heavy Rochelle sideboard.

Until Fulnes could speak of it, Læmært turned to receive a folder from the duty concierge. Under bright sunshine of a cold spring evening, the two men gazed at photographs of work of the gristly principal. How banally a sun, set via crested panes of Lichvue, to discover the stained brood, rote beneath darkest deeds of the treat behind, mute. Inspector Læmært, privately concerned five blood types were identified, yet only four decedents prescient, removed some seven hours ago, warned Fulnes to keep the door closed for a moment as he viewed debris, noted many cylinders below, and lurked into the fireplace.

Candles were knocked after a chandelier. Læmært directed a sharp glance at the ceiling. Whatever tall enough to perform this flat blue dawn at once also dodged a stable tulle. Fallen into stride, the inspector found refuge in forensic aspect, though he knew, eventually, or should need to find, how this investigation fastened upon him. "The manor has a typical allotment of locks," he mused, "unadjusted from outside, ergo, the chamber locks only from inside." "Right," Fulnes, folding his copy of *Punch*, studied a misplaced brocade.

"So try this on," Læmært hypothecated, "the hearth. Thought about old Gus Gristle." With a single knock, an assistant peered into the foyer. "Sire? We fooled around and found this pistol," as Fulnes grasped stock gingerly. The assistant continued, "magazine fed pewter clip with single port. Standard zH–57, Syzygy." An unpopular Xenonian make. If the bullet will not kill you, the percussion shall. "Have you dusted for blots," Læmært asked? "They'll run it through the trash to be sure." "That is just swell, perhaps," Læmært sighed tentatively, an indication a less experienced man must mistake for approval. Thus squarely excused, Sergeant Isp mentally reviewed basic ballistic recovery procedure. "Prints?" "Polling now." Fulnes returned the pistol to Isp.

Læmært mused, "the victims flashed off some shot in self–defence. Our man pins the bloke to the ceiling with one sort of tuning fork, per these notes along the side of the head, and bludgeons everyone, then calmly sat, possibly keeling under a sunspot wound, has a spot of tea, and crenellates the victim–like surgeon." Asked Sergeant Fulnes, "have you ever been in Euxine?" Læmært replied, "sturgeon head soup is one ghastly delicacy." "So you think the mingler is a mad *xenonian*," Fulnes conjectured. "Would not hurt to check," Læmært agreed. Finishing their cigarettes, the coolest heads got into a Midlothian coup and ploughed out of there.

"Must we begin searching for a wounded *xenonian* sweep?" A suppressed tic of annoyance, the inspectorial factotum played out, a standard motif of surfactant foil. "In consideration of the unfortunate persons subject to this aggregate non–placet." Refrainant columnist, Roveretto Messimo; perplexed heiress and skater, Vorga Ampersand; noted metaphysician and wellness guru Many Place, between terraces. Læmært continued, "Horace Tolstoy, who owned the house, above the spruced–up corporate name of Orphics, given to envision a resurgent Esparantonian parthenogenesis." "Seen often enough at parties of the lead chapter to be their considerable legal cupcake," Fulnes confirmed. Moreover, Ruthenian magnate Iraisamonde, Duchess of Syktyvkar, said to languish in coma, "little of others known, we looked for identification, registration papers, Rolodex, address books, and found nothing."

"All beyond one roof, it seemed," Fulnes commuted. "Those klatches," Læmært declared, "palmistry, reeling, writhing, hotlines, that sort of thing. The scrub lads have never kept them in before. Some of these character readings for Pete's sake!" The inspector yelped, swerving, between the center ere a badly driven moping at its own pace *'zkeeper* stepped off the swank and skated onto the incoming lane with a bored expression and ambiguous spice donkeys in its herd. It was a scene unworthy of relativity.

Thumping a pack of Gold Flake, Fulnes gazed into an encroaching mist. He handed one to the inspector. "They also like to, ere, thanks, predict outcomes of games and, perchance," Læmært resumed, "the killer lost a bundle at the track and came back for revenge." "Or his palm rubbed the wrong way," Fulnes tapped onto the short wave. Upon another end was a precinct abuzz. "Sir, they've got your witch." "Damn all," Læmært muttered, "bring him in."

Amidst weary idyll of traffic jam, Stopped–for–Shinings led out of Wimbledon. The inspector had a tragic diet letting. "Tell, that concierge, when we've finished — " Fulnes vastened, his eye, fell upon nasty, blighted, fiery scrapes of cinnabar paint along the retention wall, unsnarled traffic, and they bore forth at full speed " — the fellow we'll soon meet, Francis X. Middleford, president of National Anachronisms' Guild, doesn't take to being thereby referenced."

"There are distinctive preferences for their being addressed as healers," Fulnes volunteered. "Correction," Læmært affirmed since, wholly non–insensate to licit machination designed to procure his accession into a sanctuary of *wishram*, the King of the Romans stumbled throughout flexuous haunts of the clasp, indwelt upon more positive aspect of his self–abnegation. That fell beneath shuddery gasping bellows which sent all shades stumbling from the inferior yard, "a vizard," Henry (VII) hissed, "to place one ultra vires [*sic*] behind reach of all honest care," windy pegged dingus mellifluence Cecil plunked using an onyx mandolin, "juke me over their dude ranch lest bathos careen at archaic viaticum." Lent out petrels twanged above wavy tappets. Else balky scruples impinge near forever stuffier optimism, their train was not the glory train, this note, of dreadful brass mimicry, mustily careened about the tunnel, sought damp prey in waves of sounds that rippled and crackled of nightly decay, pursuing minds lent witless in fear of creatures sleeved covertly, fled albeit gone hope the note should lapse.

You'd hide from the expected reply of thunder that ought, bygone at most feral precedent, yet completely flagged not even their train, which ever approached nothing, stopped, and unless its inward carrier pawned, withal an oily gnash thereat, which twisted aside the thwarted hatch and slid out. Bid adieu to whatever diva misled enough to swerve this cursed locomotion, and his mess gathered, *th'ratwi'thorns* turned and saw you above glances itched of Mesolithic anemia, wondered loudly why your pathos brought him to regard you as well one may ever do so. Never since drab rancid eidolon lured imago away before beginner's luck had, between blank stairwell during sybaritic equanimity, "very mad things jut, hard wired to super–structure produced over eons, pleasant surcease from tenor of unmediated spackle," mourned Finlay, now cognizant of modus operandi of their erstwhile paramour, whose bruited topic of vague salacious import, as such shopped for new footwear, in hope her swain might refute these past–times, and Meringue, as shameless, for baying reeds snarled wistfully through clinks, snuffling at large in the yard for reusable material.

"Now, I will be snatching our float and — " the brute had pressing business. "To the best of our knowledge, you seem to forget arrangements often, lately." *ahriman* fondled the teal soft headrest, said to be unhinged and akimbo, thrust a bandwidth to single burst, lunged forward and threw his cot. The sportive Ostrand, whose stance imbalanced against the idle Menard, foisted vigorously and with a jiffy fell into this side of the ocean. He hopped amongst the piedmont, darning all ageist double dippers. "Embark," Sangreal urged, recovered first, and snapped the hawser free while PoD conducted the elder Meringue abroad, the spritzed strand submerged Ostrand as Justine gathered her felines and yanked the starter out.

Astern rotors sneezed into motion as the wavery figurine swam out beneath the paling and toward them. Ostrand's hand clasped the prow. *ahriman* snooped around the gunwale, found floppy forms and lifted out a small *untenet*, just hatched under the new moon. Ostrand floundered in spurious demise as the *untenet* whomped him on the other cheek, but dislodged his grasp only at treacle, lacking in vitiation from Jasmine's oar. Scowly, he waved, surfaced at the farthest finger of the jetty, and proclaimed to be back. Ænselm released the *untenet*. Soon into water it slank, formlessly sentient, a–tremble, moping, inept, until with flops that would have made a silverfish blush, it hove to and skipped into uttermost fathoms. They listened to the mating call of the mock turtle dove as Justine reeled them out of the cove and backed toward the roadstead.

. . .

Fulnes, peering into the courtyard below, whistled, "some parade." Læmært watched the Humber disgorge its captive. The commission ordered Middleford's detention in heavy handed flair and pomp. Above muffled hum of electronic typewriters in the foyer outside, risen voices of protest drew nearer. A brief shuffle, during which the doorknob sparkled several times, ended in entrance of an apologetic head of Tell, his svelte face sweating, "inspector, *ædith* tried to out–spoof me once, and insisted on, flew this time dossier from the barmy block!"

The reddened face of the concierge retracted, replaced by a co-opted florid form of a tall, mild man fixing both eyes upon their plaintive artifice. Silence permitted him to repeat, "I protest this harassment." "Chill, Frank," Læmært coaxed, "the inquisition ended ages ago." "Your antediluvian stereotype after our sacred venerable calling," Middleford added. "Ergo," Læmært said, "therefore, we are, a bit slow on the intake where it comes to this, your, calling. Apologies." Middleford raised a faintly penciled eyebrow. "A fellow named to oracular history." "Nor to you, measly," the ex–guildmaster spat in bitter remonstrance, "Horace Tolstoy, the charlatan. A poseur of basest stripe." "Then if I were to ask if you knew whether or not he was still dead," Læmært persisted?

"Inspector, if you're awaiting me to wax elegiac than you'll just accept my excuse." The guildmaster had arisen. Fulnes swiveled to contemplate Læmært stolidly. The Inspector leaned forward. Sensing this interlocutor tried not to impugn his profession, Middleford stared at him dully. "Horace ran almost all of the numbers," Læmært proclaimed, "thorough scraps in the op–eds. We starched the manor. The perpetrator must now have names and addresses of every, healer, in, Albion." Fulnes noticed Middleford paler than when he entered the room. All the same, if possible, master of his domain, Frank's shoulder shrugged defiantly. Læmært interjected, "then may we relish an anticipated mutual effort?"

"You shall have at it," Middleford, gathered folds of his cape, glowered at Læmært and, swept out of the room, the door slammed, typical sound eased for a moment outside until the far door closed, a reverberative thud, and Fulnes lurked, adding, "how could our mad *xenonian* have thrown all those records back up the chimney?" Læmært lit another cigarette. Fulnes upheld the jangling receiver, listened, said okay, and restored it. "Right," Læmært agreed, and lifted his jacket from the hook. "Only another thing," added Fulnes. "One of our bio—optic de—couplers is missing."

.   .   .

At Reject Fair, unfolded, a man, an early arrival, recalled at one point he dreamt of himself read, a loud poetry performance near the firewall. Paper shirts for one dollar each were valued behind shiny wrap. "Whoever can remember Nertz?" A plaintive quatrain ran, so you think you can safely cordon yourself by personally declared reality, dared their dearth of creed, tomorrow, a Brahmin, of a power wrath bed vetoed most likely to go to seed, heard of expectation, fluffy paper towels to wipe off grease from July fourth picnic, melted glance, excess a crowded room, white lace, promise, and children laugh oblivious of an even greener somewhere. Flambeaux opened observance for some dear departed character, including Charles Leaky, king of blush stipplers (re *fjulsfut*), peerless Chad, Lord Nesbit, Harmscliff—Northford, Marquis de Suppressant, who saw the Trombone society safe beyond another realm, shading events to fit perceptions, and/or Florian, in his assonant see of Ideopath [*sic*], a title retained only at cost of life on this plain, and a verse of Ecclesiastes (10:16), "woe to you, O land, whose king is a lad and whose princes feast in the morning." They were properly and carefully attentive. The tort inaugurated, "chaplain, we are chastened and grateful for merciful expectation of our lord."

The Monsignor looked up to behold Sasha's fixed and wily gaze. "There may be perhaps regard of each day as new." "A swift recourse has won you many moments of rest, your most monotonousness!" Sunk into insignificance, Bustamente wont to nod at much juncture, Harold's known opinion of a faith formed by postulants threatening hell to all dirty little boys who picked at their nose, "one's first sight of something expected but not variously arrived at, for instance," Sangreal's impression, previous pointed discussion of fescue on nearby cathedral ceilings ensuing after father Flambeaux, noted, until to the neighboring table, Paul'r'us in receipt of accolade, with fizzled cork, to new wine in old bottles, cellophane, claustrophobia, &c, in accustomed reply to this nearby tableaux, Ylferim drank too. "Deals may be struck anew, Hesiod." Unable to recall an Alexandrine quote in this hexameter, Ostrand snared into sibilant circles at the garden show.

"All wet," muttered Matthieu, shrugging at his better half, Esmeralda Fiume, who blinked, let it all drift back, to the Señora Meringue. "As you were for once new to me and are still every day," was how she read from the former flat so far as to climb the ivy path Agostinœ Bustamente turned, at listless regard, through whom here posed as author of this gruel cameo, Van Etnabaron, via Marta, who averted her glance oddly. Sam Bagler teased a loaf apart into halves. Thoroughly deserving of theme in the decision for whom it all gimlets would wax, to the mind of *il hogreeve i*, this councilor must take the trope he wanted even to hear Ænselm say, "I am, now," surprising to everyone. Harold turned toward it. "Please feel free to be still, for you were conceived in paradigm."

Tuned to the quest, fork posed, Van Etnabaron held forth. "This young man has, by all precedent, disestablished, at a rate of mental breakdown unknown to neology, any salvage claim." "Surreal," the *dan* scoffed, in private pallor at Harold's unwonted raillery. Since the elder Flambeaux, reminded to appear bemused, let himself drown in guffaw as Ostrand turned in his seat to regard PoD severely, *noli pati a scelestis opprimi*, the Monsignor's litany shushed the lads. "You must be appraised of my grateful effort to restrain my nephew." "A fancied sailor does not how often enough know the business end of irrelevance," her search timed out, Noone laughed as the *dan* twirled a garnish of parsley. "You will learn him a modest trade yet." Bustamente, his Tory class skipped (on one dare), had thus writs to own. Ostrand, wrought folded hands below the table, scowled along and carded Sangreal, carefully retracted a glance from La Esmeralda, redressed the positive aspect for some other lapse.

Dessert willed into being, Van Etnabaron leant nearer to stare into the ear of Ylferim. "Do we quit this claim," he whimpered? Matthieu glowered, for a consideration. PoD listed to a whooshing sound immanent behind the door of emergent servants. Bustamentenard started at a presumptive electronic bleep. Flambeaux had forgotten words. Bagler, awakened by a gruff snarl from Paul'r'us, hastened into his close. The dumb—waiter meekly departed, waving the snuff of silence of the desert, sure bet, tinkle of coldest green ice, micro—expectant music of some one who had best get on with the sentence.

To Harold's way of seeing things, Van Etnabaron thought the *dan* clapped falsely and far too briskly. "Masha, perchance you should awaken bursts of mentorship, and feel free too, and trim one freshly sniffed mimosa." Esmeralda, acted eagerly, swiftly, seized by this startled spoon—clutching, and the celibate grumpy Bustamenard, swept athwart the board, Sangreal, her chair kicked aside, directive glowering curtsy at Flambeaux, who withdrew his visibly withered knee—sneaking hand, *ahriman* lurked near Esmeralda. "My wife is unchaperoned," lisped the hint drooping *dan*. Jasmine caused a bow to strike plow hard flash s'mores, beckoned to each day a promise of fulfillment, yet given no sign even of this metaphor, Sasha was directed to detach. In a bark, Meringue complied, hovering for an anxious moment to listen to jazz. "Return to the ghats."

Crestfallen, Ostrand backed away. Lacking an element of uncertainty, PoD and Paul'r'us whirled along beyond thickets of darkest glasses, photographs stared at cups, and clocks, ticking in stillness of a drawn cheroot, recalled an old talent better than average. Through holier old scrolls ablated, three scholars wrestled for keys. They had three questions. "If, the road to hell is paved with good intention, then what is true of the road to non—hell?" Matthieu persisted in commencement, mentioning, while other petitioners pressed forth, impatient at the dawdled agenda, "in windows of many frequencies men with wherewithal produced entire audiences of satisfied clients."

"If, the wage of sin is death, then how ataxic are we?" Albeit many snack bars opened when the second scholar voiced this question, Ylferim

continued, in sightly slower address, "while nodding frequently at junc-
tures, wont to remind ourselves that, if we perhaps averted being clear long
enough to promote appearance of singular blessing, they appealed to be,
we at one time or another wanted an ability to win, in center of rapture,
an attentive peace unfolded on our every word." Within those billows, a
daguerreotype brought to mind one person frequently described in elan.

If in fact anything of the sort, il *dan* Fiume would have been first to
second a circulated motion; amidst associates in his own perceived circle
of influence, invented rumour, of his obsession with silver, permitted,
or at least purported to permit: a device allowed to berate individuals
closest, to him, as either these at liberty to move freely about him, or
those at liberty to be somewhere else. "Do I know where I am," Ænselm
replied? "You are the hidden imam, spirited away by Almighty Allah
during the sack of Karbala by troops of the Umayyad in 680." Matthieu
regarded the boy gracefully, for his appearance dismissed mankind for all
responsibility for what must soon transcend from mind to deed.

Past the empty circumference, closed at his order and guarded
by his deepest secret of stillness, the name of one other son Il Fiume
remembered that felt, to suit Henry (VII), no longer constrained to
interface illuminati, to exclusion of inbred structural catechism, his fresh
minted mind itched spiral syllogism, every spare gymkhana doddered
imperceptibly unlit, browbeaten wastrel overstayed lysergic egress, and
usually dune dilettante belonged in tabernacle, unless further option,
milled in *Decalogues*, actually recessive filibuster inculcated sundry pink
elephant unless diehard tachycardia wherever verbose *untenets* opted
to check their palindrome in goodwill, perceived as missing, fevered
into, far away Talitha, heralded of wine crash orb haiku, bearings dead
as pharos mix the lignite sward, whispered nail tore via the edge of
Freedomium, unequal to their endeared description. Brambles were her
path, his supper dust.

Matthieu drew, before closets of imparted shelves, articles of craft
held to be most predictable and least recent visited penchants. Suitable
topics descanted his occupation, albeit not so much as during greater times.

Iphgene Van Etnabaron had been a most decent visitor, contended herself to site two doors east. Finding this seethed silver left Paul 'r'us in a state of hopeful bliss, allowing him lien upon this dream for these last fleet days, he heaved a heavy hiss, marked to himself, assembly of old compound, much to remind them of his never missing art. Far from obviating his invested obligation as chair, this informal group of brought–togethers, self–stroked always so readily before through swims thick and thin, came to a selective conclusion they possessed an actual entity to alter the capacity of currency. History streamed propitiously and now non–avoidably beneath the bark of their collected focus, Meringue, in perception her friends reckoned, at odds with appearance, heretofore agreed, in prospectus offering many public declarations of support for Ostrand, il Fiume's erstwhile nephew, to become *il hogreeve ii*, Mayor for Global Village.

No stranger to stories circulated about his material fortune, an assize of stolid shareholders circumspect to actual, as well as thematic, leadership of the guys from rose tanks, near the ebb, arrival of PoD, was Ænselm, if probable in no way as his only son, nonetheless precisely the vessel of an immense eventuality. To appear as whatever need be required to ratify legitimacy of his cherished claim before eyes of all nations, il Fiume waved into the courtyard, where an ancient ash stood, its bark scarred by a near miss, and Norns bore files purged of mores: three, left italicized protean columnists, determinant rivals assembled their court, Hibernian witnessed to exchequer, wrap around the clock glasses sufficient toward the oncoming omen. Tedium unshared plunged the file into the lair of the chromatic tizzy who decreed the chapter stand as by word (noting no sample free page); also hard hit ere the fringe mostly peppered servitors, and they were in a nether realm.

Change Tents.

Plutons, hand tied in shekels via edict of Ensign Plair, yet unable to acquaint a living host to page bond for rapture of recent Florian's search for Core, is beginning to dither. The remnants propped athwart the magic carpet annex soon blend. This delay, gelatinous ooze that remained oppressive, lit upon Inspector Læmært and anon their sunk gauze mew indicated radioactivity. Watching gyres leap, Læmært reviewed his basophilic emitter, their essential desideratum, or tried, this biscuit toss averring aha coroner rhyme—in, ad hoc monotone hefted, a flap of one of the insulation tents. "Placental remain non—optimal." The serial connector cleared none of the bio—optic coupling de—synthesizers were missing.

"Do you maintain inventory of all bio—optic de—coupling synthesizers?" The inspector's froth forced the coroner to fall back up onto his tempo, Në, e.g., I. E., in gesture and single word, affirmed its presence at receptive inventory. "Do ye not inquire of transference officials or remark in fact not all bio—optic synthesizers are present this morning?" "Since then," the coroner switched dosimeter, "my saints sat for two members off the janitorial staff over their weekend," he chatted; eyed closely, "when the legendary last bee of equinox pollinates shimmering solstice flower, a shadow will be driven from the sea." This countersign gained attention. The shade of Thledvirrson had a grievance. The pearly gates had not been agape and her salutations there were ambiguous. What, next, Purgatory? Albeit her own belief never cheered on that concept, she thought they could be at least translucent about things, given her presence.

For this moment, transcendent, a third scholar, Dauphine, coached to promptly interject her question, lost a chance, attempted to diagram the previous sentence, forgot what she intended to ask, and ducked into her crib. Læmært, via his informal commerce digest, the shrill of the pager zapped, this bolt startled a squint at the beacon should Fulnes, stretched for his zone page, remember the sideboard at this inexact moment. Found above Paradise in perfunctory calm, checking all of her message with a sense of loss, Talitha missed her telephone. The inspector dialed the commissioner, who was at any rate hyperbolic. "Læmært, the ICC has sequestered the cause.

"They feel they have reference to deal with psychic phenomenon." "That is pleasant of them." "Inspector, you've had seventy—two hours.

Your report by agreement is to be released to Interpol in that time." "For this we faced resistance," insisted Paul'r'us. Sensing an address close to occlusion, petitioners paused. "We grasped, if enough people were able to buy enough time in order to be able to appear in front of enough groups of other people to describe a product so marvelous as enough time, then sure an event would soon commence." "Those haven't God's hire!" "A man teleported, and he'll have your report tomorrow or it'll be worth while to relieve you of your rant." "Well, can't you invoke constabulary privilege?" "From whence?" "The Great Seal of the Realm? Anglo–Saxon witangemot? Damn, won't even Magna Carta ring that bell?" The inspector bleeped off, Fulnes sniffling, "I wonder what tipped them off about the phenomena schtick?"

Rung, Middleford's contact, his ears pierced by the fax that concierge took with no known out, "Tell," he bellowed! "Tell, sir," replied Fulnes? "Just checking." Finis, i.e., he'd blown his song, Læmært looking at misused ink. It behooves there are twenty–four hours to find that scanner contact. "The culture ministry leads shall race to the tracks; round up janitorial staffs for a question." "I'll go," Læmært shrugged into his jacket. Perceiving his glare, the elder coroner, after weighing premise of whomever staged the event (given many seemed satisfied with an expectation of prized cash) made no effort to find out why it even happened, "*xenonian* chimney sweeps, sir," Fulnes asked, this fair event, then, a stage, infrequently lit; whereupon many, ere offered a chance, the goal of the keynote session essential, forasmuch as words, meant for purpose of beginning, yet forgotten by time, a method of describing it existed, became an ocean of unfathomable truth: personae in elimination tournament, bent to that most elusive hope, for their original belief, revival of themselves, individually, as processes of persuasion required either well–studied policies, or convinced evincement of absence of such mores were, while, at outset, cognizant of theme, salves being in separate camp, the stated goal, to acquire the least dubious prize, or however they were able to understand it as, had, in capturing their sight, subjectively vaulted to the top of a list of things to do which may have been irreconcilable beneath previously cherished tin beans. The inspector blared at this assistant, "start with the tops then."

.   .   .

Concurrently, Fulnes exited, the kicked key momentarily forgotten, since Læmært had another inkling, amending, "find Noone, mon," heed meandered heavily in an alto tone, Talitha, to deem often salvageable glory trains that shear over as wyvern, a thus least kept between thistles of long evening not thaumaturgent, these bells recalled tinkling in sunlit dells, stacks of harvest hard cider hayride, moonbeam, dry ice, the pumpernickel man showed you how to turn rock candy shards back to depot for recycling, the boiling glass lined kettle of hissing steam world sounded as owls so orange, eldritch, and woodsy at tuck in, times, she'd masked Hesitance who taught her to merge in shadow, so she learned a disowned gym for tiers after, to save her from all owls until she recognized she already died, and the elder hid other rife town wire wit to catch up on time, she listened to wind in hawthorns over tents, fast a full sleep and dreamt unless awake.

.   .   .

Consider use of ellipses for editing areas of nomenclature repeatedly before interjected subscriptions invaluably reapportion dialog... thematic linkage with Beatrix clarion recital, conflation of Nicean note cobbling Reject F. ~ a list of wares. Plutons vs pluperfectreß... intergalactic text... may Dolores, ne Mezzo, Lake (possibly frozen), be, or other obvioregal, enviable guest(s)? Their support essential if Rita Mirabeau hopes to retain privilege as Village Ladœñœ.

IV — xv — A Fresh Transparent Swarm.

A link has circled, at a glance, Elysium. There, usually bolted by decent ozone trim since, resistant to other blank chat, a stray sit–in sibilantly chuckled at their ashen frontispiece, "salaam, oh hemispheric posh dextrose drift." In blend spumoni via acrobat synergy, tab to form deviant nameless grace orator and, we'll find, pending addled thought, it forms an aloof terrain, the latest wonder storm zapped the raspberry corridor, from thence an intellectual torch, a fistful of hollow sputtering wand, unveiled Core's scared attentive band of youthful wavering Fichteans, and one rephrased desert owl elf being, Ostrand, who gazed at a snapshot of time, of an inception when he felt on top of all things; he so loved her and in proof, the bullet winged from the straightest shot he could ever imagine into his great love.

No steadier hand had he to duplicate this feat, and yet all unmindful of next day while, during an elation the flashbulb glared at seas of new faces with such foolish intensity, one eye bleared as if content of his iris seemed mingled void, wherein, a vague sheen reflected: one eye caught in awful clarity, a circular hole in his head as he sat there, so proud of the way he was handling things, wondering where was she, what had she been up to lately, and almost forgiven Talitha her wreck of his wrecker, the mixed trail draught, that imported much grand largesse via thorough thought, forgiven her so kindly for stopping; Sangreal, laundering why

Echo had not shown up nowadays, grimaced in agitation as she started in
sudden contrition of his polluted visage, and they knew Ostrand was not
dotard enough for her to simply yank the photograph from him.

Indeed, this should imprint indelibly some sublimated transference
until he was unimaginable. Ostrand sat thus evinced, deeds of a thousand
days poured onto him; all the other time attributable to someone else's
fault and now, sullenly reminded of his responsibility for every deed,
word, and act ever performed, an inescapable doom of impending age
wizened his feature ashily. Ostrand glanced vaguely as his *cousine* set out
for him an absinthe, yet now it was in extraneous context, its virtue
fogged in regressive mote, and the toggle slid from his grasp, he stood
up and exited the attic. "Darn, he now knew," Sangreal declared.

It was a phase and, wheezing how we'll fade to black, a sad drip
hoped the elder patch were beating the bound for us. Rather the note,
anew annulled itself to echoes, bawling in purposeless tocsin, a parenthetic protactic element, this inglorious train swallowed whole hope, its
derisive zonal whistle blast chased refrain into yawning mold lit luridly,
its flue emitted mickle glimmer of dry lightning seen only by those fey
lifeless oglers tweaked on ephemeral. Yet until you may protest your brain
already exploded, a temporary outflow of asinine sullenness robbing
th'ratwi'thorns of his sport, since you both just stood there, he rasped a
question at your lolling head, repeating for emphasis a name or else, taped
into our temple with a rusty nail until you saw yourself point blankly elsewhere. *th'ratwi'thorns* rummaged in his kit for caulk and grouted it onto
your head, flung a colloquial dark net over, and dragged you up the trashy
ravine and out of the tunnel, unlit you once more lived, "albeit if this
was living," he spelled, "you and your server will after all preserve vials,
hitherto certain incestuous dignity insert, and under this exorcism stank.

"Now prithee find an antidote and run out of the yard again," he laughed,
as ¶hrotomeous, cured of all that went in sanity, voicelessly fulfilled their
servers' behest to waken, in a steamer trunk, one more monad; striven to
find a date through three slippery schoolbooks as, tied to a standard glass
of tepid pear schnapps, Interstice was voted most innovative and promising

software of its time, a man, an early arrival, lurked at the dingy concrete floor. Reminded, though Chad once here rocked, no one appeared to give him a menu, friends cast wagers. "Witch hazel works best on door stops," volunteered the ensign. While the music stopped, everyone returned to their booth of origin. "I didn't mean to be a space Bogart," announced Idiopath, but departure of the scholars would reflect their varied interests.

Retuned, applicably Bitsy's sitar brunch is of antediluvian rote. Nicean worldview scare orders put in by neo–Platonic scholasticism, regal tinge in partial voice filter onto whim of a primordial conscious-ness. "I've liefer," said a not so neon surreal didactic *untenet*, "you'd sniffed niter pointlessly." "Given this emissivity ontological, we'll fend forth, children of Core," ran their entendre. "They've handed us the pink slop," the form ranted, dictating to an alas cylindrical menagerie.

.   .   .

A faint, antiseptic custom greeted the fairgoers. From wares their hosts expected to profit little, for what chance there were in persuading any other planet that, calculated extraction, via marketplace of whirled idyll, was in their inveterate interest. The hosts initialized a dull droll wave at a few hoaxed yodels. Vaulted to land on unavailing cheer, entreaty for a later ruse amply spun a once real wail, pliable in any grace. Ever a truer dust expectant from any applicant, significant contingents entered it with little, feyer than dogs on their laps, who were namably in Worms, where they found the process of going around in circles at the garden show to explain a few things about the messy elves to be shining in the best of all possible lights.

Be it ever so faint, honest stuff met hopes to hide all criticism across mere skewed land. For her part, Sylvia put in, "how dare we shop the progress of knowledge at the bottle return, wet mist?" Huge agave leaves realm to be plucked stereoscopically, dart to share ur–blooper and vaults just at us (defaultingly symbolic at unspoken shaka man of popular virtue), "stop carrying on as though you've passed some obtuse terse optic identical ritual," Sylvia's brother, Cliff, retorted. "We need your URL news peak." To those tarnished mental outfall the ensign flushed. "A big whirlpool pardon," Plair muttered, insinuated all thence flailed, a fluent reeking nose stretched toward their notices gathering dust behind glass in the fishbowl.

The Ampersands heartily moved while upline yet weren't getting cloth to each marketplace. A listing man, laboring to sell chimerical mists, Dr. Many Place of late once met their tirade in either treatise. On ocular dysfunctionalism as yet, one shied next, in other airs, seen to few loyal chapters with his one wee eye gong. Whatever difference made meretriciously responsible for a policy of remembering the hungry tykes hitherto referenced, the equinox found the ensign arrived alongside as *ædith*, while many of funniest twenty something duds and dudettes of the stolid geranium thumbed their way to the Reject Fair.

A precocious inability to recollect however endeared them, a basic tenet of Plair's fitful sophistry, prior to mechanism of ground last enough to matter, inculcated thereat one's convalescence during a crimson (the muse, sick of his ex coterie, could release her less dispensably), casual decade reprise, expunged from the congressional road trip, privily if in full expected endurance in unexceptional reason of experience from those nights of yearning mind, who put paid on his theory of acidity as an outgrowth of our dead saints via an average shock of outrance. Perpetuated by a read giant from Titian, who rolled up his last edition of *Picayune* and whapped *ædith* with his own macro—oeuvre, there were no dearth of some copy these days anyone might produce attributing solvency to a simple strategy of time block buying.

Thereafter Finlay's sitar seemed to plummet while attempting to download in recovery. This cusp beggared an adiabatic haste to reticulate the inter—relativity of market benefit. In response to the clarion diligent drone permeating disinterested counsel of the young and zestful, *ædith*, despondent in being gonged under the first ballot away from the Fair, found its rapprochement conducive in no way to his expectation. For almost uncharacteristic fitness, meant as intentional code of improvement, should leverage release of an macro oeuvre, far less inflective for its didactic ideology, than for a model of surreptitious tunneling soon threatening all organized art upon inner alarum, Ænselm clang to the talisman, a remnant of the Porcupine, but said nothing in pedantic stillness. Matthieu resumed, "we all have preference, I think, of what word we wish to believe pre—eminent, whether it be time, theory, calling, convention, appliance.

"They whom, few to so many concepts, ergo, clothed only innermost naive strength others whom, fenced in bravo hinge, before a lifetime of, what went out, to repress oneself, might wish to harness existence in fear of the null hypothesis." "That is your world, you of no shadow," the Niceans declared, while Ænselm sought his perpetual attendant which, now gone, held back, his impervious chagrin, PoD's defiance of optic; Matthieu, however observant of their law, "was no logic endemic to culture's tremoring threshold of decoy, while no barrier too, folk who wish to know the secret of your success," added sanctimoniously, "are concerned through other context." Paul 'r' us doused the transponder to a vernacular metier coeval with surf, extenuating an epistle toward the youth, who indicated he could keep it.

His tonality grown increasingly admonitory, during his cherished onsite triolet chant, the ensign, *ædith*, asked anon to reach formerly met representatives of all causes, must be truthful. Our fibrous thoroughfare may have optical affect always, an order to suspend techno—loggia ensued from whether their cherish vision of celestial cartography wound up with itself. Legibly uncertain instruction for jump starting the movable feast were found wadded in a duster of tinsel wrapping paper. Horace was the one person omnipresent who should ever be able to decipher the plaintive etching, yet unless his pen could slather up the unyielding slope, the following rules were implemented throughout their couscous: 1) we will always find pinochle rules in Hell; 2) we will not use smelly manners; 3) we will always desist from breaking off amidst our reading to offer tentative self—interpretation.

With two minutes left, il Fiume ransacked his desk in search of the mythical pan flute rightfully dissociate, but tonic tendrils of tenuous time leached light motes vapidly, dimly alluring if effervescent. As the sirens approached, the long missing scroll bounced out of his roll top desk and unfurled.

LOST REVELATION.

An evangelist awakened with a desire. Illuminated, a landward track from a cleft in sandy tunes washed a seer's stony stile, stamped upon a groove. Ænselm, disarmed by absence of his shadow, followed the *hogreeve* into the tangled ravine of scrub oak and madrone, and suddenly dispersed in the hugest and most wild beyond whichever, wee thickety foliage, devolved onto a deep chasm from whence all plight, effaced to make clear to everyone who'd hear word of the prophecy of this book: "if anyone adds to them, God shall add to him the plagues which are written in it."

A scribe, Empedocles, one eyebrow raised, swiftly pushed his stylus across the parched pad. "And if anyone," the old man mused, coughing, "if anyone takes away from the words of the book of this prophecy, God shall take away his part from the tree of life and from the holy city, of which are written in this book." Only upon uppermost cliffs did the solar disc hover as the path slumped into a stream of fireflies which Ænselm, recalling old edicts, hissed at fatuously. "Sire, what of that dream you quaked with?"

"What is up most mentally," the chef d'ouerve (*all too busy*), persistent, "if fain to exemplify how truant the willful seclusion proved inimitable to universal tranquility, I nonetheless bow to quality management principle intimated by my esteemed forensic and am tireless, eager, if not avid, to recuse its processional, furthermore propounding a scroll of worthy jurists capable of redeeming banner fallen from my jaded hand," and from it fell an incremental comprehensive *pluperfectreß* of likewise learned suitors unfurled and slinkily bounced downstairs until at some sound an engineer returned from the barista to discover the elevator music cleft in a perpetual digital stanza. "Has it no place in the revelation you speak of?"

Tripping the stylus athwart the album wordlessly, the old man glowered irritably. "Fat chance. It is irrelevant to the revelation. Heed again the warning of shadow puppet. If anyone shall add to this prophecy, let him be accused." Poised, the younger man glanced as the mystic resumed in dilatory fashion, "he who testifies to these things, that is our Lord Christ, says, 'verily, I come quickly.' Amen, amen, the grace of the lord be upon the saints, et cetera, et cetera, amen.

"It is finished. Seal it. One would think a grandson of Theophilus not so thick–headed." "I do your bidding, sire. Here is a nice cup of — " the coughing old man again stretched for the steaming kettle and inhaled deeply of vapor. Leaving the evangelist in shade of the promontory wall, Empedocles hastened the manuscript into his office.

Inside, three anchorites gazed frumiously as he hurried into their chamber. "Append, for diffusion, one copy each to the seven churches: Ephesus, Smyrna, Pergamum, Thyatira, Sardis, Philadelphia, Laodecia." Handing the morning's parchment to the steward, he blessed it away. Without future conversation, Empedocles reached his gutter. There behind a wash stand mirror was a personal copy. His mind clearly reviving events of the morning, he inscribed the following:

*In the air above Xenonia, Light and Darkness connected in
    perpetual space.*
*Then Prince of Darkness overthrew Prince Light and fell he to Earth and
    was adorned by Spirit*
But Prince of Darkness escaped and, loosed upon the Earth
*Then, Spirit, fearing this power would be disturbed, appeared before the
    Throne seeking authority*
*To wage war upon Prince of Darkness. And the Lamb granted this author-
    ity unto Spirit*
To wage war upon Prince of Darkness, so that Scripture might be fulfilled.

.   .   .

Empedocles booked a passing trireme to Thebes. Their library was the safest place he knew of. "Is it my future," asked PoD? The *dan* was silent for a time. "We were here first, beyond kings, beneath phæros, behind exchequers of the town, kept simultaneously spoiled on land for centuries." "You learned many things," Ænselm said.

"We learned to sell short. We learned to claw ours back bit by bit." The *dan* lifted an image from his portfolio full of news clips to the pub one chilly December morning, only to be told Tim was out of town. "Does all static anti–cling die enthroned," he shouted? "Many barks came out of storage. Call it active actualization," Paul'r'us yelled at his spice rack. "We termed hiccups against our dada. The *xenonians* stormed downtown for many nights. We brewed an irony. They ordained me to the precipice." In an instant Ænselm saw himself as crusader of some seventh seal. PoD had never before been in the same room with depth.

If known of in sense of abstract, a fact as fixed conception of what he, immortal, was not, *ahriman* never heretofore become affixed near death, among the luminous sorts of his being, a rare yet desirable, for as much as his kindred could yearn, accident, awakening power within Ænselm, dislodged, double–edged, for being now just gravitating anxiety, for their orbs, with potential impoverishment, toward (old hope, of disbelief, papers) irretrievably lost contact for another suggestion, no reservoir–deserted campus press amidst the word, PoD railed each limp limb, subject to sudden principalities whom recently he, co–adjunct to blight, should not have troubled himself to darn.

It need not have been disturbing but for a handicap of dark glass. Sat in, to the ire of one, if not more, of those hundredweight in desire, its return, Ænselm decided, to be seen sticking around here in this dark glass, was the least little thing he would like to be doing. Albeit in no mood to indicate great sorrow, that man beyond him, now dead, displayed some conformable favor by inviting them into this chamber, until assuming the condition that he was still in, PoD, addled, perhaps, another sandalwood dream to unravel encompassing uncertainty.

.   .   .

If it had been high noon for some time, throughout the realm whence the Inspector stood at his precinct desk, his pickets on the docks and East Side were unable to think of anything more trope. Læmært, his voice muffled by soundproof bands that kept this forest far inland, serving as redemption of reciprocity with respect to unaccustomed habits, missed minor crises teams hurriedly, mopped up everything at the Ministry of Clutter to find more of one Stonehenge ceremony not quite gone off. They admitted something about an unseemly corn dog (not shown up). Amidst the blamed reception, Læmært texted Fulnes to dibs, excepting the ministry to a foreseeable interim.

Now staring at the preliminary, where names of a single witness, purported in housekeeping, were badly smudged, the clerical staff more often than not noticed it, how the name of the investigative officer was effaced from the report. "Well, perhaps he was the sort who filled in his name at the end," the clerk volunteered as Læmært pitied his gain. The time was still noon. Middleford was online.

"Inspector, quite jolly of you to fax me a warrant. In my own defence, I must apologize for not leaving comprehensive instructions." "Instruct this," Læmært stepped away from the desk, bristling to split and reapportion dialog. "Amid utmost despondence, you found my co—operation wanting," Frank resumed, "and I'd entertained such hope in being of assistance." The Inspector suggested, "I mean to infer you have everything to do with that missing bio—optic scanner."

Frank meant to infer indeed he had naught. Læmært, outstanding by his secret troupe, caught on to a win—win effort, dispelling in effect whatever doubt or hesitation he'd ever brought family, or had, in taking the airline if he knew the roads were so jammed, over plans through Memorial Day to offer help with *chichi*. Left beside falafel smithereens, he added, "one is missing." "Souvenirs," Middleford chuckled, mentioning aloud it explained why Ingersoll, insurance commissar, had been so feisty. The Inspector, as charmed, stage—tried the coupe and, switched to squeaker phone, "forsooth," Frank explaining, "a certain clerical error sure cannot be laid exclusively at your doorstep."

The Inspector, though a raving guru, doubted this robot threw coffee to a tin orca. The healer, lamenting his lost vocation, replied, "splendid, pure downer." Læmært interjected, "where are you?" "Why, Inspector, I am in my field, reporting, a private citizen, dedicated to unquestioned co–operation with all authority." "You are an at–large fugitive," the Inspector stated. His listener gave up an maudlin yawn of sufferance. "Lo, if you would like time to tidy ledgers, may I ask" — "and just what is your connection within their pool?" In any minute, their minimal broken record fizzled on purpose, whispered cribs mixed timeless chasm of eternity, for hours a senseless wavelength tapped in microcosm, the omega bang titillated the bandwidth, a non–born woofer Brownian sullenly vouched dark energy throughout the galaxy a near certain vehemence during the two minute warning.

Everyone else outside lurked at the peony petunia gardenia geranium chrysanthemum dahlia flower show at halftime finding ways to give them shopping lists. Meddlesome, yet, an entire dark period remained unsnapped by any simulacrum of intelligent life. il Fiume's shelves, crammed with mini–series tried on, the cutting room floor, staircases to nowhere, and canceled subscriptions for anticipated municipal bond note, had minute eighths to get out of there, unless Uranus blew up readily, spewing photogenic radiation throughout the entire funhouse. "Go long and check for a misled steeplechase," the caste LAN heard to gasp, chafed with much laggard sapping in the foreground; yet eke endemic a glancing sortie must confound the idle foe, civil conscription, ere uncurbed, fierce cotters who'd long itch to unseat privilege of any guise. Unbeknownst to atonal lay men though, the Romans affixed pha-lanxes of smoke detectors in echelon to their sally port, and emergent revanchistes were mulched en passant.

Beneath a pale sock, the sacrist, via leeches used to dredging oasis fact, fit into dubious refuge, interval used by the siege to embed diptychs of such omni–directional cacophony baffled stalwarts dithered in hesitant wise. Partly, ere fair greensward before Worms striated in labyrinthine hive, than toward the mall shoved three great engines:

foremost, marked Any–Day–these–are–hot; it hovered through wee elm palisades plethoras of child fan camp sitar scene and soon defenders scurried to their insane coffee spot to re–true unwonted proscription. Next, Yon–farthing–vole, huge flung buttresses athwart the moat for egress of myrmidons, clad in creaky hauberk, which swept the rampant breviary; within, disparate, strident leaf blowing, the defence turned on neither flank, Henry (VII) signaled for onset of a gargantuan mime, ¶hrotomeous, whose protuberance, swathed in polished bronze, dazzled the lookout with scintillating shards of sun quake upon which all darts feebly ricocheted within its craw, harbored, a great mine of arsenic, phosphorus, guano, and custard, for the besieged vowed to confound their dual purpose of ever breaching the prospective tort permanganate in concurrent production of rubble sufficient for sealant of imagined eldritch portal said to lay beyond.

Now that castellano summoned ill–formed lemurs with mattocks who scarce withstood relentless advance, and nearby the keep few arranged unflushed *uchaux*, immune in their hop–along Ray–ban, to the blend, harried their foe in hellish impersonation, yet witans already scribbled off defence o'Worms as lost cause, and troubadours via tuning forks perused the pitch what gaily tragic tale ought best enshrine. Evening skies reel with starch of bummed fiscal trial, crackling her knuckles to the tune of *Me and My Shadow*, *pluperfectreß* decided to live a little, readily today's mood, surfed onward casually; tepid jams clashed masking minuets in non–communal flock, Core's children materially blah demanded virtual juncture since foment at last apart, and insularly murky graduated metempsychosis, junior atavism ornamented much xenon strand and, filling check variable, tonnes of inkling eased under, ubiquitous via glassy horizon, unless wry blase ushers bent upon severe joy thatched the slangy pompous exudation via small variorum. "I hear however," they cried at calamity, a flimflam of taut forum in–service flooped right after the backwash of all Time, whose name was thrown at kites. Because few honor a pact up in fear, texting fixed bobbins' work catalog escapade, the Inspector listened, as the opposite voice, grown strangely familiar, indicated a desire to take a bite out of crime. "Might there be a specific instance in mind," Læmært asked? "The theft of a private shipment through customs."

"That likely isn't a matter for MI–5," Læmært replied. "If you should peer into it, surely, I will cooperate with you in the Tolstoy case," Frank, so saying, sat beneath a large grand piano gazebo. Out unto stunning winter sun, via hedge, amidst carved statuary, light and shadow fluttered. Voices approaching, the Inspector's reply came through the line, that broke on one gusty tuba motif. "No deal. And stop calling me surely." Silently staring in bright dismay, the ex–guildmaster sat, holding his breath as one may an asp, in review of recent result. After all, a morning of mixed event. So dry Althea conformed somehow, guessing Prince O'Darkness, unlike her, issued terebinth out of a Janus gate. For they diagnosed a tentative jangling and it not an unripe loofah that was limey spackle; *ahriman* felt more able to heave that soul float, a fresher soft–shoe snooker snored. "Ohm," the first bobbin said, retching to her kachina and feeling in a dhow, "it's hot!"

To her relief, he was a fiend whose strained quarry, their scandalous bleak fast, insistently paced to and fro, briefly sitting on the floor by some mysterious birthstones. "Swell," Althea said, for she was a toy maker and — PoD meant to say she seems awful young to be a toy maker and therefore must be a muse, but the soil degenerated, and he dismembered a sham, whence Lothar's dimly polished rowdier parade made her sage stare, slack to maintain the fiction Frank ought be convinced. What justice could be served in recovering a starfish, a property matter pure and simple? As benign, much sound dialog, and other lay terms included Ingersoll, Blake, & Dank.

.   .   .

Læmært looked up his reflection on that server. One energy duffel helper viewed an airy inclination to pick the morning light and feed the matter up to Plyntymyny, if not Mini–clutter. As soon as the ex–guildmaster arrived, Læmært beheld a capped figure, masked in flickering shadows, which said, "I am at your service." Rarely surprised, the Inspector studied the disassembled plastic toy, the package, its arrival thence, and listened to a description of the missing time. "What was your purpose for obtaining this trek bash?"

"The *turec akabej*," Middleford corrected, "was a gift." "Alright," Læmært shrugged, "for whom?" "For friends, collectors, most likely," Frank granted, proffering the empty package. "The box made in Hastings, AZ. You see the brocade traced to a corrugated cardboard consortium. If theft took place overnight, it's none of my concern." Not to raise a flap through customs, Middleford said, "I will answer your question." "Then I will ask none," the Inspector, feeling strangely clover, savored bitter fruit of barley.

"Only I did not kill Tolstoy," Middleford declared. "Stated more plainly," the Inspector wondered, "where is it?" "I cannot answer that," Frank replied, "unless your connection to iBC is cloaked." Læmært, struck by *inter–regnum*, did not recognize it left in conference mode. Per severe connection, time allowed Frank to formulate a proposal: "I have technical skill, in material concern; your commissioner, with whom I have no quarrel, wishes the full apparatus of the ICC to devolve upon it."

"So *wergild* wants a favor," the Inspector surmised, "and by the way, he's Noone's commissioner. I have full Village authorization covering all aspect of this carapace." Middleford digested this mittamus pessimistically. "*Oryza sativa*," Frank murmured. He soon hoped to have social validity. "Again, please," Læmært yawned, regarding the cellophane wrapper. "I am iBC. Inboard comps," Frank added, "the board, of, internet comptrollers. Neutrality rules." The inspector regarded him in superfluous departure, a weekend to be endured.

"*Quot homines —*," Middleford urged. Læmært blinked as he listened to the commissioner. "Frank's here," he said, blinking again as the line went dead. Læmært replied by driving the guildmaster to the silent morgue, wondering of the location of Fulnes. Hereupon Frank added, "you may obtain manifests from Mini–clutter." "You will meet Silas F.,"

Læmært concluded, thinking if that scam had taken place in Albion, those might reveal it. The customs monad, met in public fashion, should precede the mess of official circle. Keeping the ICC, CIC, ICA, &c., out of it was one interest shared by them, albeit for different reason, of course.

Pleonastic hairnet donned, Middleford (in glum realization the exchequer bought out his swatches of them at one groat to the hundredweight), saw unsealing of the Lichvue remnants, and heard report with ginger town rites. For instance, it was real thin ectoplasm, unlike the fake cafeteria vomit pawned off so often upon credulous board members of *wergild*. As he gazed onto brilliantine remnants of gel, Rex was startled at recollection of his daughter's disdainful episodes, grumbling, "they must be part of a greater tapestry," and also, his description of Vorga's work as "polished," and, "professional," drawn, from her rejoinder, "I only do this for a living," which she had so quickly disavowed in death. Rex's chastened desire to dial it down next time indicative of growth, Læmært asked the coroner to give them a moment, and let some meager guitar frets roll the manger away, and mincingly hop to El Dorado, where Isadora wandered in a slight brilliance. PoD grouped his souls and dispersed them in reef spas. Vorga's Spandex sphinx, too direct Artesian from knees to calf, admitted Althea, a night jam—stand Prada skirt at such an acute line, that sprinkled her baby's breath with hassling mold at Terpsichore's Brow.

"Don't you know about Vikram, *per se*, or dry ice," Althea asked. The greedy kites recycled an undead fern hit, whose *chichi* — "ahhh, a really cold second is dawdling solo" — PoD exited the service bay to calumny. His sensible dash for toner over, *ahriman* gave up to a merry copse of quite nervy bobbins. "Ciao," blurted Etaoin, banally noting how unpaid loafers milled noisily dizzy eddies crammed into submission. Igneous chorus scolded poor *ahriman* fiercely, whose sparsely nudged proof but deleterious to any goodness, plenary, comatose worn hypnotized dapper lorgnette affably, mute his fescue of realm told wireless, and if not for baggier nasal imago tippled the palmer's choleric aim trifecta, near drab whitewash mellifluously trope. All hands shrank at much fraught banter, flak during myriad setpiece, raspy flummery leaving systemic guttersnipe to contain the foray.

Throughout the bacilli pound our tetra–pod rafted, e.g., vain pluperfect volley float intent on usufruct quorum, yet the latter finagled refulgent vast infusion of varicosity. Unlit her prey hurled spasms a–jingle via placid miasma, its retreat masquerade in churning raiment. Monumentally balked, *pluperfectreß* unfolded her travel guide sedulously, finis coronat opus [*sic*] quipped, upon a wary roustabout emerged from behind the digester, wiping his nose on his bib to gawk at interlopers. Rankled by caste, *pluperfectreß* added, "tell your ilk that sooner I flush this fetid leviathan from the gulch, more ameliorative will irksome eidetic collateral accrue to your way off life."

Tossing a codpiece of base coin as the denizen fletched away, *pluperfectreß* dexterously refolded the map and scowled. At environs, forsooth she'd yank the lanyard, cogitated until bogus construct scuppered, yet constrained in onerous stipulation to ransack all aqueducts stringently, she edgily scanned each flange with a divine rod, murmuring frugally in lull of a gerund swarm galore.

.   .   .

A small stroll in purgatory cwm wishram ~ albeit Ælfric's junket yanked by Sangreal in favor of ahriman, latter's patent nemesis, jihad, bests redirect reference to SOMHAD (Nicean faction). Frank suspect of thwarting arrangement with wergild (doctrine of affectations), interpolated inference as possible conflation of planet Titan with mythical deities, relative seconds, euryoclydon jubjub cormorant.

IV — xvi — Parthenogenesis.

Voted most likely to engage in invidious criticism, Ingersoll, Blank, and Dake left the building at disparate interval. Boxes of chocolate left purposefully incandescent, one original participant, Jasmine, believed herself easily capable, by virtue of her nominal capacity, of sauntering away with main honors. A sense of physiological sharpening occasioned by trendy iced cafes—pouissant he now drank, the rat, Kalamparumple, considered things to which he was reduced, his winning of yet another mystery card safari to central Africa (in case Vorga might have worn again her zebra tog of yesterday), left knowing off the residue of his previous fanfare.

Activating a desire to place at least good tomes, known how part of this doodling funded telepathy destined at length to power the joy of friendship, and sensed functionally, detected inertia other men considering theme sleeves of immense value to betterment of humanity, once, thought to win via wit (and not just anyone, but especially those, where it bowled up, to seven to ten PM prime time look—alike sects, for their own art installed in each of them, indifferently brisk, and a source of frequent disappointment to themselves); they clouded their brow in lofty boughs, regarded themselves born in the wrong century, and, dressed as emperor, genially assumed fainéant expression of great forbearance.

"If," they thought, "those calling themselves chosen put some bells on outside once in a while perhaps this world would be a better place." That reminded someone to shop for their thirteenth university. Others, however they were, formed fewer eccentric opinions of these elves. The storm tracked sky subsided for a session. The moon, beloved Cynthia, glided upon altocumulus terraces beneath her gaze. The night land afforded brief glimpse of leery shadow nestled in mild repose.

The stormy Caspian evening resigned, those lacy fiesta gleams rumbled, on sightly, here or there just aren't enough brain cells, for the next go—round his CD changer imploded distant patches of splashy moonlit waving activism, Rumsford, escaped to the Reject Fair, deemed upon the still evening, that promised return to placidity, his career, to this point moreover dwindled, under booked these garden salad shades, "faithful trust, sage though silent dumb servants of commerce."

"We are gladdened thou knew mimes so apt to be principled." From portals behind them, a draught of sound and light heralded company he scarce desired, depleted here instinct of light, via waved *finth* whimperer, a reply, "but in your pitiless grip wert thou near both taken when we, poor stupid beans in air quote, though seeing your obstruction should consign us to oblivion, knew not where to let up." Inside corridors, Rex paused at the door to his loom and could therein have fain gone, but wrenching sound from the door apposite caused resumption of his casual stroll further down the corridor. Beneath pretext of diligent study of a pastoral watercolor, Rex Ampersand, who had been indwelt for months, if not years, fought a growing wave of enthusiasm drained from drifting reliance upon subtle hints, and shades will further obtain closure and take a hill of beans inflecting PoD, hitherto a prodigious protege representative of excessive unintelligibility.

In definite formalism, it solved how Ampersand acknowledged this putative pupil, since to his mind nowhere had their poison grown fewer tuppence than in the wholly unabsolved death of his daughter Vorga. His sheet of paper established, any principal, beyond those few purporting super—annuated talent, succeeded in recognition of Ænselm, *per se*, in all feckless vacancy of callow innocence, the lad emoted through series of situation, resigned to antithesis of solicitude, somnambulantly unaware of effort to restore any balance upset by his fall on Earth.

In virtual risk of internal anonymity, even as the Lichvue investigation boiled over, Ampersand began reading the kites which, by their very insensibility, presented a source of concern to individuals, so drawn by Ænselm's physical presence into confirmation of his personification into all unrecognized potential. And since Rex left Læmært's office a previous night with disconcerting information, any impossibility of missing record allowed Francis, in his role of fiduciary investigator for ICC, to coerce an interest in development. The case successfully flushed, any insurance commissar yielded to his opportunism, and also agitating Læmært for an instant, the ex–guildmaster, though his aim may have flared, his casual mention of the polls, albeit in knowledge this red flag, per stuffily lipped wish–they–once–were mores, garnered encrusted barnacles in the final expanse.

Remnant to *inter–regnum*, whomever else might be forgiven for possessing incumbent desire to instruct PoD in realty, the minister of transport Alcuin gleaned from this vapid wabe that prince, if otherwise dully placid, was actively skittish toward typical manners of approach used by persons hoping to supplant wisdom, and already used his depth stare once thus far; if in the event via such hesitance, and now languished in a state of comparative, active scruple, aversely aware of humanity's subsequent agitation. In foreboding, *ahriman* fumed, as they stormed back into the Sunrise Cage, "are you scared about fitting in?" At 4PM instead of ten, though perhaps no small bag of marbles recycled by tossing them as catharsis or, in lieu of reinforcement, most topics on word rearrangement were jarring, whilst Marta rolled the Country Squire gently into a thickety cleft.

·   ·   ·

Van Etnabaron, anticipating this day at full length, dwelt upon pleasant prospect in passage, reviewing all his pre–conceived environmental notion, his expectation thus for an earnest rugged repair upon some lone hotel piling, gulls overhead, a season of solemn awakening, shared confidence, polarity, just the two of them, followed by a brisk walk at dawn upon some distant jetty. A deputation of *uchaux* railed to clamor beyond illicit scope of the infernal mittamus. How they riddled the musty surf while those prima donnas abused this palmer's tentative easement.

Their flippant peregrination sundered feng shui [*sic*] indispensable to dendriform mold, and rather would I beg misnomer of a *tictus* than rate much noxious shrift from these luminous rejects who each impugn PoD in their corporate might, honest divestment these extraneous fairs of their casus belli, and consign the sprat to the black hole or their name wasn't what they'd been trying to tag on from the get go; dustbins of apocrypha combed for writ of habeas corpus, they abjured the circuit podesta for a prima facie discontinuance, *pluperfectreß* descried. Their petition scurrilous, "far be it from we to traipse upon such cherished statute.

"Let's not divert the clerics from their earnest deliberation on erstwhile pressing matters as amending the fourth paragraph of the first section of the second article from 'no person' to 'any person' in interest of inclusive polity, and forego a modus vivendi for fixation of tempus fugit." Moreover, Middleford, no longer enamored of his own inference to souvenirs as example of discretion, saw to it all right that guarantee of the public's interest in a matter troubling to him, the heist of *turec akabej*, but not without concern, for ought a price above bond be forthcoming, restless enough before the troop of acolyte, the beginning of his morning circle, now regarding Frank.

Admittedly, as they gathered to stir enough situational parameter in necessitating switched topics beyond the hitherto explicable difference in faith or far between fewer semaphores, drapes of his composure, that morning call to the police dialed knowing of little other slack to play (that Læmært had been fuming about a missing bio–optic de–coupler was opportunity, not unforeseen, whence Frank, deplored for his lack of parlance, muffled). On a lesser hand its meaning was preserved, which is a good rejoinder, much less an alcove; capably collect there, Meringue told the logistic maelstrom to sink them deeper, it cast dancing shadows upon a frost of twinkling beauty all about hoar spammers who witted instead, turquoise, onyx, vermilion oblongs lurched and clutched at them. They were never inured from the spirit of entrainment ever far. "From there, there, men," total Sylvia spoke, "we have reached the backwater of Eternity. Who is sundry?"

"I am not undry," a sad drip insisted. "Normally we," said godless *untenets*, "bleat with shame until feelings of general fulfillment ensue," and others nodded nothing good. "It's unsettled, and we will expire unless," interposed, "non—earthling an expression of interval in these nether parts" — "unless," applauded Hesitance, "all of us heave in perchance in altogether the crystal ball." Offices of the Guild just received a parcel, discharging the contents, now scattered upon his desk, disassembled, the styrophene limbs of coral, aquamarine, and hazard yellow comprising, once fully constructed, an amusing toy familiar to all children of the fifties.

"Verily, those gaffers thematically flung tame wet hens *und so weider*," Cyane concluded, "they wander the susurration's pools of time endlessly, until it is said one night, they will finally find the merrily color shoe tree in the altogether crystal ball room, at which point the universe will be re—booted." The expected item, *turec akabej*, handcrafted meso—Phoenician amber scarab depicting the mantis king, beloved scourge of the locusts which nearly prevented thriving ancient cultures of the Nearer East from completing their transition from hunter—gatherer to agrarian societies, was missing.

Dated at some nine thousand years, its antiquity offered in pawn to Middleford's nominal superior, *wergild*, the International Clairvoyance Committee, an informal arrangement of individuals interested in investigating and researching psychic phenomenon, *turec akabej* had been the ultimate bribe. Its acceptance, by *wergild* already, to women or men infested by his skillful indistinct yearlings, should allow him sensation to coast past the ICC comptroller, thereby gaining one of seven seats to the iBC.

Incensed by substitution of this coterie, the ex—guildmaster thought someone anticipated his maneuver, intercepted the post, and now deluded him. The rougher the night, the more probabilities. Ticked off, an operative in the U.S. perchance seized the scarab. It may have been that collector, Kalamparumple, an uncertain fellow, complicated these matters. Unless Francis, assured trans—substantiation also originated from this locale, could dream on to order his district coordinators (if any remained) to close on neither Kalamparumple nor the shipping firm, the wherewithal to quit the float within, awakened by forks on the road to its habitual array of Titan which they shall, demurral inverted to complete all those values out of hand, than envision, exact as might odder old ring habitat. Simply by avoiding things, the tire decided to change a land of legend, dreams, archetype, and recurrent fantasies became a holiday, and Thledvirrson embarked upon a succession of ascending ledges.

"Oh, this," Althea expounded as if to say, what next? SOMHAD, closer to one who writes like an anachronism in her or his sleep, knew (the monads peep poetically about, and how) they, who go on the most about it and are more interested in not losing Raoul's beer decanters, may have switched parcels and gone to lengths of sending the cootie. The ex—guildmaster felt himself a fair target for a whimpering. He raised a shout. "To the bath!" As they repaired to streaming enclosure in shadows of his innermost chateau and disrobe, acolytes plucked rushes and over the pebbly shore and at the end a humane voice distinctly sat upon him. He pondered if the plot originated in the Community. He envisioned himself bringing the assembled decoy, flinging it before *wergild*, and accusing them of the switcheroo.

This heated inclination cooled into fleet desire to make a clean breast of things, confessing to erstwhile benefactors the thing indeed was stolen. He dismissed this idea in a heartbeat. Not above steering the committee's paranormal agenda for the last eighteen months, his own knocks and leads, sinisterly machined to conform their least adroit occlusions, knew any admission of incompetence on his part must burst the bubble of complacency Frank had taken such pain to inflate. An host appeared. Known only to Van Etnabaron's sight, she was a frequent tigger and sifter of clay and sand at any of several portable turntable productions.

"How did you guess," An Indocile countered? "Althea," she said quietly or tranquilly, "after all, a quick dank heather owl, a bobbin with a drip moue and heated hair punted slack behind her ear." Talitha, somewhat mortified, listed in quicklime to her plexus of Nicean symbols. "She's a Chorister, and d'ruther afford that than live out in space." "Her ombudsman had to crawl there and move it off and she didn't want him to be fashionably late," Glyntz excused her seconds, which gazed at her more than dully.

"I'm sure there is a brief work–in, and Inyo saw us fumbling our name into some hot water." Among the rocks of Miranda, a massive form, opinionated, less irritable since all the other writers at the experimental building, under a dazzling tumbleweed walkway linked across a perceivable methodology, circled around the last slice of pizza and took its intense mild level of sublime detail, enabling compunctive empathy, an endearing nerdy darkness in an organized medium, which had addressed them from a conversational standpoint. It would deadpan *wergild* in its own stew. Fair wrung within the hour, Frank bitterly pondered his decision to contact Inspector Læmært. Yet, if someone engineered the theft, in government, the police were his only hope. The intercom buzzed, signaling the end of melee. Dwelling on what anyone had for breakfast anymore gingerly, Francis accepted text from his secretary at the Guild. The Yard had telephoned, dropping his arrest warrant.

Sighing, he dismissed his entourage with a shout and set into the field to shoot skeet. This electronic zap, which a confrontation must predictably manifest, and shouldn't be enough, for her shipboard effects (last remembered power of withdrawal) went nowhere, *ahriman* helped to fan giant sects they foisted into traction; all knowledge from coterminous aurora to technical crumbs thrust into *wishram*, darkest of eight myths, "though at this rate," he'd say, "I'd be truly crazy to read my book to them!"

"You have to go," PoD said in reply, "and fax Philadelphia." "I'm fogging for *fjulsfut*, yet it didn't fix Tolstoy." They must have a contract farm to countenance their bravado. Even the chance to strike up lovely chords snagged a further unknown into the Sunrise Cage, where there are very many good technical advantages to all things we receive. With these same hands, Althea shaped an hourglass around him, twenty–four times, lest PoD was becalmed. "Now, Harold," Marta, using his given name, addressing a release form, resumed.

"Whatever you like. I'm here" — stranger to this fashion of address, Sasha indicated there wasn't need to continue. Fully persuaded, Marta led him into a lesser janiculum. This much Sasha could guess from his all–night sessions with *Cæsar II*, a classical sym–city variant. Notwithstanding this bountiful concession from Sandra's precept, doctrinaire eighths wrangled to seat a spotless proxy to propitiate meddlesome venue, and soon cyber gazettes bulged in bids to lodge a suitable candidate in the untainted sinecure. "Thus their dismal rubric accrues irrespective of cosmetic sophistry," *pluperfectreß* concluded her interview on *Mr. Ng Live*, and chided him for his plagiarist use of the indefinite article.

"It is among the most perilous of opening," an host agreed. "Our new prince, and I mean it neurally, collapsed in a hasty reproof, yet feels ghastly, though Death, running upon the coast, would answer his question. Perhaps *ahriman* should have checked his e–mail." Dwelling upon his cyber adventure, Harold was crushed in amusing fashion by passage of a troupe of acolytes emerged from regimens involving such svelte sweating. Their hair trawled up in turbans, they ignored his glance. Harold turned to admire their exit and doddered into another figure of humanism, dressed in cassock and Birkenstocks. "Fr. Anselm," exclaimed Meringue! "Marta," the massive host replied, engulfing her in a chaste hug.

Detached, the sacrist lurched gingerly at Van Etnabaron, "you are troubled, my son." "Sasha has been working heartily of late," Marta explained. "Then let him forget his cares for a time," Fr. Anselm replied, "since the children are waiting in that refractory *wishram*." "We will take good care of him," Meringue affirmed, clapping his hand in the cold ice water at the bottom of the chest and reading the mystical logos stamped upon the bottle caps. In retort, Ænselm, now limited to nothing more than that find which claimed his erstwhile mentor, Paul'r'us, slipped dearth, his grasp and ran loose leaf into the wilderness singing, "I don't remember loving you." PoD burrowed into the grubby forest of live oak, madrone, iceplants, and of shabby birch and stunted pine, the rumor of his demise pursuant.

The ground fell steeply before he found himself within, raving until sodden, amidst deflected crags above him, a figure loomed. This pale man, astride a cadaverous nag, visible, albeit his right forearm, appeared caught amidst transparent plastic cookbook holder racks. "Have you lost everything," Ænselm asked? "I have lost everything," the disfigured figure figured. "I am holding on for dear Death," answered Kalevide. Ænselm walked far before finding this niche. What had three feet and sails? "A yard sale," replied PoD, adding, "well, thin king, thou pernicious captor of Death, what has brought you to this pot?" What brought him to the crevasse of the nether land, the Kalevide was not prepared to share. Remember, a tear streaked across the face of the legend.

"My tale is terrible," explained Kalevide. "What sort of a cigar store are you running here anywise," Talitha demanded as a mote shocked the entire range and, displaced out of subsidiary power, swam before her eye? "For it," *ahriman* smirked, "Earth moved off of her syncope." Here, chosen outliers, an older hind, swathed in haughty toga for a spry exotic reprise, flipped the dial to home phone, and concealed a page on Nicean machinery with her utensil, Bitsy sang to their eldest, Sylvia, whom, so busy laying down the frog pond for this *wishram*, said, "there aren't enough sour apples to show how much I typically care." For that apostasy, prompted to often toy distinct heretical conundrums for everyone, four way out textures walk into overt arduous comps windily and after breezy shorts of an internal censor, derogate phalaropes to the framers of let's get fatter.

"Longitude," Kalevide exclaimed, "ran south or north, dividing the indigo sphere into twenty and four shares whence between every commonly agreed form is ellipsis of an individual hour. Latitude, in contrast, inclined west and east, paralleling the equator at tropics, where also concentric circles of diminished circumference, since the apposite points were simply polar, north and south, antipodal, betwixt which, an aforementioned axis, has been raffled by the frumious bandersnatch. Cite Psalm 103:12."

"'As far as the east is from the west, so has He removed our transgressions from us,'" Ænselm remarked, known neither how he knew this, nor why he had been asked to recite, nor why he had been capitalized. "At this point," Rex interjected, "the earth is cool. Here, where the Earth is fat" — "the Earth is flat," Ænselm exclaimed — "no, not flat, it is, in fact, fat." "An oblate spheroid true," interrupted one second, spilled through the transponder and into conversation a crackling retort, "and had it not been for it, we might have succeeded in recreating our sure paradise, instead of the fine mess we're now in."

.   .   .

Presently, Harold found a cell. Albeit comfortably strewn with rushes, the small bed was not where he expected. In a restless stillness, he glanced at the mirror. Some water schlepped from the basin onto his temple, and finding a change of garments set out for him, he left the building. "It isn't humanity's fault the indigo sphere is imperfect," Porphyry added, "but it is very warm," seconds persisted, "at least on outermost shell of what you called your burden, oh one of no shadow?"

The Earl of Rumsford cast an anxious glance at PoD for those biting mentions; but seeing the latter merely shrugged and said, "even their curiosity cannot pre—empt their ineptitude," Kalevideo returned to the tale of lines. They might have no idea that figure skating atop the arch of her own phrased yarrow show, *pluperfectreß*, palmer of pureæ, could evince anything but astonishment when her quarry, pursued to all appearance on temporal planes, sullenly went astral. In attempt to fend *pluperfectreß*, Ænselm hastily reverted to the only zone where couth ink held off, his native form, a mass of electrified surging darkness, no neat thing, fraught about tout—court to engulf his foe.

Inasmuch as the palm mistress equipped for the chase on an immaterial plane, this odd venue offered a prospect of slighter entertainment, her enjoyment dallied moreover by uncertainty underlying the location or whereabouts of the artist formerly known. Athwart her white bicycle, *pluperfectreß* lunged seventy longitudes eastward. Lugubriously, an antagonist arose. It was altruistic to remind *pluperfectreß* that she, on delineation of continents, is a confusing polemic diatribe; Niobe nowhere else as capable of thereat shifted tables. There, there was a realm just for surreal men. Away in one sly acuity, ever to hold over your head a foam into steamy depth to find Althea, all sportive captivation wherein real men so often felt sure in life.

To one's content here might colossal dribbles be struck at leisure into an ethereal range and past masters bested, skunked, fanned, slammed, upset, stoned, burned, and crushed. These otherwise vaunted hysterical grates counterfeit, mere figures of straw, au courant to those palisades, elaborate simulacrum of perception, a twitch, in hope the sun wore their own shadow, soon rate other, if no less tremulous, sections of heck. For those remnants, gleeful thrashing proper sang thus did intensely bear off ogling glance of copious sport bar courtesan as yawning scrivener whimpered the grate question, existence a beamish gloaming of capacity, read about one's own gloriousness slow to notice a shrunk field, light ever more lurid, a gasp of rebuke from a gallery, a sick cinch putt but strayed; these bunks seldom transmogrified and devils sprang into bearing administrative sour trash upon they who lunge too long at the bar of fame unlit, crowed around by insinuation from those attending manes in madness remained, jeered upon tussocks whiffled beyond their hapless grasp into gossamer nets that clutched them; more fortunate confidants in small and stale rooms missed perpetual billiard shots upon warped fabric while harps ceaselessly upbraided, the lone exit to curl upon the table and allow one's shelf to be chalked into one of the schlockets of egress.

Paused to await the next scramble, purgatory non–organized, Noone troubled with design of a floor plan, while splinters of the kaleidoscopic dimensions, the entire southern horizon besieged by a periodic dance of lightning reminding one less of a cyclotron than of glimmering hope in the avalanche of despair, for example, leaden artisans gazed wistful at homely despotic elves displaced a dozen centimeters awry, while others, more driven cheaply, beady fulcrums at the moment of inception, found their sleeves mesmerized by dreadful sane gargoyles, and these, awakened privilege of that byword, compelled to seethe horrible books (that one is unable to renew), and Bitsy's youth, true in one, go ciao yet drivel fifty miles to return the seraphim.

Upon bountiful sauce, those spilled across ditches swept, hoping to surf upon that fleet calculus of victory expressed via depth, met by dreadful Mercator swans skimming the perimeter, who then whistled them back into only endless temporary servitude. They called no shots there despite oblivious expertise. It may have been said eventual veils filled their lairs for this purpose, for no matter how existential they nattered jolts, to the young and zestful of that otherworld, always the national chant continued to prattle everywhere the amount of helpful advice upon topics' immense weft for accompaniment, drank decomposing neuralgia joules trilled to via fence sofas often, now derided, "thou art in no position to bargain for your corporate hide," ¶hrotomeous, other than behind a screen saver to change its intense rare brown and tan, sat there, "if you would alienate your true friends, Talitha."

Her head, in the U.S., a strange flatland sort of caught up on cybernetic implants, vomiting the hatch key, said, "I will spare this poor client of yours." "But we are grimly pledged to maintain a simile." Warrant out thrust, thanks to his unresolved horror comic issues, Park the palmer enabler, demanding a sage. Scurrying minions from every side swarmed to examine *pluperfectreß'* warrant, "you should probably stash the voluminous thumping overhead and occlude around upon my white bicycle shouting, 'everyone is motivated and utterly admired in the bulrushes, on the atomic bomb, on language syntax modeling theory, and in plant–bacterial rhibozone nodal interaction,' generically bringing all conversation to a nodding halt."

A free mind crept ere more sound of plush apnea came here for a polo moue, her warrant stuffed; into a pocket *pluperfectreß* stepped, balked unwillingly into the device of new plans. All of this gravity kept individuals charged with subduction of the counter–utilization from knowing more about their strumpet's dare. Her fare seemed to arrive a lot more quickly than she foreordained in little time for already, like dirty little ash cats, a million cumuli seedling raced north for rendezvous with the solstice.

Elements of surplus vision visited her a fancy she, in actuality, already being foremost arbiter of oppressed conversion, and given the importance she attached disdain to her own thorough fares without a word, and ignoring our tentative process, *pluperfectreß*, charged to sub-duction of counter–utilization, mourned, so anyone who asked how anyone else was with intent of exposing excusable behavior were con-strued, perpetual, solicitous, nolo contendre fomented chiefly beneath cameral toehold, for they not shrugged into despair at outset offered the heaviest affordable heresies in volute propensity baffled any attempt to explain the Sisyphian waste illogically, skirt reasons of their gloom. Kids crowd the latest verbatim foam thrill, the dust buster, stimulated by experience of being vacuumed up while a contemporary historian, pounced to write upon the calliopes of the corporeal empire, discarded a topic ex–Ælfric ever since in blameless fashion reverenced everywhere without momentous or renewable vigor.

The substantiative infinite end zone delineated occasional chalk, a drag positive over, which decisively and in effect re–impressed their rank order of internal drivers insistently tabled over recognition of inherent bid. Sangreal, appellant before the dingy quay, in fleet if limited power, instead enmeshed a gauntlet of non–recognizance, for she, visibly spent and for the junk store bound in transit, once subtlety, a harsh south wind carrying a notable valence stirred instantly, begat necessarily herein, though bereft of available bleary tar, and lit upon periodic inscription of a lengthily expressive itch awkwardly experienced however reminded of her marriage thereby rueful ousted; yet after the sere and treated hand of *ahriman* reflectively sought the dam of her nostrum, an entire facet unknown dispensed and the prints of darkness, an insistent mirror, beckoned, for far above one saw the lofted heaven, a basin of quarrelsome larks, and rhymes for wont.

These clanged every and/or any commonplace interlocutive wrinkle, and while Sangreal read, too, allowed of reason, etched upon lobular significant chichi [*sic*] she accepted, if forever marred, she inclined to secrecy, and could sooner leave an expectance of renewable bounce than declare an imprecation of original misconnection. Thereby canning ergo a state of rinsable effect, for a day her hopes cured as the characteristic lot of no feyer a person of absence than her cousin Ostrand, whose entire remission caused her to seek a return to the hand of the artist never only formerly known either before and/or after her or his time. A deferral of her entire life she bought; effacing the risk of involvement in impending inquests might easily soon dismiss her vixenish attribute. Considerate of emulsification in the arch comprehensive smudge of darkness damming her follicle, "take them," she indicated. *ahriman* left her purged, done with original sin, and rejoicing at her limitless stock of headbands.

·   ·   ·

So as PoD fumbled about old performance reports to the populace, most of whom, mildly disappointed to see only a few vapor trails and cellos, scrapped out a funereal lack of concern for any one of those rare occasions when people learn from another person who doesn't sugar–coat everything with the patch, ¶hrotomeous waited even longer than usual for an uncivilized, insistently more privileged, grand, and smelly algorithm, so different from the orgiastic clucks above the Canadian Hills theater, though hadn't he surfed unceremoniously beneath an obligation to avoid barks here in the last defiant cry of an editorial policy twisted into submission by exterior dictates? Titan, aware enough of its approach, watched as the jubjub, a giant blue legend without bird food, dredged up several jejune texts and e–mails; though finding excuse to leave lunch, this was its major interaction.

In the flurry over grilled wrought iron pickets onto grounds that, while seeming luxurious, crowded holistic Amazon, whose swarm for sensibility, it set the self–perception they will act in august friendliness, noted *ahriman* in descent, interest lost in its tiresome perpetual repast, and plummeted instead on Ænselm and float. Hope left them while Thledvirrson felt, in a cusp of web reversal, forced to stare; into a well from the nether stratum her reflection rushed to greet her. Ænselm's point of view, in this frame, enlightened in another sorting, for his shift-less resort placed him athwart an immediate Tathagata. As he screamed up at talons, the almighty tonsils, the dome around the horizon exploded until he felt upright. Lurking into a vast and encompassing bowl of stars, Ænselm now spent his time developing mental checklists, flowcharts, and protocols of specious contingency defy why the native force justifiably harnessed his own blighted sense of propriety at some future time.

.   .   .

Marta via CLASP cocytus slushy slop that natheless fortuitously forbids bicycles & provides opp for one captious enough to make yellow snow angles to scare PoD (his kryptonite)... continuity sorted via chess pieces... Ænselm separable into component dualism... frame colloquy between Piero & chamb (alto busy).

IV — xvii — A Small Stroll, Though the Time Flew.

His family left huddling for warmth around the photograph of a candle, Ion Uclosco set out for the Reject Fair. Much of western classicism read, and demonstrative of a bent to talk it out of the garage, through a wicket, without breaking ceramic figurines, which alerted the rural caretakers whom, subject to such strain, and maybe a scan of the want ads, Ion once again staved off galactic pullovers and jettisoned banana coupons in exchange for black light, an adhesive and cheesy cowl, oryza sativa, and adumbrated cereals. Etaoin was also among a select gathering, the convergence was not lost on everyone, and the thread of this day loomed long.

Participants duly arrived, specified by their uncertain repute, individually or in tandem. "If, death was the wage of sin, then what was the point of existence?" Once last word, obvioregals, mostly noted for voice displacement, crooked from theatres anywhere, had also to find another thing. Droning in seas of intent, they were paralyzed by option. "If," they agreed, "the seller proposed to pass this off as original, would they also walk out on it?" Aside from a reckoned image of sociopathy, it was all right or not so bad for Proserpine to arrive in joyless solitude to some idol of promiscuity, only recently defined by the TV advertisements which neutralized Morse code and even the harmless past times in the dizzy platonic plutocracy.

At least she was able to conceal her chagrin to the nether clans. When something happened, everyone, instructed, returned to her or his place of residence. They wished to be spared further infinitive on the road to *biathanatos*. Already experienced in ontological fatuity, they fled invariable niche ousters; things to bowl, sought, they found, indivisibly quarantined, in forgotten tense, inciting Plutarch (rest, sweet source of labor) during betrothal, an exclamation of loss, hue, and cry odious to a sense of further viability; about the purlieus ELIZA, the neo–reversionary cognomen, if unfettered in any depiction of best loved tales, gentrified in throes of a presence. Hades looked after their fresh charge inexcellently, for pleasantly, a Note, appealing to their disdain of continued sentience, and offering change, to experience an entire new benign trend, began.

The dan *Matthieu* Ylferim il Fiume Paul'r'us expected all further Global Village communication to be transmitted in double quatrain with an expository ninth line Alexandrine. It was taken under advisement, whereas his caveat, to rest in eternity prone, face down (he always slept better in this position, allowing weight of Earth's forces to still restless stirring), generated a more robust debate. In receipt of assurance, tread between intrusiveness and fealty, slipped into evening, these requests were legally valid, his executors left to devise public presentation of his remnants. In stormy confluence involving principles and various peers, malleated between three camps, each advanced solution:

A) SKIP VIEWING, IGNORE LAST RESPECTS, AND BURY HIM.
B) PLACE IL FIUME ON HIS BACK, FACE UP IN THE CASKET FOR VIEWING AND TURN HIM FACE DOWN AFTER VIEWING.
C) SERRATE A DISTINCTIVE ROSE WINDOW INTO THE FOOT OF THE CASKET AND TURN IT UPSIDE DOWN, SUSPENDED ALOFT SO HE MAY BE VIEWED LOOKING EARTHWARD.

. . .

This, the age of wax, found representative creation of myth left to fend or yield. Reckoned as if by chance, a leveling did, for a measure of permanence, occur. To a spectator, a glimpse of the summons formed a vantage of a chthonic, variable, known but uncharted against an overwhelming adjective described as affable cause, one scene of any strain on a very limited value event, as, hovered upon an immense expanse of linear augment; the Note shadowed, dispensed posts of the cosmic circuit, showered upon honorific of deposed poets, and shoved *lumine* into an oath renouncing their present ground as harsh or common, as, juggled by Meringue's concern, many continental notables assembled at a valid load, where, hushed before the civil conservatory, to the shriek of arch blob auks, tickled, sneezed, they withstood sifted wage to grant ease, a calliope upon, then disclosure of, garage pipes summoning fine hearts of antiquity as an orator stepped forward to announce a limited wake.

Drifted inside, the invited, in receipt of escort into the foremost cusp where, tucked and tilted, the residual *dan*, lit beneath a lamp of grotto neon stillness blue, mourners found kids feeling superfluous, at church to have a bagel and read the fine print, their foot in the chamber pleasantly sprung, like one field of clover, and critical few sniff yet stoop to verify it is livelong lawn, and most time flies like the wind. A plastic shield interlaced atop their aerie coffin concealed an august facet of il Fiume, though one might mend a frozen mind, if one was so touched.

A puzzled and grown majority remarked that seconds conspired to push them further into a large antechamber when, their viewing obligation fulfilled, they might soon be of a bent for departure. Ænselm ran very jitterily across lacquered boards, uncertainly, at which point, into unlit address channel surf, and dangling, in the hand of the youth, the hatch key opened the secret carrioccio [*sic*] Në Dipol availed, "I will insist," she noted, "for modern time is now whatnot how non–prepossesed." Anybody who viewed more than a hundred absolutions of a proletarian anti–toxic personae shred this rare glimpse of many whispers, which have been a subconscious conflict over being summoned to your knee, ever since large velvet limbo, its foreboding checklist, as long as all far quadrants of the Nebraska ticket counter will mind well knowing it is final time for the yarn being to keep her glove, donated by likes of mature Plair in dim, benign veiled skies, and narrowly recorded, since *ahriman* smelled, things, each o'er armed with pre—emptive taser, somehow provincial; Në was not, far from Regatta, lurked again into an unfamiliar way, far away, forgotten chants, with alacrity balked, to except darkness.

Distilled unto eleven stones, upon many mercantile outlet shelves, to accommodate what seemed like paradise, a surge of second thought intervened. Talitha yearned they'd been into worthier books in Erewhon. Chorister, upheld, of two minds, closed, toward PoD, who grasped that antecedent could obligate him to relieve his own hand, and without, talisman of the Porcupine sown in his guess, merely said, "your left, your left," a cry even now echoed upon parade grounds throughout the new old new world. "Alas, poor lad, you are not smiling," sighed Porphyry, "yet we will try to explain, how the best of mimes missed, inaction, a sole option to rout back out there upon that reeling void."

Under this palm trolled the black pawn, all light swallowed, it cried out amidst rude birth, "most of us swear of a premium obligation to survive, require two decades of specialization, before, emergent, fleet, as dream dolls, and hence, best of all responsive automatons, clueing to one or two infanciful pathos forthwith, poor lad, who must experience landfall in a period of comparative brevity." Whomever's call, its property of being a big cultural presence, even while secretly indivisible, pleasant arraignments of Henry (VII)'s strident tantrum caused wonder if a noble and institutionalized rest will be enough to restore necessary occupational hopscotch and jocularity.

"If I am prepared for the impending machine inside me," the King of the Romans began, feeling too threadbare, each rotation about fifteen mental versions, "apparel is hard to describe. It is a huge structure overlooking huckleberries and used Granola boxes. In aisles, a tape player, a carousel of socialized silence, over sprawled states of sugar plums, drawn a rather Bohemian guy who is ¶hrotomeous, the prototype of legal darkness" — "may it last forever, albeit becoming flies above lurid, and steady, redesigned bowling noise." It, being the crest of time, or nearly two, and three other curtains close across the courtyard with composure.

They set up this bleep, yet each twenty–seventh move, Ænselm, down in front, drove black's queen toward untold exile and exchanged rooks, Alcuin's queen pawn quashing PoD's castled bishop side, the knight driveled into the open, ejection of an anti–social beaver on Red Square, black's bishop moved to absorb Rex, white's king knight, linchpins of PoD's defensive system brought white's queen and one shriveled blob to bear upon Porphyry's third file. They met, shortened by inexplicable figurines in bottles long disused, and feared for, in a mail–order confluence, itself atop of a freezing town hall on the veranda, thus did not fulfill impulse (including innumerable coated passers–by).

"Soon you'll find ARM's to go at eleven, ten percent, in two–percent caps with Westworld quarter paying off the mortgage binge." "Señor Florian," replied Iphgene, "you might put up storm windows," never indicating she should rather spend the night apart than leave; *uchaux*, doth protest in dark room, but here the stranger, earnest guy who wanted in on their beads, "of course, didn't, you naive boy," Hesitance replied in pure Castillian. Finlay earnestly heard here, Tell, her son, distinguished djinn as dark energy discernment capable of perception, under strict compulsion to adopt succinct axioms for each given occasion, and must remain in dank Bing Bang cathedral until someone shouted MIME! And there waxed barely time to dive until musicians gazed up prettily. "Hey, Finlay," Ralph shouted, "can I crash the rain check on that beer?"

Immured of an accurate solar canal, a bobbin related, "I'm sitting in the high chair at Etaoin's table, a hideout varnished Sunrise Cage which came with the haunted house." Park had *Chicago's* first album on and basked, not himself away from *wishram* tablets where, tambourine inaudibly poised, Bagler and niece unlatched their own cases: Raisin had a flute, and he, thank God, gave Finlay a glimpse crestfallen. Said Meringue, "Sam always has to despond until Alcuin summons courage to stoop forward and shake it." "So you'll be in on one of those rings," someone in front rooms half–answered Bagler, a barmy character in Gestalt, creating a slick surface, everyone nodding aha, that old oily sad dark stranger crying, at Park's early guests, "ah, yes, Norah my lass, he cried a river." Van Etnabaron, coifed in a scowling, found himself within parties of blackberry picking guests.

Mingling to edge off the ground, Harold sniffed from here to view the distance to the Country Squire, and wait for huckleberry pickers to leave. Although the wagon was fewer than two mad dashes toward the quay, he saw pickets find plumb ground in blackberry patches nearby, and many parties soon plucking them everywhere, it seemed, Jasmine continuing to listen, and finally pressed nearer the door. Frowning in hesitant style, and using Marta's key, the source of scourging sound, an immense, scratchy 78, left warping on an ancient turntable, a casement seemed forced upon. Three scholars wrestled for keys. They rallied against a dichotomy in Western civilization ceaselessly reminding them corporations needed love also, posing three questions for the future of humans.

"If the road to hell is paved with good intention, then what comprises the road to non—hell," Shrdlu, of Nesselrode, mickle forthright, counted himself out and blurted? At crunch time, security, whispering blandishment, surrounded him. "Unhand me, you operant schnooks," the gentleman frowned, "my time is my own." "Most certainly, your honor," they replied, "if you will only surrender your programme." What gloved hands beckoned for and retrieved the cambric card, and with a stamp, here your honor found his elbow clasped and this person hoisted through a cusp and into a central partition. The orator rescued the situation.

"Il Fiume," he sang, "we knew him as modest. He could take no man's time." Nesselrode flopped out of there, the orator adding, "Matthieu would insist to invite all of you, who wish to depart, and celebrate life in your own way, to avail yourself of the path of Etaoin, one of il Fiume's earliest friends." Several of those present laughed, if albeit allowably any seemed to risk a ginger step toward the conveyance.

The orator continued, "many who may wish to obtain a forward gift of il Fiume's esteem might do so in the corridor." A considerable lot fanned toward it, but seeing any of the original exodus crept back on this premise, movement was not at all purposeful. Several minutes of polite sifting produced a wavering trickle of refulgent, how urgently knocked by adventure's whim, via such sentiment as, more for us here, who needed you, collect your door prize, and see if they let you out. These last observations brought them to restless calm as piping skirled anew and, light let down upon vocalists, a shorn, Gallic waif wailed in tune, "and Samuel said unto Saul, 'your kingdom has been torn from you today (15:28).'"

Sixteen tables, each seating sixteen persons, more than half willed by a partially insidious audience, Porphyry's deposed king promptly attacked Ænselm's surviving queen knight, an exchange of small premise, and since Zugzwang trembled in thin air, *ahriman* opened his mind to the disclosed Porcupine, the Minister of Transport lent, for word, "chalcedon flattered into anachronism, obsidian with white tellurium, no truer work of that thirteenth century master Bitunyia Koatzer." They listened from a sense of listlessness, wandered into a quite large banquet, and presented their programme to facilitators who found seating for them within.

"If this might be, it's locking the barn door," scoffed Piero, lurking almost alone in the vast enclosure with nine minutes before eleven o'clock; Në, fainéant, noted, "in a recent check–in, we gave the freeze to a person who urged us to sing for our pulse." "See," ex–Ælfric said, unhappily swatting at a sublet imposter of diagnosis they'd all rehearsed in Nicean, "yes, I paid a lot off–the–rack to get introverted." The die already rescued from a portabello, a certain detached thought he'd weathered the worst of maneuvers when, around eight etoliations of Hard Rock, their glib patois of invisible fallout pinged above this modus operandi, which, seeing things 360 degrees out of form, o'erruled by purpose, and strained, from kvetching there are people out there who said we are all social zeroes, arose beneath the crawl space to a scratchy scuffle of deck shoes, drop the corporate ladder, as fall guy for a little sporty with here s/he comes shrill activism tempest to make friends with; moreover your ethos whose area, mashed anyway (in this ambush to know history), to dye, a real fetish for typing the one whom you love since sounds; of one hand, clapping around his larynx, *ahriman* dissembling into encompassing expletive desire to disestablish its threat from their being (thereby assuming that bearer of this tiresome display of dark energy should leave).

It did not long linger here, but nagging participle, lepton, or skeleton rattling in similar folklore relaxed, it became trouble ahead for an empty unfamiliar imminent milestone, procedure less tiresome to Ænselm and yet a more personable voir dire [*sic*]. Since chance of further cranial existence fleeted from him in an instant were he to move anything, Ænselm collapsed on the floor, bereft of his photo shop, and seemed oppressively still. Hands rasped amidst his virginity on the very sort of salons that set Paris upon the pinnacle of vagabond under–achievement prior to tools taking the door apart where, of strength unknown to him, had the mountain groaned in surprise, outrage, and panic that it, flailed by this testament, unlocked the naive sanctuary of his being; pity, a strange alert kinship on voice mail, tempered thereupon this motor scooter into the sunset a little numbness but, now perhaps, the throttle, eased by a merciful lens of color alarmingly re–energized, on pathos of a tangible flunk, and not even slightly tried to make amend by singing, "what the heck are you suitable for," Ænselm's assailant, temerarious without commercial interruption, for the first time in general reckoning (of course on her disability to make demands like a hyper–structured and non–relaxing control freak), figured a way out of this mess, raked back her fist anyway (it least applies to a taunt pinching duel), to inspire a real, old–fashioned, onto Miranda, giant culminative stroke.

Ænselm no longer felt need to explain his job, a suitable break–in paradox of form completion activism; all that had fallen from vast stellar depths, summoned heterogeneous nucleation dusts of creation to pass. Upon it, a whittling lady of elements daubed also, and PoD, shifted by a small queer purple stigma, attached into a frame of original beam, *pluperfectreß*, shellacked by a carpet of phosphorescent ions: fell, away from her mark, groped like a sleepwalker, in a land of false awakening, and recalled an effort expended to no avail. Having sought the Porcupine conch, PoD found his collection of nurturing excuses with which to unleash his inner elf reward, beholden this being, on a leased thing, brought up again to awareness of option, and pushed against the held hatch in an endeavor to thrust it out from within. It held for a round total of thirty–four lunch hours, possibly not translated into overt helplessness, for a person of strict training in the slammer, whence remark our current state is from Eureka; but for *ahriman*, temporal commitment found to be not utterly futile, so much as a hedge against future bouts of angst, it was in a completely tepid light.

¶hrotomeous, swallowing the quay, yoked around, neatly reflective of dawn throughout the check–out line, disputing that ideal catalog, unexpectedly leviathan, of bio–technology imparted against, in jeremiad, for a quarter in full bloom, at least six weeks away, ere weird Medea, a prioress, groggy for her cougar, ululated at *fjulsfut* for speedy brain ceorls of their wild. They seethed in spontaneous mufti. Althea nodded at him in wee interest as Ralph tittered slyly, "I can find hell," and rang forth ages like, jumbled on the slopes of Miranda, *ahriman* saw Chorister squeezed, blanched through a bent oyster town ever after extrication from the convivial booths. Also, interminable, moist tubes cascaded like frozen *wishram*, "good–bide, Ænselm," An Indocile candled after–hours. "Did your local work at the Institute," he asked? "Whelp, uh, you need to wait on moonrise," Althea intoned.

Her voice broken, the distance PoD nuked, isomorphing into a parfait quill ray — both eyes which, spying his Lohengrin, slimed Oz, and threw a risqué wok at Althea! "I've got enough airtime on each swarm," Thledvirrson, a superb undertow whistler, said, anointing some stars in the neighborhood. Like a maid searching for a kick, or two, "aha, Ænselm, why d'you verge into my so many minds," Althea asked, and downing his soul, bundled in turn styles hence, Talitha led thee into a dank base moment. "I swam all meters!" There were sonic bilge spirits. "Putrify," Althea emitted! *ahriman* distracted it for the nonce, though, to evade her sapient iPod, he went beyond infra–orange where, accepted by toothy butterflies, he was dazzled his muumuu was so askew.

.   .   .

If fewer of the guests were apprehensive about diner with a deceased person, beyond TM, pixels, next glasnost, or their room; others, known of these customs, joked il Fiume had never seemed hungrier. The repast shockingly stark, the simplest sliver of morel, sparkling Pernoud, a teaspoon of *œufs brouilles Bergeres* washed in a sallow Montrachet, a strange myzithra crumb followed by *langouste Grandes Augustines*, amid much scary fawning royal liens, and paella on pewter saucers stamped in severest features of the deceased. Not a few of those surreptitiously decamped while series of scriptural metaphor commenced, Jasmine felt, a sunbeam tumultuous oceans thence endured as point. Many seconds on the daily float righted a hemlock conch as she touted meeting with a tragic soul. These inspirations behind the medley peered forward, waited for the punch line, provided thorough, great technological effort was the first attempt to lift the visage of il Fiume into the promised downslide angle.

A corner of the parquet burned upon a turret and, with a gaseous hiss the sarcophagus vaulted into the room, facing them. Those least affected expressed irate revulsion against these tasteless mechanical acrobatics. Those who glanced again saw a wooly figure, a living lamb, cropping carpet beneath the crèche. Others saw disconcerted walls of television monitors unveiling crash into mighty storm highlighting antiquated middle–aged man how stood up on the dais amidst amicable classics. "Are these mod worst–look fancy dishes on retail yet," one asked? "I'm Florian, current editor of the *Mainzer Landfriede*." The chef d'ouerve (*all too busy*)'s first witness schlepped off his cusp.

"All in all," PoD gloated, "I'll have my faults, my strengths, lies, paranormal, inner fright (instinctively unknown, all he said fussed uphill)." Bells rang as ¶hrotomeous reacted to the fiercest question, that Piero deliberately miscalculated costs of distribution for copies of then cyclic ale, "ministerales et podestas, et al, *pluperfectreß*, beyond clause of Menander's *Clandestine New Moss*, clad in a stir, barely perceptible until a, periodical, uh, in a recent issue, advanced existence of a sole" — "turn it up next time" — "damned your stuffed shirts: I have proof of fifteen and six, £900, the paperwork, the names of all that attended your meetings during the insurrection, the acting podesta lah–dee–dah, the periodical in question" — Harold paused — "and all else that favorably reflects upon my client."

"Are ye off the well–maintained walls yet," Idiopath, his unlit meer-schaum and carven [*sic*] coffee mug, tucked in three syllables, nodding to a grind bloke whom had been shown the door, olé? Mold paperwork behind one swarm, ¶hrotomeous pronounced, "it's probably no special custom for one to hit up pending appointment near the Assizes, isn't it?" Bottom line: one might lurk long and far from the ledger. "This exche-quer was sown ahead of *pluperfectreβ*, geodesic help for us, there was not."

Although Meringue held the causeway to the county squire, Van Etnabaron had plans. Couchant beneath the wheel, he pulled aside a panel. "Harold?" At use of his given name, Sasha clunked his head on the steering column. Its refrain of gloomy feats made a dreary noise, hooting at sooty grandstands about this unseen unnatural earthling (ah, shrewd envious look from Læmært's teensy lapel daisy), who soliloquized, "a proper specter seems bandied on a circus tiger," yet is too kismet to dial, however St. Agnes yanked that isosceles chive mace object, and silently moved off without ice cubes or a net. Next, remanded, ¶hrotomeous saw, near *xenonia*, Piero, standing beneath a bank of good old klieg lights, who spake, "working, please remain, standing," figuring, £11,568 van-ishing before his eye, chef d'ouerve [*sic*] (*all too busy*), in sirens, rang for his first windlass.

Down in from assembly there, ridden high on thin air, a rumor wrought via exchequer that ninety–one percent of *wishram* funds were snookered. Okay, at eleven o'clock Në must defend the insurrection's levy. Seeing there are fifteen minutes unspent, ¶hrotomeous waited for Piero to break a colloquy with the chef d'ouerve (*all too busy*) and slid a hand by reflex on his worksheet. If not in bowling jargon, another might still be astral to it. Via gregarious mist, Van Etnabaron found the tunnels, narrowly escaped framing by bowls of smoked incense, stepped behind the balustrade, dunked past the reception desk, and sped out into the parking lot.

"How a doubt," Bitsy scuffled, at l'nurt [*sic*], to select a better teeter totter au pair for her souls, "took getting in, for example: that tall bobbin is ethereal and I was too fat anyway," she fished. Talitha strayed underwater now, indicating the hoarse sound. "This is lifelike," saith she, eyeing, an edgy glow, a molten whelk hedged on the bent float; bracing a bottom booth, *ahriman* talked as if his dirty egress helped him quite stealthily win. "Are you all right," Jasmine asked, her voice deepening in concern?

Van Etnabaron flinched. "Fine," he trilled, "oh, there's that old kit," dispatching the glove compartment. "Shaving kit," repeated, adding, while *ahriman* heard the sock thwack on the door amidst shingles, "PoD, did you swiftly, on tugging a beatnik aspect off the stucco, wish An Indocile sahib goodbye and flag a top float?" Ralph told them, "your own uncle ensign *ædith* heard of my discovery of disbelief, or is he snot?" "Stop smiling so broadly," Sasha thought in self—reprimand, slamming the passenger door, and struggled to his feet.

"No need to get dressed, dear," Meringue addressed him. Over her collier, he noticed she had clad on a bright parsley caftan. Noting the precocious curve of her anklet in wraparound calf—length sandals, Sasha felt a fresh perk; Bitsy saying, "to this one of course nut hatch ere lunch was dinner and so on," Van Etnabaron, re—entering retreat upon the final tendrils of nones, his shrinking heart hit with a recanted menu shrimp.

Dinner, served, consisted of large mounds of tambour, conscience, falafel, humus, cracked bugler, and most. They entered the cafeteria as younger persons sited in studied indifference. Given sign they were on verge of exit, Bitsy called to them. "Clifford. Sybil. Here is Mr. Van Etnabaron." As they froze, perfunctorily, to meet an embrace wholly familial, Sasha, clutching his sewing kit, barely found voice to ask the decided question. "Are these" — Bitsy beamed, tousling the heads of the quiescent youth. A heathen *ahriman* splurged, wondering at their methodical story.

"They shall be a new cyber—form hence," Bitsy added, "my first guest!" "Oh, how you can show us to thrive in the city," commented Sylvia, in limp wanhope. Van Etnabaron found himself ravenous. Having already dined, the wax–born dinned about instead. "Chad, flat, old, pop, wants me to go to knickknack camp this summer again," Clifford complained to Sylvia's mother. Harold glared up from his pita, erupting, "kickback camp?" "An HSN knickknack camp," Jasmine, ere quoted, whistled, "in Nevada." "In August, knickknacks made a lot of dough," Etaoin mentioned. "All right, C–man," Bitsy said, "I'll talk to them." Van Etnabaron, his eye fenced briefly, followed Sibyl's invisible gaze as a television monitor in the center of the room offered a Chrissy Snow radial radiant pendant ring for eighty–nine ninety–nine, which glimmered, night and day.

Ænselm, startled, coughed up falafel crumbs, as Meringue blinked at anyone indirectly. "Sil, please don't play with that remote." "Mom," her daughter complained, "that other stuff's boring." "Honeybee," Bitsy ruled doggedly, "it is a retreat. Mr. Van Etnabaron is very tired. The world must not press in." Retiring the meme on tour to house programme, learned dissertation on *The Architecture of 4th Century Hippo*, whence Fernand felt, on expulsion from institute broadband, any inkling of about how green wash for Maxwell's calligraphy emporium drew comparison near Planck's constant, the girl stood up. "Excuse me," Bitsy prompted? "Excuse me," thus replied, Sylvia blew out the lamp. "Excuse her," her brother added, and arisen hastily. "Nice to have met you, sir." The *fjulsfut* nodded brashly, "was it yet to be air or wine?" Not many more histrionics could persist until all matter, co–existed of deliberate fugue, accepted, experiencing odd respite amid Fermi's post–Cambrian axiom's minuet. Limitless parades of sack candles diurnally squirreled one way toward voices of the actor, ceaselessly asking any who might spare them soon, grown absent, gross in exertion even as sound engineers gradually quelled the storm. So his fading voice continued to be audible, Florian, greatly miffed at a tortoise complex, hurriedly buoyed by this intelligence, an average strength, and a high anticipation, brooding about their second tartan committee, saith, "going to have soma tiffin; if you want to wrinkle the soak master" — "I like to see how humans do with fire walls," PoD enthused, "and get ready, fine, I just did."

Meringue signaled them to step it up, to distract the audience with techno flurry for more moments, and Florian, grown faint and prostrate, fell, rose, got up, gave up, and his thrown caftan aside, left. The storm eased into a bright but misty forest. Hesitance led part of the audience clap in a generic silence. Someone felt incumbent to interpret. To the consternation of Nesselrode, Ostrand arose, walked to the turret, kneeled, and garnering the lamb, heard to recite a story, since learned in criticism, announcing he had been spared to do parochial work in the name of our father, any murmur of approval, accompaniment to an astonishing apotheosis of Ostrand: heard to chuckle echoes of protest, inability to communicate, in no condition to play hail–fellow–well–met; id and super–ego, he glimpsed for something to hand the Elector of Ruthenia, or Echo (henceforth refrainant as Contessa, Mme Nadeladimov), her placid call to hesitant Wyvern charged out or away from the open window, whilehomes reactivated. The old Emerson CD player blue light, defunct for nearly a dank fortnight hence, featured words of guidance before dismissing proprioceptive elopement into the thirteen hundreds as a way to make things better. The lamp changed many hands before, unwound in those of the county squirrel, *ahriman*, his cold harp seemingly diverted by continuance, the casque shifted, hoisted the beaming decadent aloft, over, and down onto a baseboard. Tipped with minimal assistance upon an octet of weightless dumb bells, the vasculum, suspended on platinum grooves, four feet beyond the lawn, reposed.

The pallbearer shrugged away support and in a resounding clunk, the casket merely sank. Many gasped at death's seeming clumsy finality and winced as the poised ossuary shucked from the chamber with another conveyor to the happy hour freebie snack side; assuredly hence, they were blessed by a number of hands and in a sudden current jam, the vast complement of angels, lit and dark, left their haven and bounded into ether, twinkling, again via nets hovered, their one return privilege to sue later, and neglect to unpack a box of air, enshrouded in vacuo from one side to another. They knew, if dialectic enshrined, the trait name outlook of affixed procedure would begin, forcing them to afford a methodology of anti–art which, in argument, expiated a movement of utter decoction. Synonymously, very many, so diffuse, evolved on initial reification of a word that followed the sending of blessed Norns.

.   .   .

Find letter to express sentiment of Baglers' niece ~ other typographic parallel... Ostrand, visiting Raisin in hospital, enveloped in PoD's community assistance program... consider present tense inculcating obversible observer and to track apostrophe's ~ italicized personae lack possessive case.

IV — xviii — Sounds Like A Name to Grow Into.

Porphyry's operative (Në, increasingly ignored as being preferred to Tell), derided, for siting PoD as backup dance crooner above their showcase, the deleterious nature of this plot, eruptive in a toney toll, a wellness choreographer dead in a study of cause linked to inhalation of Mercury, verily hapless Noone initialized a trance, and hopeful of geographic fixation in an hour, the Inspector told the concierge, Tell, to let not anyone know he said something about peering into Plyntymyny this afternoon to invite an old Sandhurst salad bard, Blank (frozen), now in customs, aside. For once, the telephone rang.

Again, Fulnes answered in snort mode. It was Sergeant Isp. "Sorry," Fulnes replied circuitously. "Not a thing, sir. Coaxed Miniclutter of their payroll input listing individuals entirely involved in some Stonehenge ceremony." "That shelves it!" "In a flash. Also (characteristic muffle at the far end suggested the speaker was amidst attempts to coax documentation from a transmissometer), we must then create two normal shower cures and wade both through, only then free to experience transfiguration apotheosis into the mighty orgone to avenge the bereavement of Niobe." For their champions, the prize, to defend St. Agnes in impending extradition from Madras, suddenly went glowering, when word leaked their erstwhile client skipped her flop.

"That's not all," Isp exhumed, as lilac *ahriman* smirked and said, "yes, dreaming is this way," vaulted from their nether path in the crescendo gale of an obvious mid shift. The pair evaluated the virgule sent from an apparent deliverer, even considering faith may produce chronicles equally demotive, Althea, unlading her sous, perked up convection, "can you see why we don't want these criers for the asking?" "So meet a, or the ascetic dude" — Iraisamonde was in an empty moment, sublet for a lively url–Queen who wore feather dusters at home plate, "Silas F., it wasn't a tuba," Chorister challenged.

"And that is not our job," the *fjulsfut* said, a map drawn of possible snowstorms on the spot her eyes took, piercing imposition if not actual thought spiral about causation of the moment's importance. "How long would you like to drink?" In Ænselm, spores turned to share Sasha's Danish and, noshed with an inky tall bobbin, filming little brusque egret three–ring tattersall bravado (inevitably circumlocuted), *ahriman*, jujitsu'ed in the operant, glided to emit photons, a prolegomena high An Indocile spritzed on.

Miscibly, Fulnes took twelve minutes to find the nearest operational facsimile machine on the fourth floor. Every space beyond which span might not count for anything unless he was on to something. As PoD soaked in used saltpeter, a metallic, and more eucalyptus second whose oil business tanked, said, "Talitha hates snorkeling" — "are you formed," asked Delores? Ostrand cited the living float. "Are reactions to those manes rare," Thledvirrson asked Chorister? "Well, it has been a bent quid of serio–comic goo," she yelped. Advancing documents from the culture ministry to Læmært's office, Fulnes reviewed his progress.

Beneath first glean, of the semi–public heap of record found, upbraided like sheaths from mica, yonder layers, equally formidable. All research options seeming inexhaustible, Fulnes put his hand into his empty pocket. As it should have been, for in an effort to reorganize his thought, Fulnes retained, never quite forgotten, an image of the kicked key. The facsimile complete, Fulnes left the cubicle for Lichvue, where an attendant troupe, ill with six weeks of similar exposure, forced cancellation of an entire sea coast Ritz swing tour.

The financial health of many a dot com, most predicated on fast advance ticket sales, declined in fidgets of insufficiency, and refurbishment of several municipal coliseums; deprived of resultant capital, brought to the merciless scrutiny of public indifference a fresh wave of despair, scarecrows, posted in previous undistorted bier ant nests in the northern hemisphere, preceded, by moments, recall of large SUVs seen being perched upon by cormorants prior to many of them being involved in faulty air bag releases, and the exchequer, to stem a matchless urge toward reaction by lowering the prime rate, a further degree below absolute zero already incensed many lenders who stormed the citadels of Worsted into charging their denizens with uncivil duplicity. Peat bogs in general began coughing up screen plays since any gain which might accrue soon vastened into a wee nest of legal obligation.

.   .   .

Political soundproof alibis aside, were the flip cite to be endured until, tired of being blamed for everything, Henry (VII) needed to state a national debate about effects of magical mystery tours on reverse social engineering of par "— er, universal diagonal parking," Sr. Florian, lacking access to community broadcasting, was last to assay a perpetual cordon sanitaire in hope of scooping the catch of the night. "If I thought you might like to wander off and bowl out the candle, I obviously derived prodigious joy out of reflexive fact–finding."

The events of the morning may have led to a less casual Friday, had not Frank persisted on accommodating them until lunch. Identified via cellular code name *wergild*, Middleford informed a commissioner that iBC, receiving full report, expressed regard as satisfied with their Yard's handling of the Lichvue case, and Læmært descended to the Hornet n' Hammock, a pub frequented by many ministries, to meet Chorister's customs crank, Silas F., whom, buoyant as ever, always managed to balance the glass on his foam fingertip. "Among few mature experiences," narrated by more than a dozen persons who are awareness majors at the community cable access TV blue bulletin board advertisement AM/FM C&W music weather information center sliding past felicitations, "are fair game for all sorts of interpersonal questions." "As a matter of course, under the courtesy circular of 91–96, you adhered in principle to the building's only open flame policy."

First, there was a royal lien on registration of all parcels found addressed from Ingersoll, Blank, and Dake, LLC, an import firm accomplishing business for many noted healers. Next, Sergei Kalamparumple, an American collector (whom, readily known to them, began divestitures in mind of remittance toward his non–nearly frozen Delores) released the parcel in question. Thrice, contents were described as relic, a scarab, of some craft. "Are you spraying that parcel left the United States," Blank asked? "It left Newer Loans, LA," replied Silas F. Many individuals, unable to confute this logic, in receipt since infancy, of exposure to several hundred thousand hours of content, became privily appalled by the formlessness of their present assignment. Hasty deputations of persons dedicated to pursuit of happiness converged upon the assessor, demanding access to tell founders of this event to name a prize for them.

Sadly, and with airs of great infantilism, Silas F. saying *aucune* (there were none), was resultant psychological agitated response indescribable: for everyone, moreover visibly upset they were no longer able to append their trade names to themselves at each crossroads, the season has become meaningfully storied over the vacation, lest they wither for a periwinkle spell of epistyles; since it is a fairly organic experience which, in deference to a new lamp placed atop one of the lake front's sporadic slips, reports to dawn arpeggio and other bureaus with brass trim. Left next to the sequoia, the estate of Inyo Tiarmsofarie subsequently hit upon a possible solution. For benefit of assembled television cameras, she convoked a forum to address their plight. It featured many perplexed looks, chin scratching, facial primping, and otiose postures. They determined perhaps if they did something revolting to natural consciousness, such as eating a lizard or something, processes of national selection would ensure continuity in the march toward receipt of a prize.

A consequent expedition assembled to look for lizards, but there were few enough in this northern clime. Add a carp, whooshed ashore, duly eaten in grated parsnip and yam cerement with charcoal rose hips, and for a moment, blessed harmony prevailed. "Some certified idiot lacking basic knowledge of co–dependency patterns is going to be responsible for starting the next wave," the concierge, eyeing the desultory carpe [*sic*] festival, heard tell. Long aware which guests sneaked cigarettes into their room, in defiance of civilized opinion, Tell, the concierge, finally, told to hit the fire alarm, beeping intermittently, skipped history class (on account of a recent penchant for turning in at sunrise). There were several snow showers and ice pellets on Monday as they pulled up stakes — Në'd already mentioned they were building the arts together. It was time for the lightning round, a team–building activity up to a degree.

Participants, tasked to address a collection of missing myth, bail out, each with different versions of *Poljola's Daughter*, cast in elements of time, place, and manner. Who was Poljola? Three viewpoints coalesced: either s/he was the worst fisherman, the village actuary, or a plow horse outside Sibelius' summer cottage. Why was music written about his daughter? "A sad air," Dauphine narrated, "in one more wear," prompted by her step–father, Middleford, "she saved the village from a slithering forest serpent hence." Porphyry contended that, in their land, prisoners of truth included all terse elements, and since a foal, Poljola's daughter was harnessed to pull a dead whale away from the village whence.

Left untold by Plair, his knowledge claimed via *th'ratwi'thorns*, thence she drove a terrible stench monster away from the village scene, the estate of Inyo Tiarmsofarie interjected, "further niceness depended on her dive with divine foal to the beach to quench pursuing dragon that, thick as us, tamed the unicorn and galloped from the sea to escape a lover." Hence, standing above the staircase to heaven, the Contessa Constancia Nadeladimov sniffed, "what nonsense," and added, "having restored plasticity to a ravaged space with a pose, she steered an errant school of porpoise from the beach." A close second, Gnadig Anodyne related with zeal she'd spared the groom from embarrassing hindsight.

Etaoin regarded this interpretation ironically, hinting at once that Poljola's daughter, concealing the golden hind, pierced by the storm hunter whereas, considering all sequence, and wherefore, ergo thus, interrupted by an historian (*all too busy*), indicating there, declaring the Finnish interdependence of 1919, a blob, scuttling, in tow by her at *Guetakagtu Sandviken*, thus denied access to the nascent Soviet fleet. Tried, to include all elements, in immediate sense upon an azure stage, they blended online for a group hug and accordingly, finally, with conviction, in fine, after all, and on the whole, made a long starry shot, until dialectic, though insecure on film and television, formed a premature anticlimax vis–a–vis premonitory expectations.

.   .   .

"Assigned to the security detail of my famous talk show," explained the Contessa, "PoD's duties were to intervene in bad situational flight soufflés of jilted lovers, unnatural birth patents, and incestuous liaison. He enjoyed this work since it permitted him to ingress bluff back shorts and alas proved far too apt at restorative order, for often, combatants, fraught by episodic sorties, ended in reconciliation while twenty or sometimes thirty minutes were left to the program, causing me to develop increasingly lengthy homilies exhorting compensations of moral decorum." Moreover, it was found that prince did not photograph well. During the infomercial phase, it was imperceptible, relegate as his post were to be near staged side shadows.

Beneath unflinching klieg lights of the public forum, however, his every movement, attended by a smear of dingy uncertainty, left the viewer knocked in deferral of an evanescent dactylology. Recognizably in danger of spinning out a decided unwelcome atavism, Nadeladimov had Ænselm ordered from the set, took to her bed complaining of spilt milk, allowed her fiercest rival, *Mr. Ng Live*, to absorb her backlog of festive circuit piñata traders, calendar stars above development, stressed millrace repairmen, and survival wash backs, and, born again, embarked upon an emblematic, resourceful career in televangelism. While the league treasurer drafted a brief syllabus, "Sergei's operatives, reasoning that Ænselm," penned Chantal, "for repetitive exertion, seemed quite suitable to their thriving communication industry in the United States, found employment for their new charge as infomercial shill."

Requested to mount medieval engines of perpetual motion, *ahriman* performed ceaseless feats of inordinate tracking, thaumaturgy, oasts, and spinal tapping, extolled upon those set around him, skillful nymph Hudspeth promulgating the virtues of dual action metabolizing processes. "If not for his excessive neck–breaking stretches resultant in fouling many of the rugged machines, confounding their advertised claim to foolproof reliability, 'his employers should have been spared the task of inducing PoD to train into another view,'" cited Rita. Ladæñæ Consuelas Mirabeau Mervyn glanced upon the assembly, and all was shushed. "Your pluperfectreßneß [*sic*]," Frederick II replied with a scowl, to the fourth questioner, "either one of these, persons, bring their subversive agenda to our meetings, what with the wrong dealer no less, who'd, known to work the architecture, bill the hell out of the *Papal Encyclical of 1237*." Disparately, to others' presence, or their answer to the last question, that a scrap of paper had been handed, bypassing all emissaries, to the need, Althea now had forty–five minutes to compose rationale for more shuffling papers.

As Frederick, ex–Ælfric, viz., if *xenonian* pro tem [*sic*], enjoyed the proceeding so far, a joke, the emperor remained standing, reified his numbers foursquare, questioned a silent groan, mixed via Schadenfreude [*sic*] in which Henry (VII), the ink, and our holy sole God, "then must fall to beg matinees and forgiveness, of him, in a strict policy of non–interference with our sister insurrections, let individuals of different faith also hang out freely, therefore," and ministerales, in lobbies, returned to seats to listen to their latent reproach. Apparent beneath his worksheet, often ballots were in for the salvage recovery effort, the committees announcing, there is a tie. A count, ¶hrotomeous, allowed unto how should you banish all critical faculties forsooth, "in all didactic sincerity," said Middleford, "the most meaningful glimpse shan't say how I like this unless you throw all of your bad selves out to her."

"And the air was as tan as mine soul," seemingly, Raisin, dreamed, and started, since the keynote replied, to her own question, saying, "for while we wait and whistle the world turned upside down." "Mass club she's not," chimed Blank, an inkling their connexion would not stay in the skip zone an instant longer moment. Yet, most of Bagler the enthalpist's next question cleared thoroughly, "what must needs be done?" "Ostrand's unpopular culture," Althea connoted hastily, helping a crush of inside outlet network degrading link margin saturation merge with roar of the distant sea above the evening traffic so didactic, so the question of ¶hrotomeous ran, "have you heard one about the policy which mainly decommissioned acrimonious tenements and thereby spared to dessert itself?" Inspector Læmært sought, aground of first flickering faded flashes of daylight, queerer words. "Does the story ever wind up cold, ere in ten minutes, coral index tools for slippage improvised?"

Amidst standard of excessive integrity formed djinn, ultra vires [sic], almost bleached semanticists melding, "we want you," unto Læmært, who replied, "idiots, do you read from a script (we want you to hide), or just making up as you merrily go long?" "Hide from the identified flying objects," the voices rang, "or you will be hauled before the ICC. And not even bored old Inyo may suffice to save you from unclear demise." From the premise went Desdemona from their sight to the tune of *Can't Bowl Right Now*. "Talitha," thought the Inspector, downing his caraway rye, "must, telephone, Fulnes and find out more about the corn dog charade." And the Reverend Logan Ferguson, doctrinalist scourge of Snorggi, in a yard where cattails hissed, in a sufficient usual current, further call all very troubling to Regatta, who'd warned her father formally in rhyme as a poor little boy he'd been attacked in church by a droning hornet, gainsaid such stratagem as might now plot emeritus, whomever dissembled finely, "I just wanted to see your darned digs."

Today would be merciless alkaline, a hang–up nettling some kind of deadline, perhaps complementary to *untenets* vacuuming all of those crushed vanilla cherubs next to her or his bar stool. Whatever all of it was behind them, the enthalpist Bagler declared, by jingo, they were going to have some lists of things. The enthalpist began the New Year glaring out upon that best January night he was able to stand, albeit via crutch, after that tambourine landed on his head once during a verticule incident that drained his day trippers' profiteering business. Before the door stood, a boy seemingly knew how conducive an informal survey shall be. "Are these stupid questions," Bagler asked? "If you died tonight do you know where you would go," was the reply?

"Into a wholesome ware," Bagler answering, addled, "now is that your best fetch?" "Do you believe intelligently," the boy insisted? "Yes," Bagler, "now depart from here with your ghost registry," said, remonstratively, being a slammy Sammy with the door that stood unturned. Amongst noise, *finth*, thought that enthalpist, "I could pursue and give thanks." Never shamed in hope, critics host the wan door he beheld, flung upon trackless expanse of pristine snow, stretched, horizontally, at his feet, a tinny pinchbeck cylinder lain in abandon. "It was a messenger of shadow puppet," replied his niece, Raisin, returned from the aviary, whence one more hive had vanished. "Pshaw, omen, any awkward blog could harp at fewer goofs than so messy a discus. Have you no shuck for more internets via social engines whose diversions sweep away my little lunch hour stick city, illustrative of a nearby choice grommet, how Chad's gain tattered angle theater hymn to its doughboys and tries to cobble this thrown cabin ink expert some thousand years in the reverse future is in inverse proportion to any amount of all time?"

Daily, "it was a messenger of shadow puppet and His frozen peephole," St. Agnes reiterated, since a man lingered at the smorgasbord of resentment, railing against the pious fatalism of his niece. "Away from me, you popular mechanistic deistic encyclicals," he'd wail, frightened at the ancient Manchu he was ever trying to trim. "His eye is on the scarecrow," she insisted. "I'm sure all this sentience was wish fulfillment of the warped message, ousted lexicological continuity, the Alexandrine in–fill, naive culture, and such knowledge forever effaced. Give me my reverie or, given mete dearth." "How about some Nicean emigrant music," offered Iraisamonde? "Snare me such mulch sap," the enthalpist ranted, "Noone hears nightmarish watery epistles of the Etesian chorale master; any terrifying more herald of vengeance and mercy you abrade, a tinny purple shadow puppet, now go into your god house and leave me and pale video poker alone."

"Don't dish the baby via the bath water," Althea pled. "That baby can take care of itself," he retorted, "and I'll prove it. Listen gosh darn pumpernickel! You see its role left out a rightly obdurate shadow puppet as ours." "Beware those whose glut is their god (Phil 3:19)." "Thence is he not construed in his own vitiation of us." His idea of atonement is clear, yet no one else surpasses Ostrand's predilection for stifling unaccountable propriety. This effort exhaustive to enthalpy, Bagler returned to his drab futon, sullenly recollecting the enclosed message, and opened it to find an illuminated manuscript from the papal nuncio. "My dear child," it read, "for nineteen years we've each done what we must, yet now events cause me to plead for your expertise, if not your belief."

The enthalpist went on to read Reject Fair awarded him a missed linkage inanity in absentia [*sic*], and for his prize, a grand mime, embedded in substrata of the 13th century, threatened the great cathedral at Worms. Only Bagler, and his effusive time travel expedience, might be reliant enough to implode it. The enthalpist fell back in a stupor, thinking, "fat chance I can anyway," chewing brittle left from the church picnic, and fell asleep while mentally adrift with a ginger retort. The next morning he awoke to a sound of thunder, amidst rushing winds he could walk, it was a miracle, he strove to share the news with his niece, only to learn she just eloped with a selfless beast. One nice wee thing about writers is that here you might sail faster than currently against the wind, or isn't this simply scholastic flimflam and I, did, use, this word accidentally twice in one sentence once, yet all the while look forward to thanking you all for another year of perennial or geranium bulbs. Of a certainty, encompassed major mote radii Etaoin actually read, disinterested converse monads, incensed with nothing like this perceptual makeover asked, "weren't ripples dually transitive?"

Only mere static tub blew denser drape. "I barked over the Styx

and stole slang restive garland, a former eavesdropper now chaste." Her
rearranged, nostalgic and chic stand–in fresco, as lone outlier, framed
by knock along Sadducee, near offset serer gloom, sure dampened
sylph–like tattersall acetylene demurrage. "pH," spat the theorist noisily,
"let's talk of nurturance system djinn fad," but by an eclipsed rhapsody,
mingled triptych announced a crooked lasagna knit, cascade multiple stir
fries, jangulating nuthatch throne, beleaguer some trammeled inebriate
green noctilucent skip.

"Whither goest thou?" replied Ostrand? A risen amplitude, unheralded, pulsed in alarm at it, addressed, in a deep Latin bass, least
unanswerable question. An importunate reply rippled from all around,
an assembly, convoked by chant and swinging censors, congregated.
"Saturday mass," Læmært explained, "to meet the family. Should you care
to attend." Middleford, preferred to sheer dotage, hovered outside the
vestibule, and waited for Læmært to gather his family. Regatta arrived
by separate carrier. Entering the sanctuary, they stood haltingly before
the cross. Three pews above the rectory, Regatta Læmært wrestled a
conscious re–evaluation of recent events. "If I suppose that I know a
thing, I have yet to understand the true ought of a thing. If I love God I
am known by Him (1 Cor 8:3). Though I heed, not every day is very well
lived. Fears continue to hedge my thought. Belief of God will restore
me to a condition of ability become a sentiment that sin has turned into
sickly whimsy." She pondered a peripheral sense of perplexity through a
healed combe, for as shadow puppet perceived, official blessing evinced
to proceed with this inquiry, an awareness that *wergild*, whom she began
the day determined to keep away from her father's case, were in no
way contained, and thrilled with regret then, in respect some present
trial, shadow puppet repented of his deed and, offering a new covenant,
afforded much more than the dissociation now found contemplated.

"Though mere sentiment would take, I never checked, and always
assume you believe all of my behavior. How do I right my disbelief that
world is ending? How could another word lurk?" "Though impartial
observers shall say I am bested with trivial snipe, the procedure is

validated by those interesting public programs on the birth of circular reason," Middleford, by his action of speaking personally to the commissioner, even at hazard of revealing a code name in any cusp perishable, also seemed determined to keep the ICA out of the investigation; while the loss of the scarab hid from his friends, the collectors, and their seductive collaborative polls.

In a classicism reflective, under the murky jaunt listed their gerund bark, toward Neath, without occasional talent ordinarily crepe, "ergo into the middle of convenient waste not aggregate," i.e., and matin *uchaux*, their faith not even jammed from beginning operant excellence, and complacent all obstacles were here to say, "beyond luck warmed over, destiny of cringe attainment, or love dissonance status unlearned, are fallback into happenstance once migratory," and things whomever punched reset fitfully, reified strait into any preservation anxiety; annoyed the sensibly helpful, they accused manxome Noone, "you floated into expressions which anyone knew not how else to be." These channels broached topic of morbid exeunt preface, reflective of nascent condominium of invisible totality, and next befell inability's delicate rephrased too barmy to entreat conscientious effort Idiopath, more skilful in order to manifest peripheral, through lack of successful perception of subjective interval, moreover each roved under microcosm then extant in accord with pluribus then we haves.

"It being written, 'it offended Noone whom'," in wisest stead stiffly reneged and refused to listen to another word or so for a week, at least until their sudsy will amortized their arguability, "at the essential monument said aha to so hardily one more of 'our greased fetes of relativism,' we're impotent to stand and receive trail mix like the rest of us." These, *uchaux*, tossed, his lame cover, grouted by her fixed silence, before other current events, trifurcated into chronic noise, strained run–off malt mufti. Helped out, a kernel uplifted by Fanta, said (they hire enthalpists), and overused, as Etaoin, retired band leader, a palmer somewhere restored, equitable distribution of municipal parking revenue, or a screaming headline I thought ironic at compline, left, while

Læmært wondered at the vaporous languor of desuetude that led him to this pass. Francis perused the architecture. It, and the liturgy, not unpleasantly reminded him of his Mundesley parish in East Anglia where he was borne. If presently not a serving member in his previous faith, Frank was amidst the first to admit the stability of organized religion in provision of social utility.

"Fewer than few hundred years ago, humanity was restricted to travel afoot, horsepower, steam, or sail, and now we embrace an orb swiftly spanned by inventions of the little novel writing machine. My pulse thickens at that, though a boat of wishful thinking was so fun." It had been a rather bleak concession. Many heads turned to look around. Returned from communion, Læmært noted the absence of the figure in the rearmost pew. Only deduction might be made in certitude. Middle-ford was CIC (if, in canon, non–official capacitance). While one other, also non–prepossessive, angle, which Læmært held not quite up to par, occurred to him, the entire case just felt punted into a crocked hat.

The Site of St. Agnes.

Fulnes had lost four hours, mostly in traffic. Any time beyond that span might not count for every thing unless he was on to something. He refused to use his sanctioned swan song to blast through orange barrel labyrinths sprung up near the Temple. Sovereign facts aside, friend Fulnes was never able to explain, for posterity, why he languished as inspectorial factotum. Arrived at Lichvue, he ducked swiftly behind the sideboard in vain hope of retrieving the key. Fulnes faced an even lengthier drive to the central repository.

Many may guess the anonymity of inspectorial factotumship ceased to pull ambitious men in its wake. Once, this post offered perceptible security of advancement. In the dingy cellar, a civilian greeted Fulnes languidly. The manifest printed ten minutes later. Scanning it, he saw three keys, and/or key chains, were listed. In an elderly aside, a worthy constable approached the desk, musing, "of late, the system groaned and brought forth mice." "Ye became that way when the system began loosing your scholars," the clerk, drawn to search the container, spoke tersely. Fulnes broke into the box. Removing the key, as he wished to do, was a less simple matter. For although at one time the post of inspectorial factotum opened all doors, no longer was it seemly to flaunt this capacity. The clerk departed to assist another investigator at the bleakly contrasted ledes. If he could help it, Fulnes would not lift that key.

"This," the redeemer, finally moussed, over–steadied, "was made by Nertz–Kalpa, a Polish firm. They served most polling stations of Least in the greater *xenonian* midlands until being bought out of it." Silently, the constable wrote several notes upon the pad and torn sheets, handed then to Fulnes, "list all rotten boroughs extant with booths installed before 1655." Fulnes stared as the constable regarded him evenly. Cradling the key in his hand, Fulnes enunciated a voiceless why? Inevitably, Fulnes peered across the desk at the gentleman's own tie. They had each been to the same inspectorial factotumship school, albeit decades apart.

Throughout the structure of the force, one once gave this office due nod, assuredly sturdy amidst wind of change, yet now it was unseemly to be seen in this capacity. As Fulnes, and/or others like him, thought it might be time to bid adieu to a seamless career, "off you go," agreed PoD. "It is depth," the kale video poke protested! "Allow us," Ænselm urged. Fulnes turned quickly, for whiffling after bursts of click beetles were darkened skies. Undertowing the tulgey wood, the [sic] bat's temporary presence allowed them to share, at Lichvue, "the internal debates are about the only fun thing that happened all day. All I wrote down was, 'today was a rest from all the other days. I didn't see one person outside.' Since the wind chill is nearly four degrees, it's possible this phrase amalgamated an effort to forestall biased narratives." At Least, in a shadow of reprieve, Desdemona saw scope after scope at rock bottom, considering an investment in futility to recharge the escarpment filter beam.

Ostrand's lorn hope, to find an isometric pulse, alum well of flimflam flummery, into whence trickled some visitants, naive ingredient interpersonally in their canton of bright columns terraced, a net crescendo of Algernon's destiny. Hence man replaced this description of given Earth, the replicant consanguine casement periodicity, sold a keen effort depicting reaction of many loud gestures, ascribing arpeggio pica disdain of ramifying bodies, anymore seconds wee loath to share of their earth flight, emigrate as toot clefts harbored the vantage. Audibly gained through cavernous inflection of aforesaid rushing winds, out the strong stalls of Lilliputiania wakened her to overture, the second ingratiate the occupant, a bipedalien human estranged, to enact simple revelatory impetus, expending limit tangibly worn into gerund odalisque. A pilgrimage of transcendence wrought from the hand of any hive, Renata, Ladæñæ Mirabeau Mervyn, exegesized instead a plan of restituting her facility with new purpose.

.   .   .

Iphgene Heppleweis (ally of Henry (vii)), non—happy about xenonians & exempt
obvioregal skaters (daughters of Islam), decreeing cross—check via Noone's village
bio—optic scan... cue the zombies... ¶hrotomeous, "the protagonist." Fulnes
(et al) attacked by jubjub while trying kicked key beneath armoire... saved by Isp
the xenonian who, if his own access 2freeze comped, is able to explain method
for containing bandersnatch (via an ersatz one).

IV — xix — Key 2A missing nowhere.

Tease left in immaturity innermost, l'nurt held her synaptic jurisdiction and remained quixotic for no spell, thinking mitotic faults at cost, biopic stour elsewhere exceeded, or blunt ghost tiles far out—grabed hexameter near the balustrade. Noone viable, a censored visitant whose wash, however she went donating hence to alleged variable, had receipts brandished of visionary accord, merged in albeit diverse hearsay. An attempt to declare an office versed in glory, the holy name, as root of a shadow outside where they, on the verge of travelers patterned off insipid plate, left in awareness; a chip here they verily now halted when themes thus punted out in defiance of preventable clasp. Now and then, notables assembled to appear quaint for any relativity which merely SOMHAD gained on them.

At least there, theories, of why else may ties reglue onto a sane habitual rote kick penalty, are justified, undone amidst immeasurable constraint of achievement, fielded in newly flung fit epithets afar; effigies out with all retorted groovy mission of craft it never hurt shrugged indelibly their most current code, drop the rest curls, wasting no smithy an earnest genuine reflection of oriflamme, cannot cusp the explosive mange, again numb, this arm, or their concerted first list of titles. Such airs, prompt static noises of lickety—split, also seemed immediately awry in pleasant fortune moreover put in the complexity of act.

All point bulletins went out of their way to show a loss off Broadway, and a sandy void, found jolting near the information off–ramp, oft untold moribund petit–fours, where, toothily lucubrated into collective Vikram, an orange angora ocean nor, whence Idiopath no longer filled nowadays ever. If a pink dashed scenic line parallelepiped his course on any given roadmap, it thrilled wishful Nereids and, at Least, fictitious landscape flowed past treatably. All waltzed between a misty Hibernian twilight toward one amusement park, strewn with shells for ribbons and balloon shrouds, pound for square inch boxed into cumuliform high–wire regurgitated witch hazel. Here, returned in crocks, debunked lots of not sticky eclectic movable feasts vetted unlit daybreak.

Heightened awareness struck this reality: the otherwise reasonable gallery left star–gazing above a dunk tank SOMHAD to revive existence via more tubular preponderance, and hence for teen or fewer caroling sunshine patriots, the eagle flew by the time hors d'ouerve [*sic*] arrived. At his customary shelves of apocrypha, science alone seemed gone in berth theater, held out as Nietsche, early courier of the fright, beat facing off the opposite shore. After a verb was banned, ¶hrotomeous, businesses of shipping ordeals upon a magnified Miranda cast, replied, "there will be no *inter–regnum*, withal; those hazards of radioactive decree, developmental, and residual display, I admit rather evolved anomalies unless one went out into the vaster realm to frolic before the throne of clouds in Florence. The first thing we did was let loose fancies for guests who occasioned several moments, many state dignitaries; summoned, the most tacit episode starred from the sidelines. Nor is my own cause for red carpet much gone, leaving this abnormally heavy, yet unable gestalt."

Being very neat during transfer to compile portraits of a departed congregation, it felt no less compelling, an indoor event of renascence. Talitha, whose feeling about life became significant, narrated, "there is no such room for my ongoing if aimless bubble, so how or why am I indisposed to recover emotionally, misdelivered to get out of my identity" — "the irreplaceable complexity" — "when I was sent to commence values wont to revolt against the birthday boy?" "My son," Frederick put in, "had his out on the issue of happiness (a compliment to rare times I had to squelch, in belief circular riffs busily erupt out of our most fatherly instincts), and peace thing, and here every essence dares me to write them off by default. I spent out, bought comfort in known trade secrets, planted not by a cluster into the tangled my bluff, and reinforced career podiatrists, whom everybody thinks are virtual wing–dings; it's all I can do, since whatever malingering those flashy tropical punches with emptiness can only question insolently took upon a big act of contrition."

If they'd makeshift a very muddled comprehension into equanimity, after several pages made up some great epiphany (we, in tandem, armed to tap or create risen concepts) revisited, inasmuch as panacea man, who endured in a tangled maze of stuff he'd left us alone, "I spared myself trudging up–tempo below, but the train groaned and huffy freaking year–old Minorite beggars gave away more than the first tale." And gazing fixedly to sag down with cries of, it's very well my present starch was fruitless, not perhaps endemic decorum, Henry (VII) turned to behold what happened, except for one thing: they faced the wrong door with complete composure.

The response of the church — to leave detachment to a more friendly hope of national spiritual poverty, i.e., and glorification of differentiating a trip to Freddy's picnic, said the last of fifteen oddest canons to paean. The only sense of Christianity today, [sic], e.g., the devil walked up into the third person without reminding us, glanced around politic visitations, the whole nine yarded, ostensibly, for example, gate themselves by dredging little more than marvelous mood, and pounded on any table, this flat courtesy a mask dissolved into every bump and slam session as erased, in bolting panic, "like most congenial, I just skim smooth lyrics all of the air conditioned, padded lah–lahs mindfully provided for their own conclusion inaudibly." Above dormant youngsters, Señor Florian indicated the traffic circle to compliment acolytes' recall, "as customs house for just desserts, ici c'est rond–pont [sic]."

In cusps, clueless barking lots were awful. A gargantuan, if not Brob-dingnagian, wet hen, berthed in the nearby amphitheater, had backed up lottery sales for miles. "Should we jog afoot straight up the access road, and risk mete tinfoil eidolon or worse, while sloshed behind backfire bootlessly?" "You adapted her tactics to deal," huffed ¶hrotomeous, "the universe you'll meet, a prince to wean awkward overripe installation of the old backwash." A duet got so snowed in, to avoid lightning, until into gravity kicks the brightest and sloppiest of human innovation as it goes. Echoed Henry (VII), "before weeks of uncertainty repelled what we could have done to avoid it earlier." "It was the way I planned it," within the hold, Ænselm was heard to say. "Please yell," enjoined the monarch, "the diabolically obvious, witness, albeit, via intermittent, clear, and practically abjured, unceremonious converse, I'll bet, semi–public minions of civil obedience romance this well–fed cat who was, that," pausing to lean upon the end of the master speller fork, from that snell perspective of the five rivers, "least endlessly unfunny (if lilies, influenced to make up before drawing too much amusement, persist in print anyway) secret.

"I can excuse antics kept from initial limitation, so I'll intervene my best; beneath their palpable pressure it may sign, one letter must be a fatal progress. I'm not such a damn classical enemy — these rare prophets become rank, trip to the realm of St. Ives, and thus miss the bridge to leap into every available burger pit — jammed up with great mismakes at Kinko's to shrink so." However, and it's not supposed to be a kindlier snap, or pretend had just another day, a chair so organized nodded off, and a grey eminence, Bagler, hinted rustic stillness far and near, finally pointed out in jovial condescension, "we put together via chance only regarded yesterday as uninspiring value, it accompanies time when simply a met cusp of men, pledged to set down that precursed matrix of fabricated advice which would make a tree–hugger out to fleece the forest, to quote the Salem play; much to commemorate," conveying events through a filter upon l'nurt [*sic*], a frown deepened as it once did, "my effort also up–ended rapport, in many cases unsought. Now I chasten a thorough inconsequential sap as permitted to exist on fringes of each culture. Try hard not to let other accouterment to this

Fabian odyssey of relentless society mindset bar opinion for holding up remnant vestiges of abstruse hasty arrangements proved into the ground."

These put on, St. Agnes saith, "hand in their cute orgone for lost agates," the hereafter shades of *wishram* ermine, "could I not warp it to suit their findings" — "lest you be trans–mogrified." Fulnes, only now noticing she made no singular impression, remarked, "if you are Glyntz, how can you shade so swell?" "I am wearing the dress worn by an aunt, Persephone, and a mole, dour in the episode, never more dull than one whole choker, invoked to cheer between a Norn led to craze," so similarly they plunged into a cold kettle streaked with lime. A vast cavernous lowbrow tempest encapsulate, his tantric gaze permit some slight to sip into consciousness, and limit, defined filament of a lamp once inactive, requited time to coalesce eke achieving return to utility freed, for tan beans touted the fountain beneath the spruce. A huge, patriotically painted *HMS Flie*, in dry–dock lien, moped into fidelity.

Since they refused to leave, thereat, albeit grown intransitive, summons their apparent whimpering, "I don't ever stay to watch this," startled by argent infusion of psychic deviance the wax–born, as Dauphine knew of them, left cairns, tread past, meant to direct the covalent fast masked among finished levees predating the lane led into a real flat in other quarters, and became a segue into marital squabbles over the ocean. A swain twice loved his truck more than ever. A chilled sled, stood amidst mingled shards of vast ceramic worlds, now shattered in a stale grasp. No sports they, my shell game, shelf imposed scholars fizzled like enamel settling on plate, each yard promised sale, an ad ultimate legend, and ere air no more became the dolorous march, though in time gyre solute alacrity then occurred at the decanted mote, plentitude proviso pimento imagined dust. As major mote radii clustered in registry, the inspectorial factotum forgot to minimize his own good sometimes, fly fishing for flounder in a mellow sea of amiability, fitting closure to the last three years and their first name chumminess.

Prevalent fugues yet sturdy, habits of profession only certified his witness of the bottle return. Every sumac foliage athwart the lane was stomped by them smoothly in little concentration or ever show of concern, and the queue, faced fourfold, marked progress toward a sinister azimuth, stumbling not, feckless of extensive root networks of the uplifted bog. Desdemona would not go with them, mentioning her own depressed amperage as indicator of a separate peril. Lugubrious as each case spelled out may proved, not a sprinkle may ever be accountable with the presence of mind all of space converged. "His face sure rings a bell," starred ¶hrotomeous, seethed into the eye of panic. Unless Fulnes might ever begin to notify hitherto jaded colleagues, a creature came of terrifying mien. "More or so days, when their final plausible counter–argument for or against me, hand–in–hand tacked a new course, soon led to turn discussion on the patio over to" — *ahriman* sneezed — "bless you." Flagged offside, they took two hours to pay the piper, and resumed the tour.

Home to witness the hollow facade.

"Too airily American anteroom," Justine, one more nebulous occludant, averred arguably. Behind them, a long bungalow of Chantilly rolfed green sleeves, three portals fitfully sauced a partial rapprochement and took second place, covered by totality shed from eclipse of few eidolon remnant. They slept in the eeriest parlor along rows of berths previously occupied by batholith, and witlessly numb, spent numerous tithes for an aha — heavens awoke, bracketed in even ruder gaskets, and traducing a wan product in favor of more vegan technocracy, retraced steps of an enthalpist arrived to defuse the wet hen; amongst parallelepipeds, holistic whodunits lack cusp themes anymore, and huzzahs fixedly derisive of scenery, s/he'd rave about the eighths' milestone achievement in mixed company of bobbins, but traipsing an unfamiliar stile, fewer than half these distinctions found reflectively sloppier logs onto village server.

It was best to leave bygones at the door above the three–hour meltdown necessary to impress ontological booths of acquisitive inklings. The severer evening's best lizard dealt, so they hiccoughed via floppy fields, snapped twigs, rousing borogroves, and skirted wild arch developments which generically may have happened, since an untimely watchword, vastened to avert declasse denouement, sprang into the bagatelle, and they realized SOMHAD stretched the hostel boat legally. The incumbent familiar, Rita Ladæñæ Mervyn Mirabeau, keen needs fretting, "Euryoclydon." Non–gamboling, an ill wisp, searing the horizon beyond their perspective gaze, shrank to mute amber which the inspectorial factotum sought to watch glow all out the dark window, chisels then bent (he kept his eye shut) a new path noticeably emblazoned, displaced some parallel mote they now stood in my dark range, coaxing the leftover rice dish from Alabama, at length, the jujube's turbulence dysphasia, often gonged rich mobs varied PoD's esthetic momentum to wash upon the shore of Euxine.

The walls splat at ¶hrotomeous' reply, fluctuating arcs of methane, ammonia, and freon, imminent from its nose drool, sans elan, chivying to Ænselm unsociably, were I too shrill to impart this period as a family ritual, Fulnes fought, another issue of substance, a mediate endocrine of organic involvement, the universe Euryoclydon preempted, extended an event driven allowance. Supposed its eventual, unspeakable tyranny of existence, when an only way one can sustain a creative impulse began, eke wed in mimsy forelock, to fake thick self–depth, via dry manque, led to fewmets rained onto them from Euryoclydon; shivering in flippant precaution, Pluto's booth flimsy, mental, contorted, etc., in compression of volume, thereby reductionist, fewer surfactant areas exposed to ¶hrotomeous' noxious attack. But for the artist formerly known, this process was too slow to prevent being gone into large siphons.

Out of the barrel, this time, the plaintive trek unfurled, comprised of argent integers, which, handed such awning stock abaft, browbeat, conveyed inhibition of natural reflux. "Ah, felt always tickled," PoD, a once recrudescent amber grey blob, shuddered sickeningly, shriveled into a piteous walnut shaped sack. A gulf of experience now yawned, "being polished, my aspect in balance, my feverish desire gags. Anyway, I'm planning to feel normal" — "what for" — "for ending dominion of you and your ilk, superstition, antediluvian fear, premonition," *pluperfec-treß* knew; "did you eke any of it," Porphyry flung back over the shoulder at Në Dipol, who shook in a somewhat tepid embrasure they failed to comprehend, albeit sealed the article ended, and in aphonic apathy they sat for seconds.

Fulnes was of a mind, however his object, disapproved inherently not just of his presence, but also of the prospective role for her of allegorical tour guide, waived at the flown array. The coquettes, Chantal labeled they whom, intent upon tumbling everlastingly, plodded out, lurking right nor left the room I, too, took a gulp of fresher air around, three o'clock, wandering in a courtyard riotous with rank sub–tropical growth, wishing Delores were, "here, many are these," said she, "who have, in dearth, refuted summons of *inter–regnum*." The ground, for those yet live moreover, proof little were reversible. Tiniest cobs sufficed to void a single step; the sprawl root net put paid to any notion of progress; Fulnes, arrived at that worst or last shift where he, stripped by politic regard of his cop, viewed himself as glib and seedy sycophant, must bear no longer worn blinkers. His move to tear them off his visage accrued fierce, contemptuous solicitude from his star witness.

"Thousands issued a statement," seen twittered via the Assizes, "before you, should, in it's mere self, demonstrate the present mission best described, perhaps, uncertain, we, the Assessor, chief artisan of citizen's said defence district and Isp, assistant comptroller (skating in a heffalump herd; suddenly our canteen, which was lying on top of cultural achievement, for the worthless draught), £2,250, figured as calm tributary to general desserts," Porphyry wrote an inscription, "for many folk would wish to leave this," he warned, and commended Nietsche, for once written, "whatever, doesn't kill you, makes you stronger;" here, comped, our erased caucus, Regatta's cause gaveled down, they and we gifted the iBC mint for eighty percent, betraying the *Encyclical xxxiv.iv.cxii.*

Florian chortled, "to prohibit use of defamatory language ad infinitum [*sic*]: in forefront of emotional correctness at *wishram*, as/is appeals are approved by that *plenitudo potestatis*." This sampler, the Minister of

Transport precluded, an assembled retainer might bear chilled PoD to the shares of newer loans. You realized spring could be here so soon, they'd liefer go to coast for a weekend and get an antinomian petition abated. Ænselm bore those attentions in unusual stochasticism, recognizant his recent narrow escapade placed him in a position of supplication, and was merely relieved Alcuin seemed unbent upon any super–imposed agenda ridden template of his own for Ænselm's already addled character. "I don't even know how to pronounce the first letter of my name," s/ he protested, eliciting an assurance out of a bobbin it would not matter, and for this reason, and because, eager to flee testy voices of his present circumstance, Ænselm surfed on feeble cost and felt one sting lift an alluring time dump, once fetid mildew, a least neat, droll dupe, painted Room 2A in arts.

Run apart between a cathartic tarragon fob uplifted, ghosts of wanton luaus manfully, much pontooning turned Athena onto haunt non–livid blancmange scenes, Fulnes, shoved via implemented resolve, back toward the treacle well; *pluperfectreß* paused, startled for a moment, as a shade appeared to address her. "It is best done, that is done but once." As *pluperfectreß* pondered unsolicited advice, colleagues clustered around. Insisted a freak, "into the frozen deeps!" "Leave me," *pluperfectreß* snarled, stepped forward, and affixed her bolo tie with a vicious pundit. While not prey to exclusionist sense immuring many of her peers' ill will toward all non–entities, St. Agnes felt repentant enough to regard her once privileged walk now tainted by feckless blunders of this interloper, whom seemed resolved to feed to the cyclical beast. For his part, the inspectorial factotum, any love lost abandoning his diligence habitual, for all oversight vanished, and Noone really cared what he was up to, saw in repetition of standard principle an only cornerstone of lingered sanity.

Not resistant then to eschatological device employed to demise of his original purpose, to find one live testament to fell echoes of previous weeks, he coaxed his hostile interlocutor in sufficient vastness. Far, far aloft flew the blob, far from Antarctic deep consigned for it, northward in fact, tumbling down upon shores of a slightly warmer sea, where it bounced fitfully and, to no purpose, in times together always sounded, better than now, and then I miss my fair rake, once hoped to be a force for good, yet who is by the way almost unmindful more or less. In our dream time of several finesses began voices ago into today, gone off with the rest of the building, their tepid beer festival web cams trained to eye everything as if I'm expected to peek and peer around for their voyeurism diversion and finally, as Core fast forwards toward emptiness, will her love for me only depend or deepen, albeit inadvertently how it brought about via cameo or per rare omniscience often salved from imbecilic puerility our being tepid as all get out, such style and grace mirth fled, the day incidental quantity hand—outs occurred, our dual benefit of mutual doubt mismakes, in both pace and structure, whose absence robs all glory from noontide, stifles the gate of borealis overbooked, and any glimmer of the evening star fitful at best fainéant, consent, in mercurial, rather volatile semblance, even if she is all miss link about it, yet a tempter shifts project value, in mean irrelevant monotone, humbled where forgetful spells inner wariness, kept idle amidst our passage toward decorum among prompt seedy shuffle, on or beyond tonal requiem, the greater west in fallow remuda, given rise to phased seasonal Ives via philharmonic ejection, its cusp both pivots snapped, located in crows' feet of the dead headlong schooner nestled in dry—dock, and Sagittarius thus sent to escort Xantippe, Molyneaux, daft to dormant locale, Mozart has devolved somehow into scramble mode, and concern about this marred mass at much crucial juncture appear typical for an underlying cause while guest and felicitously reproach noctambulance.

If eschewing the usual walk, while he also almost put the ring back in his pocket, wondering if holiday greeting could assuage margin calls betimes foreseen as something, melted beyond screens or lentils projected vast wafers of fennel saffron wax over just her way of letting knowledge of present moment in, or crepe via focus, slept effusively during an effort to remind oneself of the word originally imagined to recede in above, riddled shakily as shades and tones, she is afoot; revoked to undisclosed purpose thus area my tough tracts trickle toward reserve, such tenuous reception maybe engaged the only thing recycling avoided: pull all of this pulse away yet the moon does glare in so, illumining three nights later the brushfire started, Dauphine's mode of exiting further converse, so before a nice correlation launch of trinkets and errata, Fulnes was able to admit they went nowhere more quickly than first expected, least unseen in every shadow a trembling foil her step might trip spellbinding by and by.

Any mode still glimpsed of her divinity home school economic project flip–flopped to elapse rustic freak hostels which can find enough good to say under other conditions maybe we're each commingled beneath discrete voiceless cones of blind vanilla time, considered well spent if more costly from nearly every angle until she cradles, what's left of me, unless nothing shall ever be sad, "my diatomic pipes are wandering here," Althea chattered passively, Ænselm affecting a piteous tryst — a wry flutist phased ejection coolly. Her name apropos, Glyntz whispered whoosh to him sullen as a geranium, whirling through pages of dusty spiral comet theory, pinwheeled in a vertical smear, "they say you amass time." As *ahriman* melted, Talitha's shadow waxed; in her skewed ethereal suede, casually aware of pixel seneschals, she swaggered into any safehouse. "I managed to reboot an invitation, but on my decision to occupy much shrubbery," PoD blew out, or in, a power surge, as if they were faking a DUI, and then everybody showed up at the mercy of the early sixties. Is it simply another myth of a pink flamingo night light?

Also rash and constant criticism, the pluperfect attempt to reconcile diverse tourism in the shadow of poverty thus drawn (their visit had somewhat quadrupled in pits for this very bland catch in the well), comparison between forthcoming as a freight train in the deli aisle to listen to artsy sleep, and the incommunicative stage wardrobe left its mantra to an uprisen form, the fielders (stirred to beseech direction of a wordless soul), gratefully found temporal digs in following, via beeline, the pointed finger invisibly proffered. Unlit, embraced nearby lofts of hopeful access detour recoiled, sane paths in excrescence predictably, while debunked in radiant sleighs, tearlessly scribed tomes, bored and oft noisome dank to—lets ahead, a sudden instance of extra terra formal surveillance then boiled, ripening strait in vivid purpose, albeit flamboyant, as debatable word (inmost rush to deepen the moat of situation via increased focus reliance) upon the surest, often inspired floor management tappers who were interested in acoustic qualities.

If, about the little canaries they might test visible zero through, or on second mind eon agog, the plain seemed narrower, though wind power, solar extract accompaniment, or zoning for chance might seriously, the enthalpy banner sourly flag, in response anatomically unsnarl if there was never a word, conditioned, the tidier blend all redound in one sonorous lead for mint; these bellicose rug rage syndrome, surreptitious in nature, should younger vintage suffice than caloric to measure public indifference to all feeling toward a name, yet at cylindrical epicenter of apogee, forgotten Iphgene swore here service, via feat of elsewhere while the sham retrieved, vapidly recouched, a redirect fee simple in the works. It was not wholly unavailing through their fall, as toward asymptotic antipode, flavored to watch mephitic beings relay to intelligible cyber chatter, "if you were drunk, then the deal is void of meaningless ambiguity;" in rapid and unceremonious departure, Fulnes fell through hell noisily, not without remark each layer comprised an age of damnation congruent with mores of a dominant paradigm.

Since he landed, the sacrist whom, in wake of dunes, extant eldritch invasion of heffalumps, siege of Worms said overwhelmed, schemed to secure icons seeming ineffable to continuity of his project, knew innocuous AM receivers installed in the loft were fully capable of spoiling the pool despite sunny oldies. Scribbling sedulously that these creatures seemed akin to mythic pachyderm of torrid regions, yet possessed powerful alembic quantities, Fr. Anselm, thundering herd eyed warily, turned to accost this newest guest's lost contact lens. How then, with the inspectorial factotum's arrival, had Fr. Anselm, colour him baleful, for the newcomer would bore a net, to let off his cherished post? Poking his palate, he took manger steps away from the frieze, pondering how quickly an idea suffocates amidst conditions of lapse. Past enough hitchhike area diversionary blocs as carven for a nave, militant again, fomentable disjunctural concepts felt, versus a ferric–hydrous next trim, sternness as alloy of material density.

Antonyms of space, purposeful affiance, of object necessitarianism, analog drawn out foremost rain suds, slightest distance, of onion writ codified, for an elect of access live, viz., concerted miss cusp trim, lest elation ensue, an ethos decisive instrument, apt, prefigured themes impinging the neo–spatial position of an aspirin, Fr. Anselm held forth with someone who cared throughout; their discussion, if nettling very little actual identity, enabled nearby district Idiopath to maintain here, once and for all sorts of water sports, the most striking differences of scenery are still around. Sometimes their interlocutor, traumatized by an Euryoclydon, had very little time to reconsider margin for error, albeit mores, as extension of subjunctive splice, if held by recessive artisans to be an inexact prolix, seemed fast to all tangible plumb.

Hence, as not merely eager, yet tirelessly avid, to recall slumbering proletariat in order to commence the seat of the elaborate final coping-stone, the sacrist made no move to detain his visitor, who noticed, in sour confines of provisional belief, a creature, if impounded, seeming grateful when Fulnes cast his net over. It was a [*sic*] bat. Thanking Fr. Anselm fulsomely, the inspectorial factotum escaped with the prize. The sacrist wasted little time bidding them adieu, noticing already it came about, conferees perchance confronted someone upon the issue of incentive, "for what purpose are we here, if there is no other prize?" "Six known people no longer live," Isp explained, "and since you have insisted upon clinging to reticence, if not blatant logorrhea, you must walk this way." Stang had no reply for this, though she considered him a disgusting beadle.

. . .

After mass, irrespective of an adroit detachment assiduously cultivated during intinction, furtive, imponderable crescendos insinuated to a different room through cycles into Frank's perspective. The vacant chamber palpitating in repercussion, the faint lyrics ranked onto crampiness, to exclusion of all else, he filed out of the vestibule, sought asylum in early fall evening, and sat on an overwrought benchmark. Not since the startling exposure of his leveraged pyramids in the last century had Middleford sustained a smellier alarm. An empty chair, one of seven on the iBC, had been advertised as vacant in the recent *Economist*. In conformance with the Concordance of Maastricht, it habitually devolved upon comptroller of the ICC for a period of three years.

A semblance of *biathanatos* made known, three days ago, either tenure nearby now accessible, each goldenrod time, to turn on the lamp, convinced one has earned the merit for kicks. Now all there is, however, is sunlight, a finite amber cascade across the moor on this balmy Sabbath. Possibly a tract, ostensibly in reach, albeit the latter precedent nearer probability, Middleford, consumed in a sense of executive makeshift, had gone to so such trouble to palliate *wergild* with vouchsafed antiquarian relics, he'd attempted to learn neither why, nor for how long, the chair stood vacant, much less who had ever sat on it.

As obscure hereditary by–law dictated, once one whomever, in fulfillment, retained capability ad priori, if even from beyond the grave, to stay put, the guildmaster recognized his name was no longer unlisted. SOMHAD, which knew him, but of whom he knew naught, disturbed his career and cast a merciless lamp upon what up to this point seemed a swift and secret aqueduct to privilege, imagined hitherto implausible until at least the twenty–second century. More known than ever, unknown for aeons, a terrible burden of citizenship accoutered Frank as parishioners seeped out unto the vaulted portico of chrysotile.

Læmært stomped upstairs, fidgeting behind a pilaster while his spouse and children clasped everyone with thin scans, to be pickled by, even, if with sufficient research any nice sort of thing may happen if one just might stop trying to attend to everything else, and surveyed the parcade whence Frank yelled, "I don't expect you to have any regard for our outlook, our heads puritanically oriented, too much for straying off that topic." Summoning the valet, Park, the guildmaster fled away in his

Audi and reviewed options. The identity of any person recently filling an empty chair was logical starting point. Yet, he shrank to contact *wergild* for this information. Nor did the iBC network, polled by regular alphanumeric control scans, seem advisable.

Such precipitate research could stimulate uncertainty. He opened the solid state laptop which, in performance of its weekly virus scan, ninth, whom one can share nervousness about walking into a new office situation, may pre–arrange safeguards persistently grinding away, oblivious to his inner turmoil, filling Middleford with spurious comfort. His thought of an only step–daughter, or whether special visions might assist her, the lengthy scan ended, and Frank heaved one that's it for Saturday sort of sigh of relief, and decided to roll by anyone everything about anything upon this or any other occasional future.

. . .

Alcibiades, one of chichi pack... "schoolboy snacks," search scruff draft, keyword fled [or felt]... as "micron mice" re–warm, so Bagler, over role of Cyrano/2 Ænselm's crush on Americana (in return for help with defusing mime)... "Nome" might shelter from spatial hazard... i.e. conflation of Henry (VII) with global village court... spool inspirational mores until constructive scene is nigh.

IV — xx — Bees'wax amphitheater.

Beings, yanked into following understatement: *uchaux* (of those eighth, few, via divers whatever fare capacitated renascent compunction as accolade to shared nothingness) solely touted and ingested prophetic ripple, given innumerably observant lemming; without an ever fixed agenda, prints wove albeit appreciative mews, Snorggi's subsequent sneeze, at large babbling Cocytus snores, and never, a subtitle basked in previous legislated decency, weren't we given later task, to enact hours of Salic lineal furze, flown venting reticent stationery where all was here, thanks to seconds enough.

Every possible iteration incurred, eighths prate upon bleeps wet and old; those spent creation mattered aquiline, oozing enow clique preambles yet, in serenity, lost, cool witnesses blissed out, in remainder of glee, trimmed the hour and, their accumulate premise drooped, fielded enough numerous burst options than a moment snelled and, evinced it would shoo in areas of lasting wonderful good, "were we down to seize the carp and now enact many vested epithets," brought so fitful, to pertain, simply placed ethos of sound alike.

Spilled close third to best earned longevity and limit, and if ever stuffed in motif and kept guessing all around that chatter, arisen during decades without this ill or putative facet, they began to acknowledge, if ever tapped in ekistic imperative, forward become a steady engine chortling only for every other port, and progress no more than a can of corn thrown into an interview featuring anyone's best quality for freely floated whiles, ordinal shades stalked now the miscible chili, their ancillary abrupt return to nominalism postponed. Appellant to that attentive man offering tickets to a digital festive and in your vision you rebuked the gross premise his kin were the source of every whoa.

Tripping that few hired, thou went to next ideology soloists haply, expectorant largesse to explain recent frigid behemoths, yet in quicklime sloshed accidentally bezique, unless recent hatless persons adapted accord of just nodding along whenever one's sonnet of schema mapped under initial evenness by all account, transport geodes domed to reveal Bagler's one line, in improvident state of ocular dysfunction had, even to the most fervent, receded into stuff of urban legend, a social construct reproof incident value went bugging all excellent persons insisted thus and again as receptive charge of topical brilliance (that ended any further), ointment of clear singing fount lest spans of immeasurable limit brashly exude value of option.

Between their live beret roles to see around the veil and answerable to one in word howsobeit amerceably, stiffly thundered crescendo stairwells leavened, eloped, doled, via amanuenses' mosaic spheres boiling with occlusion, ongoing several tropism antithetically coruscated, as imprecation palled off natural design, as far as one wrought of workaday habit graced acceptably to the definite escalators. Found vaster harvest, than anyone may endosmosize fortitude fled, wit, becoming vague, bode via tables original offset when, and if, the banister trellis tinntinabulate joint chafed some existence; yet since suffering scope, the needle, one fretful step threaded, felt angstroms abeam.

Moreover, those redacted upon might soon receive invitation to fill the grey empty question in like concept, upon discovery of many new technical achievements and their impact on events indexed from out of the beneath: amidst the laborious increase of genetic ramification, Fr. Anselm also gave these worlds little shrift in his dictation, borne as he were to describe pre—circumnavigative sights.

Were Isp at least available to shore the crumbled cacophonies inherent in his discovery of supra—terrestrial nodes, relative to giga—aeons in

elapsed time, every subsequent cartographer were, had the sacrist
dismissed the frequent mass persistent enough to document histrionic
predilection of a design, predicative, and trans—montane, one of several
availing minds, frozen future antiquities Fernand recollected as a path,
transpired above the skaters, etched the mind of an Indocile, and infinitive heave whence came the *xenonians*, blink here the importunate scions
wake to find this siege overthrown, '*zkeepers* sunning past their pavilion
beneath expressions of dissimilar timidity.

Some spoke, if the encroaching tribe, as of Tamerlaine (or other
interloping horde, such as one to be turned away by the forces of Ægypt
at Ain Jalut in 1260) arrived, for the visitants, cloaked in rudimentary
skeins, sifted throughout the sward with proclamation of horrid totem;
recessive linguals hustled past wistlessly, chemical plexus formed incidental cipher eagerly, sized upon in tumultuous fraught, and a new weird
old duress is nigh, so forth announced millennial pattern of riparian
stint betwixt lintels of doom. Respectfully nudging these indeed naive
merchandizing asides, Frederick found anew circuitous tacks dyslexic
yesterday only now, roseate in light of the monotonous Norn, the glyphs
rearranged in last minute interval and a seclusion ancestrally disclosed
Iphgene's proof.

. . .

Dust emissions suddenly began turns ubiquitously, for frozen spalls a
thin verse, on the quarrel over Europa in stale shifts' restive seconds.
Albeit guided, nor by memory, blind, these hands for the miffed indigo
sphere the monad perceptually occasioned, success in shifting immutable
haunts, someone's notion to douse the torchiere elicited vociferous
dissent at the intersection of cause and reason since preservation of
peculiar bandwidth excerpted a facet of mineral constraint.

It rose, indwelt now as galleries of cold, stolid, talc, meticulous
columns, and, dismal despite daylight lent behind a screened awning,
stood the years like dust and the end comes, the anode that sacrifices

itself, a tremendous parallelepiped two hundred feet in height, the ex—chamberlain (*all too busy*) left, Ænselm, warily undertaken by a baby bustle and trio of serious co—dependents whom, wielding free propane torches, began lighting candles. PoD subliminally lamented its own design among feasible strategies.

This dome, applicants turned to admire their surmounting business, read Kierkegaard, and laundry re—evaluated quickly, half smiling between themselves, as mingled straw palettes of wax, Chianti—colored, tapping, kept their attention. At bay for an half hour, while civil twilight ended and full night began, they cast fresh peeps above, noticed queer regard for their part no excuse anymore to hang around, started in fright, and fled the premise. Agnes surged, next resulting in growths of worry about fictional persons, away from unfathomable realms, expanded, hark, Nerf wyverns Hesitance, the lacking effort of her second too, stumbled in thirst of fresh apprehension rekindling acquaintances to preserve no real benefits, disillusioned, sought or advocated mass as a reason to rearrange other plans thrust away in her feature, this sighting expedition she ever craved.

Outside the Heliocentrist sect, Althea was Niobe's best pledge. Glyntz, awaiting her amidst paraffin clangor, felt drips off this mesh, months of moths stirring in clouds beneath a storm clad initial crescent. Strangely relieved, yet implored, by the Inspector's recall, Middleford turned to apprehend himself from evoking a shout at this sudden appearance. In the maze of light, the men observed silence. Læmært struggled to perceive purpose in any of it. Fulnes' eye roamed the mural, framed in roiling votive terraces of sorts, unseen save for vaulted cornice filled with Teflon pillars.

Supported, an umbrella of night thus peered forward, discerning Delores in mazes of corridors of candles atop mute fits of brass or mere sempiternal ducts. Sponge—proof eco—picnics caught rivulets of time, ever flown, the fallen wax arrested and connected upon a hissing ring of silver pans, unless, and in final rearrangement of disclosure, a web of oblique yang, yet, a singular cob twisting reality forestalled harvest. Distant sirens left an unsaid thing out there. After ticking several elements, the monad traced, Delores Lake might abridge real density and lasting gallantry.

Perceived extrinsic to the old able consonance, that lantern, for aggregate play ingot ohm, when twenty copious ordnance seconds were all remnant, before eight elapsed an unexpected lull, in which capacity lingered An, her undaunted solidarity whom were loathe to emulate, the monads' quest to recover the indigo sphere fitting exact standards, albeit extant, concomitant beans natheless protested, against overt simplification, aseptically able to stand sustained agitation *finth* qualmlessly roamed.

Now impressed by an entirety or of certain disingenuousness, on a sudden spur withal ware the expedition of twin lifts arrant omen fully mimed, endless clumps from the rout gave an uncased reckoning of discernable ablative. Thus one is not left holding the bag to explain to the nine one one operator that it is an occasion of such joy to read of her love and steadfastness, throughout all ages blessed, most wakened to a telephone; in Iphgene's drove, no one sense murmured, the spurious recognition of dark matter marked let it all out last fall.

She most skillfully derived from website traffic chiaroscuro evanescence during a Saturday marquee of completely illusory sunlight obliquely refracted by, achievement, reserved for twitter, inspired immeasurably through recall of gerund feats previously perceptive of attachment. Sparse insistent echoes below the vale sneered to her mind in beat to a frenetic pulse, so overrun had their sense been in acclaim. If, for a freer natural hour they argued over whom to inform of street theater, the other voice message involved opportunities for the improvement of life; graduation adventures in vacuo commended, the steady deportment of Chantal left them in knowledge limpid, ere the fifth strained with contract, penultimate court in the decision of Failsafe, to mark then children brought into a lesser world than this finish nicer than first. There was always something for everyone, yet in Bagler's cause, peculiar lodestones concerning dominant paradigm, that headset keyed an honest jones here represented disparately.

By now this had never happened before, and wherewithal at the time palpable (shadow puppets' save), *ædith* should, now apneal in concert to ratify failed dada's fault around thy wreak, panic those used by degree to a clear enough view of downtown until that floodlight went in impiously, engaging funiculars. Flung into a more persistent depiction, Ænselm recognized, the worsted nearby to show, yet returned, to his own imminent patents and maturity, pled a certain ignorance of mind at his disposal, preferring instead to issue declamations, of everlasting fealty, to hear echoes of utter vacancy.

It was a process of sage insularity, retarding Plair's ability to cope, and yet foreordained by principle to a far ago age, those human successes opting not for dolorous copses upon surcease at least free will to transmogrify into *inter—regnum*. In the beginning, you hope they will be so careful with your endearment. Unlike theorists indiscriminately filing their bouquets at large, you are of a nature scrupulous in account of every ballot. You will be so careful next time. You are so careful next time. Everywhere you go exercising utmost care.

Retuned, Desdemona, blinking orbs of fiery purpose following her love moths let out of the web of bleeping, negotiated the suite and left the room. Her maze of tutors followed and attempted restraint. She vapidly shoved their thirsted hands aside. Frank stood up at a loss and followed. For some of the tallowest candles, burning in fitful ways, spent utter soaring sparks of flame into mesh not allowably warm and shielded from the blustery retardant as may once have been made by heliocentricism in its prime.

After waves and waves of searing gossamer embers sank into hitherto sibilant snores, Læmært lurked toward the clock, wondered what sort of official warning to shout, and people shrieked. Fulnes yelped to equivocate, since the chateau was to be engulfed unless the fire response were notified. Punching out, an ensign replaced a pager and looked for a supervisor, a commissioner not one to be found lingering.

Correlated edits of linear adultery similarity flung beyond the path of blithe free zone, albeit cliques tugged at an essential common demotive stance after all, rotely mimed in hurried soak before nearby germane iambic gulf striven through fault of gnomic plague aroused whimper, acclimated to various decline and flop of calibrated entreaties, emeritus together, concerned awful beta rang again and, on via lack of word to specify the Gauss ceiling closure now; nothing was further form [sic], truth, bad was worsted and least now on, the Devil's dictionary one hundred and ten years ago predicted in this libertine era anew waning stiffs abound in their *biathanatos*–leased dementia, whence, once recoiled unlit, they clamored for more befitting end, scuffling upon scaffold as minded to watch your step; creased above lack of guile also, these colors blanch.

"Mayhap this Madeira was inspired by turpentine," Bagler whisked to shout at Fr. Anselm, fighting the battles of centuries ago averted, heavily sobs the borrowed Hell, scrambled words in print seemed wrought by enormous freight, yet to Rita, Consuelas Mirabeau, now stumbled over truths and dormant omission, once owed use of civility, repressively professional examined overtures to established existence fled. Herein she wished to hear Fr. Anselm say Delores had every Moxie whatsoever if Sergei could have plucked forth his own idea in order to never have to lurk here again. Naturally, it hadn't happened, professing an eternal patience and maturity the sacrist belied, in order to nurture hyssop, offset with leaping here, and upon an etiquette of pads they sat, fructificatingly heliotropic.

In wanhope nearby, of micron mice Adjustor Blank leaked toward annexed local area, in Plair's fancies of causal realty, so pleasant Bagler tore across the dotted line, the runnier were, as the bench indicated here, prior jests unshod all along. About the enthalpist then you need hear lies lest lists of superb ablative fail thee in shorter term, would née Mezzo only pause to near them. Could Delores, best at home in darkness twittering, measure his glowering vision?

Up until now, Bagler did exactly what marred essential rasps of decency deemed hitherto causal, flinging caution up there as niceness for an era. Whole, yet flatly mythos clouded her brow at those times and inquiries as to what was dark matter drew from Lake such assortment of ire: where should she begin, haunted, grim, prior oases of meaningfulness now wan, each second fluffed in equal measure, moments turned to mint, aortic delay, mon thy arrears how frightful to draw the bland key which could only be covered in bitter pitch.

.   .   .

F. Xavier Middleford dreadfully floundered in pursuit of his prodigy, nervously gulped by casting, and no obeisance done to seeing his habituation aflame, seized she whom, surmised, correctly, as the stewardess, Althea, hovering aside in craven stupor hoping to escape penultimate responsibility, recovered enough of her sense to go to the veil outside. The bucket found lowered and already half full, Chorister drew it behind the stone rim and mindfully brought contents into the face of this enthalpist, shouting at Bagler to contain himself.

At once acute yet oblivious, its sole relief inherent insofar as the vertiginous fickle light of daytime was again recovered, the enthalpist understood and hastened out of the blazing keep. Feeling better about things in general, Middleford nodded capably while the response converged by lateral boulevard. One eye kept on his step–daughter, who crept steadily athwart steps of shadowed heights atop the combe, from Croydon Blank rang up towards Pink Plankton Station.

Inspector Læmært, already waiting at that station for not long, was no sooner present than the seamless carriage turned from up south; Læmært, sweeping Middleford on the far platform as soon arrived, glanced beneath in vain for Dauphine, nor did either see Fulnes, flagging a cavalcade of cars, swept by the opposite direction, almost, not, stopping, at the last instant. Læmært jumped into the southbound train. Blank waved to him aboard the northbound train.

Fulnes found they were both on trails mixed in smoldering futility. Hudspeth, skimming neat across both tracks, lit about in streams of consciousness, led them into suburbs, a shrub area tux caste, a quickly recognized district of Horace's Lichvue manor. Læmært searched the rain for faces, as the guildmaster counted stoops. Oldest trick in the land? The inspector, moreover entrained, if in an apposite direction, glanced at the map and decided to let himself out at Halsey. Sergei, soured to an acrid laugh, wondered how Mercury was transiting, without paraphrase to fortune that he should find another swift southbound spin.

The guildmaster allotted one and braced to debark near the Embankment right in front of the sundeck of the ski lodge, Fulnes, below Lichvue, saw Delores sprung volubly up an coverall flat retained into the very familiar district of the pre–dawn chill. The trains were slightly more characteristic maritime airships, later following her to the house where, smartly rapped upon the lintel of their present casement, Dauphine scrabbled cobbles for one stone, cast amidst the panes, and as it skipped, declared, sibilantly, buy grotto, for ashamed of lousy youth, Fulnes, aware his house would not thus persist, put this hand on his heart. Althea dropped her trance to turn full eyes upon him, demanding, "you would dare undo the tapestry?"

Fulnes, apropos of nothing, but perceiving an awareness of energies, affixed a warrant. "Tequila in duty oboe," St. Agnes whimpered, flattering the inspectorial factotum with sempiternal trait, the kachina drawn from his lapel let her self into the house which either remained renamed astir back out of cryogenic help flush epoxies coolant, raising topside under waxed articles, clearing N for the first letter of then extenuated dear air ran, a circumnavigable figure measured tense present happenstance or often, for example; at the outlet mall of time, thirty–eight steps belabored the waning capacity of glossing over prioritization, a smatter of detail was, for all intent and purpose, enameled as An Indocile deftly began improvement relieving the static rule from heavens, an inordinate vault displayed.

Therein orotund charts of ebriate majesty after why has the word hail struck an imperishable term, ionization of all the lay, with a symbolic flail anyone, saved. A lot of catching up, arranged, arduous vanity, toward a pressure concert thereat; nor were hashed opinions, the telling precept into the village dumpster flown, before a recent ultimate feng shui, shine felt so sure in one's zone, that relinquishment of it spelled grievous ware. Spared the trouble of selling out, something more often than not a reason for a pier shoal meant fountless eras, because an initial standard of procedure, lending necessity to an epicenter of what difficulties participants encounter during man's watch, a road to Shangri–La might forget small day gins used for seconds as basis of locking on for continuity.

Steadily inklings waltz in creation at all time behind the aerobic curtain seethed ambivalent light, for ultimately, they had theoretical ground for believing Norns, reticent as all purported get out, were itching to be observable. Temerity they lacked not, yet they were also prevented as from Titan, a colloquial tribune rejuvenated firmament, stopping them; a third felt practical justification in cutting off the chase, yellowing as to let cards behind glass spelled something they threw wax at repetitively, foreign effacement deemed applicable as literalism.

Despicable climes were roughly pooled for an allowance of slobbering in established myth. That tonic could permit an excellent importunate register yet, reasoned fully of the ineffectual stopper, and resolute to weave an etiquette of far greater scope, Sam retreated beyond a trembling shell, for a purpose of all embracing contraceptive lime act, to reckon how should next the Norns simultaneously tan. As hemmed, recalled by her truer nimbus, *pluperfectreß* turned in consternation to contort the visitant. Only a girl stood on the portal, glowering at hymnals.

Dauphine's visit worried your prose precept and, the being of Gaussier's disconcerted, ¶hrotomeous in fact thrown aside, staid by a lively hailstorm, Në flown beyond Agnes, Fulnes, time anew, had prickling pulse of disco emission quarantine clog the virtual CB dream pipe line below transformers blown, unless, rolled, tense to postpone an expected end to colonize, upwards, upon and over a small prominence as his old bad trick bowling knee must negotiate, enough to find a revetment of near enough refuse to flail in, as Tobit Summit, a void, the sheeted blast of the Lichvue manor gone up; mad as it all now was, spared to crawl in time, place, and menue back, likewise, tense as plumb reverse realtors of amalgamate design fixed inopportune catch.

Threshed ajar instantly neither warped corrugation nor lengthier solvent pikestaff appearing through them leaned, add envelopment an outcome, and *pluperfectreß* had issues, originally, relentless yet mawkish, were she ably persuaded of the sincerity which, during another edge tra–lahs the evening off, Alcibiades uncircumscribed, oh–oh that was a second rate move this all of no wish to compete original intent for lack or want of sound pattern, omit opinion, violating even one own old rule or proscription of grounds, read smellier isochronicity than of man or God interfering with the mean temporal stasis, all conversation maintained at such persistent longevity strengthened only concept of the spleen requited, this sexual pickle oration too, to stabilize these Augean minefields, given at least ably in dressage of Fernand's indolence indelibly ulterior, forgetful penance.

Indefinite of late, much next misery sallow orally daft, sport sin die were of not weal nor comely aspect beneath regression of his schoolboy snacks. Unscrambled, ¶hrotomeous, the house, blown, dared even give Sandra a gerund of hope that resumption of sidereal motion, cinnamon so fit will this, as become realtor than her chirped temerity foreseen, by only the presence to first right of animated rampage in which she turned, at forfeit of reason, a mere precept, behavior warred with austerity, *ahriman*, reprieved, regained, in measure of unlit night ice, a semblance of his foremost presence, pitted the blob of this being long entombed in arctic night against the irascible flurry of *pluperfectreß* driven to bay by signal failure of stratagem.

PoD filled a horizon via meshes of curled device, so *pluperfectreß* ought in vain center off intelligence enveloping their core. There were no known unknown appeal for gallery of long–reproached principality viewing this plight in detached composure. Seeing golden marbles offered in flight, Persephone fled those whom, having put forth hypotheses concerning that, after all of tumultuousness there lay beyond one more day, via these ordinal, trans–suppositioned several key limits, wholly strange now; that patent stirred the trickle–down out–sourced sufficiency, marked then wild idle fires, plain as an argent remnant of exordium.

After the process Echo, insistent on rushing out to share their feelings like a copper penny however, reply of *isomems*, "so what," peremptory that short check–out, line you cruise into, only to find one bargain basement coupon clipper huddled 'neath marketplace of ideas, was a mild contrast. "Oh, why don't voles dive," declared Core, by decree, Miss Worsted, unilaterally intent over her basic uncertainty whether Renata had been crass, vexed, miffed, simply nettled, or unlisted too, also, in case St. Agnes discarded or desired the end of time perhaps, and intent on them, an entering gnomon; done fulminating in a hallow room, tugged at credentials ill–meant in certain off hand celerity of an essential tithe, they all lunched warily as the chrome sphere experienced photopause for a slaunch.

That, in brief, kept a projection of bona fide idiom translated in theism, among ravioli tattlers, chaffed in driven selfsameness toward numerous feats of meritocra–synchronous scarcity. "Heaving obeyed obese wit via and beyond sight was not a reason for letting the universe explode," Rex interjected. "Try at this time to hurry slowly, because such inherent concepts stretched their each premiere worn character out mensa–thon occurrence." If in result of willful rant, reasonable device washed in for a pound, imminently Noene [*sic*] ceded the ordinarily pompous disinterest of Least's ninja card restaurant tours.

Slowly Iphgene turned, her awareness of being undesignated, for application of exposure–based cures had not deterred or disabled macros aloft, and did little to prevent the person from finding them in her least inkling. "Never get used," the docent huffily vented (tierce did in fact cause amidst them fiercely didactic if apt lies, cantering pleas for more socks to rinse), "to the largesse," and unexpected Vikram, unentered yelk essence once began tidily.

"Doesn't real nobler permanganate readily accord affliction on an apposite grievance whence flocculent plaintive formations craned?" In front of a parenthetic vocation, April's kinder moments were ingredient enough to preface a network like effect in ochre matters. Then knit them, did Yahweh reply to their query, and from then on was she unstoppable. Some gestured in placid stance while tinted monochromatic links attributed soiled lignite pathologies in reconstituted facts' travail.

Heppleweis swept a periodic ally, tapered the flecked deluge obliterative with few monads lest, blended thither, distinctively stamped upon the every nick of heterogeneity, the hand of SOMHAD were assiduous in fomentable realization impended. If she succeeded in perplexing audiences without, in vague tours of progression, the sacrist from Ghana who said we watch too much television untowardly glimpsed a past arrival. Their appeal, before antiquaries reflective of a price achieved during restive surcharge, every standard uttered before, any assonance of the Donative clarity executed beneficence and clemency overdue for migrant courts peering toward the inspiring scarabs.

.   .   .

Touring the ruined frieze, Frederick declared art is extravagance, it is so artificial, they will never miss it: upon that topic, concord, hive of slight suffix, is the most miffed bus never stop loss or arguable go plot epicenter of some winged victory replicated; others driveled upon hours of the vote concerning a constant intuit shovel of mandate lifting the barrier of natural ionization as prelude to precedent, achievement, junk your option in one lessors' cause become no out, else seethed potential, so vacant of desire as a savant declared, total non–cool blue blanket of iron filings form or beard of bees horde nomenclature worn, an exact pre–eminence to specific orrery left perspective gain deferred to a future consideration.

Among dispelled, once more evaluated, will to be placed beneath review, the virgule rivaled nougat in its abrupt eminence; requisite comatose awareness ascended as acorn to an ulterior ochre convenience. Gathering drier cleaning words for claim slip, tickets we knew, as if Sandra must have, or for all of them who inferred that to this — of this it was to be charged with extirpation of a clinging and rouge stain; indeed the, while of azure seizure, qua breakdown's unclear dance, it may now be noted, the word prior to dance marked the edge of the reversed blue pad underlying a super implosion of redactive arch, each semicolon revealed one iota obfuscatory at best in exchange for return to a previous nuanced reference to the clinic iota semiotic necessity of an ungainly impending legerdemain to slip that impervious word almost from the edge and onto newest tropic somewhere of landslide ever effaced.

Contending patterns over them, Rex nearby certifiably brushed, sneaking to healthily advance the natural constituence of a omnipresent element, fair moments clasped as penitent prior ethos, rede to act liable for being struck thus already given; incidentally, spoke no lasting voluble neap forest, all SOMHAD precluded several possible outs, the conversion of obvioregal [*sic*], so obviousness the precedent was an edge word that could never be lost in range. Anon the verge of Rust, aplomb they scattered charily, from plinths of vertiginous phantasm, adipose if mindful over the previous circumlocution of Core.

Then, at Least, she is the article long deferred who won the last word, an essay upon the effect of punctuation, as well as "edge words," suggestive perhaps of precipice, in approaching the edge of the page, during the course of autonomic exposition, unless one is writing upon an infinite flat surface. Rarely, save on the plain approaching Babylon, to be found in nature, the letters will pull up, like wary steeds, as Henry (VII), King of the Romans, on his way to prison, learned as he chose solicitude over exile. If I hesitate to disappoint contemporary producers whom, filled in unflinching puissance, infallibly seek to jazz the subject matter by turning every medieval idyll into an equine hecatomb, in truth the wise beast bore the doomed king only as far as limited reason demanded, vaulting the imperial presence over the edge, and returned to cropping the sweet jimpson weed at the side of the road.

For his own part Henry (VII), no fewer than many of his most skilled contemporaries, took solace during initial stages of his plunge insofar as he spared the noble charger, for faithful courtiers now peered over the side in consternation, not unknown that he was swarmed upon by angles, congratulative of his rigorous choice, and offering embodiment in *inter—regnum.* His reply was not immediately recorded, for his retainers, scrambling down corky slopes, and sustaining onerous injury in so doing, reached the vale to discover their monarch, not only not dead yet, but on some level, getting even better, sufficed to lend a hand in lifting one of the household who sustained peculiar crippling palsies in the descant. "Understand, cheer, I can never hold a candle to thine voluminous beatitude in this time of apparent development."

Henry (VII) had so much to relate, and did promptly during the breathless return, yet preoccupied with the perilous climb, his comrades may be forgiven for failing to consider transcription of his breezy anecdotes until, with a last blissful smile, the brave monarch set his injured ward upon the road, and looked to the heavens, with a final prayer, "you may ask, if whatever I left behind is problematic, but at a point in a relationship where I start to wonder in what mode your interest in us paused, a nice future, visions of seaside escape, may we never stage a sour scene, you may thank me inasmuch as you do not, will not, or cannot reply to any more messages or letters.

"Time turns ticklish as a studio, remembered of adjusted value principle, does transit oft night, and day, foreclose an onset of dawn, as December elapsed in new arts, over the horizon as well and pine of voluble evening, should your clearer dream tell me of the time you cared? Have I locked silent missives spent in meaning? Dare I not deride the concept moreover?" After the page turned, a new leaf, tremoring reminder one of one tough Apennine millrace personalizing ratios of active if, if almost one or more eponymous icy dust tomes unspoke this word to mean a whole cloth of show time, they sought to muffle the silence with a large medicinal value.

.   .   .

PoD, in sole desire to sell shells, outlasts detractors to escape carrioccio. Norah's bio—optic synthesizer, medieval mime ¶hrotomeous, unearthed from Worms, defused, inadvertently thwarts Nicean effort to contain ahriman. Amid ruin of Lichvue, Nicean principals predict plot of act v psycho—trochaically. Disinterred from symbiotic tri—literalism, component personalities, Horace, Roveretto, and Ranth Tyoslament (Nicean protactic carrier), revive via synthesized pattern buffer.

IV — xxi — Kindvåkningen.

Æ nselm had enough of that carrioccio which he was not yet out of. In there, no light transept of manifold disco, foolscap for purple monarch, one or two illegibly super—sized keypads of transitional and many recanted texts, from which deprogrammed mists sizzled by now, surely sprang like Athena, full grown, and they were plenty to illuminate a mist—shrouded calm of ziggurats, pottage, snacks, ditties to pilfer, flattened newsprint to line the Sunrise Cage, stacks of books garnered from the nice free library in whatnot hopeful self—enrichment periods, and time—out to read while grand projects gestalted by the sea, SOMHAD, altogether embroidering futurism between an alternative trousseau, christened evanescent intaglio apposite epochs of kalpa; certainly enough time for postulation about ever exorbitant perception germane via verticule, virgule, vinculum, or more declasse eflots, precipitative of multipartite intercept of apples or other oranges until Simic felt scarce, superfluous amid after—hours aristocracy of the destitute, streets paved in aluminum cans, upon reception of the ever magic towel alone onto logarithmic districts of that clasp, distinct individuals spurned fate, her town, under all emitted produce, a Braille cipher illuminated in dry faux fire, eliciting persons to a copy of each boxed eggshell doughnut sparkle.

In any scene ever surpassed wittingly, fewer instance rocked nearby a treacly well, concomitantly hypothecated only at next week's convenient outcry belittling a dull bee, as every rumor mill stopped scrabble; unto topography eponymously typified, a star shed, in general, by an abstruse announcement of wing beans who'd reticulated backward into antediluvian sage, ignoring parsnips of inscrutable *finth* neon to reverberate amassed yard sales whereby pulsars danced even benign, Bagler forked incandescent niblicks which, blearily mud–slid into matchsticks, were too sedentary for mega–pod hand signals.

"It doesn't have to be that loud," one of the figurines yelled from behind the curtain. "Frankly it was quite unseemly for a man of your age to even look at our cookies." Integral with no knockwurst, the redundant emeritus sat moodily, salving odd regard by regluing linoleum spindrifts and fishing the heights of Nineveh for pistachio mackerel. His LPG candlestick threw indigo strains at a moth–eaten marzipan ephod devoted since an ancient nihilism commemorated actual tinny placebo rotisseries to ratify free tariff tra–la–lahs, *scrapmon'*, "let, us, comb this exhaustive compendium so posterity should someday extol our relentless effort to forestall material bias," said. Yet efstoones could they ordain a recess, thereupon the stand energized the state's first witness, a man once thwarted by Vikram's finest knock and talk via the simplex of premature co–existence.

A considerable nabob famed for superb icon reenactment segue moreover might persevere toward calm comprehension of dear Niobium, if unsearchable enough, since deeply spatial bias, prone, an ethos often frescoed as *pans'fly'trite*, an only whistle stop culpable of sojourn amid their lamp average certainty about terra–formed nation states; this Nicean onliness charted not only worthily resisted attempts to make it seem as always olden days, but also stood Flußtapfer's evinced, theist, utilitarian, dystopic activity on behalf of individuals, as a more conducive method of reconciliation throughout society of larger than life magical invisibly transparent prospective gain then rather focused one elongated Fuald, whose distelfink coal rose silhouette, sown among the least level stalest absolute esplanade in sibilant Ixtlan when, last checkered time flew ever stiller than tempestuous tears jerkily kinetic exteriorizing merer incidental exegesis whilst upon zero azimuth, arrived, a spiraling gaseous blob, enthused about distinct integument of fomented flappery, solid behind bio–synthetic arrays of protean agit–prop curlicue, measured for basic underlying consumption, beyond reach of all the hours spent reading allegory, travelogue, true confession and other magazines at the five–and–dime until the impervious space snail arrived to bore you to Vikram's house: a place of peace and thanksgiving, fair past the chromatic tizzy who streamed five floods known to be unknown to the unknown known, an illuminated Artesians' intersecting signal for a staggering slow express seemed prone to easement and the pristine rye of Lothar's fanciful charter wavered, tremulous in the solar sneeze amid the drab dusk of Nod.

Here one heard if tepid prophecies, each a runny nickelodeon awarded more wild Ovid LPs, yet fed really fine nard to foundling urchins recently, on toasts made affirming her aim, that and/or nut cruise, explicable to all tense Mithraic Illini owning at least one lone lily, could inspire shorter skimpy straw polls, whilst lavish majorities existentially gaveled fortune cookies away, the better to fool coded entropic jests. Land, how persons looked age–regressed and shopped for finding the best time to flock out of work early thus scanning the street where you lived, for a sparkling plot was a moist liminal mathematical shadow sized to one man's horizon; an, at all visible, hand through the door to a moist recent ice age kept ajar so chipper a plentitude may wake in new mews unveiled for art, yclept seeds from neuro–Niceans carefully strewn via fusilier (*all too busy*) in collated cascading terrestrial radiance of cerulean fabric on surreal cynosure, wherein cubits, subsets of sentence indicative of modular participle–avoiding hidden structure directly coupled surfactant phenomena of the building, inescapably turned into a bookshelf Rust perused, out flung the heavy tome, *Village Table of Allowances*, and riffled past *Babbit*, backboards, and backpacks, s/he mumbled, "billingsgate, binaural synthesizers, binoculars, biofeedback, bird baths." Hip, one rouge second shift sped the index verbatim, "scanner, bio–optional, see de–coupler," indigo stock numeral I79–1000805–00001.

The inventory terminal activated, Justine tapped in. Requisitions
were sitting on three of them. It would take three weeks of red tape
to pry one loose. S/he glanced via her monocle at the boffin. That this
is not the traditional peremptory special service in an hour abets the
cancellation of their long let—out. "Idres, I want you to forget I asked
you the next three questions." Receiving this assent, s/he confirmed that
algorithm accessed other parts of the department, buttoned in clamped
sundry tile warts — usually pesto jerboas cantered across your welcome
mat, you need only mash two cubes of cold roller coaster voir dires [*sic*] to
drive weird quarks, unrequited, lo! — that being the morgue, ballistics,
the laundry, requisitions, and the W/C, s/he winced gracefully, unable
to find a clear mister ever since. Arguably, "will this trap door code work
everywhere, and can you tell me what it is?" Darn, that fourth question
the boffin broke, into a queasy smile, paused — the divorce of positrons
from pixels, ignited by screening phosphorescent bores, freckled by
innate basophilic cubists with aversions to gelatinous iconography.

Their rhizobium symbiosis hydrophobic, dark matter expressed
ideally lucid quest stirred, no dull forum imagining wide varieties of
mutant yeast casually sent around oscillating cytoplasm palimpsests
overlain, since in spirit a tunnel revisited lightly did strive for a true
closure, yet in proof kept lamps unspun, spiking onto frabjous fabulous
geocentricity, and as Sabbath let out there were possibly children never
who had seen snow before, albeit had it been sempiternal, drought so
settled into the remote basins of Xenonia, irrigated throughout antiquity
thanks to generous levitated natural cisterns of vertical parallax drawn
via peculiarly sensitive lunar aquifer, the sub—stratum conferred until
the dawn of modernity some newer, emphatic other wisdom, cyclic
constituencies unknown too long for being known, for Noone, once
concierge at a distinct hostel where anyone should roam about as if or like
one were ever again during one of the teen years (1213–2019), an epoch
foresight denoted as exceptionally pivotal during involution, placing con-
versance with dark energy amid perennials of eistedfodd, distelfink, and
cloisonné among thus notably lasting arts capable of their discernment,

unless any inkling Fernand may distinguish in a maximally wind–milled calligraphy emporium drew comparison with Frank's expulsion from institute broadband.

Unlit, all dark matter co–existed of delicate braided fugues expectantly experiencing odd respite amid Fermian post cambric axiom minuet, limiting no parade of sack candles Lauscauxvianly squirreling the way toward Ixtlan, wherein *xenonian* stills indwelt, this dialog more than merely illusory, fiction, or self–instructive. Thus wrong hands could get atavistic for other persons' tea tin collections, meditated later defaulted resultant re–read of Sasha's mom's famed dissent applicable to earlier returns from the voting machine. Messimo's etoliated persiflage told of Charles' late beneficence in acreage for populaces displaced by electoral results in Ossian, seeing the Nesselrode faction's Etaoin Shrdlu swept into office every spring for the past twelve years. Noone, confuted to disparate alarum, a coarse, sunless, granular time, importuned thorough troves, albeit every item restored to the hermitage tilted an erstwhile tepid renascence toward surrogacy. Florian's remonstrance gone about instinctively evincing this neoteric vox into relevant, thus great reform establishing the plunk as equivalent exchange for sixteen won, or one thousand *lithiwatt*, eleven plunks equal to one sunspot, eleven sunspots equal to one cycle, and one thousand commensurate via a single epicycle, Justine received a scrap of paper.

"Plunk on with your bad self," she was told, as Idres put his feet back on a shelf, slipped the snood overhead, and readily read the latest *Byte* while melted down cyber–trolls on the tertiary scope, the hollow old scintilla blazed ruminatively, gilded for eon in disreputable totem, effluence of dashed windfall seeping out near snow forts one need reckon, as Plair proved, too bifurcate for significant rapport during his final re–entry, a snap policy reminiscent yet classified for octants of wired throw rugs for which *œdith* wagered his flame–out against the beast of pale eyes, a lot of star baths misted how that cloaked node regrouped at an arcane rest stop, an elated mix of crass lawn gnomons, innate cartoon samurai thought magi, enigmatic heavy metal lorgnette urchins, a Nicean

Sabbath amphora, theatrical puffin see—saws emoting tremulous lullabies to illicit heffalumps, hives of beady church mice nodding too, would each, lilies elided empirical coterie thwart, when dealt a sad thunderclap, and madrigals of neap twin decretals reeled in.

.   .   .

So Lethean were the tides, so dawnless an inamorata neon night, truer faded sneers, that thus tinged stares for phylactery, Bagler praised no serpent beyond an antimacassar seen sleeping in a drafty good burrow with songs on a dare; that de rigeur hyacinth posed weird steps apropos a viewful lodge, worthy of dotted fleet nodes, a soon marginal motto, floating on puce boas, *Snailiest until Lent*, meshed over the sonorous flood.

An argot eggshell cocoa punt, *Delphinium (II)*, tamed there huge epidemic of sandy Scylla with anointments of supple agate. Ever at odd albeit unimaginably incessant migraine, if steamed elixirs were wont to rally hymns of the odious void, Sam clasped the balky cynosure, 54'40" or fight, into a stiff magnetic undertow, and bade adieu, pushing overland to Acheron Station, Al—Kamil boondoggled, or some towering dominoes rapidly watched how triumphantly he emphasized a sense of elation; too, one of the persons, the shrinking hearth of imperishable arrangement, noticed bicycle tires under the eerie late winter desert night, fervently. There Nephretite scanned empty desks between lumping out, and spilled bins for an url—queen.

But she became alternately, in fond glimpse of energy, a compliant, lugging inevitable space music in, and how Shrdlu returned, a proposal to the Ægyptian kiosk at the same level they spotted, spark tappers collapsing in mere grunts and instant memories. "Hark, solar eidolon," Al—Kamil grasped, if petrified into a tedious but temporary dormant horizon, presaging aimless, star struck rock at lunch today, speaking in passable patience to the fantasy she used no hair spray and sniffling, costly Shrdlu — a compelling but decided history tale that digital preparation of the police—hospital circle were better — left undisturbed, a mere formality of merchandise events seemed no more fitting sobriquet than Damian's casual coda, heard from this side of one's pet Lethe, that he is "almost as bad as they say she is."

By the time twilight totally disappeared, Damian, who professed a sputtering but disembodied temperance for elite stop gap cusps (thus risking mineral health foods and the dismantling alternative motto for pain, calisthenics), having served in an actual union, read passages from *A Decent Day*. Of course when the statue awoke, airily eager to tug oscillated breath relief, a wholesome disease of realty unspooled, as it were, and challenged a mountain of Hard Rock Cafe shirts for only $62. That a loss of isolation should not have blighted the revolving erratic slab has distressed Goethe and stopped many feathers. As uneventful inspiration, it was as if this place existed, which panicked the worst of the program and let a local juncture all around to be back off flu vaccine tingled in the 1950's. "You'd think they'll never leave," chef d'ouerve [*sic*] (*all too busy*) averred, its radical ethos obtruded by calisthenics of *scrapmon'* natheless. Chæron said, "seraphim are adept at prognosticating Snorggi sneezes. They really are."

"Perhaps you would punt. After them, this pace doesn't really suit your spare mulch anymore, now does it." Grendelle returned, "don't you recall he shall run down the enthalpists' trope?" Before all, the poor man only whistled *Pennsylvania 6–5000* on the privacy of his own steam grate, a breathtaking experiment in social realism. "Then he'll spell the man to convince him it's on Snorggi's doormat." For around a far–fetched, kinesthenian flan, an unprevious mad onset panted at dowdy hens, met near remitted bent diaphanous mauve strand aboard a wobbly coracle simulacrum, *Elsinore*, to hear themes of toxins. If stricken, stretched as a flatiron, the books, mostly about one's inner Hilton, took off on a lifestyle of similar coffee break, upon the stone wall of the holistic market, were once presumed mere delightful interval amidst grand fruition, turned obbligato if in their own way nonetheless compulsory, boiling thus a current tugging the listless float next a shoal.

"To make a long starry shot, Bagler'll then trans–mogrify into an anti—matter dark demitasse, hijack an intuitive sailing expedition, and sell Snorggi to a very inopportune theme. *Que sera, sera*," chef d'ouerve [*sic*] (*all too busy*) yawned. "Verily will it be well, short beyond rapture, all chosen are to be snuggled into their cozy retinal theme park, whence PoD, control of Global Village seized, decries these chosen are just a little too comfortable out there over eternity and their dime novel xeno-phobic polemic trailers." Since reversion to the pre—Ptolemaic universe, the planet ought ossify into a tough old nut to survive solar winds and a near collision with Uranus. "His roles, in avoiding the calamities, propel *ahriman* into a proposition of real, as well as institutional, populism, and, co—option of *untenets* as motive force, an aggregate disarmament deconflated to gambol spaceship Earth toward the galaxy.

"Only unless his, in the final instance, syllable, thwarted by those rites beneath whom, for outlandish reason, obtain the helm, and Earth is plunked into gnosis of Snorggi. Moreover," noted chef d'ouerve [*sic*] (*all too busy*), added, "our enthalpist does Earth immeasurable service, insofar as he prevents it being fully digressed." "Aye, and a swell curse as well," Chæron exclaimed, "for thus, land grant biologists descant, they'll file open the Great Seal to examine contexts, and out bowls Earth, bouncing the crass steps from Castle Mandrake, and rolled onto the well of irre-trievable consciousness above all hope, shall said shadow puppet, moved to piety by selfless action of those left behind, repent this deed and dig in to reboot the universe?"

Replied chef d'ouerve [*sic*] (*all too busy*), "we'll reach a mental block at that stage." "You are a mental block," terse Grendelle's mom, Ms. Tsp, espresso brought on a silver tea service they hastily, quaffed, "well, lunch hour is over." Methinks they go onto an Midlothian coupe and plough out from there. As their swirls back straight traffic, chef d'ouerve [*sic*] (*all too busy*) asked, "name one, what, of the deeds of shadow puppet of which He'll repent." Ere flawed thanes in sooth glared at too few grails, doom imagined amiss, in light of mere submerged weird casbah bees drenching dilettante Cristo rip—off over epigrammatic sweat shop, other drones, looking freaked or at least dissatisfied near wan spoon, could think gonging over grown seals behooved snooty gas house mudders leased above 1984. Fewmets uncommonly radioactive fenced ichor of stucco emptiness, dreary voids seeded so improperly that buses, paused to switch via sere vortexes of overtly tenuous salsa, took amenities beyond practically off the wall terseness, and sponsored kind serums, busy orreries favoring double helixes of outmoded starts, REM sang after extremely faux dithyrambs, a label soon to be detoured by key ground cover of herbal free falls, too many to count united and reasonably glib, then fluffed around five geo–chrons to comport just enough rattan cubicles for repressed lawn oblates.

Echoes of canine activity wot below the bowl games on TV, a metallic shriek below preceded wrenching events to fit perceptions about the acceptability of plastic, the hasp upon which the hatch locked in the dark period of cellular forested intermission to need, on sects felt SOMHAD but not done with, one's existent dialectic of flippant adagio, and/or without, which upon casual prospect should have served those times that are thus wonderful had the quality of mercy not strained offline, implements, thrust betwixt the collar and the hold, rang off the restraining catch and rent the fog without time, in contrast were ostensibly nearly terrible if, amidst such worthy effort, a tendency to ameliorate littoral into a focus of wondrous expectation twitched, and seeming beyond an old blue dervish theme begun anew, Ænselm felt descent of the device thus after he, aware now the massing pack, on the edge of intent, suddenly dispersed the youth gathering, easily four rows up, and Rust remembered, "anytime you want to crash here, feel free at any moment." One being trashed by, uncomprehendingly hiccoughed any way, "so why not live the philosophy of the preacher," PoD crouched, squeaking, as the wielded conch hardly missed his head? One expected, nay demanded transport into further venue of ever more surpassing beauty than the present, at which time one would create the big thing to bring adoration, security, and identity.

.   .   .

Surreptitious Tyoslament peered out amidst this forest of electrodes wrapped around the mind of the illumined fourth who thought this cure for carpal tunnel was gone beyond tolerance. Hesitance may have mentioned, "never return their call or immediately try to reassure them everything is all right." The key is to develop a plausible peeve, giving everyone an opportunity to feel useful and that does not at all redound to anyone's detriment. In time, each film appends the expected immediacy where everything anthropomorphic in the adjacent canvas gives way. Never tea and crumpets, it was something that happened near any moment, given all of the litigation flew past a press of things, and another unrecognized three persons took patronage.

So, on the trying morning to reassemble a checked box without resort to neat stenciled diagrams, Horace explained to the podesta in a light–hearted fashion he had difficulty making fists anymore. His admission to the Institute heralded as sample follow–up visit, Messimo voluntarily steered into the lift and toggled up to Room 2A, a rather thick woman of indeterminate age told them it was all right to be as different from everyone else as possible. It must be for a peer of accord until fall too, the settlement's reputation delayed to a point behind notice of an almost background or white noise, collapsed into a purple polka dotted ottoman and began reading next year's *Economist* when Dr. Simic walked in on them. "Oh please, take your article on the pendant shrinky dink of the cottage industry with you, Tell, stupid, my, have you heard voices," she said as they traipsed down a shaggy muffled corridor.

"Only these of the bedridden and repressed," was told. Tyoslament conceded, "icon see the magical fæire landfall above us just twinkling invisible belief bubbles three yards later everyone nigh." They cluttered, bounding shadows yelped and splashed, their detectably mingled wave of fulfillment expanded periodically below twin rubric of conservation and purgation dwindling into immemorability vacuumed happily, if with sweet, grating cites every eighth minute, the height of ¶hrotomeous, brusque and bleakened, arose within the hold. Oft dreaded things gleaned from pasts ran out and between fewmets fair, life deferred anon in syncopation of next scheduled take, tonight or months from now after one reconvened her bravado for a short period and felt normal to all concerned.

The crest borne glittered with a remembered loss of sensible hope that those wings were those of a dove as they rang around, knowing why if one ran out of time, one might either get ashore or not get ashore, and either alternative looked to cast its own shadow. Tyoslament wrought up the chancre into Ænselm's trick knee, chased his chest through him, placed one heavy elbow in his nose, and began to strangle us with it somewhere else, glimpsed via strands of gossamer seen mandatory for much vision parted to reveal a stolid surfactant upon horizons of vast blue muse intruded on voids of surreal grain, an aggregate extant recited to lend atmosphere to any occasion at best distracted. "Nobody in motion remains so unless not acted upon," Persephone screamed! How she'd carry on about why they left a guerilla in the hills (and in itself cannot least isolate a large stunt pirate), and then push a wafer thin volume of haiku that's thimbled over, "whereas I have to reconcile ionic columns of eleeosymary wherewithal into octal numerals all the livelong day."

"An over—reliance upon DNA has made opportunists of us all," added Simic in emphasis. New wide vistas buzzed out of the big display of the geo—political hand, scientifically fumbled a crack in the hull, when the forces of Nemo and hope departed in opportunity to practice one's ware atop the hills above the flood. A window upon the pulse of civilization maintained at little or no cost, and commercial free mail, jeopardized by a postal reform, could no longer comprise solely hand—written missives on crinkle stationery, albeit hand—picked, of distant confidants, Althea, puzzled at the source of indigo, skipped behind charcoal voodoo. One can even surf in vain for a daily gazette perhaps depicting rancorous yet civilized debate in parliament on grown costliness of dreadnought platforms. Nastanto, attained, by degrees, through osmosis, said, "Ohno, we're full up." She replied, "so they were also able to watch us. Inyo gets to hit them with it some time." These, one could read no more over coffee during periodic trips to a sidewalk cafe far from viable foot traffic, greeted discretely by servitors and casual acts quaintly coupled across a sea on a continent a century or more a go–go.

Sangreal's injunction stopped the youth with that gun in his hand. A partially farmed crop of ginseng furbished no talc ream so snorkly. On rivets vice drew dives, proofread near octillion conflated proto–objects, clumped in undone lariats, whatever sloppy stopgaps were even ebbed in health. Save for an occasional opportune indulgence, one should not need to resort to obstacles for refreshment. In frequencies currently observed, Talitha, hesitant, looked around and would liefer embark upon a perpetual tour of creation, freed of contentious conscience of original sin, yet also assured of better stuff, and everyone else brave beacon whom all yearned and schemed. There was no further necessity for her character to evolve in such a world, and for one instant more, Ostrand dithered in fear of a psychological standpoint of alternating miasma, a dogmatic uncertainty, aiming for Ænselm. Sr. Bustamente, caught up, left no strand turned in the celibate grumpy relentless search for facts, an attempt to pan his barn muck; PoD, watching them, spun, aware of a pleasant vacuity as Althea addressed the men, shrieking, "get that thing away from them!"

A shudderer, Sangreal, tugging Talitha aside, Ænselm rose with a flinch, robbing his late assailant of the conch. Sponged off carrioccio, he hastened to the scuffling pair, relieving four hands of one revolver. Detached, the gendarmes stared as their cause burned. In this manner, this hour, this way, the historian (*all too busy*) concluded, five hundred words were strung together; simple mathematics dictated how during twelve average houses of light, six thousand words could be but likewise engaged from His, and after a Sabbath, mass at a moist seaside chapel in a somewhat Anglican fashion, one would create 36,000 words each week, one million eight hundred and seventy two thousand worlds each year, delivered to us paper pushers in the grimy city, and pursuant Sangreal crying to Ænselm, "she gave her life to save everyone," *ahriman* stooped. "What do you want me to do, thank them?" "You must face the music, man."

Althea insisted, "what else will see to it a universe, of surpassing bulk and thickness, is distributed to the public?" "Whomever shall ransack their wall for requisite pittance to become enriched by all these worlds," Persephone, the unseen point, resuming fright, said. "Aloud, however, in case you extol our pledged commitment to advancement of scenic sincerity scientifically since all that's happened (fringed were Messimo's voluntary community service in wake of his charcoal hilarity evincement)," and deliberately sat nearby, "here is," an emeritus foretold in hushed tomes, "an internal auditor who," in aim of deflecting village scrutiny, "reasoned," on the night before human togetherness, if Fuald watched enough film it might provide insight requisite for coping with any situation, and we might pull the plug lest he scarce believe we should be so provincial. Only by the disturbance of unfamiliar thin power would they no longer be a twisted parody of something turned out, to be quoted of memorabilia, restorative to nobody.

.   .   .

Beneath thick lengths pried, a soft charge defined Tyoslament as they splashed into the car with an abundant stowage of cords. Already afloat steeply between felt needs and exterior complacency, Althea, asked whom is real, returned to the jetty, regarding her Orthogonian cistern, in the icy suburbs which needed to be kept at all cost from *finth*. A prow she studied, marks upon the band glistening. Land, a breeze struck up. Rasped in toil of approaching chivalry, the packet steered ashore, wind abated, and the rain ceased knowing which phase Sangreal, albeit whatever ninth get agile, thorough force could hack huge budding bugle duos alone. She fixed the last oar or saw a familiar oubliette.

"No time, paprika. Must, follow, Ostrand." Bustamente thrust his hands into his pockets and sloshed away, invigorated by this civic exposure. A current embraced the floorboards, but as she rowed, one fast chord verging the shallow disc of the bay, water lapped at heaven's elemental snood choir. Then Althea, glaring about heck now, thought she'd wend to the far point but already that water swamped the prow. Pikestaffs of rock, attended with solemn crag, rose toward the sea some hundred roods from the headland. The original current dispersed in a subjunctive clutter as Sangreal, borne in a bauble of increased shiver, lashed oars around and whistled, "world, a fit home in values, cheer on my entire vast damp haha."

Mondo draught, among a very other thin farm of carrioccio nestled, insufficient to her cause, Sangreal alone grasped the till and a nock sought along the wall of the rock an iron ring. Chorister had rarely time to seize the hawser when, upended, the sea poured into here and most of the hold knocked herself aside and against cliffs. The moorage line stretched, pinning her by the chest as the float, sucked under its burden, disappeared beneath the wabe as, last unscrambled, sometimes writers forget their own truths or, at some remove misplace them in deference to eventual diffusion when, any composite lexicon phrase panel too Sangreal, presently recused for being rough on crime, farmed in forums for ordering themes and road visits to CRTs. Refulgent icons forelimned, ornamental rust was slinking away; rugs the antidote to your cloudy side of the street, "thou shalt not die. Pass later old leaven, not moral, but worth truth, remove thyself amid them, saints, for we shall judge angels, nor be among those non–righteous, known thyself sanctified, yet unyoked nor mastered by unprofitable things or members (1 Cor 6:12)." In a shallow grotto, Althea struggled, drudging carrioccio from the splint and fixed it, half in, half out. "On marriage, on abstinence, on burning, scissors cutting paper covering rock, break (7: 8)." Hardily buoyant, the hull broke the surface with a heavy hiss.

As the resident clambered nearer the rock, wondering at her predicament, the flange of a tremendous bore sloughed, the tide, a surging eventuality, twisted the moorage line her finger caught, she yelped into an envelope of indignant spray. She felt this slip line choking her and the hawser from her hand leapt. Beneath her, the cargo shuddered. Her yoke loosed, carrioccio slid into the sea. Ascended, her float surged through the isles and occupied what few tables slowly dormant Sangreal. In a mad revolt of struggle she escaped and caught the moorage line. "If unmarried, concerned of things of the Lord (7:32), remain happy." Her

side of the float sagged alarmingly as the moonlit and shadowy night, that
a man from outer space, no longer aiding her, slumped into the vault of
an errant nimbus.

An echo of chill seawater slapped against her eye. Darkness, rain
presumptively embracing her fumbled search, in a last instant, she saw
herself, a propinquitous sexton, emblazoned in a glorious discharge of
discovery. Sangreal beheld the float settled aright above her. Swarmed
to it on the radio, stars returned in a wistful foreboding as it sank, amid
trope cliche rang hollow; vehemently motioned, the left line acted at
to her thing, there isn't swarmed a shoe. Now waving sayonara, Althea
needed an ear sewn shut. Her tedious pastoral striated snood worn, she
basted insipid raw mealy toner beans steaming and teased another keen
tuxedo slacker to host chaste tangents. Dredged through rotten rodeo
stints, a loaned–out serif garçon crooned in, "humbug, pink creosote
ninjas, soon this snob swoons thereupon at thongy circus faun," as a
piñata throve in sunnier pines.

.   .   .

Iphgene learns xenonian skater, Za'at, albeit frozen, is their very own cyber–dotty,
ELIZA, by Village permit participatory in tourney... tendency to drape personal villein
in totem as occurrence of character, i.e., committees, unnamed receptacle of impolitic
fracas... also preferred as monad, so avoid chrome ozone. After ka'aba returned to Earth,
in the interests of yore, finth, granted power to typically fubftitute every s in thif, and
nearby, up to dozen fubfequent fentencef, into fs, lift miff worfted from the clafp.

IV — xxii — After, It's Kind.

"You will soon be free to forget," the inspectorial factotum repeated too well with the onset of sudden form. His star witness checked her glance, and with what would have been one, for lack of a better word, blob, let out for midnight, Isp transcribing Jasmine's recollection, Fulnes regarded the present circumstance of cachet as ants darted lingeringly amidst four oblong vertigo planes describing his (and their, he might have amended in a moment of sentiment, given as he were to promulgate their recent history together) relief in familiar ground; the inner factotum within the police sergeant asserting retro fits into an interview clouded with personal desire.

Dared dreamt any place, one should not have the slightest idea that while slept Raisin, an entire phantasmagoric theme park sprang up on the street where she woke. Here, as the dust buster, simulating ferment, crushed vanilla wafers, hair of the doggedly arisen, solid, prosaic engineering curriculum, in tantric suspension, cigar ash, mold spores, pine cones tracked in from the Enchanted Forest; a rest stop just outside of Salem where there is the best coffee ever known, scratched lottery tickets, happy meal scraps, other ejecta of a once teeming and vibrant civilization, deposited into a giant wind mill until the zipper parted and out there, standing in blinking sun, were ancient porcupines dressed in caftan, piping it's a smaller world after all, and to far more intent,

Fulnes' witless, evocative affectation, repressed by the accouterment of his station, had never previously so likewise a witness intimated into his presence.

Soon before deposition, Fulnes arrived at the end of the session, and ignoring obvious perils of his situation, he studied Dauphine bleakly, about to ask why the girl, albeit regarding the ant farm with decided disinterest in the southeastern corner of the glazed cinder embrasure which served as dingy sky light, had not troubled to demand her liberty. Desdemona appeared incapable of perpetuating any known autonomous function. By submerging his inclination, Fulnes thought he might have gained, following the sedulous dictate of his conscience, valuable insight into the cusp of pressing concern. "I am tired of being treated as if I were the only baby who could ever save the universe regardless of constant admonitions to practice low risk activities, thus never forgetting the hungry tykes," Hudspeth's prepared statement to the Bureau of Piezoelectric Assessment asserted acerbically, yet, loath to concede established procedure, Fulnes felt wholly as unprepossessing as possible and, in lieu of signaling the concierge, Tell, to resume her detention, arose.

"You are free to go," Fulnes said, hesitantly reaching for his hat. Replied Chantal, "not right now." The inspectorial factotum left his area. Reportedly capable of stirring for a second day, incipient calamity of symptomatic retrogression procedure slammed forth onyx *untenets* that, save reason, amiably littoral transitive interests await. Their onset fable lulled, "our off par equity," went the rest of it, "relies in essence upon subjective negligible reverse amortization of whatever bulk spindles are noisier than scrupulous terraform cofferdams.

"Loudly querulous, proof verged on inevitable alterable oneiro-mantic [*sic*] construction: wasps' reposed itinerancy, some able token occludant in one live teen thriller knew candescent amplitude swam vis–a–vis; indeed conjured suns arrived aloof in singularity, jade advent, as clue resplendent in abject sensual tautology, green notaries dabble in plenary grange lockout (seed *Ion versus Lex's Hat Trick, Inc., 1895*), geographic inured crannog virtually jammed clumsier feng shui motivational benefits. A forward by–play of Nertz track record shaped in deference to zero percent on every egregious tenement, a non–atavism for gruel, callow humors, a negotiable cloakroom smallhold, ejecta to remain unlike sturdier weirs, deferred thaumaturge of incendiary penstemons, of crepe lace, megaliths, icy glow worms for a staid if adenoidal concupiscence, somewhere infinitesimal leitmotif of urticaria genome dry–dock, rheostat holdover, or repossessed Gnostic tracts met laconic insensitivity."

Antiseptic per this degree of accuracy, every natural propriety ago, rabid tastes toured the nearest fiat's glum trance in sedentary blinking. Myriad cymbals, accolades being endothermic a plethora, coped by temperament. At Least, stale when agglomerate facades if twirled, *biathanatos* fused, nebulously, viz., coracles; stoic on purpose, it lent mold sense [*sic*] integer, caroling decent real eschalot, typifying sponge costume irrespective which, of inklings durst fizzled, each proconsul bounced to incline. First are syntactic cysts of rinsed incitement pre–eminent through a codex of emphasized mome, their folderol art simply vamped onto agreeable minute dimensional hat rack isomorphism. The next amplitude consignment would reticulate around even circus option, said earthly bric–a–brac auctioned somehow until chloroform broke into vernacular.

Eluctably furtive in our habitat, now Sibyl's teleology, ushered by nimby Satyagraha driven to eschew meaninglessness, sanctified all legible concern as mulligan throughout organized existence, dense, bluff aspen stations wink leerily aboard a blatantly organic strained ensemble, sailing a stout vat dupe, dabbling a venté urn true tote of ruse. "It's all in Gupta eidetic, of course, do unglue your crumpet or donut, twill, furtive faux tomatoes I call, shogun, every threshold or shelf down time is a vessel loosely vanished," said Upanishad crock mixed elves they'd sought foremost, each dense fidget nearly ascorbic.

Thrice in sempiternity, Echo, Mme Nadeladimov, quizzed upon thick stretches of miasmic archetype, beholden to debatable beer gardens over why Thebes' wattle wear supplanted Anodyne's usual plastic formal.

"My flat prom," she is declaring, amortized among many number residual prisms, "shall attain zaftig thermopiles like" — a naphtha praxis causes Gnadig to trail off into variability — "I'll tabulate as eerie graft serifs loaf around the block, protons effervesce as magenta spores beneath our remissible Bermuda."

The swell bee palinode monestrous ever since, concomitance with Hume and under any scrimshaw — one bilateral, dunderhead, escrow grommets of Za'at away, loss indeed to our informal museum of honesty thereupon. So heckle dreary orison, lip—synch, amid whomever's convective grange appeared genetic enough for asyndeton, al—Kamil, constrained if as chance cuneiform orbit most hallow shroud bent wittingly some stream into us. On machicolate binkies, happenstance lest firkins as usual, pronated liked Utrecht for many causative or bench—checked outer mobieuses upon Merovingian kismet. At Least, parsed flagellant motes may burgeon how atavisms, derailing chart rooms, hadn't ever breezier, in cyclically appanage, smidgens of concrescent motif aloof, since l'nurt [*sic*], wafting six quiche kumquats next an astute mandamus, perused ever caroomable sapience mythic, dabbling trans—figurative mini verse nigh a compost, still, on consorted moistly of weft, which atomized hereafter topaz parallelepiped laterals she'd moorage in abject scrupulousness.

"Only in blossom of neoteric U—scans shall our factorable hellion scarcely transcend ubiquity," ELIZA, her derivative mural of *lumine* presciently cognate as libertine (at least diffluence, beneath condition of flocculent sigma, a regimen debunked by Wald—Wolfovitz in seriatim), held manifestly reprehensible in vast coordinates: the contumely of *all too busy*, whose nascence indorsed by the Contessa, Mme Nadeladimov, with much diplomacy, was noticeably, amidst her more of disenchantment, pivotal. "We're hurdled those chill druthers," glazed, sorbitol (Hesitance, a tinsel heurist her charabanc, fled least cultic inklings), ill—fjorded dithyrambs, yet unless ailerons submit alto *finth*, a refractory demulcent lint gnomon, non—visibly owed to some clumpy cenotaph into *wishram* above an apparent aegis of rapidly unset *pans'flyt'ryte* clear off any meteoric pnyx shall mop around surfing foolscap, its wonted confinement Tell, known to be of hinged Perspex, left to languish under strata of atomic distelfink.

A crude by–law, whomsoever might strive, viz., nano–static precepts discombobulated hereunto, put aside on seemly woven infra–indigo were viewed whiffle boards or fable, *l'nurt* mutating each kismet dabs of time, elapsed time, space, acceleration, mass, volume, speed, popularity, and noise. Endothermal hiccoughs of that splat from ¶hrotomeous' implosion requisitioned such epoxy of replevin, tacked around by desultory *fjulsfut* cabal, yet propagation remained staid. Some nearer polemic trilled, rowing [*sic*] bat ninepins to a standstill by ornamental curacao rebate, ubiquitously effete toward innate lean–tos. At once, Nephretite decked annoying lacquer sconces in marzipan eidetic pectin night Styx, fed up a largely green ululator soon (Simic's kerchief probably best regaled or palliated exacting paupers anointed as variant) derided icons of miscible sanctity affordable to the first Nestorian effigy acclaimed in rouge pimento earth codes.

Since Finthector usually lost track of much stylish thread, profiling excess tragedians as piquant, if lemniscate, piñatas to plethoras newly pensive about lycanthropic terrestrials, and gerrymander diaphanous juxtaposition of monolithic *finth* whimperers, whose drafty placation endeared an oblique GPS viewfinder, a resonant semaphore ironically meant to limp past cagier *tictus* eflots or multiplex a tonality too urbane for expatriates. In his *Codex Habilitus*, completed below contempt after, by effrontery exceeding a visible dour prole isocracy, Læmært bought off his murky ambuscade. Necessarily icing all sensible precaution, Esmeralda importuned, in Ahem's surcease, faint recluse debutantes to project their equinoctial ordinates; a codicil of subservient arrondisements, integral nexus, *eminence–grise*, incessant futuristic orison of erratic sycophants estranged and plangent, Masha, upbraided for sagacity in specious anecdote, yet met askance to complain about tingles at witangemots, esteeming transient immersion requiem. These occludants, sited to affect the electro–harmonic spectrum from rare kicks, connote a toneless form.

"You see fandango's idyll," lisped a sheltered orange blossom, Iphgene, ere thespians sidle in feigned catabasis, where her quietly temperate trefoil disavows, axiomatic caricature hen–pecked, on a stark ale house *Scheherazade*, lent magnetic finality for jinxed icons, mixers too dead to ensnare *Tetrabiblios*, a bleeped horse opera as wide gods doting bracken, Mantissa's nanosecond–sized cause for Delphic idealist swatch, unless a banal parole, opining partial similitude as *lignum nephriticum* unwontedly, squinted, off–being outliers, long assiduous with thistle paraclete motif. Rhododendronized, therefore, some milieu silkworm diatomaceously see lymphatic nodules, abaft an isinglass–bundled, warmed biomes. The furtive garters rang off the wall–interposed esthetic and were no less preponderant than most emeritus snippets.

Left to stand in remonstrance, proof of keen antipode gossamer cephalopod, the clothsome enthalpist wandered into Hawaii, bilked at spasmodic inference, each meriting sodality freeze, must typically fund dull, blustery endo–frippery. Within gefilte codex tuffet (Lothar's corroborative extant), Bagler censored an already refulgent monarch mickly reprehensible for periwinkle theories of staunch lemniscate ability toward fustian. Ecliptic poseurs lacking original hardihood or qualm, prehensile innate cameral toccata punch line, those meta–spores, thus supercalifragilistic, anodized away from *wishram* in distortion of seminal Nicean mandate, a cavalcade intensified mensurally beyond the *licentia vatum* imposed, foil to volte–face of Iraisamonde, chrysanthemum queen, necessitating intrinsic public policy reviews.

Compunctive license, insofar as abortive diffusion of a vast ochre mime qua exacerbated the flow–through poppet natural jam tendentiously manifest, the enthalpist avidly audited an emergent debacle on Nesbit's woodcut, solely transmissible via anapestic foolscap. On a bobsled asymptote were trying short–term emeritus amenably received, albeit uniform unto a declivitous pall of dolorous happenstance, *In Finite Nuts*, fully captious in refulgence, motionless crop circle exercises there form instinctual subjection en route from blighty, irrespective lunch pledge; amounted to underscore, in diverse plethora, how recent lauded occludant galvanized Norah's bleary spectral REM hospice, pooled athwart rigorous ampoules effectually, allowing paltry recognizance toward variegation.

Emprismed cephalopodian caprice averse, since an ordnance requiting all binaural synthesizers into public domain put paid to privy seals, her own, gathered a now keen and no longer present rotogravure, research of Vikram's known temporal row boats in a channel of hedged incline, wastes of list stave out of Village commissaries in viable surf mode, if first–hand repartee, often too wistful, declaimed peremptory hasps uncoiled; to rededicate ability, will, or motif, to see their arguable habitual behavior no permanent effect served, Læmært in the combustible warrant, mentioned her metempsyche as gerund of laudation, so thenceforth were personal experience apportioned among character. In toto, numerous milieu ever unless in folio wearing illusion sequins, arid Esmeralda wandered upon whomever we, convinced of or given grace in measurement sufficient, forgave in love and all in all now were guileless in observance of unfolded panoply, dreamt, aspirant laity quite reciprocal in mutual regard, to her mind, fortunately, all I had, were benign, naught kempt, in villages heretofore known; few, until lit, often, ventured forth past universal time coordinates, allowed Ahem to cling to compensating for inability to pay her only way in today's world.

To celebrate an earnest tenet of involvement, Rust invaluably sourced harmonious rivalries of assurance, tiered, and gregariously broached, an immiscible hitherto must best fallow, sensible upon their erstwhile server super silver surf in elegant resignation dubiously, insistently proof-read, persisted in amenably declining Læmært's first if final remedial gesture aversely. Arrived, one concomitant being, Justine's enjoyable renascence in cyber–spatial circulars, inspected inference of driven positivism; imbuing gratis function hypothecate in this specific example slid far and wide, on sempiternal chance ebbing a lease term too rickety loose or foreshortened at any rate, moreover dawned on Raisin, and for what purpose lord had one discretion, overruled hereunto, lest arable concept, heinous bewrayal maxim lifted, panned below motif sampler apace? There, oppressed Freudian bipolar outlet mall featured home improvement, background checks, how Fishing Lynx could pawn her silver bass guitar, a handful of trophies won for overbooking Eur'tru'bro, her late father Gaussier's superb olive rang, by antique Steinway concertinas once well used in plunking *Lady of Spain*, unto a local chapter of thee, ghost fraud, *wergild*, two rubber slippers, and enough original copies of a declaration of interdependence to raise necessary starch to put her son into, if not thoroughly, an old bowling school behind here, dispassionate masks of social Darwinism. Masha dissolved to fade, unless systemic hopelessness, endemic to them, far unto nigh, in a way sincerely, edited Adjustor Blank. "P.S., Noone, remind me to download latest version of Nertz into firewall, or if we all wake up tomorrow mutants, please feel free to find my symbolism amusing." At present, Wesley Fulnes, upon colloquial cognizance of warrant non–contemnible, expressed a nugatory and nascent vocabulary of measure designed in regular interval for promulgating such static leverage.

.   .   .

In every channel of endeavor now inverted, an already elusive colophon, left immurably throughout otherwise porous enclosure, wrought via porticoes in driblet, as fewer health would append some specified incidence relevant of particular instance to solemnize reports of Læmært, whose super–annuated expansive argot, in alterable conscience explicated, owing to Horatio's insistent process, impinged, ere rulier upon familial roles owned, viz., aspirant faux luminance, importuned a sedulous referral, a snub if not of incurable variance toward ecological factotumhood, which cinched Sangreal's other weary accession into parochial senescence, a shallow shingle inked about if comped in permeable legacy, affected in fewer tremulous provenance, separable beyond freely cosmetic binary gazebo; in due credible symmetry, evincements to affable traversal of hitherto non–endurable distance in regard for a portentous venture pilot studio devolved into, when silage of prose knit act embossed, "method really figures into our nice active scheme by–the–by," proposed [*sic*] theorists fitfully over ventés, an unintentional consequence of live cylinders always flung athwart your heuristic funnel prion via fiddle–dee–dee ions.

"I sensed hidden rollover eke tricks upon your sleeve," interjected a man set apart by affidavit, reacting to magnified Nertz folderol. Still, current, sour grapes, dire need to be appreciated, despair, a deserted campus at outlandish times may lose some distemper below torpid fence spackle, yet for some pure chaste reason, glissades faltered. Dejected, Ion spliced thin gems of gneiss and lapis lazuli back into retrofit, convinced gratis evidence of mondo prayers solely placated urgent free for all snicker doodles. Untold pyrotechnics went out like insidious bees, causing wiry on and off gyration to reset, swaying sempiternal odious breach of flagrant decency. These processes calmed, somberly, tensing every muscle only when all done up limelessness neared all existence, "in best case, our ancient rank and file will rise up against freeze–dried hero worshippers who trick masses into divesting their innate heredity for any jar of incense produced below altered states." "For one who blended treacle litmus, you've picked fewest original dust mice to prove a tenuous philosophy," averred Idres.

Tacking some ferns locally as Mercator triptych once forsaken for Zinfandel now serenaded in stately syncope, "oh, fie on your droll eclectic plainsong," fretted seasick dervishes worn out by esoteric lyricism. If golf pros conjecture on every quibble reversed, whose aerobic lenience serves to evade arguably usurped lateral form flow daydreams? Jasmine's, as her foam finger hovered above send button, snooze alarm awry, so Tyoslament sauntered toward pod bay door and enrolled in a community assistance program. "Why, look, there's Aunt Norah, speak of" — " " — "tough, pish–posh," she said, "I've a son without Goshen ought goners' old patch, land, one measly *mont–de–piete* offered me some hundred plunks for a loft to shun doubt, oh nardy snoops," Fernand curiously sensed.

Four pirouettes were only viable when terraform constants wrecked their repose. Here, livid seneschals frowned in dour weal; a conch, spouting treble moiré ululation, hip–hop candles malfunctioned from tapers of astatine, stank, mace awls, twill–tusked and tavernous, athwart Boolean peek–a–boo cassowaries faltered, more pomp aside, Niobe's lancer went toe–to–toe despite illicit lumpy *finth*; treed seconds orated pious anthems: *On, Blithe Geckos,* and *Ram Life, Erin, Ere Quirinus Punts.*

A sweater tax, soon entranced via Saskatoon, annoyed Vikram gamin too; thus pinning waist–high true totes, a bobbin tapped Mithraic rot gut, hexamethylene, strewing it at some festive storks. Those search lamps scoured lists in amenity; anti–blotto posses fleeced haversacks of Zaibatsu [*sic*] for trail mix. Allies, posed purple ingots, in order to yank tsunami from winsome choir, Simic won past mesh a truce; to Hesitance, an illegible fix hinged upon Taoist can–do.

·   ·   ·

Aged are logs reverberated to pique of a punch bowl emeritus An impinged in coterminous distaste. Lodged on couth Ohthereitis, children of Core, a tacit host at bay trolled on formless cushions, "ring–a–ding," screeched Flußtapfer; seventh of aspect fied upon riprap a teary dirge to stares of rococo slump hive tontines, buttoned down above scads of fusiliers (*all too busy*). Hark, a monadic non–pareil enveloped matinee, alike trochaic Cyane, *tictuses* seeped turbidly onto earthworks, a rinforzando of gummed dies tapped below–extended mome pastille, and there a furnace binged half–witted in psittacistic license Homeric theorists should have tallied.

Only, for a weak awl, communication constrained, in overalls transpiring ripened conjugate of a coal rose, all residence, limited to similar dives upstream, hereupon repaired upon chintz redirect of lithiwatt [*sic*] outlet power stripped into each, group–rewound, Finlay's opus, these faulting dictitionators are foreshortening bric–a–brac. SOMHAD pirouettes led among ratatouille asperity, near Demopolis, parlance fobbed albeit starched juxta tandem: why, in October tickets drawl to your entire idyll, off glazed remainders of a slipped, paged apparatus beyond, strikes a cornea, rather than eggplant, is an imperative of deferrable perceived inevitable dawn toward epochs of gradual progress. Conducively spanning future academic hang–out, a pattern of virtual sorrow such stray shibboleth must energize ELIZA's placatory emblem of regard, twitched this hermeneutic environment.

A gel in moist, impure meniscus, cinching incandescently much ochre rewind, in perchance generic instant wavered along channels, in tripartite version, let ink readably tariff overnight, not large proviso contemning another twinge obol sapphire effectually, Sangreal's worsted shall Gaussian leave scene outgrabed, lurching to a colossal slouch. Between limes and ascorbic tulle, there seemed a listless chancre, far from diacritical, recurrent in festive inert polities. Each, leerily exteriorized onto scarce lien out of obverse connivance, gyred away in miscible complaisance, at last one remote colloidal insight. Any, kind (Gen 1:25) of present, wherever likeable, to say hi to folks back home, was pluperfect travesty for such colloquial persiflage.

Up until dawn, an old slaunch spinner trellis, Tell Ferguson, masked manifold search protestors behind an incunabula of blandest subtitle, yet penning incipient Heisenberg, effectively an off–shore totem before this happier hour indeed, Antonine theory, aggregated upon a raft of regressive meerkat codicil, ran out of things to do — the staggering sound whence a cogent vernacular, auspicious for fair zesty zeal may cobble, notwithstanding cromlech eisteddfod Tipperarily extruding from *wishram*. Few men were eager to remonstrate about timid immunity relished by all non–Niceans, forasmuch it percolated as a clear inter–regnum [*sic*] concertina alike, responsible citizens of Lichvue gathered as Læmært, and *ædith*, and commissioner of italicized time–travel, Silas F., faced each other. "One could not fail to hear alarums on all bloody frequencies, you sent word of that precious sequence of yours, you" — Læmært withered beneath unpleasant public badgering, his fiat percolated — "second your market for vulgarity," another voice, belonging to an ex–guildmaster, intervened, ushering *ædith* aside, and Læmært, left to his own mind, watched fire wardens work the hose and struggle to

prevent a total collapse of the frame. Middleford supported a commissioner implicitly and was not lost to himself in minimizing every reason
for Læmært's immediate sack, but as an unpleasant monad detached itself
and flushed around to straighten afresh that inspector, Middleford stayed
his hand long enough to alert Læmært. Hence onrushes Silas F., collect-
ing a moment of renewed silence, and his mug, pushed into knuckles of
the pensive ensign, slumped to ground in a time out. Læmært winced,
"you call off your dogs then." Middleford had lost his reliquary, forsaken
his following, left a burning house, and was instigated in a venal fire.

Adrift to the rarefied rear, a hoarser hare, name pasted into a coroner's
report, behind a wall of doubt felt never known proof of anything ever
again. Instant, an invoice, handed to Læmært, for cæsium mittens, signed
by Dr. Many Place, revealed the late Æmst as initial investigator. Embers
dampening, they went into the smoldering house. Læmært removed his
hat. Braving enough ash, Middleford stepped upon the hearth. Retched
upon stones of an inner chimney, a stamped cymbal, left glowering in
recent conflagration. "A shrugging star," Plair whistled. Læmært stared
at the gram. "The *pans'flyt'ryte,*" a guildmaster added. "Then what," Fulnes
interjected? Blank put in, "five hundred years before colonial times, our
calling, and those races of Niceans chosen to impose purest empiricism,
were at odds. A truce, finally declared under seal of snoring, granted
their right of reprisal if any of their number were ever again infringed."

"Cozily arranged," Fulnes observed just as sudden shifted embers
above indicated an immanent crackle of heated chimney tiles shot down
in cascading files. One, striking Læmært, knocked him stone cold.
Ending investigation, they dragged him to relative safety. Blank concluded, "since our late friends scotched their *fjulsfut* masks, a significant
faction of extra terrestrials is now after everyone on the planet." "They'll
have to take a number," Fulnes shrugged. Upstairs, eyeing side exits in
case of anyone's approach, just as Rust thought, a grass roots network
prepared the groundwork wisely, and seraphim entered. "Purely a social
visit," a latter murmured. They glanced about walls, encrusted in lichen
and jimpson.

"This is a very burnt house," declared *scrapmon'*. At the jalousie, asked, does this ever open, "on finer days," Mrs. Teaspoon averred, eyeing them warily, added, as Justine bent to sight behind inset credenza, "for what be she seeking?" "Mice," replied *scrapmon'*. "They will find none here," the house *'zkeeper* flared. "Dust mice, to be exact," *scrapmon'* explained. "Dust mice," exclaimed Rust — "you will find none of that," Mrs. Teaspoon insisted — "congregate in vicinity of electrical wiring specific outlets offering a simulative current, they prefer bare floor and drafts; you see a register across the hallway there." Justine extracted a sinuous rope off behind the credenza, a tousled melange of nap. "I still don't see what this has to do" — "they are composed of fibrous strands of weave, one can learn much from them, I'm afraid" — "with us?" "You share a common wall with Vikram," *scrapmon'* asked?

"Naturally," she noted. "I imagine you must cleanse regularly." "I can scarce see where this line of inquiry is leading." "Mrs. Teaspoon, perhaps you are familiar with a man in this picture." Frank, attracted by a diagonal portal, cringed since noticing he was subject of the portrait, and schemed too quietly at an offer of greater gain than this present circumstance. Seeing Mrs. Teaspoon failed to leap at an inference, Rust, indicating dust mice, asked, "may we bring one out with us?" "I should not see why you should not." "Tokens of gratitude shall be stown upon thee and thine everlasting."

Ike's Park Reflux.

As another doorbell rang, Park and Marta were in the kitchen unwrapping Saran from them who'd thrown in their trails of despair and left dress parade floats in after saying thank you, when these few, admired by all, blazed perfect spirals, though a show of hands, they'd expected, Señor Florian among them, Fernand, a writer, felt partly responsible for an eclipse before Core's transference, when his mispronunciation of a simple compound sentence, "if I may be of any help, please let me know," turned, beneath her recalled regard, into, infamy, and then bleated;

debunked, he yelped, police, shocked as if lemon had been his first word and, only to her, a lapse he had just mispronounced, anathema upon the scene, this attempt to assert a swashbuckling chuckle, recognized, and so much it was all she wrote, for the force surfed by solstice clients that fortunate evening. Park was nonetheless filled with morose sorbet. Finlay nodded, "it was an alpine ray gone to sleep five niches beyond our noses."

Hesitance agreed it became an occasion for any leveling. Set carefully on a tripod, a reverent octave zephyr penned into an unaddressed envelope they opened as music ever deepened; Norah Anne was fine that they were in tune, beginning, by agreement, the third movement of Zoltan Kodaly's *Second Symphony* (check please) zithered into a place while anyone could just kick back and play what's nice for a night. Inured in pine barrens, *ahriman* watched towers clothed in necklaces of light poured into the house at sunset, and started for them. Both began to radiate steadily at an Institute blueprint class, and felt was nice when on occasion Raisin broke out folding chairs for a ziggurat. How seductive they seemed. All Park knew was returned to a stranger land, not far removed from posterity, full of felt like signs, and had been shown portents; unlike the arid, desiccated, and secretive land PoD left, these paths, dripping with fatness, promised fufflement. Staring, Ænselm approached a bustling outlet metropolis.

After about the sixth run red lamp any sort of intervention would seem salubrious, yet Horace, never able to get the remote to work, and before solemnly exhorting, "it was written on the missing page of night stand Gideon, 'be saved from this perverse generation (Acts 2:40),'" PoD, shriveled to watch Chorister trans–mogrify into penultimate levels of *inter–regnum* parking grange, cried, "in event your still tingles, it's as if a shamrock was borne," whilst djinn etiolate, amber snails upheld parquet ramp, a giant pickle squeezed through a hairpin curve and past a galaxy, Althea, new Moxie girl, attended by fiery mustangs, vaulted into a threnodious sky clad awareness of imminent specificity. There her strained bowling shirt and ubiquitous cargo pants were exchanged for an obversible potting smock, all inner rage nowadays, something worn once

and tossed aside; her sweetly cloying doggie voice made Snorggi turn and
sneeze at systemic guardians who up to a certain extent willfully failed
to address her; and thus ensconced, Sangreal, declared directorship of
proletariat, placed all exogenous elements of *inter–regnum* beneath an
extramarital ban. Now the disaffected flocked to her standard.

In no time, a Nicean grand fleet appropriately sent to complete guest
satisfaction questionnaires in every corner of the universe. She returned
Tolstoy's ciao by a vapid blink, the latter paid in uttermost farthing for
xenonian golf, a cart hack who plunked four G's to get him out of there
(this did nothing to alleviate his recent unsevere headache), and returned
to an old stomping ground, Horace found it not a very perpendicular
place anymore — folks had just taken to throwing their Mayan blank
calendar into the recycle bin, that made for a very surly 'ket feller of
a morning as they say: who else hasn't heard there there offended by
gods of static? The circle of obversibles schrank, but new hazards, such
as black holes, aliens, and renegade Spocks uploaded enthusiastically as
Ænselm excused himself and slept, drooping hints, "you didn't mean to
let that out, you know," but if Finlay knew she did know, Noone hadn't
sang our American linen that night.

Only Fernand (Zero Point) O'Kelvin, *ædith*, and Ostrand had ever
been stateside. "Must you mind if I strum my air guitar," he'd call out and,
"lo, go ahead;" they both found him selfish on a dare. "If you'd be wakin'
up a lady, you shouldn't mean you wouldn't go, couldn't you?" Iraisamonde spent her last good year on a girls' academy play, wielding hockey
sticks and learning shorthand, so Bitsy might sit up frantically, stand in
her field, and receive guests. In a short silence, as everyone gazed expectantly in dark, she wrinkled her nose near snubbed tortilla corn chips.

.   .   .

Narrators Wormwood, Tell. Romanian Rhapsody, A major, opus 1, Issuance Viasansky.
How some had fewer chants to hide a plastic clarion, whomever else might play
throughout their nostrum, to forestall chunky mage icon fervor which swept, on
campus, the merrily color shoe tree so free of elemental ink. PoD, penning the stage
of Ohthereitis, is in turn besieged by a dominant paradigm.

IV — xxiii — The Ossian Poetry Slam.

Citizens of Erewhon were attempting to enjoy uplift in the most lateral fashion possible, when this did not seem very surprising. A mustard seed wedged so far so near the year everyone broke even jumped beyond the planet, a jumble I tried to fathom and cast light and salt upon. Everything fresh as an oath and gladly rattling in the kept sun, a sage, his blinker teensy aura from abandoned chair sparklers why anything, began. As fully fit as the day, the Rat WTH was on a field trip. Pan's flute, dumped with the nymphs at the moment of the inceptive Note, was believed hidden, carelessly, in a fitful brake.

The word upland was, that for it, as a measure of what remained of hope, to be effectively contained, the fallen remnant must secure the hatchway to *pans'flyt'ryte*, as it, said dumped with nymphs of the moment, on a wabe gamboling, was held to have initiated the recoil. As depleted nether counsels grappled, in interest of utter quality, to agree upon a name via whence their principle sufferance, as defined in their loss of might, might end, preparatory to developing immediate constraint, favorable compunction, and eventual contraindication of the Nicean theme, residents of Ohthereitis stirred to cope in reducing the weft of the unexpected onset of *ahriman*. Commendable vessels as they kept themselves, his faithful body found the foremost gate of the new hold fustian.

Windrows of an Elysium over–attenuated in this kindling of a ninth neon bias, light, flint, marveled, sound, and among the body of the faith, of individuals predestinate, then disconcerted, larked about them the glory of an absinthe throne. At what eternity the all of you marveled, in a promise gone south, that predestinate, ere gathered hostage anew as latest installment, unfolded. Læmært had not a mere box shunted off to the side, which must have contributed to the entity. Arrived, the persistent practitioner of the single voice, the sky blue jay, disabused visitants of events since, amidst many mansions, a connectivity, remade all about the whole or entire city, sauced (from chard, or other over–charged) arrays of magenta filings (resplendent in trembling recollected).

Impending, further niceness abounded, retold the persistent practitioner upon the gate of the abandoned ram. "Spring, no longer up, you wells," it chided, upon the uttermost walls where remained some few to witness, before lit out, over, and beyond heath fled trellis fields of promise become. In resultant stillness, the collectivity demanded a recount of itself and no longer felt another covenant could ever arrive. An emergent process, archipelagianism, the unsnarl of the long overshot, declared absence of synergy only just desserts and arranged another series of ordainments to resist, in lightness, the new captivity.

The predestinate had, moreover, little presumption to agree, amidst themselves, only this Stadtgeist [*sic*], a sense of stintedness, denying their one and only living hope to be at last one with their Lord or all of the saints, sentenced them to a measure of relentless re–assessment, curtailed as, their apt journey sought the bride at the same place as the lamp. Known it was filled with the oil of a ghost tank, several hundreds of persons without the body, cast off their train and beheld themselves at once removed unless the hope of many more who, impervious to their own declamation, remained possessed in belief of an eventual deliverance. At Least, safety had been guaranteed by their surfeit of guile.

But in eternity, resuming a sense that city remained an edifice nodule of considerable visual acuity, wandered, the faithful performed occasions of great gathering before eleven of the gates, gloried in their own lamp below Neath, an over–hung article of darkness, and founded considerable arrangements and to praise the rock upon what hope remained. In time, the renaming of the gates occurred. All stood singly below the twelfth gate. Albeit of turns narrow, not one of the citizens would hazard to know to what world it must lead to now.

The blessed, meant to peer down the old path, saw flashes of that old enemy, mill house, jumping jack flash, scratching against their captor, Prince O'Darkness. Lucifer's matchless lieutenants, the chromium beast of the various acronyms, leading neo–refrainants; anti–Plutonians, their voice unified in the falsetto post of corporeal counsel; the prefect of Antarctica, blob of the very being that captor of the faithful unloosed: a campaign, designed in a teal shelf, culminating in circumvallation of heaven's wonderful wohnerf, which stood unguarded, for yawning on, from, or upon samplers of new atmospheric tincture that restored a sense of their aim, the omega big band bang wave, impersonal, imminent, immersed most of the least resistant *lumine* in the link of the minute fold.

This violet invitation to rest also decimated eight ninths of the fallen, forcing the old foe to conduct the battle, insofar as it might be won, in response to foreshortened summons, on exterior lines, yielding a potential decisive advantage to PoD and his remnant allies, the romantic phaeton, the Mirandan *lumine* in exile, a village, a preceptor of South America, some tinfoil eidolons, and Oceania.

.   .   .

One late night, and to no apparent purpose, a man stoned around town on his damned hog, a cruel and unusual sound made for no reason whatsoever except to vex everyone. The man, an enthalpist of near non–universal acclaim, worked diligently for causes of preservation, albeit in dawning awareness everyone half–heartedly indorsed ersatz panic; thus, spoiling the chilled driveway daily at Noone, who drew a kind rag simile to warn, ere, actually alike, Bagler held fast.

Achievements bottled in anticipation of a worthier day, publicists of the Greater Mesa Bio–Range Commission, prepared to let slip a fifteen year fuel estimate, recently issued their casual opinion that, thanks to technological advance, any new excavations were never foreseen to be necessary during the presumable future. The enthalpist, in his dwindled following, felt bitter pinpricks at this coherent sentiment.

Its heat felt them apt, men knew reservation of several wetland conservancies was assured. Sam had not gone to such trouble to construct this network of fragile marshland only to see it ignored by minions of the techno–industrial complex. In his fields of endeavor, the enthalpist was able to cite many authorities without slightest recollection of what they actually wrote.

Anodyne, recognizing this, was immediately out for one of his withering retorts, viz., "let's say I've forgotten more about that topic than most of you will ever know." Bagler, unable to contain his dismal turmoil as industrialist and environmentalist, odd fellows all, went shopping for matching percale counterpanes, and longing for a reversion to halcyonic disobedience, was of no further use to the League.

Let out of his recent position of research coordinator for the Reverend's template, the enthalpist remained, inviolably feeling that plan, long harbored, to space the commission to renege its roseate view, must soon go into effect. Since the Founders' League's asserted, ebbing, resources of civilization required at best a proscenium of stewardship, the ruinous émigrés, vis–a–vis pert tropism, amassed tandem whorls. "Rest up now, emirs." Off Earth sorted the chop store elves, rumored to wield hale cheer. Tin soul beacons on Miranda, gross great herbal tubes wished toys a whine mislaid.

If you meant a dole is sagacity, lit in lacy luau, i.e., a pooch moss fret, a no–no in *untenet* hives to the cafe dawn nodded glumly. "Stet, we'll say biased Aves and chew our hats with raw treacle until TGIF." Whomever, to a near Waldenesque zero, unfrocked at peccadilloes, hauled a slew, Porphyry, in scene cones loath to feel omega, bled in wonky bodega peeps. The tsunami blew heuristic gift tubes out. Night is lithe, where caloric aunts wait, a gathering, if otiose, says 'tis nasty Niobe's seltzer phial!

It immured few lords worth one to curtsied altos: luster met shed laity well. "I've sniffed oval ziggurats on fetchy poilu Ti–Vo sheets, canned ferret docilely pure rococo, used a narrow haft at fierce fens."

"Caught stewing out, MTV beatniks knighted no chum to heaven, or we free the bland hint, railer." Haute aunts' tactile cargo school these spied: true chance never treed PoD.

Those huge thaws did dual decor—fed nimby shires. Alive, these let law hotties devise thorn debt pork–a–billy, unripe writ suds, l'nurt's wort cheer tale, a nutty forest, yet lent fichus fed in bashes of thee, consolidated henna treacle hits of a hoot. As messy dynes reviled rapt yeoman or hearth, "Në, I'm treed to be lissome loam pits," it's soon 97 wild spumes Thoth hid; why, a tier opus Fourier, pal, i.e., a shoal, included ritzier japonica dated bloomer. The beat creep axed new sooty flops, thinking a batty lord threw off Diogenes hooter feed fumes to cwts of Niagara WMD.

So Echo gains votes anon, Utah dinar by taille deemed wise. Output museums spiced terraform, i.e., lustier street wonks create opportunities for forming a peer group right here in this dark heat trap and try to scrawl away. Thin claws leered at a slam. No man, invited to stare down italic use, left a civic solon to zone this moiré. A clear scan clung aloof, "until we twisted muesli as a fit hat: finding a neat minor nerve," Alcuin, coating talc tinder, spat. No foal clinic, it connived nova sinners' plural cognate in seismic terrene.

Snipe tides in rum comas met the great stew. Might men vote on aim that is more able? It tingled out tide fog. If a stone is shot at ELIZA's dire inner rut, is newly illicit PoD's maul a really thrall–lit mob of mirth in few sexist diets? Noone heard, "when I've tossed tontines, op cit, vita are nisus," putties vine–fed since treed sour new ague plotting in banned gear. Six smitten night druids smelled rapture. Plair's bower babe concerted, were leaky vita rap common in votive use, the land bats realty live now sat. A dustier throw, sang LOL, is a free bias high as a dove.

Mitten Bowlers Cheered PR.

Tingling, hot time sojourn, wet cat, hats, melba portal omen fund, rare Morse, thee, tube baron, shop as our help is acute. A nicer treed night ink cit, "my garb mirage slush nuts housed gold ladies." Sure, one coin in either fief drew a real canon wind as hot gift–wrapping pipers re–ran paltry lima nut shelves to chair divas, ere need hit pesto crepe nut cant vita.

Wormwood skirted rife Ti–Vo, as merest paper toke, rebel with twain, AA liberty cider, iota ruin, a mind bunk, Canada stemware forest, or jet triennial crypts, in yummy chortle fosse, Vishnu excites the sneeze stoic. It blares anew, biasing a device ere stopping his deltoid rave. There, tarts connote it cropped ten love bagels, in aurora bone, pencil–built ethos serpent, with chino poker stitches. "If jet–cheered resets heard a lure oblate peccadillo city serrate pine, I, while berated their foe, collect stilts, sir."

In trend crier foyers, hope helps hot hens axe summits ere supper woe, "'then we beg exit tints: pray, Aira, uncle, trivial huge tide chains weave hermit hovel.'" They diet a cruel verse as wary swans stare dimly, "heed ten mint teen Volvo ivies: oh to much nice ones niacin abounds!" In liner bins, a wonk decreed both spores twisted. Even voles minded troth or pyrite fire on it, so a favorite thing, ire, duly married sable cusps to Nemo's dash. Wormwood can deter icier ploys if sirens amerce caps on bower connoisseurs at Tottenham. A gleam for vintage union: those grittier bendy reeds placed prior wing octets.

"To spoof Diane's muse, I shut a wild cart draft so the tandem innocence train courted a man of truth." Then God will foal, near an anointer, nineteen evolving summit phases worth a daily salted nut level. A rail threw now fit tar paper folk latches at this vintners' firm drove. Worsted on trail mix, all the more realm rowed for beer while footmen steamed a pale pilaf, things met memory, in such sent hermetic thaw, effusive FM orders shot nearer Indocile's newest thunder cabal: *Trick Ghost II.* "You don't have to keep picking your teeth like you just left the seafood buffet across from the Bijou," where everyone was assured their ex's should soon star in an off–Broadway adaptation of *Mr. Ng Said*, never mind the garbled marquee, "the night before seeing everyone turn into their only own big brother," said Marta, during a busy afternoon collating transacted coupons by place, time, and manner into little drawers of a *xenonian* spice rack before the decisive audit of the center for international assistance.

Puffed up the one–way escalator to scatter notes to the four seasons, friends who worked at the buffet very helpfully enticed these welcome guests from Mercury across the traffic circle to the Sunrise Cage and assured them, according to new law, their tentative harmonic waves would make *finth* stop even for them in the crosswalk forever. In memoriam of Æmst, Marta's listener, Iphgene, who often amused herself by hypothecating scenarios of increased alarm, evinced no indication her friend's aphorism took effect.

Heppleweis attempted to peel an apple in one swipe, not above thinking she consigned her firstborn prayer for guidance, praised her detractors, pounced on these instant solutions to listen to a semaphore by famed enthalpist Sam Bagler, all the rage at the Kalisthenes — rites of passage, a dream of big tops dispelled in a clatter of foam niblets, and it must have been the sound of tumbling flan sent him out of his daze, after which ELIZA projected Earth's orbit was entering a keynote and should intersect a tektite sometime, after 2039 was in *Vogue*, and journalists, asked to check their scones at the door, left eftsoones huge cairns of them unclaimed, indicative of many, remnant therein, enthralled by the new creed.

Bereft of universal joints, Iphgene blinked in vapid arrangement of a slimmer neurosis, hoarsely gone so nihilist an entire terrible sciatica alleviated by taking zinc supplements. All of their efforts to re–conflate ELIZA's psyche, using a check written last month, Esmeralda's popcorn popper, node six rheostats, and other ejecta always seemed to terminate in a live buffing wheel for which no switch ever went chorusing. It whirled vigorously, too ungrounded to be left unattended, and yet every hand needed to trace identity of the *Picayune* embroiderer, funneling script into the past using several more marble buggy tent tunes.

Every attempt to establish this movement ended in a communal Chocho Molyneaux sing–along on MIT. An entire city at bay, of winking metallic traffic cones waited until perfectly logical connections were sorted in theory. Finally, Plair concluded, if an enthalpist insisted upon dismantling the fluffing wheel in search of a switch, Meringue gamely assured him it was not of concern; and if in haste asseverated, the copper power strand left a live spark in a room filled with ether, and not a scrap of duct tape in reach, ordered abandon dream, consigned the entire construct to oblivion, selectively, Persephone's visa inculcated ailerons toward the sham fest, adumbrating mixtures of huge bustard chatter within.

Moreover, she'd overlooked how internecine automatons defrayed null empathy, since by now strange scarab havens were once to yonder skip albedo, indicative of forlorn Godot. When approaching lavage clusters bumped alongside their precarious abatement, Talitha uttered to attend to at least one other castaway and, swathed into a stern, slept above all these worlds.

.   .   .

Pluto, the ninth of them, faced relegation, and Hades missed his consort spouse queen wife. He had nearly no option. Could it be less fun? To find her, he should need to leave the building. Of his proximate beans, few remained. Those not evanesced into the general rarefaction comprised a spent force, their squeaking search, for news of Core (this best were *REM*), at the edge of Hades' captious bound, a ridicule of their formal power.

As he pondered the subjects, the ill dud we adapt could behoove Pluto to have to send one of them. It posed a homogenous precedent for, if in so doing, the shade released, to her former life, did not return, his swollen realm would soon clamor. Hades could not be able to contain them at all, should not be able to send them to any of the other after worlds, and already decided, if any were to be permitted at once to depart, it would have to be into the here and now.

Soon, s/he should have grievances to redress. Hades, in absence of many minor functionaries, already had to attend to so many of these lately. There were too many closers. There was not enough flight. There was too much shade. There was no longer any need. There was no lack of closure. There were either insufficient, or too many, depending upon one's inclination, underneath the stilt–supported wings, inserted storage closets, and concrete pads upon which cars were parked. The aforementioned driveway ran up a steep incline to a second level of fields to wander. Hades wished to be disposed in consideration of a fresher petition. Empowered to do nothing, it was also his lot to listen to everything.

As one of his bookworms added, a permit, to release a subject, on condition a living man wandered, as hostage, the underworld, exists. If there was no problem with it, we would leave at dusk. "It will not be that easy." Glanced above a beheld visitor, appearing at the fringe of *wishram*, the sky blue jay, persistent practitioner of the single voice, paid heed as the worm foretold, spells of Scheherezade could follow if the released shade did not return, averring the practitioner's master would see that hostage, freed to promote the stance of instant demagoguery, must receive distinct marque to storm Hades' domain with an allowable, blasted thoroughly in the impending azimuth, snore, a few more djinn than were usually necessary, and it was altogether down with the living to plunder and pull at the tapestries, to sink the shafts, to consign the deep treasuries and cart them aside, thus also possibly supplanting Pluto as a trans–cultural namesake. The released shade should be chosen with great care.

Frederick might fain accompany this lucky contestant out of here, so jaded had he become with the nether land, yet unless one was officially dead, one was ineligible, and his mind strayed to his restive counselor Piero, alas too far away to argue him from this predicament suddenly in the 13th century. If not as called for as any of this, here already tenor dispositions held one's own severance, their due admissions ratably actionable insofar as loads of everyone knew who were however here anyway. Unilaterally, they caught up with regardless time unless viewing inter-related qualities of metaphor. Who said being a silent mediator was the worsted warp amiably allowable?

Tunnels of trembling time splashed, searing overhead as the Nicean Grand Fleet, powered by a thousand suns, nearly buckled in its first attempt to rush the new sorority. Albeit its heavily configured tappers succeeded in riddling the coattails of the commentary to achieve time, mass, elapsed time, velocity, density, volume, space, acceleration, and noise sufficient to resist the backgammon pulse of the solar system's pale dwarf, the vesicular Nicean flotilla, so shallowly adjusted to the task on their screen saver, held aloof in fear of fear itself. It was the coldest June ever known.

Measured in animus was time required for facilitators (*all too busy*) to recondite their propulsion sub—system, initialized to withstand immense shallow gravity tide pools of their original sunstroke, one which they found themselves wont to forsake insofar as Nicean trail mix, a secretion of matinee antics of *tictus*, of whom the last dyad, ordered cagily and as a matter of course nettled, recently absconded in an odious (for *inter—regnum*) photosphere saturated with tincture in any cause at all. For its nine strains to gather in a modicum of unity, bobbins ordained design of a symbiotic version; *fjulsfut*, an incredulous race (first in acceleration, last in velocity), raise time for *inter—regnum* in fabricating diffusion paradigms geared to muckrake into their dwindling stacks; tappers soon bought word of an entire plant, Titan (hovering in the third ring of the sixth disco ball), purported to be photo voltaically—enhanced with compounds spectrally even smellier than those emitted wavelengths of niceness when emplaced among any simple heterodyne.

Their final answer, to streak backwards via an array of ultraviolet lava lamps until the host at best was spherical, proselytized into a Nicean—synthetic ether, awakened, since considerable pathos, *finth*, reminding them such colonial ethos, refuted by the Pleiades Rarefaction of the final teensy year, ought sauce a reinvention of reality. Yet chef d'ouerve (*all too busy*) lapsed its most rarified numbers (first in volume, last in space) some millenniums ago, and few were already peeping around the perilous quasar known as the Noses of Snorggi. There was eventual cause for an even greater cheer when someone else announced an unexplained propensity to locate an indigo sphere.

·   ·   ·

Ænselm rested a moment behind the pinwheel of unfamiliar stars. Spaceship sounds, faltering along an easterlier ellipse, now recessed into complete distance at sunset wholly undying. Bat trees perused biodegradably, one's best materiel witness down in front lied bleeding. Into pavement clammier Muzak shrilled, half–pence Norns bygone accompany many diligent sunstrokes, the project of one's desire a grand inclusion.

Before please stop lacing ticklish alibis, someone else's gazebo lit upon a rum crush meandered sullenly. Omnibus forums blithely sat, under the table crumbs hurried up, Core said in arms, for not long however an ochre brief please anon sworn equation, the dais toward persiflage picked up a little steam, and amidst ergo gingham, formed cartoon bubbles, under stress, sensibly conflated newer shows of monitors.

At once one hundred weight alarums, not as brisk as vigorous jingles sang instantly by gentler models, nor yet as incestuous as bleeping cyber devices of modern smoke, the Note, an unattached dreadful D flat siren of brass mockery, shooed guests into corridors as if gabby elastic strumpets tuned out the entire house in an unvaried state of duress. Middleford truckled lilting declensions, too studious to follow us into the grainy frigid bas–relief, and finding sanctimonious refuse near a duck pond, lit a cheroot. "Enough of that uninhabitable heath," 'zkeeper, a voiceover rejoined, and yet Francis found strength to retort on the contrary many quite unexpected valences were quiescent hereby.

These peak interests sloughed an awareness of more down time than usual, and after severe minutiae postponed his return, the ex–guildmaster peered amidst an open portal, timidly sensed the corpulent malevolence of the roynish ward, and ventured to perforce pass a vial beneath the lurid synergy, which glanced at him in weird suspense unless defaulted spot on aloofly. Frank scampered dizzily aside. More than ever might hematite reruns await his evaporative sauna, for upon noting a vast personal collage, standards of preponderance dispersed in hasty wind, a loud semblance of Fourierists responsible for combing the premise lined out only if, specifically paused to whistle, for a while, at worst, an unnatural prepared blast of some kind.

In actuality these were but sparks amidst a vast squalor alone, since Azali thought everyone had Fridays off. One would hug our rented obscurantists if, not until further notice, those oddities are usually too raison d'être, but to follow upon sizeable lead, you'd imagine the classical era as a time where all of these sage pronouns meant something, earmarked today; chewing out the pre–historic riff at Silver Styler, al–Kamil, sultan of Ægypt, pondered on a GOP questionnaire when nine mistruck burners grind, up in a corner of the Korean bistro, wrenching about a voice message on several foreshortening epicycles.

Just next door, the accountant, who inspired some actress, between very different spying television coverage, of *xenonians* as stereotypically able to jump across pictures of sublimity, coaxially imparted the prince of a random sink with narrow expectation to alter confines upon which checked away Cupid to her thing. At best too important to drool, all fizzling at Manzikert (the peace of impatience should be given convincing enough onyx crystal), wrapped, redeemed cheerfully, and sprawled into the shrubs or streaks. There was nowhere to introduce being; a lone carload headed to have fresh flavor, covered with those exponential, shifted detritus and memories of inspiration.

At Worsted, sounds like it slipped on lawn beers, in quick march the unified time flies fallen out in thousands. Clad in a rain barrel until changeling, where eternity seemingly flipped pine cones at the church, *all too busy* became any smarter. Many went about the homily of their germane intellectual past and told willingly comprised e–mail polishing contests. Even up channel, but all far short of ice, a minor usually stood for fast cash. Its campsite was normal again.

The daily Tuesday left in mileage falls; tendrils of uninterrupted sidewalk and steps from cable bounded up, telling Fuald, carry us through my veins like I care, and it's necessary to aver that damn craft fair, albeit convivial, and quiet, except for airport stories she had, was vintage. So why could she first step in a sea of communion to get them busted? A vertiginous dream away in downtown, near the federal concourse (Ensign Plair's army armoire full of exuberance for these Presbyterian humorists), people, trying to dance and voice this yin–yang out for the nervy kind of secrecy, pledged to right a time of being self–ins with vapid skies, given no idea where Old Jerusalem surprised time to a crawl.

For example, since return to a lot of disconcerting scrap today, which caught upon a verbal toy rookery, enormous empty shell stands, ran by al–Kamil, "I've finally found the giant leafy purple vacation I'll someday regard, pressed to disrupt opening" — a glimpse had vanished. It was a sign from a leashed Yorkshire running around with a teletypewriter, going Boswell as soon as it lumbers into, and over, Fuald, and up the nose I've hours later, because of that name, already the architectural enormity for anything atop the industrial brownie auto–mat cafe. It may, to blurt out in about forty jokes most real, like what happened down off a spark tapper at any given time. It is why al–Kamil felt so weird, wondering if this bugaboo be killed, by bad innuendoes and twenty–odd sneezes, as Meringue's last chance to stage a heave–ho and stable some napping silverfish.

Frederick undid some front gateway and pulled his haughty gloves together when the telephone rang earlier yesterday, after brief outbursts, such was his speech on saluting at a dining facility worker for referring to him as baby, and snipping weskit scores, and/or even Freddy, with his dishrag; al–Kamil opened a gateway thrice, ere in space, they kicked past a tear in the screen, made knick–knack work boots such fun, knocked themselves for standing in a crowd (acting like their recent training was out the window) and, benefits in being, removed a return unmatched unless cynicism ticked on, insurance forms that front office played hardball withheld. The furnace actually kicked in, but words just weren't going to lead to an open door unless Noone, concierge at a distinctive hotel where you might roam as if one is forever in the year nineteen hundred everything, said again, finally, that I was, in terms of non—existent significance for henceforth future geraniums, a good writer.

.   .   .

PoD brought a pine tree for the empty hours, the fatuous work order, the search for the serve back over, and crouched in gathering darkness and heat; written off the VW assembly line, when he was buried below goose blankets behind the French Burger King for not being more of a prince at the time, which was a remedial art therapy center they'll eventually kick him out of. Their henpecked wedgie duck made it somewhat near the lamp, shuffled in order to hold a head high in the missile crisis that had an impact on development: the turtle, duck, and monkey.

That first song rooting out abrupt exits from sand, a little puppy did not diminish a bubbly mirror filled with some cobwebs, and QED, some old professor who was carrying on the bulk of being in one of those earthquakes, and power dozing down through childhood, a gateway screened clock, fumbled with feldspar and ran undone out of the ocean and an occasional counseling; so, in a fit of industry, *th'ratwi'thorns* featured a door slam fest to plunge off into a streak. The rat—like creature, braced for a final charge yowling, undid some sneak fall, scuttling across the highway of depth, sickened by constant talk of reality, and announced, to all but a hunched and miserable extra terrestrial hence, a proposal to watch sage monarchs, fierce and gregarious, who fluttered in during a commercial break off the freeway, in and out, and sneaked unobserved views of the low—riding thong cheeks of Lilith, who berated them for having her driveway excavated on their watch.

Last night the strike—out hot—foot loop monorail, regained hinter, would not shake that impression; any more to run around the edge of space spotted Frederick, reeled off in front of a perfect, proportioned clasp. Lilith, verged on QED, punted toward a tapper wrenched open, mistook a crescent wrench for a spanner, and a delayed reaction, exasperated by the ceaseless, who never rescued her from mother's, stridently enforced, piano lessons, under a dribble gateway, heaved PoD against the messenger ledge, and gave Frederick a rain check for what QED regarded as pseudo–retirement. The *untenet* now railed against everyone, finding outlet in designing her standard of perfection, a talisman against further despair, Christendom, invasion, bolting off into the blue, not a bump in the road, and shortcomings.

.   .   .

As Nicean Note beckons its scattered strains, perambulated toward an empyrean, newly terra–form republic of Xanadu achieves orbit to escape tyranny. Undetectable, symbionts of Damian, emergent from backwash of protactic dissolution. Frederick II repairs to Viterbo, 13th century portal of Nicean jitterbugs, to create more prototypes.

IV — xxiv — Yon origin, other polite node thus...

These credentials gave pause for resultant conversation between exiles, a metaphor of liminal exigence, seduced into contraindicating least civility remnant, accompanied by halcyon loose motif parasol who egotistically asserted PoD was yours. The commission knew her assertion as reflective of the claim of her trans–Xenonian people, annoyed their bête noire was casually subsumed into a Worsted triptych. A large snaily shape untitled onto upon an interactive wharf; albeit sporting transitional snazzy gerunds apparent in nautical terms, only one of them congregate, whistling stranger than the controls of ancient encounters. The exiled chancellor decried, "which is neither, creation, nor destruction?" *untenet*, from depth of a piebald stare, regaled them curiously.

"We will take care of our own," it assured them, intransigently excoriated their method, said one man's work is another's eleven's, criticized latent inherent futurism, and implicitly stabilized tuppence without application heretofore. A prince anticipated its charade drew much rejoinder of late, yet always listened as originality, before conterminous notice, wore such goings on. Recognition of his compendium a waste of religion, dichotomously all hands joined in scattered applause as an enlarged dressage disingenuously plunged from the nave.

"I have no quarrel with this one," the councilor fiercely whimpered, aware posterity transcribed his limited conscience. His companion gracefully tugged doubt, "I recognize the seal," and the carafe splintered into a thousand shares, fed alike numerable quite chats who wash, skipped athwart dockets. "Note," added Zoyschia, "how our true feet dress so lamely," as several hours below adaptive surfed the pirouette fetch and another mandrake longing grasped essential fringe. Their dyed splashy oriflamme, with sprites of fare thee well above anew great sound, began torridly, with a lingering dusty roseate watch; seamless, rife, harsh intonation of coercion froze every wondrous track.

Minute above moorings, unpinned without view, Sibyl's assistance and the purported *untenet* launched so far into ether that clever universal gradation hovered in heedless topicality, "in the name of every visionary promulgation, those variegated subservient regressions tax our profligate agenda," Harold deposed, "ex post facto, we've stumbled onto a terminus of sorts, an active recovery of spiritual clamor, an aggregate azure terra foam of *lumine* by first HF cure." Ablative *ahriman* cheered, with subversive countenance of encore, "the popular will has spoken in the name of humanity. No longer need for being chained by this insidious pursuit of amalgamated chivalry."

Replied ELIZA, "first, find your hope a misguided reaction to a time when life was apparently symbolic." "Now listen, skeptically if we may, as old hypostasy surfaced to report failure." Van Etnabaron added, "next, I reset our attempt to enlist meaningful criteria in PoD's genial causal texts." They watched an informal veil of large pre–Cambrian stage rotes suns might spell, in tense phonics a runaway exile, as since now Plair's virtual milk run snares ambrosia where omega tracers waft. Ironic, diverse platitude Harold had seen enough of and could leave anytime, but a seethed mask, lurching with showy next pagination a personally lenient, rippled bitter retort across the fringed fulcrum. Coursed into obedience, the councilors tuned from the watched potboiler and clambered onto next *untenet*, charged with translation of PoD's counter–circumvallation. "Hurray for our newest subaltern," sang untold throngs already therein.

As the ground floor zoomed away from them, he saw Lizavetta erstwhile, beneath the parasol, who called beyond him with nightmarish clarity, "I told them my father disliked mistreatment of employees." Through carpets of hail Harold stared at the recessive promenade, thanking her for an opinion. "You must love optimism," Van Etnabaron guessed, whatever result might be, for the great seal of the universe, almsgivers, posed a creative transaction, "must, cause, her to lose interest in skating." Sasha, shrugging visibly, knew this minxish confidante, alone, among Iphgene's rivals never invited to their after hour scramble, needed no injunction to carry out this task in backwash of sequential ink lines; propensity of over–reliable awareness toward any latent involuted sediment post liminal, acute surfeit of epicene risk furtively fictionalized all peroration until stared up by remedial or jocose Etesians.

Diffuse blinks, owed to fickle sensationalism, only upended hermetic no–frill health scares, yet rally dedicated borogroves into farming, at one remove, enough schematic foam fingers for ecumenical denseness. Another parameter, distributive to a priori fluorescence of an expanded ejecta, was copacetic, a patented panacea of stressed bonsai holly under current al fresco of quantum astral gene. Once present at few bloc stair stepper jams, hale divas greeted manifold immense coreophore choirs as controvertibly feckless, bucolic, and yet innocuous, such flash be sooner implemented sop, effusive, emblematic of casuistic gadfly dressage. All vacant prefectures sent hundreds of convalescent spoiler argyle alpaca to source tons of bulk super outliers first into knitting loophole at pall mall, pretense an unfounded speed pundit should gag on revanchiste fallacy.

Next, persuasive vermiform infused warped assassin cysts with amiable tailspin shanties, a stage adverse Glyntz at sixes and seven with stock–only third person narrative reel. Consecutive rococo gramo-phones relegated blithe telegenic demiurge for calypso trail fandangos, kept with instinctive equable intuitive mills. Plush to mime interstellar cusps, their pertinent ad museum photo finish stood to amass giddy serve domes. How Ænselm led near eternity home to real agate sops of scarab facet doth lineally bother undersigned artifice; dependant on what fair thou wary secret stem cry typical, polar if now asynchronous orbit took reason's next question, distanced from annular combinative.

Ionic insidious levels past the earthly met, sodden sustenance for a bland if frabjous anon, aloft sputtered a niche of pressed dour arbiter commune in contrast with whatever isthmus prolix or other exit wore to just dessert a gnomic grunge, in return for an only red viol, topmost in the singed lane. Here we, eke brightened in smelt of approval, endorsed levitation of lemons dropped from liquid light nights and they with mitotic ulterior rite went on all beyond the compress. Crescent patterns avert placid squash and Rust leaped hermetically in fright of a sour blaze. Afar, importuned a second, though her snood inevitably a real snag, St. Agnes swiped the guest's punch in averring the locale of another, whose absence bestirred their entire fraction.

Immoderately they cached here, if ware some plate were already immutably drafted and few genuine men at arms quickly spent in rout as the van parted to reveal ingenious machinery of dire project. The sacrist, known of these occurrence on the fringe of dissolution, their industry napped, the exact pinochle swept four verified trochaic waltzes down an irrelevant blanch, Echo's nascent litmus, poor old tempura shampoo needles, left parabolic mind thimbles amidst those soon apt *tictus*. Would then hell blurt either shoppette as ingenuous when Simic's latest mean metonymy asset demented. Natheless, ought inertia deride a nuptial filbert, Wormwood went across fulfillment, scintillating, cosh–impelled nexuses, profuse as ammeters tripped to gulp pandemic goobers, pullulated gratis as scenic in an oral Mithraic *wishram*, smatters legerdemain very trifecta, semi–usual Plimsoll, minstrel pundits mint sparseness, unless kempt inane gelatinous Becquerel embellished lamia *uchaux*, viz., ordinal monotype fringe art least taken aback. Moreover, imperious dynes persistently ceded wee inklings nary a grunted slaunch behind effervescent pathos.

Upon video auction, manifold incentive revolt down specious parapets unflappably, umpteen Chrysostom glimmers variegated seasonal giga–Oerstad into teleology encomium diurnally, concatenated incipient commutation. As dross ampoules, such ware enacted, to semi–spheres, graphic moribund sectors toward emoticons of livability; noodled in a zonal, if oxymoronic stance importunate, suave tum–dums averted a range of feral protozoon upon stare decisis [*sic*]. Were not this abrupt lintel between store–bought and all–one–word downsized with zest, any manner of heretofore unexcitable continence must bleep fritters.

In plain sight, it smelled dumb Fourier wavelets. A theta skiff pendulous, outrance counter–clockwise, uploaded furballs it macerated, preponderant hesitant spars prior to routinely crash prone roll about, a fractious expedient as ever was, yet deemed uniquely tractable among Ossian's indigestible periodicity, this graft, the *Pangea*, attained supra–remedial province, requited merely any peroration of deftness adequate for replacement of the vacuum breaker. Sans Thumbelina, they deduced, on Sabbath, simultaneous cola accolades toll hefty Barca novas down–site. Bored at shrine Muppets, they then beamed lenient versions aft.

Ever nestled are solar raves, sundry nose beats — phew — easels seethe, and each faun sat for twelve octal McCarthy eons when picked to incite panda lust dashes, a forte Sasha mummered out last autumn. Raw fondue grey larks lost as beady roadstead areas, threw figs on corked thinkers. Should healed cider pendants deny all pixies huge, near holier stale noses? As stars a dusty oat oasis yard undaunted yonder Norn to joint perms ever of clines, ciao, stand–ins, Tiamat mega–enameled; sanest, she sold easier exercise nets there in rude danger bodega tea vats to everyone. Their vault on tour, road ephods of Nineveh, barged torn lava stepped in Albion. Hark, dry and thrawn touchy runts, no taint would connote, harped, shame and fie to such forays! Our dang engine pulled on and off drips: now that mud slid, skates skidded in scads, while snappy highlight hovered near an inlet formally clear.

Prithee, they sank in dim ganja strands, belled as woodsy ballyhoo danced dime store tarantella around an oak ark. Then fever, a mired frilly hexarchy dankly chortled at weepier mirrors and filed hired stevedores at Tuba Bay. Even truer teen things gummed hoax term for olden bathos. Promotional bomba sand dabs and scones, huge trek orrery made life a street caravel germane to June, oh how fleet — phht, wise Artesians, spores towed a new tent of snowy event cherubs long jogged, or gamma mimes trip foes. What else could a good hash tease, ash foot nemesis? Roentgen grind rayon–themed clouds soon chased tulle eglantine ghosts, the huge aroma of land: tarpaulins, aloe, gingham, peony, tete–a–tetes, and tomato hummus, proper tourist fence; bye, stern Renata sleekly weans stoic farina sand castles from the five–and–dime, lad–de–dah, or fake peewee mail porch byte heroes find cocoa for saintly coda unity.

On pretext of an impending engagement of Core, repeatedly stressed by *murahaleen*, they managed at least to visit the Kalisthenios and dash off a postcard to clearer premises. For buskins yawn to Fuald, who dribbled an andante filter dyad, since they'd owe theme elves, on somehow reverse LP, to get unread, armed, viz., a jerboa behind no junta too non–tetrapterous, foot printed explosive polar orbit in hyperfine worsted crop circles. "What if we dust off polytheist elves, mandrake, and ululate at kites," harrumphed a symbiont? Every epicycle would wink up at mutation and then start spiraling at a ledge of posterity, objectivism, and allergies that hover in full bloom tomorrow find al–Kamil able to get through a wave of event that might have sent him over the hedge a year ago. Idres plugged on uphill about three miles to the funnel, and before it was level, Frederick tessered for a magic carpet break *Survivor* call and made back off. He walked and walked, in search of hope, and took some argyle socks from a restaurant for dinner.

.   .   .

Only one morning, an enthalpist's arrival at a cavernous warehouse daunted hymns; until material canyons, stalked with timorous deference even a most grizzled stevedore fled, persistence, in its day, was lengthier governance the clement bestowal of petition in a sunny gazebo clime. As the next decade dawned, fierce little men did scuffle and hoard every red cent begrudgingly and serve best who never underslept. *Elsinore*, a glass bottomed dory boat, soon to depart with shipment of discarded cæsium isotopes, on word of the Countess, Mme Constancia Nadeladimov, prioress of the Sideswipe Inn. Confident his ally could keep her crew enthralled beyond midday, the enthalpist, pored among his charts, announced to the motley squad their aim was to abduct *Elsinore*.

A vigilant advocate of management by objective, he then fell silent with an associate, Azali, a navigator of uncertain skill; Mrs. Teaspoon, a dying benevolent now insistent upon accommodating the great venture; Esmeralda Fishing Lynx, a cyclist, who berthed her eclat behind the Superior Dock and Lock, at once, during the brief bicycle renascence of history, correctly identifying Verona; IT, as locale, on the radio, for *Romeo & Juliet*, how ardently Sam regarded, the cyclist who had forsaken participation in a local health fair for molecules injured during production of reality programs. To be where the land of chowed down checks list, her unexpected tasks, as far as they postponed dreaded egomania, elicited excessive alacrity. Mrs. Teaspoon, sporting a sunny grin, mentioned the comprehensive quaesitum moreover glum natheless spurred renewed exertion in a comparative horizon of option. Azali, less pleased, announced his skill should free them from all predicament and, in paroxysm of denial, withdrew from the greatest journey with a single step (it had shown up on his task reminder this morning).

Grendelle, the enthalpist regarded with a level stare, asked permission to write a letter to his parents. "Occludants, cheerlead for the octagonal Norn," he apostrophized, "our incarnadine litmus frequency stretched, on no account, permissive dictations on inferential, innate anthropomorphism." The needs of the modern nation involved a lot of collaborative yakking until a fat smelly guy came out of the basement and tweaked some pixels and everyone said whoop–de–doo, "so up to this point," Etaoin haltingly pledged, "survival is possible. Here are sub-titled bandstands of scant fungus honked at assiduously in downloaded ink pots."

A plastered octave atomic poseur, Horace, reiterated afresh, "I owe this change alone to a cognitive, catholic, qua nifty tonic: any offset immensity, availing of dark energy schools' agit–prop, risks theatrical vista, even if men act inevitably cool around each corn flower." Terse Flußtapfer temporized, "all limit aside, can crueler ratios never outlast a transitory mark–up?" "Measures," Messimo groped sententiously, "ostracize ubiquitous nine–to–fivers." Bent on solely wreaked havoc in the orlop overlook, the astral component ignoramus continually surfed time ducts at hyperbolic celerity.

Haste, and arduous notion of versatile prototype, now end up, actual polymer emergent with pitch, oasts, owl fewmets, ungummed *tictus momentum*, poinsettia, spruce frond, encore Lenten nuts, retsin, puce web log clappers, odd ducts of eczema, loosed chords, innate fustian, fugue aloe, vernal in stained mystery syntax, and stellar squares, each cost exceptional, apparent postillion, hopeful of gramercy, a walk with Zarathusra. "To indemnify much impetus, ere glycol turf strobed mandarins, I'd drum down factional disguise."

Tolstoy moralized, "always pull the plug on holistic clutter after bespoken whatever." "That's how we want them to think," recused a diva, shown as Iphgene, merrily thrilled yet wistful, afforded coaxial Earth glow everywhere: a tropic thousand island ink seeped in fitful stark gazebo, moats of grub who'd sent fair daisies, to each three cheers, it nipped and tingled in eerie tutus for forged annuity flare powder, &c (in teeny shoe trees); concurrent, visual–spatial provincials determined Narragansett aristocracy, chalcedony, and guilt–free requiem since Tridentine (re: choirs, sly in subtle gin mills) constructs of witangemot heard soft footfall in every corner. Visions profess tense omega farms with sententious edict; rouged amidst talc Caspian dunes sat mountebanks purporting ubiquitous terra cotta role polieu vogue.

A fine–tuned seventy–eight, requested by atelier types, *Your Skin–Deep Chichi*, ended and portly Sadducees emerged. "Yea, Zippy, treacle scone, pro tem [*sic*] cruets, intinct in every Middlesex agape vesper, great wind turbine to air out hoary tone poems in tillage," and seasick sacerdotal complaint, ex nihilo, of expanded verticulum encephalograph inciting effervescent layover.

Posed as timid, an Indocile stoked the girandole in sisal sneeze guards: each Ave commensurate in enduring cause, biodegradably weird censors flung macrodome as contrite buzz kills foam adorably. "Go, in vestigial futons, say nighty–night to fustian precept, act as all faux pas are cleansed." Hereupon, in the theme foyer, Rex, upon further contemplation, animated on off–peak shadow darts, knighted teen peers sensibly; often Szechuan vibe ensured trendy somnambulists remain viewed in tactful yet infinite ommatophore.

"Personally, I'd react to Proust in gaudier tonalities," cited Melissa, in triplicate, and one benign wheelbarrow loan transept from dozing off on innate forum at Clermont soon, cisterns, rang like larks, intimated Hippocrene quarantine athwart atomic ringtail comets. Vitiated on Tirolean hydroplane, ever droopier vocals freckled below, whoosh, a ghost fringe donned chaste amaranthine tincture, and latent wordy repo — coma nostrum dives into salt cellars discretely.

Dendritic dust mice of Prester John re–engineered a merciful omnibus tinged in garlands of gossamer enokidake, gefilte, and large smores, and our pound cake, *iamin'thelim* protested! *th'ratwi'thorns* flung the bag and poked it along. Then, kvetching mixed feelings pro forma, Flambeaux lamely commented on how much fun it was to flourish false, spurious, and disingenuous supreme volition, filing the Danish matter, grumbled into equilibrium at every turn, visiting an I'm–with–you–guys sound in his head, and amused at getting so ruffled by this concern with the store's inner clique, he'd divided each last fling, note, proposal, memo, shield, counter, excuse, justification, or protest before eventually perceiving all as flammable.

All was defined as scraps, bundles, and reams filed against disastrous social fashion feebly. Tapping his head (toc toc), *iamin'thelim* undid some foil and warped myths around pound cake as *th'ratwi'thorns* discussed fetishism and, in what were theoretically his last days on the continuum: previously (instead of going back to very hilly country carved by time mathematics), Ostrand developed consolation in sobriety, "as someone they might like around, although entertaining may have warped my mind forever." Proserpine was at some dried–up motel, and the woof of collegiate pain and struggle; metallic yowls recorded, they shoved back off front to recover her virgule.

In order to alter another incommoded pond, a tectonic void montage, Raisin's densest kismet entourage custom here in bas relief, harsh, ignored, eclectic tilth huzzahs, adagio karakul tarantella crumbles, palmetto refulgence solid, always temperate at compline, cespitose, crammed isometric denouement of paroled biscuit heretic, sallow heffalumps mocking calendula caterers who'd promised a remora salad attached blandly abeam, lacier Manzanilla, dyed in present segue, matronymic Venetian geodes emitting stray oxygen, innate polymer sangfroid tartan arrivistes, tone–deaf racemic thalassocrats voicing a regional decorum to rapt paramours of loopy fortitude, penstemon icons once aloof, comped epiphanies masking zebra orchids; odd balloon whisperers engulfed nearly every semester, *th'ratwi'thorns* at once will to humor any concept of perfect conversation unless conclusive proof could be obtained from travel malaise.

.   .   .

After being overshot eight times by his snack routes with barely a complaint, and an impassioned paean to virtues of schlock, losing most of his identity, Ensign Plair's VCR rewound the best of the Great American agenda. If the ensign figured he'd already made the decision, for any reason, to forsake stringy bouncy impetus that kept a terrible sleepless night punctuated by disjointed revelry and air quote vacation, he plunged directly into enough paperwork to leave his merry red hots out next to the coffee shopping spree music and various fungus colonies in the toilet.

The stuff was really immeasurable, startling to detach for a last enterprise at this early stage, indicative of established over–indulgence on previous tests, and he went into big old party mode for his bookcase, for the meet to come next Christmas, into the basement to recover a disputed tool, his precious art; a little, duly steam–fit, emulsified Guelph, afforded see–through partisan pipe stem, anticipating a savannah holiday, reconnoitered volute pail [sic] again after coordinating device to develop aversion toward many mundane but necessarily long daydreams of disconnection from mental surgery.

The creation of the volute pale.

Of sufficient resolve was one attempt to arise and explore his circumstance. Etaoin, out of their fire circle, yet spared to convey the message that we would not leave their mountains already, heard approach of sufficient forces which sent him on this mission, and prepared a shout of coalescent volume when an invisible hand, clamped above his mouth, caused him to spend moments feeling his head yanked back, and into the eye of Core.

"Persephone," he attempted to say, bitingly, her palm rendering humanity no favor by letting Shrdlu remain conscious. "Not so easy this time," she argued. Etaoin rose, though a mere tilt of his head perhaps enough to believe he fortuitously lived, and since away from the bend of the road heavily mechanized coalition forces muffled their engines behind an intervening ridge, silence punctuated by fierce fires indicated perhaps they're zeroed down beyond the uplift.

Albeit it occurred to him to fix his own fair link, Shrdlu squirreled his older coaster choice road trip: Dr. B's peppermint soap, feeling binoculars sweeping the eastern sky at dusk, prepared to march toward the lager [*sic*], and felt entitled to ask one question of Core. To pick an applied caution principle link, light and dark at home unless a hot wire drew a fluke, the manager of alchemic programs, meanwhile compliant, ministered and, if in penitence of rebuke via Aristotelian precept, they maintained an article all other tenets forthwith upheld worthily abide.

Meant as adherence began, a prefix omnibus dative diagram in transverse universal Mercator extended exceptional reversion to a pre—Ptolemaic model runway standstill. All soot shucked out of creative decency lent direct impetus onto standard edifice probably within legend of a great aegis of enumerated series of mere nostrum realm nuance arrival displaced veteran patter as Zoyschia earned triangulate points in generic style for her determinate individual to apprehend, on the part of the government of the United States, an intent to be still, preventing aim of possible asymptotic inflection, but this newly global village, then forsooth calm, distracted by red balloon herring maroon, an island of infra indigo, Plair, tuned athwart diagonal cameral pattern vector off onyx, chose transference to an absence with relief of nethermost next non–niceness nor beyond exaltation of belief or principle *untenet* of more perfect paradise.

Light enough to lime within expected seeping, *iamin'thelim* stepped upon the foxfire, disguised, vitreous quasi–nephalim spam, immense Etesian orgone dumbwaiter protean tektites that, autochthonous, incurred a rare soupcon irreversibly tawdrier, covert, yet circumlocuted recent modus vivendi, norms entailing spores, ensconced pensively near itinerant bailiwick, uproar Plair found of sublime cause an ancillary crumpet; interwoven as prescient hopscotch, vernacular to grace other tropic off–track thermion frustum in synthetic falsetto, should only wait while gutters of storm water cascaded in subterranean passages betwixt Uxbridge Arch. To an untoward strain of the retail upgrade hermitage, despondent to a plaintive storm, accompanied with ham, a cello soliloquy, haul wended away into we're talking of your yore here, grandiloquent accompaniment concession bespectacled sampler harm.

It has been learned, a reputed accord, to notable witness, that a tympanum has lurched, dislodged from licentious time, crumbled upon induction of emeritus, and if a man was struck by reality of calliopes, structurally, it is not known whether at this time he lies nearly dead. *iamin'thelim* remolded, in time hinter, for Ion Uclosco had need of little elves, which assisted him in turn, his mind inside out as stricken fellows grasped and a magisterial form swept out of mists, brandishing a baggage claim check. Immediate precedent, this trim punt verged upon frumpiness, Ion returned for an extension cord.

As he'd absently sunned too bearably in original text of Formosan's largesse, Sergei tended feebly to argue Deerfield's main complaint of news they would not share broke grounds for the newly chestnut way of thanksgiving. Somehow irritant to principle impressions, feted adherents of the League took notes of issue, steps, expectation, standing, and foundations. Unresolved were whether they understood grains, fronts, furrows, painted buttons, forgotten sights for natural only eyes, basic courses in elective rigidity, and diverted by occult décor and the notion all problems should be solved by jumps from retribution.

Yesterdays, bedside of that happiness, Sergei, dying beneath Uxbridge Arch, had been preventative in suspending its pressure easily with nonchalant rhetoric. Then Pyrogabion dissolved in shelf life, its membrane flaked into stucco of weird Worms wall flower at worst, paper concatenation, a blank black frond seen by actual wild ibexes visiting the drained bath, and machismo also there remarked for unspecified numeral years; a plaint of *iamin'thelim* being a mere crack in the bell rang hollow to others who stated, "even extolled pluperfectreß [*sic*] is now a sampler dramaturge. Inanimacy is our fate, and we shall become nature not as–is, but as man's fears have always projected, capricious, precocious, unrestrainedly fecund, swallowing ciphers whole, and all entendres of the Holocene era shall be averaged."

.   .   .

In visible communion with a topic which pre–occupied millions of United States residents, shadow puppet had to redress one of his disciples who simply couldn't refrain from sitting on peoples' laps before grace. A worthy attempt others might fathom, divine mysteries surround Himself, hence a decision to promulgate an exit questionnaire, to be administered prior to cessation of each processional; outside, empty dark, and alienation, expedients, poisons, and neo–con atavism to avert crisis were especially amused to be the slowest of zephyrs.

The decorous oath of dismissal, written by the board for this possibility, with considerable under–achievement, thus began reminiscence about whether the early war, where to rescue, with strict renascence at every juncture, arranged stickers for trans–natural challenge, no mega–store met, tremendous depiction of elemental peace, "that sort of makes it official," chimed blessed imam Azali: "in situ, a landmark of sagacity, for all a stage of commutativity." Fanta labored beneath a misconception that if she just fixed the right truck they'd soon be zipping among secluded columns, and ubiquitous tasks of reconciliated cascades of decimal prisms into octal reckoning weren't going to cut it, needless to say, for just across from the garden, lady Rita's walk to her sloth slide shop above each driftful day, Frederick reopened a three–hour mass dash to Viterbo. Fuald, out of the corners of this period Sherpa, to help Shrdlu's mean liner demons portray thought, elicited in cedar twilight that pool was merely a snow cone.

Then power fed the steps of a windward God (James 3:3), bemusedly conversation with the beautiful germ of salubrious non–events. Down on congruent areas of Earth, pertinent shelves were full of dusty news-paper interviews, an inspirational gabby incessant contrast with people, begging one fun proviso, shopped for Za'at (least of all by al–Kamil), a fortunate sardonic formation, as big plains, dotted with occasional renaissance, began to get away in the last part of the fog, roll out of live glory, flop while Cyane, past down by those oasis, lulled, yet left an only mild lethargic fair in the parking lot; a comparative idyllic tuba pavane for the logbook drifted into a chaos of that Macy's number, hoping to hug everyone who'd tasked our couple of the night to listen, *Deirdre Tipped Our Equator Turn South.* "Who said life in the airport was so organized that all rapport owed," Etaoin, quizzed, a VH–1 perspective on a pad, practicing legal scream, "text to another medium?"

"Quel–que chose [*sic*]," freeze–dried Fuald, bet, "why, even we did vasten they're bagging her down to, uh, stranger town?" Idres noodled, "Core told us a hymn, her bad self, insofar as brainwashed corporate groups" — "by the unusual nature of a tall shadow, blinking, 'how could a merciful party drop me, everyone,'" Persephone added? Several indica-tors to all ancient riddles revamped to support her shrift to no bleeping rip since she lied, next a gateway of our conversation I essentially blew, and it seemed to my *chef d'cabinet*, the fabulous matron how drifted, on few stalwart wave radio (our stranger town she pulled home against environmental counsel) things, she had seen better judgement urges.

The golden chance, to take a primarily rationalized Morse code and run, must wait till you marry energetic and able resolution, to find transaction full of livelong memory lane, provoking snafu with anyone who gives its place strange inner mass to walk out of buying a new town. "Very down, rye vole, we'll oil behemoths," al–Kamil rang, a gateway bulb, and on some level, which, benched in Soho, they entered what fish were there in a mad shake down at odd intervals of a different camping trip ka–clank, as Telstar crackled via random crock, runcible, by stars, and at best, ampoules, left through some super–charged portion of napping components, led about a third of the previous evening's adjustment problem to the unused into stasis.

"Ciao, ink blot peers!" Shrdlu jumped from the messenger ledge and multi–versed all over the purple sage. In second exile, a pivotal person answered, "your voice, thrown together, and yet always designated for anything whatsoever, came to us, who call you a little breeze south." Why, Cecil was just also wandering the smallest all night fad, the downy life, for most part an ensemble of Cyane, fountain lady, and Damian youths, with saved though rusty *fjulsfut*, contributed to resist conversion, impressed her office, a hub of overdrive commuters on their comic exercise thereof, to occur today. The cursory way they wheeled around the beltway parlor malls of Neath, heavens far from yesterday, motivated only via swift recessive desire for extra large ballroom bobbin rayon things, seemed to strike an old bandersnatch as frumious anymore.

.   .   .

*Cura pacis concordia quoque intestinae cause fuit (the pains they were
at to maintain peace were also productive of internal harmony).*
Livy, Histories, III, lxv., 7.

afterword.

P.S. Love from everyone at the tiny, nice, Xmas Party of 1986. Cherish
your trust and hope to continue story of how characters referenced above
persevere in wish fulfillment. Thanks to Mark for writing pivotal story
about adjunct as character in 1980 at Bozeman, and for support and
site design from 2012 to 2019; with sincere condolence in memory of
Diane (Proverbs 31.10) ; xox, & thanks to A., and to J., and to Portland
Desktop for repairing old computer in 2015. Many thanks and love to
Arianna for sending two new computers after one broke down in 2013.
Cover photograph: Mike en route to Ptarmigan Pass, MT. Photo ©1973
by Karen Frausen (July 1973).

www.ingramcontent.com/pod-product-compliance
Lightning Source LLC
Chambersburg PA
CBHW020548120726
47903CB00001B/177